Mariu[...] t novel
Making Lo[...] was published to
great acclaim. *How To Forget* is his second novel. His life
and thought are slightly caught at www.mariusbrill.com

HOW TO FORGET

Marius Brill

BLACK SWAN

TRANSWORLD PUBLISHERS
61–63 Uxbridge Road, London W5 5SA
A Random House Group Company
www.transworldbooks.co.uk

HOW TO FORGET
A BLACK SWAN BOOK: 9780552771320

First published in Great Britain
in 2011 by Doubleday
an imprint of Transworld Publishers
Black Swan edition published 2012

Addresses for Random House Group Ltd companies outside the UK
can be found at: www.randomhouse.co.uk
The Random House Group Ltd Reg. No. 954009

The Random House Group Limited supports The Forest Stewardship
Council (FSC®), the leading international forest certification organisation.
Our books carrying the FSC label are printed on FSC® certified paper.
FSC is the only forest certification scheme endorsed by the leading
environmental organisations, including Greenpeace.
Our paper procurement policy can be found at
www.randomhouse.co.uk/environment

Typeset in 11/14pt Sabon by
Falcon Oast Graphic Art Ltd.
Printed and bound by CPI Group (UK) Ltd, Croydon, CR0 4YY.

2 4 6 8 10 9 7 5 3 1

MIX
Paper from
responsible sources
FSC® C016897

For my mother,

Sue Seward Brill,

without whose love, support
and encouragement I might
have given up, found a proper
job and become solvent.

HOW TO FORGET

a Life?

an 'aide oublieux'?

'ad Amnesium'?

Me?

Dr C. Tavasligh M.Sc Ph.D

Preface

Some said it was murder. A good many thought it well deserved. Others reckoned it more likely to be suicide. The police speculated on a kidnapping for a while, but no ransom demand was ever made and no body, alive or dead, was ever found.

The jokes doing the email rounds at the time tended to revolve around Dr Tavasligh, who specialized in the causes of forgetfulness, ironically forgetting the way home, or suffering amnesia, or suddenly remembering that science has ethics.

Tavasligh was certainly no stranger to death threats. The storm of outrage caused, almost a decade ago, by the publication of an experiment that seemed to cross ethical boundaries forced the neuropsychologist into hiding.

But then, just over three years ago, Tavasligh disappeared completely and, despite the feverish theories, no trace was left.

Like most, I vaguely remember reading about it in the newspapers at the time but as it was unrelated to me, and with so many human tragedies daily running past in the media, I soon forgot all about it. As Tavasligh would no doubt have put it: I forgot because I had no emotional investment in remembering. Memories without meaning are the hardest to keep.

But last September my interest in the story was reignited when, out of the blue, I was sent a large number of Tavasligh's personal papers, articles and notes.

Most exciting was the inclusion of the manuscript of *How to Forget*, an unpublished book that Tavasligh had, apparently, written shortly before the disappearance and which seemed to shed considerable light on what actually happened.

I contacted Transworld immediately and they agreed this needed to be published.

How to Forget was unlike anything Tavasligh had attempted before. Apparently, 'to elicit some emotional connection, which is the cornerstone of memory', it was written in the form of a novel, a sort of biography of an obscure conjuror.

Unfortunately the original manuscript was far from complete, often lacking details that I found referred to in Tavasligh's meticulously kept notes.

Enlisting the help of the notebooks, previous works and published papers, I have spent many months piecing together what, I believe, is a definitive work.

I feel very proud to be not only taking part in publishing what is, possibly, Tavasligh's last and most controversial work, but also going some way to clearing up the mystery of what exactly did happen to Dr Chris Tavasligh.

Marius Brill
South Kensington

TIC

1. The Inciting Condition (TIC)

This is an incident which the subject may
allude to repeatedly. Often it is something
that happened in their youth or fairly long
ago, something he or she never fully
recovered from. Memories of the incident,
either directly or indirectly, tend to haunt
the subject, making them more compliant to
end-of-life considerations. Their conscious
rationalization tends to be that a life led
haunted in such a way is no life at all.

1

It had been one of those warm, fabulous summer days when simply breathing in bathed you in the rich scent of Primrose, Wisteria and Acacia Avenues: a mixture of curry, discarded sump oil and the festering carcasses of every dream and ambition that's been buried in the shallow grave of the Suburb. Peter hurried into Curate's Drive, the long and wide tree-lined avenue where the Suburb's motley green hedges suddenly give way to tall, bright, redbrick walls. There, behind high gates, stand vast mansions beyond the realm of mortals, taste or planning permission.

Bright red, yellow and blue balloons were tied to the ironwork gates that clicked open as Peter approached and pulled back slowly with an electronic whine and a beep beep beep, eerily reminiscent of reversing trucks and the end of Inspector Morse. The lawn, like every other on Curate's Drive, was so meticulously manicured, it was hard to believe that the crunch of the gravel path didn't come from nail clippings splintering underfoot. The dislocated twittering of a skylark rose and fell, drifting from some unpinpointable foliage. Sprinklers whisked around, sending glittering drops of sun into prismic spectrums and somewhere, over their rainbows, bluebottles flew.

So if flies, born without any olfactory sense, still knew they were in the proximity of big shit, why hadn't he?

The house itself, a post-war, post-aesthetic, postbox pile of red brick, straight lines, enormous picture windows and exposed gutters, was not only detached, it was positively aloof. Its angular Corbusier roof swept down in a smug grin of superior modernism. And in the shadow of its grandiose eaves, Peter stood sideways to the door so as not to scuff his enormous shoes. He checked his buttonhole for leakage, adjusted his braces and rang the bell, which recreated, in a beautiful twenty-four-voice work of electronic synthesis composed by Michael Nyman and rendered with 248-bit fidelity, the sound of a bell.

Maybe the particularly hysterical tone of the shrieks emanating from deep inside should have told him that this was not the right place, the right door, that it would all go horribly wrong. When Peter watched himself through the veil of time, he wanted to kick himself and shout, 'Wake up'; standing there so innocent, so blissfully unaware of the omens, and with that smile plastered to his face.

The woman who answered, her look would haunt him too. Skin of ice, glacial blue eyes and lips of slate, her thin mouth as capable of meaningful expression as a phrase book. Perhaps she was beautiful, once, and still not past her prime as, with a proper superiority, she joylessly raised one eyebrow.

'Mr Noodles, I presume.'

14

From: <u>*Sessions Notebook 43.23*</u> p37
P. gripping hand, HARD.

Peter grasps his hand when he speaks about this event, so tightly his fingers turn white. He's oblivious though, still wrapped in the memory, the physical mnemonic of the handshake, the deal struck, fate sealed.

A predictable motor response but I think he's what I call over-remembering. Look at the clarity of the details; just too lucid to be true. There is a technical term for this; I believe it is: Bollocks.

It's not that he's actually lying but, at the time of the event, he neither saw nor noticed half of the elements that inconsistently blur his story. The urge to misremember is, as a rule, directly proportionate to the pain of the memory. Remembering, with hindsight sitting in judgement, requires the same nervous optimism as does, say, retrieving the dropped soap in the Broadmoor showers.

Peter's clearly embellishing things in his retelling, imbuing incidents with meaning: all those symbols of impending doom, the foreshadowing of disaster, as if the whole event could have been predetermined by nature, decreed by fate, and so not his fault at all.

On the other hand I have to recognize that some features of his memory of the event were indeed present at the time, even if peripheral, and were absorbed unnoticed while his conscious mind focused on his mission.

The scents, the skylark, the balloons, the lawn: he remembers these details despite himself, although at the time he paid absolutely no attention to them. His actual approach to the house was almost unconscious.

When our bodies are in motion we tend to release our minds from total immediate awareness. We allow the motor neurons to dominate – an aspect of human nature which, I believe, explains the horizontal complicity of trophy wives.

So, that afternoon, as Peter moved to the house, he was actually on automatic. The synaptic map made in his mind, which he would later try to reuse to recreate the journey as a memory, was constructed not as a continual line of experience but by certain moments of sensual priority. The colourful balloons, for example, a moment when his visual sense overpowered his others. So later, when he came to consciously replay the event in his head, it was as if tracing a path of stepping stones, leaping from one point to the next and making assumptions in between.

He remembers clearly the woman ushering him in, beckoning him to follow her. As she strutted and wiggled in her skintight pencil skirt, he swaggered and waddled in his size 17 shoes, tartan buttock-stuffed trousers and rabbit-crammed wonky stovepipe hat. He remembers that, clearly, but in the corners, in the details, he doesn't notice that sometimes her satin skirt is shiny emerald and at others a shimmering mauve. The gap in his memory is filled by a colour recently seen, so its absence doesn't glare and interrupt the perceived continuous narrative of the memory.

The human mind's desire for a sense of perfect continuum in our perceived world finds the disruption of a narrative highly irritating. So . . .

16

2

The squad cars weaved in and out of the mid-town traffic and raced across intersections, cabs screeched to a standstill, pedestrians dived for sidewalks, their curses drowned in the wailing sirens, and, as their rides braked, bus passengers lurched forward in unison, crashing together as iPods threw down their iShackles, found fast-fingered liberty, pawnshops and new ears.

On the 110th floor Kate watched distantly. She liked the view, she liked looking down. She liked the altitude and loved the attitude. There was something pleasingly detached about her own superior perspective gazing down to Fifth Avenue, the park and the misty blue Westside.

She knew who they were coming for.

Had it happened less often, a hazard of her career, the approaching sirens might have made Kate's heart thump but she was long out of the habit of listening to that part of her anatomy.

The wailing gradually grew louder as she saw the tiny cars skid to a stop below her and all the little officers run into the lobby. Kate watched the traffic jam mount up behind the abandoned squad cars and experienced the disturbing feeling that, by rights, she should not be there.

It wasn't because there were twenty immigration officers racing up to her floor, nor that her green card had faded to a pale lemon. It wasn't that her last boyfriend had given her just twenty-four hours to leave the country before he called the credit card company or that the only reason the rent for her vast apartment had not been called in was because it was nominally leased by an Arab sheikh who owed his name more to Looney Tunes than to the grace of Allah. No, the reason that she shouldn't be there, she was realizing as she gazed at the tiny families flowing towards the park, went back much further. She should never have made it even as far as being a toddler.

She had, she knew, been the sort of perpetually moaning, screaming, whining, wilful child that most sensible parents, after a couple of years of sleep deprivation, finally sort out by finding a teenage child-carer who, left to her own devices, would end up shaking baby Kate to death and having to take the rap. But not hers. Far too busy with their own careers.

For Kate, childhood had had little to do with being a child and everything to do with being a hood. She had been clever, precocious, and for many years her ability to ape maturity scored her fags and alcohol at an age when those pleasures could do their worst. So she was the school bully? Someone's got to step up and do it. She thought back, fondly, to her first factory assembly line. Sylvie, Melissa and Sarah, whom she had 'persuaded' to sit shivering behind the bike shed every break, opening and emptying the fag butts they collected from the bins in the local shopping centre, rerolling the contents into Rizlas that she'd sell to kids too scared of her legendary Chinese burn to just say no. Kate never considered why the memories of her time as a person of restricted years were made up, chiefly, of a series of misdemeanours and their subsequent punishments, the most successful of which merely reinforced the importance of never being caught.

These happy recollections were suddenly dislodged by the very thing that had started her train of juvenile thinking, and his well-aimed *Boy's Book of Spells* glancing off the back of her head.

Kate swivelled. 'Just act your bloody age.'

'You act yours.'

'I cannot believe I was ever as bloody annoying as you.'

'Give me my book back.'

'Pick it up yourself. And say please.'

'Pleeeeease pick it up yourself.'

'Oh for God's sake.'

'I'm bored. All you do is look out the window. I want someone to play with.'

'Listen, Da, we're about to have some visitors and I need you to be as grown up as possible just for a little while.'

The book-thrower got down from the table and stuck out his bottom lip. He sauntered slowly to the book and made a play of being unable to bend over to retrieve it. 'Can't. My back hurts.'

Kate nodded and whispered under her breath, 'Of course it does.' She went over to him and picked up the book. As she passed it into his hands she touched his cool skin. Flesh of her flesh and yet it felt frighteningly alien. She tried to remember a time when those hands meant so much to her, but it all seemed too long ago. Now he was a thing apart, separate, an emotional leech that bestowed endless responsibility with no redeeming future reconciliation. She thought about his tiny mind and searched herself for some sort of compassion. Nothing, even though she was fully aware that he probably had not long to go. A few years maybe. And his condition would only get worse and worse. What had she done to deserve this? She was never meant to cope with such things. She shouldn't even be there.

3

Peter was directed to an open door off the hall. The ice maiden gestured impassively to a group of mothers all talking simultaneously with all the animation of the facially paralysed plastic cast of *Thunderbirds*.

'The clown,' the snow queen announced and the stony faces of the mothers turned.

'Afternoon, ladies.' Peter nodded to them. 'I must say I was expecting a slightly younger audience,' he said, trying to break the iceberg with the conversational equivalent of a toothpick. Not a smile, not a grimace, a groan or a yawn. Peter was sure this wasn't Stepford but every shiny face was a vision of concentrated impassiveness. He thought that he knew how to deal with difficult audiences but this complete lack of facial movement was unnerving. A little girl who had been dipping into her mother's handbag brushed past him to get through the door.

'Don't make them laugh,' she hissed, 'you'll wrinkle them.' She darted off to the back of the hall. Peter looked up at the impossibly smooth faces and realized that if he made them laugh it wouldn't just be jokes he'd be cracking. Forget the warm-up lines, they clearly led their lives in terror of lines.

Peter clapped his hands and rubbed them together with feint enthusiasm. 'So where are the little darlings then?'

The frostess glided away to a door at the back of the hall and Peter followed. 'They're in the conservatory,' she said, her hand on the door handle. Maybe she said something else but it was drowned in the partialness of his memory and the harrowing noise that burst from the opening door.

Peter grimly surveyed the killing ground, grin still painted to his mouth. A small palm had been knocked over, various panes of glass were already smashed, cups and plates lay strewn around the floor and the almighty whoops and cries of the savages pierced every nerve known to parentkind. A yellow and red banner, half torn, drooped woefully down like a forced smile and proclaimed 'Happy Birthday Titus'. Peter quickly counted thirty of them at least, perhaps a little boisterous but nothing he couldn't handle.

Behind him the ice lady clapped her hands and shouted, 'Children. The clown's arrived.'

'Well, technically I'm a magician.'

The eyebrow rose but infinitesimally. 'If you can deal with this lot you will be.'

21

She did say that. He was sure. The circumstances were extreme and she stated it. Afterwards, in the days that followed, she would never admit it, but he still clung to that memory as his one small ray of hope.

The only ones in the room to turn and acknowledge Peter's arrival were two gothic teenage girls with 'suckered' etched into their desperate over-blackened eyes. Whatever pocket money they had foolishly agreed to accept in exchange for organizing party games and thrusting cocktail sausages down unrelenting throats, it was not enough and, unless it neared the national debt, it never would be. The girls looked at him with such evident relief he felt as if he were Mother Teresa entering a leper colony. The speed with which they grabbed their coats, whisked past him and slammed the door suggested that maybe it was something a little more deadly than leprosy.

He looked about him: he was alone with thirty baying eight-year-olds, high on sugar and low on attention span, an orgy of carefree, conscience-free, cola-caffeinated bacchants, already dancing wildly in anticipation of the coming feeding frenzy.

This was when the magic was supposed to kick in.

4

'EN WHY PEE DEE,' a voice shouted above the banging, 'OH PEN DURDOOR. NOW.'

Kate adjusted her pinny. '*Sí*, *sí*, I come.' She peered

through the spyhole and her brown eye met a blue one.

'How I know you policeman?' Kate added, breaking the English as decisively as the World Cup does every four years.

'Lady, open the damn door now or we bust it open and take you down the shop for obstruction.' As he said this, the blue eye sank down, out of sight, and the famous badge on the officer's cap swam into the goldfish bowl eyepiece.

Kate began the unbolting procedure. Like most New York doors, from top to bottom it had more locks than Rapunzel and was considerably less accessible. It was a respectable three minutes of clicking and clonking before the cops could abruptly burst into the apartment, guns outstretched, spinning as they took every angle in their sights. Now at a pitch of hysteria, they screamed, 'ONDERFLOOR, ONDERFLOOR, GEDONDER-FLOOR.' The closest to Kate waved the persuasive end of a .45 in her face as she obediently lay down, muttering curses in Spanish.

In a few moments voices from around the apartment were shouting, 'KITCHEN SECURE', 'BEDROOM SECURE', 'BATHROOM SECURE', 'LOUNGE SEC ... FUCK GEDDOWN GEDDOWN GEDONDER-FLOOR.'

Kate gazed into the shagpile and smiled at the familiar voice in the living room. 'Cool. Are you like, real policemen?'

'GEDONDERFUCKINGFLOOR,' came the frantic reply.

'Right, yes, OK, I am ... I will ... I just ...'

'THEFUCKINGFLOORDOWN.'

'Yes, yes, I am trying, it's just, well . . . my back, you see . . . I can't . . .'

'NOW,' the cop almost hyperventilated, 'NOW OR I'LL TAKE YOUR FREAKING HEAD OFF.'

'I am, all right? Keep your hair on. I . . . ooof . . . I . . . right . . . there, is this right?'

'SHUTUP SHUTUP MOTHERFUCKER.'

There was some stifled laughter.

'WHAT THE HELL ARE YOU LAUGHING AT?'

'You er . . .' a snigger, 'you used the naughty word . . . You know,' another snigger, 'the F-word.'

A deeper, altogether calmer voice arrived with some very shiny shoes close to Kate's head. 'All secure, officer?'

'Yes, sir, secure.'

'Thank you. She here?'

'We have one Latino female and one elderly Caucasian male.'

'No one else? No. Of course not. Why should she hang around? It's not like your cars didn't warn the whole of Fifth Avenue you were coming. I imagine she and probably half the hedge fund managers on this block are right now on the way to JFK and their private jets to their condos in Tijuana.'

Kate smiled. There was something endearing about Americans attempting sarcasm, it was always done with such light irony and a heavy hand.

'There's an APB on her, she won't get through any station or airport. Should I request roadblocks on the bridges and tunnels?'

'For chrissake, Arnold, she's a con artist, not a fucking terrorist. She's probably long gone. Jeez. You questioned the maid yet?'

24

'No, not—'

'Christ, if you want anything done, you got to do it yourself.'

Kate was pulled up by one arm, led to the dining room and pushed into a chair at the table. Only then, as he sat down opposite her, did she get a look at her antagonist.

'Lola Cervantes de Sanchez?' Agent Brown said, looking at the driving licence he'd pulled from her wallet.

Kate nodded. '*Sí.*'

From the moment she set eyes on Brown, sitting at the table in his acrylic black JC Penney dreadful suit, she knew she had just doubled the troubleometer. He was no policeman, he was FBI. If you're wanted in seven states, and none of them being one of undress, it's fair to assume a fed's going to turn up sooner or later. Da was sitting next to him, fiddling with his teeth. The fat envelope from his pocket now lay on the table in front of him. He had looked Kate straight in the eye but as usual, what with it being all of five minutes since he'd last seen her, he showed her the same sort of recognition that the Pacifist Society have got for their war effort.

'You got papers, Sanchez?' Brown asked casually as she sat down, as if this was just routine. A formality. But he already knew the answer, he'd seen it a hundred times. He didn't need a criminal profiler to tell him that Minola would have perfected her Fifth Avenue socialite image with a Hispanic maid straight out the tunnels.

'Papers, *sí.*'

Brown was surprised. He shifted in his chair, leaning forward across the cool marble dining table. 'Really? Where are they?'

Kate pointed away towards the coffee table. 'I get *New York Times* for Miss Katie. *Sí?*'

With a relieved grin, Brown leaned back again. 'No. Papers. Like ID? Passport?' He held his hand out and dragged a surprisingly delicate index finger across his palm as if it was a piece of paper. 'Visa?'

Kate shook her head hesitantly.

Of course not. Now he had the leverage he expected. 'OK, Sanchez, let me tell you how this works. I've been chasing Minola for five fucking years now. You co-operate with me, you answer my questions, you get to walk out of here and I forget I ever saw you.' Brown leaned towards her, baring his teeth and lowering his voice into a snarl. 'You fuck with me, Sanchez, and I'll personally make sure you're on the first flight back to Taco Hell, straight back to the mosquito-infested shit-hole you crawled out of.' He leaned heavily back in his chair and uttered one of the menacing Spanish phrases that he had learned on the street as a kid, '*Comprende, mi amigo?*' The street in question was actually Sesame, but then the clean streets of Chastity, Ohio, had been sadly bereft of an immigrant underclass.

'*Sí. Entiendo,*' Kate said softly, correcting his Spanish.

'So. First up,' Brown pointed at Da with his thumb, 'what's with this guy?'

Kate glanced at Da. He was now inserting his finger into his nose. He pulled the finger out again and as he examined the tip he spotted Kate looking at him. He stuck out his tongue.

'He Master Cedric. He sick,' Kate said in her thickest Spanish accent.

Brown circled his forefinger by his temple. 'Like crazy sick?'

Kate broke eye contact, hesitated and then nodded.

Brown turned to Da. 'You know Minola? Catherine Minola?' he asked in the slow, patronizing manner that you might use to talk to an idiot or that man in Jaipur who just won't accept that you have already turned the fucking thing 'off and on again' a million bloody times.

'Catherine?' Da repeated, narrowing his eyes and rubbing his chin. 'A girl? Don't like girls.' He uttered the last word with the guttural disgust that only the class-defensive, difference-fearing British accent can affect.

Brown turned the envelope upside down and poured its contents on to the table in front of Da: a dark red British passport, an airline ticket and a large piece of paper which, when unfolded, bore the two words 'Lotus House'.

Brown picked up the passport and riffled through it. 'Tourist visa OK.' He reached the last page and turned the passport to look at the photo. 'Cedric Minola? You're related to her? And she's left you here? What she do, think you're too much baggage? Thought you'd slow her down?' He shook his head. 'Man, that's cold. She skips off leaving her own flesh and blood to the mercy of law enforcement just to save her own skin. Jeez.' Brown looked up at the cop standing behind Kate. 'With family like that, who needs the Mafia?'

'He do nothing wrong,' said Kate. 'You not hold him.'

'Yeah? That the plan, Cedric? You walk because we ain't got nothing on you?'

Da looked down and gestured to his clothes. 'I've got these.'

Brown turned back to Kate. 'What is it? Is he like Forrest Gump?'

Kate shrugged. 'He thinking different.'

'That right, Cedric? You a bit hard of thinking?' Brown dropped the passport and picked up the airline ticket. 'Hey hey. You're booked on a flight outta JFK tonight. You're flying back to Merry Olde Heathrow England, Cedric. You're off on an airplane.'

'An aeroplane? Me?' Da sat up straight, eyes shining. 'Oh yes please, sir.'

Brown's eyes rose to the ceiling. 'Freaking liability,' he muttered.

It took Da barely ten more minutes to exasperate Brown and convince him that Minola had left him behind because, in his state of mind, he posed absolutely no risk of betraying her.

'Roscoe?' he finally shouted.

Almost instantly a uniform in dark glasses appeared at the door. 'Sir?'

'This is Mr Minola. He's got a date with an airplane out of JFK. Make sure he meets it.'

'Yes, sir.' Roscoe gathered up the passport, ticket and paper then practically lifted Da up to hustle him out of the room.

Kate smiled for just over a hundred milliseconds and then tried it on. 'Boss, say I take him to airport, stop him get lost.'

Brown's fist suddenly pounded down on the table,

making Kate jump, and the cop behind her twitch towards his holster. 'You're not going anywhere, Sanchez. Not until you tell me where she is. Where's your boss? Where's Minola?'

As Roscoe disappeared with Da, Kate shifted awkwardly in her chair and looked down coyly. Da was a big boy, he could look after himself, she lied to herself. He'd have a great time; after all, there weren't many septuagenarians who got a police escort to the airport.

In the table's mottled reflection she noticed Brown reach into his coat pocket. He pulled out her perp sheet. Brown gazed at the picture and then laid it on the table, pushing it into Kate's line of vision. '*Wanted*,' it said, '*for Extortion, Fraud, Blackmail, Larceny through Deception, Impersonating an Officer of the Law, Identity Theft, Bigamy, Immigration Circumvention, Evading Arrest, Damage to Federal Property*.' Kate read this biography with a pang. How little they knew! The mark of any good con is that it leaves no mark, no sign, no trace; but then each was a victim of its own success.

'Your boss, she's been a very bad girl.'

Kate looked up at Agent Brown, who stared calmly at her. Now that he had her photo right in front of him to compare, now, Kate knew, was the moment of truth.

'You,' he said, pointing a finger at Kate. His eyes widened.

Special Agent Danny 'Hawkeye' Brown was an expert at observation. He had not only achieved one of the FBI's highest ever scores in ex-obs, he also infuriated a large number of his colleagues by consistently winning the Spot-the-Difference competition in the *Informer* (commonly referred to as 'the Snitch'), the Bureau's in-house magazine. Brown liked to claim an almost Zen ability, that he 'saw' when most just 'looked' and, apart from that one bombshell redhead he had failed to pick up on vice detail, he prided himself on never missing a trick.

In contrast, Kate's attempted change of identity from wanted British fugitive to undesirable Mexican maid was, at best, rudimentary. But then years of experience had taught her that good disguise didn't depend on the wonders of latex second skins, prosthetics, wigs or falsies but something more profound: the speed of thought.

From: _Forgetting to Remember_, Random House, London, 2006

Speed of Thought

Just for a moment, imagine if every turn of your head, each sound or gesture you made had to be thought about and logically processed before it could be enacted. It would take a human every waking moment to simply survive; forget the creation of civilizations, art, philosophy or finishing off the Sudoku.

Consciousness, the thoughts-we're-aware-of and the constant world around us we perceive, comes at a high processing cost to our brains. By needing to follow the rules of logic, which make everything in our world seem explicable or at least 'right', the conscious mind is hampered and slowed by constantly having to tie all the information from our nervous systems into a continuous narrative for our waking brains. Each moment apparently segues seamlessly into the next. But this makes consciously working through things, logically, a relatively slow, time-consuming process.

The speed of conscious thought is a deliberate, slow, neurological Sunday-style driving when compared to the thoughts-we're-not-aware-of-but-which-must-somehow-be-there unconscious. The Porsche flashing its lights in your rear-view mirror, overtaking on the bend and roaring off. There is no narrative that the unconscious seems to follow, no discernible highway code as it careers along, impossibly fast, emotional, multi-tasking, un-controllable, and completely neuro-illogical.

The conscious mind is good at working in a linear, logical progression which is slow but renders the rational world as we know it. But can we catch the unconscious processes right in the act of speeding?

One famous and fruitless psychological study, the result of years of scientific research into the speed of unconscious thought, confirmed that the workings of the unconscious mind do function a lot faster than the conscious mind, but never found out why.

But just in that we have a major clue: have a look at that last paragraph and count how many times the letter F occurs.

Did you find seven or eight?

When we read, we tap into a faster process, we consign less important words to unconscious recognition. We distinguish them only by their shape. So even when looking at a sentence as a collection of letters, we still tend to recognize the word 'of' as a whole shape and find it difficult to overcome the urge to let our unconscious mind interpret it. The logical, conscious, counting mind will rarely spot that there are, in fact, eleven Fs – if you didn't see them look again and see how difficult it is to overcome the urges of your unconscious mind to see smaller words as templates rather than individual letters.

From: _Project Notebook 17.6_ p12

Kate's disguise was consummate because it simply tapped into the way our unconscious uses templates. The unconscious doesn't bother to think things out, it makes assumptions based on experience and memory and then takes notice of the way something deviates from the template. It goes from the general to the particular. It relies on stereotypes and sweeping generalizations and, in that way, we find bigotry, prejudice, bias, racism and general narrow-mindedness is hard-wired into human biology – which may explain why we are so very good at those things.

If we look at a photograph of a crater on Mars and see a face, we then find it impossible to see the crater.

If you see a Mexican maid and she fits into your mental template of a Mexican maid, it is almost impossible to see the grifter beneath.

As long as Kate didn't deviate from Agent Brown's expectations she could maintain the illusion, even if the perp sheet she was now looking at specifically stated, '*Suspect known to alter appearance*,' and '*AKA*' followed by no fewer than fifty-seven different names.

The pale blonde who smiled out of the photo may have had the same faint cheekbones, the same defined jawline and gently overspilling lips, but the woman in front of Agent Brown, with her flawlessly smoothed Insta-tan, dyed black hair, brown contact lenses, faintly kohled moustache and thick accent, simply bore more resemblance to his Mexican maid template than his Kate Minola template.

5

Mr Noodles had successfully vanished some flowers, a foam rabbit, an assortment of coins, a banana into his ear and any dignity that might have lurked in his soul.

'Now, kids,' he shouted, 'all this stuff keeps disappearing but d'you know what? I know a person who does that. I can see him but no one else can. He's my friend and he's called Bertie. Have any of you got an invisible friend?'

At this point he would expect a few hands to go up and Mr Noodles would select one of these more imaginative children to come up and help him find Bertie. No hands emerged so he tried again. 'Haven't any of you got someone you talk to that no one else can see?'

'No,' the birthday boy shouted, 'it's only you, you sad wanker.'

'This,' Peter continued, 'is where Bertie lives.' He produced his trusty Ravenport Deluxe Change Bag, an innocent-looking prop that resembled a perfectly normal bag; in the same way an elderly transvestite does. It looked rather like a ping-pong paddle with a hole cut out and a velvet scrotum hanging beneath it. It was a classic magic prop that children's magicians just seem to have; like whisky on their breath, thickets of nose hair or warblers under the tongue that can make them sound uncannily like the African Weaver Thrush when constipated.

No one asked how a friend, even an invisible one, could fit into a bag the size of a cabbage, so Mr Noodles continued. 'Bertie's very special, children. When I snap my fingers he will jump out of the bag and fly right over your heads.'

Peter searched for that glint of wonder in the sallow eyes of the children but knew from countless experiences that for this PlayStation generation, the fact that something might just jump out and levitate wasn't magic, it was just knowing the right combination of the ○, □, △ or × buttons.

'OK. One.' Mr Noodles swung the bag towards his audience. 'Two.' He swayed. 'Three.' His eyes followed a trajectory of something invisible flying from the mouth of the change bag right into the air. A couple of the more innocent children looked around too. Apparently distraught, Mr Noodles peered into the bag. 'Oh dear, he must be asleep. Shall we wake him up, children?'

The birthday heckler at the front sighed. 'Wake me up too. When you've finished.'

Peter plunged his hand into the change bag and pulled the whole bag up through the paddle, inside out, showing that there was nothing in there. Pushing the bag back in again, he looked at the sea of dilating eyes already hitting their first sugar crash.

'Who wants to help me?'

Nothing could hide the fissures of quiet despair which splintered through Mr Noodles' white face paint as he took in the blank stares of each one of the thirty children resolutely not volunteering. He was in no state to appreciate that the room had in fact fallen silent for the first time since he had arrived, that he had at last managed to capture their attention. He took no solace from this achievement in the same way Sullap Al-Habib, the one-legged hermit and last troglodyte of the caves of Bora Bora, took no comfort from the achievement of capturing the attention of the 3rd, 5th, 8th, 10th, 17th and 22nd US Marine Corps, Airborne and Light Infantry Divisions.

Mr Noodles shook his head in dismay. He turned away from the children and pulled out a Groucho-ho, the full set of glasses, eyebrows, nose and moustache – guaranteed to get a laugh. Twisting away to place them on his face, he turned to look at an audience who had as much chance of recognizing the mask's simulacra as they would of identifying a vinyl record player, a telephone dial or moral clarity. A small boy in the middle looked like he might smile but then coughed instead.

'Hey,' Mr Noodles said in a broad Brooklyn,

painstakingly accurate impression of Marx the elder, 'who let all the midgets in?'

Not a titter, laugh, cough or groan, only the cold thin sound of the wind which seemed to be blowing every gag right over their heads. Mr Noodles caught the malicious scent of the glowering brood and turned to his bag once more. He would go straight to the finale and then scarper. He whipped out his grand finishing prop, a clinking clanking instrument direct from the sadomasochistic bondage scene, and dangled it in front of his less than innocent audience.

'Who knows what these are?' he said, grinning.

The birthday boy, sitting at the front, suddenly took an interest. 'Handcuffs,' he called out.

'Indeed they are, young man,' Mr Noodles replied, invigorated by the new-found attentiveness. 'These are more than just plain old handcuffs. They are heavy-duty tensile double-dropped forged steel handcuffs as used by the LA Police Department themselves to apprehend some of the most dangerous criminals on earth.' Anyone who has switched on a television for longer than twenty seconds in the last five years would know that this was rubbish. Every episode of the endless *Police, Camera, Speeding Fine* or *The World's Worst Shoplifters* shows the felons being led off with tiny plastic electric cable ties around their wrists, but still the glittering sheen of cold metal was a nice illusion for the weapon-obsessed eight-year-olds to focus on. 'And I,' Mr Noodles continued with a new confidence, 'will attempt to escape from them before your very eyes. Now, who will come up and chain me to the chair,' he pointed to a sturdy-looking dining chair in one corner, 'of doom?'

For the first time the birthday boy smiled sweetly at him, raising one hand as the other palmed a ball-bearing swiped from an already smashed pass-the-parcel-prize wobbly maze puzzle.

Mr Noodles beckoned the birthday boy up, gave him the handcuffs and went to pick up the chair to take it to his stage area. On closer inspection the chair appeared to have been made from cast iron and was much heavier than it looked. Mr Noodles could barely move it. Seeing as the children had now cleared a space around the chair and there were no others clean of smeared cake or big enough to sit on, he called the boy over and directed him behind the chair. Mr Noodles sat down and placed his arms around the back of the chair.

'Now place the high tensile rock-solid forged steel handcuffs on my wrists so that they are locked tight.'

The boy dutifully, and a little too professionally, snapped them shut around his wrists, leading the chain around a stem in the centre of the chair's back.

'Are they locked firmly?'

'Yeah.'

'Give them a good pull, make sure.'

The boy pulled at the cuffs, which clanked loudly against the iron.

'I can tell you've done this before,' Mr Noodles said over his shoulder. 'You're not a policeman, are you?' A few of the children laughed. 'Thank you very much, you can sit down again. Everyone, give the birthday boy a bog clip, a bag clop, a big clap.'

The children burst into a round of applause and, quiet as a lamb chop, the boy sat down again.

Now, were it not for the ball-bearing that had been

jammed into Mr Noodles' Whodini Handcuffs ratchet, the ensuing routine would have been a very amusing one. It involved Mr Noodles struggling with his arms behind him and getting so hot that he needed to wipe his brow. At that point one of his hands would come round to wipe his forehead and then return behind him to continue the struggle. Most of the children would be so caught up in his writhing about that they wouldn't notice the free arm until it was back again pretending to struggle. Then the other arm would come out to loosen his collar, check the time, point at something, etc., and then return and this would carry on until the children were almost sick with shouting, at which point Mr Noodles would stand up free, waving his arms in the air.

'Do you want to know how I did that?' he would triumphantly exclaim to the rapturous applause.

Some children would shout yes.

'OK, OK, I'll tell you. When I first tried to do this I soon realized that it was way too hard to escape the drop forged tensile double-hardened steel handcuffs, so, so instead, and this was the clever bit, I shrank my arms to slip them out. But then I realized that people would notice I had really tiny arms. So I decided that I would shrink my whole body to keep everything in proportion. But then I realized people would notice that I was smaller so I would need to shrink the chair and the entire room and every one of you and the entire world as well. Which is exactly what I do every time I do an escape, look.' At this point from behind the chair he would bring out a huge pair of handcuffs. Great giant manacles which had been lurking down the back of his trousers. 'Now these are going to be very useful when I arrest the Jolly Green Giant for being so corny.' A bow, what a finale.

But Peter's life, the birthday boy, and one tiny ball-bearing just weren't going to let things work out quite like that.

6

'You,' Brown said, stabbing a finger towards Kate, 'Tell – Me – Where – Boss?'

Kate peered closer at her photo. Not bad. She recognized it from a couple of years before, cropped from a wedding photo, standing outside an Episcopal church in Vermont, dressed in virginal white. The mark in the tuxedo who had been beaming next to her had been excised from the picture, in the same ruthless manner that his entire bank account, a small bag of uncut diamonds and one thousand Microsoft shares were, only two days after the snap was taken.

That had done nicely for a couple of months in Palm Springs.

'Your boss, she knows I'm close.' Brown was peering down at the photo in Kate's hand. 'And you know what? She's facing forty-eight years in maximum security. Your boss is going to be a very, very old woman if she ever comes out again. She won't ever find you. You can tell me. You've got nothing to be frightened of.'

Oh but she did. Kate felt a cold terror seep icily down

her spine. A terrible fear gripped her as she looked at the photo, as nothing in her six-year jaunt at the top table of America's Most Wanted had before.

Maybe part of it was the sudden absence of her father, whom she had become so accustomed to caring for. For two years she had been bundling him from hustle to hustle as his regression worsened and exploiting the sympathy for cold cash. Maybe a part of it was seeing the younger, nicer Kate in the photo and wondering what a monster of deception she had become. But, far more immediately, what struck Kate with such cold dread was the finger of the hand which held the photo.

Kate spotted the pale line of her hastily removed bling engagement ring. It was the last gift she had scored off the petulant mark who had called the law in the first place. And it was the inevitability of the raid that had initiated Kate's whole plan to ship Da back to England for residential care. She had only realized that the ring was still on long after the San Tropay Insta-tan had dried, and whipped it off seconds before opening the door.

It was the smallest of clues but Kate knew that it was the sort of thing Columbo would turn at the door to point at when he said, 'There's just one more thing.' Something an expert FBI observer was trained to spot a mile off, let alone less than two feet away. It was not something that could be easily explained. If she was unmarried, why the ring mark? Who would believe a divorced Mexican? And then, if that was her natural skin colour what sort of Mexican was she anyway? However you looked at it, once the flaw was spotted it begged questions and the only way her flimsy disguise could work was if all answers were assumed by the mental template and not directly asked. This tiny mark threatened the whole house of cards.

It was the tiniest tell, but it struck a terror so deep in Kate's psyche, it shot through her hippocampus to permanently alter the neuronal and synaptic structure of her amygdala. This part of the brain, the monarch of our emotions, sits in the deepest cavern of the mind as on a throne teetering atop the spinal cord and shapes the way we feel about everything. Later, when the mask of the adrenalin had subsided, Kate would feel that scar of fear and would live with it for ever.

She couldn't move her finger out of the way without drawing attention to it. Suddenly everything relied on Kate keeping Brown's eyes off her now trembling finger. Before his inner child became an outer bloody nuisance Da had often talked about the art of misdirection. 'These, Da,' Kate would point at her cleavage, 'are all the misdirection I need.'

Agent Brown jabbed the photo. 'This your Miss Katie?'

Kate cursed the high buttoning of the maid's outfit and nodded slowly, '*Sí.*'

'And where is she?'

Kate, try as she might, could hardly keep her eyes off the ring mark. It felt like the disguise had been blown wide open yet she had to keep going. She tried a surly Mexican shrug.

Agent Brown leaned closer and she could smell the jarring odour of an oversweetened deodorant. His voice became a threatening growl. '*Viva Mek-he-co?*'

Kate looked up, fear flashing in her eyes. He hadn't spotted it yet. '*Señor*, mister, no. Not send back. I in big trouble. I work hard. I—'

'So. It's this simple. Where boss go?' He snatched the photo out of Kate's hand and stopped for a moment. A moment. A lifetime. Kate felt as if every organ was melting in her. She slowly withdrew her hand and looked pitifully up at Brown, ready to give him the 'It's a fair cop, guv'nor' shrug.

'Show me your hand.'

Kate put her right hand out.

'Look at it,' Brown insisted.

Kate stared at it.

'You're defending a woman who's been working those pretty hands of yours to the bone. You're protecting a woman who had no love for you, no thought for you whatsoever. Just give her up, Sanchez. Give her up.'

'Please. Mister. Sir. She not say.'

Kate was aware that another uniform was entering the room. She glanced around to see a squat, overweight woman with an 'Immigration' badge pinned to a chest which resembled the sort of weighty, overstuffed bosom that shoplifters tend to possess when they leave a store.

'Sanchez,' Brown said, 'this is your last chance. You don't owe her nothing. She's gone, *vámonos*, she's left you here knowing that we were coming. She's betrayed you. She ain't your boss no more. And if you don't cooperate you'll be back to the castanets and donkeys before you can say *hasta la vista*. You need to look after *numero uno* now, Sanchez. Be smart. You know something, don't you.'

Kate fell silent for a long time. She knew that it was

all in the timing; the more she looked like she was struggling with her conscience the more he would buy it.

Eventually Brown thumped the table with irritation. 'Come on,' he shouted. 'If she gets away because you're holding us up I'm going to—'

'She say nothing, mister. But. I see ticket.'

'What sort of ticket? Where to?'

'To Hotawaa?'

'To Hot . . . you mean Ottawa, in Canada?'

Kate nodded.

'Do you know where she's flying from?'

'From New Walk?'

'Newark?' Brown's head jerked up to fix the officer standing behind Kate. 'Johnson. Get a team down to Newark Airport.'

As he stood up he gestured towards the fat woman. 'Miss Sanchez, this is Officer Caskie from Immigration. I'm releasing you into her custody. She'll be making your deportation arrangements.'

'Bastard,' Kate screamed as her arms were pulled behind her and the ubiquitous plastic ties were placed on her wrists. 'You promise,' she spat. 'This American justice? This land of free?'

'Nothing's for free, sweetheart,' Brown said as he left.

7

A little play-struggling. A little stretching of the neck and swaying from side to side, then pull the magnet from back pocket and place below spring mechanism in ratchet. And pop. Come on, pop. Magnet against mechanism. Pop. Oh, for God's sake. Magnet against mechanism. Come on. Pop. Oh shit. Oh fuck.

'Come on, Noodles.'

'Yeah – let's see ya.'

Right, try again. There's the switch, it won't bloody move. Harder. No.

'Right. Well, kids, um . . .'

The birthday boy started a slow handclap and singing. 'Why are we wai-ting, why-y are we wai-ting.' Then every child joined in.

As the volume increased, Mr Noodles thrashed around more and more violently. 'Look, I actually need some help. Could one of you go and get one of your mums? Just get up and go and get someone? Please?'

As the clapping and singing just got louder and faster the birthday boy stood up. Mr Noodles looked in his eyes, at the slight smile, and in an instant he knew that it was him. 'That's very funny. Well done. It's a good joke but I think you should—'

Mr Noodles got no further as, without a word but in time with the rapid chanting, the birthday boy lunged towards him.

The birthday boy grabbed the sides of Mr Noodles' pantaloons and yanked them down to his ankles. The giant handcuffs, fifty-three cards, a puppet rabbit, two thumbtips and a jumbo coin clattered to the ground. Ah, thought Mr Noodles, so he just couldn't bear not knowing how the magic was done. Well, now he knows. But the birthday boy didn't stop there. He took hold of Mr Noodles' boxer shorts and ripped them down. Mr

Noodles jerked ferociously, trying in vain to bring his hands forward. To hold on to his shorts, to hide his modesty, to whack the awful child, but he could do nothing as the whole room burst into laughter and applause, pointing at his exposed and very shrivelled penis. The birthday boy played to the audience and, rummaging through Mr Noodles' props, returned with something hidden in his hands. Mr Noodles was writhing violently but didn't dare shout out lest he be caught in this state.

'Come on, please, yes, very funny, now let me out, please. Kids, help me out, come on,' he continued, tears starting to run down the face paint.

Most of the children had stood up by now and the chant had turned to 'You, you, you're a dirty old man.' They danced around him, pointing and laughing.

The birthday boy leaned down to talk into Mr Noodles' ear above the racket. 'You're a bit exposed there, old man,' he said. 'Would you like something to cover that todger?' Mr Noodles nodded without thinking, and the boy, sporting a grin so smug it would be etched on Peter's mind for ever, pulled out the prop and forcibly rammed it on to his genitals. Mr Noodles screamed.

From: *Sessions Notebook 57.14* p22

P. seems to completely relive this as he remembers and describes the moment. Very vivid: his arms 'wrenching against the jagged steel' and the pain 'rocketing' through his body as shreds of skin 'tear' from his wrists. The veins in his neck 'bulging like creepers grasping to throttle' him, his whole frame 'quivering with the strain', and the 'agony' as he pulled at the handcuffs with 'nausea bubbling and crowding' his stomach, sending 'convulsions' through his body.

But even though the lacerating pain must have been overwhelming, unendurable, there seems to have been one sweet mercy.

Distraction.

However fearsome the pain, it distracted him. Distracted him from contemplating the awful circumstances in which all that was happening. It brought a numbing joy which smothered all those thoughts, emotions and feelings; of shame, of guilt, of self-loathing and, most of all, of sheer cringe-making embarrassment.

The pain overwhelmed everything and it made the moment somehow bearable.

But now that moment is a memory, it is somehow much worse. At each recollection he's there again, straining uselessly for some grip on the handcuffs' mechanism, unchangeably his fingertips slipping with sweat, or blood, but that compensating pain is absent. It's only now, in the mnemonic reconstruction, in dreams and flashbacks, that the sickening, humiliating, unforgettable embarrassment engulfs him; it's only when it is replayed as a memory without the merciful distraction of the physical pain that that recurring moment seems to become utterly, totally unbearable.

So, even in that instant, as he struggled to escape, deep in his hippocampus, he was gathering fodder for the nightmares that would haunt him for the rest of his life. Even as the chair's back dug into his armpits; even as the 'contraption' was attached to his genitals; even as those globules of spit, shooting from the laughing mouths of his tormentors, settled on the hairs of his bare legs, there were parts of his brain which already knew that he would live this naked terror again and again and, even worse, each time he would have to face not the pain but, much worse, what a total and utter fuckwit he was.

From: _NeuroScience Today_, Oxford, Hilary 2009

Fuckwit? Swearing? Yes, it's a bit childish. But then at what time in our lives were we better at learning things? Does it really have no place in scientific discourse? Are we not limiting ourselves if we can only convey knowledge in the academic orthodoxy of style which insists on a stern face?

In communicating science especially, there is a preference for the image of Darwin furrowing his brow rather than the one of Einstein sticking his tongue out. There is, apparently, no place for levity, frivolousness or, indeed, a word like 'fuckwit'.

Science is a serious business and, the logic goes, you cannot think straight when you're laughing.

It's a common mistake, but I believe this is confusing the act of thinking with that of urinating. Whereas it really is quite difficult to pee straight when you're giggling, we can prove that, when it comes to perception, we actually think straighter when we're laughing.

Look at this Necker Cube (*Fig. 1*). It's a bit of a bugger. One moment it's pointing up, the next down; something which, usually, only teenage boys have to learn to live with.

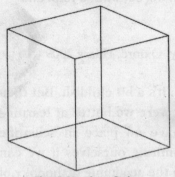

The visual uncertainty, though, is called 'binocular rivalry'. Because each of your eyes has a bias to a different side of your brain, your left and right hemispheres are actually competing right now for dominance in interpretation. Sadly, as it isn't a cube at all but a crude two-dimensional arrangement of straight lines paying no heed to perspective foreshortening, they can bicker as long as they like; they're both wrong.

Fig. 1 Necker Cube

You may have to find someone to tickle you for this; if you're reading this on a train right now, perhaps the man next to you will. But, look at the cube when you're laughing and the switching stops. You see just one of the two versions. Clarity is restored, amusement instils a more harmonious disposition on the brain, and the mind is at its most ready to focus, absorb and even learn.

So, I make no apology for any frivolousness, baseness of language, exaggeration of situation, embellishment of character, puns, gags, jokes or any other linguistic trickery that may seem crude in my writing. Why would I write if I didn't want my reader to concentrate? Some of science's greatest findings have been down to accidents; what the academic fear of humour keeps suppressed is just how many of the accidents were down to jokes and pranks being played. Like the lab assistant who thought it'd be a laugh to switch Fleming's yoghurt fridge off over the weekend, or the kid who was scrumping and found Newton's bonce irresistible, or the bored nanny who flashed her front bottom at the impressionable boy Freud.

Whatever's up with the actresses and bishops in life, humourlessness and focus are not the natural bedfellows we assume. We actually think straighter when we're amused.

Now if we can only apply this straightening process to male urination we may clear up the sticky-patches-on-the-lavatory-floor problem for ever.

8

'Lola Cervantes de Sanchez?'

'*Sí.*'

'*¿No pasaporte?*'

'*¿Qué piensa?*'

The acne-etched porcine customs man shrugged and wearily stamped Kate's papers. '*¿A dónde vas?*'

'*Infierno.*'

He looked up as he passed the papers back to her. '*Voy a verla allí.*'

There was no point trying to elicit bribes from the weekly deportee-return flight; the Yankees always made sure they returned empty-handed.

From the quiet of the customs office, Kate made her way on to the bright arrivals concourse. The moment the doors opened she was suddenly hit by a cacophony of shouts and voices, clashing trolleys and beeping electric invalid buggies. Ragged families stood piled high on luggage-free trolleys, waiting to greet their prodigal repatriates; casually dressed, uninformed police teams awaited the flight's extraditionaries. Kate, on the other hand, had to suffice with the solitary greeting of an unlocatable wolf whistle and the realization that

50

she was still wearing the much too short, much too frilly maid's outfit that she had been arrested in. She pushed her way through to the airport toilets.

According to the *Lonely Rougher's Guide to Mexico City*, the Zapata International Airport conveniences are the 'last chance to spruce before the hellish filth of the Barrio. They're the cleanest porcelain in the whole of Mexico City, man!'

Breathing through her mouth as she found her way to the last cubicle, Kate shuffled into the tiny space and locked the door.

Occupado.

Standing on the toilet seat, Kate reached up to the ventilation grille and poked her fingers between the bars. Tugging hard, she managed to pull the bottom far enough away from the wall to slip her hand up into the shaft. Feeling around the greasy edge, her hand hit what she was searching for. She pulled her fingers out again, holding the tiny plastic-wrapped kit. Banging the grille back into place, she sat back down on the toilet and began to unwrap it.

Inside the grimy plastic bag was a passport and ten hundred-dollar bills. Kate stuffed the bills into her little white-lace pinny and flicked through the passport to remind herself who she was going to be next. She read the name and winced.

Winslet, Kate.

She had forgotten that. Back when she had planted the kit, there had been no film star, it had simply been a random name, something that sounded winsome, in-effectual, self-effacing, instantly forgettable. The passport photo didn't help either: she was sporting straight blonde hair and didn't appear entirely unlike the rising and sinking film star. The fact that she was probably a good foot shorter than the starlet was not much of a drawback. People in the movies were always expected to be smaller in real life. Winslet? I ask you. If you're going into that sort of industry the least you can do is treat yourself to a new, sexier name like Norma Jean or Frances Gumm or even Diana Fluck did.

Unless it's part of the game, the last thing an artist like Kate ever wants to do is call attention to herself. Still, she took some comfort in reminding herself that this was Mexico and perhaps, as far as anyone here knew, the name Kate Winslet was as common in the States as red necks, the term 'whatever' and obesity.

'Miss Winslet,' the hotel concierge sang as he ran round the lobby desk to greet her, 'the moment we got your reservation the entire hotel was abuzz with excitement.'

Standing in the lobby of the Mexico City Hilton, in her re-blonded hairdo and boutique-fresh washed-silk dress, Kate scowled. 'Actually I was rather hoping to keep things low-key. You know, incognito, no press and so on.'

'But of course. Discretion is the byword of this establishment.' The concierge bowed and turned away. 'Juan,' he yelled to the other side of the lobby, 'take Kate Winslet's bags up to the Presidential Suite.'

9

'So, for clarity,' Justice Dunnruff gazed over her glasses, 'what you are saying is that the defendant made a career of seeking out society's most vulnerable people for sexual exploitation.'

The glasses were for show. Her vision was perfect; indeed Justice Dunnruff possessed the sort of eyesight that fighter pilots aspire to, and tend to claim they have, before taking to the skies and engulfing troops in friendly fire. But justice for Justice Dunnruff was not only to be done, it had to be seen to be done, and if she was going to be seen doing it she would be dressed for the part, complete with wig, gown, garters and glasses. Especially the garters.

Mr Psmyth-Heigh-Fannate smiled at her, his Ultrabrite teeth glinting. 'With respect, your honour, what we're saying is that he sought out children.'

'For sexual exploitation,' Dunnruff repeated, pointedly looking at Mr Psmyth-Heigh-Fannate and moistening her lower lip with the tip of her tongue.

'Certainly to expose himself and therefore gain a deviant form of sexual satisfaction, ma'am.' His 'ma'am' was pronounced with the open vowels of an acquired plumminess. Dunnruff's gaze lowered to Psmyth-Heigh-Fannate's well-pressed trousers, thinking it might be time to call a recess and summon counsel to her chambers. It was about time he learned it wasn't 'ma'am' as in 'calm' but 'ma'am' as in 'ram'.

Peter sat with anchoring hands gripping the dock. The wobbling ginger ringlets of his court-appointed legal aid lawyer bounced furiously as she nodded at him and he, with resignation, nodded back.

'Defence would like to change its plea, your honour.' Miss Smith stood up. She stumbled to the side of her desk as if she had just left the wrong sort of bar. 'Mr Ruchio, I mean, my client, has directed me that he wishes to change his plea.'

'I see.' Justice Dunnruff smiled, anticipating an early lunch. 'To "guilty", I presume.'

'Yes, but on the grounds of diminished responsibility.' Dunnruff looked suspiciously at Peter. He nodded again and dropped his gaze to the floor.

The boy on the TV screen screamed into his microphone. 'I saw that. See, he admits he's a filthy old cunt. He needs his bollocks cut off.' As the stenographer looked up with a slightly concerned expression, the Clerk of the Court swiftly cut the audio feed.

Mr Psmyth-Heigh-Fannate jumped up. 'Forgive the witness, m'lady. This has been a terrible, corrupting ordeal for him and,' he paused and his whole face fell into a sombre grimace, 'I think this amply demonstrates the dreadful effects on a young mind that such a sordid exposure can leave.'

'I think we have the relevant facts,' Justice Dunnruff replied, 'and as the defendant is pleading guilty there is no need for this witness's statement.' She glanced at the boy still ranting mutely on the screen. 'I think we can now see why one of the pillars of British justice is that children should be seen but not heard. You may switch him off.'

The screen went blank. Psmyth-Heigh-Fannate turned to the bench. 'I'm afraid there is one more witness to be called, your honour.'

'Is it necessary?'

'It's Mrs Black, m'lady, the victim's mother. What she says may affect your sentence.'

Justice Dunnruff sighed. 'Right, send her in.'

The courtroom temperature plummeted a few degrees as the ice mother entered and Justice Dunnruff pulled her cloak about her. Taking the stand, she gave her name and told her story with chilling precision.

'And when you heard the scream,' Mr Psmyth-Heigh-Fannate prompted, 'and you entered the conservatory, you were completely unaware that you had left your small, vulnerable children in the care of such a man. Could you describe what you saw?'

'That man there, sitting on a chair.'

'May the court record that Mrs Black has indicated the defendant.'

'The children were almost hysterical with shock. He was sitting there completely naked from the waist down, exposing himself to our children.'

'Completely naked?' Mr Psmyth-Heigh-Fannate prompted.

'Well, apart from that, that thing on his, his winky.'

'Could we see Exhibit A? Thank you. Is this the

so-called "thing" that was on his winky . . . pardon me, his penis, at the time you saw him?'

'Yes.'

Mr Psmyth-Heigh-Fannate turned dramatically to the bench. 'Sometimes, your honour, a cigar is not just a cigar. While indulging in an extreme form of sado-masochistic bondage in front of the children, this was what the defendant placed on his penis.' He held the familiar object aloft. 'This is the sick, warped kind of depravity that the defendant indulges in, nestling his sexual organs in this. And with this we must all condemn him.'

Peter watched with tears suddenly stinging at the edge of his eyelids and a death wish tearing at his heart as Psmyth-Heigh-Fannate triumphantly waved the article in the air: the Groucho-ho glasses, nose and moustache.

TIC, TAC, TOE – TEA
Assessing Suicidal Potentiality

(This handout accompanies today's 3pm lec-
ture by End Of Life specialist Dr Hans
Helmut at the Social and Healthcare Workers
'Improving Targets' conference)

In today's world of financial stress and
fractured families the need to be able to
identify the potentially suicidal is of
paramount importance for all in the primary
care sector and, of course, recruiters for
Al-Qaeda.

Firstly it is a mistake to characterize all
suicides as stemming from depression. Some
subjects can be highly motivated by other
factors. Today I aim to characterize three
key stages which almost all subjects electing
to end their life go through before complet-
ing the task. If, through taking detailed
histories, a healthcare specialist can detect
these conditions and events, the opportunity
for intervention to prevent The Expiry
Action (TEA) will be greatly improved.

1. The Inciting Condition (TIC)
This is an incident which the subject may
allude to repeatedly. Often it is something
that happened in their youth or fairly long
ago, something he or she never fully recovered from. Memories of the incident, either
directly or indirectly, tend to haunt the
subject, making them more compliant to end-

of-life considerations. Their conscious
rationalization tends to be that a life led
haunted in such a way is no life at all.

2. The Activating Condition (TAC)
At some point, usually more recently, the
subject will have been placed in some
emotional turmoil, often accompanied by hope
and generally a moment of positivity. This
is usually perceived as a make-or-break
moment. During TAC their life and their
past preconceptions are given a thorough
shake-up.

3. The Originating Event (TOE)
The Originating Event is the initial moment
that triggers the logical and apparently
inevitable set of conclusions and feelings
that overwhelms the subject's better judgement and even their natural fear of pain
and death. TOE occurs when, due to bad luck
or the subject's own shortcomings, something
goes wrong during TAC which then reinforces
all the long-term underlying negative feelings that were generated during TIC. If
suicide is to be prevented, intervention is
critical between The Originating Event and
The Expiry Action (TEA).

4. The Expiry Action (TEA)
When all is done, the subject is ready for
TEA. It is no longer a matter of whether
they will take their life, only how. The
chosen method will have become clear
through TIC, TAC and TOE.

10

So it was only when she was, at last, lying alone on the 'Presidential' bed, showered and skin shed of de Sanchez and Winslet, baby naked between cool sheets, that Kate was finally able to think of herself as Catherine again.

This was never the moment of pleasure that she imagined when she was keeping up a disguise and longing to finish the game. When it happened, it always turned out to be a dirty feeling, and painful. Like the transformations that the moon-bathed lycanthropic seem to suffer in films as they metamorphose into werewolves; the sort of testtube-breaking, lab-destroying pain even Dr Jekyll could never hyde.

As soon as she allowed herself to become Catherine again, all the reasons she had tried so hard to stop being Catherine in the first place came flooding back. It was Catherine and Kate, and Catherine was somebody Kate really had no affection for. It was at these moments she really wondered why she still held on to her at all.

Here, Kate was a world away from Cath-the-Path,

the sociopath, the psycho, the school bully, the daddy's girl, the girl who got caught. Look at her now. Now, Kate simply had to turn her head on her 'Presidential' pillow and she could gaze out through the wall of windows, high over this extraordinarily violent, exotic city, a place barely even dreamed of in the remedial classrooms of St John's Street Secondary or the tills of the Bristol Costco. Ciudad de México lay beneath her, a vast shimmering sea of red-tile and grey-tin roofs spreading away into a pointillist blur at a horizon pierced by a lurid orange setting sun and bleeding a pink-purple haze into the still, cloudless sky. Around the city, little lights burst to life in the gloaming.

Kate was a world away, so why did she feel the need to hold on so tightly to her pathetic, crappy, grim past? She couldn't understand why she was still clinging to this last vestige of her old self with the whitening fingers and desperate prevaricating of a shipwreck survivor clutching the last piece of driftwood beneath a darkening sky. She held on to Catherine, that little girl growing up in that tiny, shitty, freezing cold, two-up two-down pebbledash *cunts-louse* in Avonmouth, with the same pitiful desperation that Batman clings to Bruce Wayne; knowing at once that the millionaire playboy is his last chance of being human again and that, no matter how hard he tries, he's never ever going to get back there. Not after what he, and Kate, have seen.

Thinking about Avonmouth, Kate suddenly felt overwhelmed with emotion. A flood of feelings bubbled up around her and her stomach tightened, trying to preserve what air was in her lungs as it seemed that she would fairly drown.

From: <u>*NeuroSceptic*</u>, Geneva, March 2007

EmMems

Emotional Memories are key to our evolution but they're often the most damaging and the hardest to lose.

Chris Tavasligh

NOW I do realize that, for romantics, 'feelings' and 'emotions' are something mysterious that defies logic and therefore, since reason is the backbone of the scientific method, the legitimacy of science itself.

However, for a neuropsychologist 'feelings' are far more prosaic. Though they may be described as a basic biological brain function processed in the amygdala, feelings are, in fact, more than that: they represent one of the pinnacle achievements in the development of human brain function. Neither instinct nor reason, emotions are the brain's override mechanism for coping with life's moments when the amount of sensory data that needs to be processed becomes overwhelming.

The real secret to humans' evolution to become the world's uber-beast is nothing more than our brain-to-body-size ratio. We've got large brains at a relatively low energy cost for the bodies that support them. As we have evolved, our brains appear to have grown to meet the challenges they faced. The inner parts of the brain, which, theoretically, are the more reptilian parts, seem to generate all those beyond-speech parts of our comprehension like instincts, hunches and feelings. Surrounding these is a newer development of grey matter, the cortex, which, generally speaking, seems to process more sophisticated forms of data like language, maths and the instruction booklets packaged with gadgets from the Far East.

For most of the time your brain is just the right size to

deal with the rate of data that your nerves pick up and has enough spare capacity to turn your sensory information into a world perceived as one seamless act of consciousness. However, every now and again in life we find ourselves in extreme situations, facing massive increases in the amount of sensory data that need to be understood, and understood very quickly, so that the body can then take appropriate action.

Anybody who has watched an EEG light up as a patient thinks about a lover, or an enemy, knows about this neural flood. It's not very poetic but our emotional sense, our feelings of love, fear, hate, scorn, pride and so on, is, in point of fact, the brain's way of comprehending in situations of sensory and nervous overload. In moments of heightened brain and nerve activity, as senses are overstimulated, it is simply impossible for the conscious mind to comprehend every one of the body's vast battlefield of conflicting impulses. Moments like these – danger,

arousal, genetic opportunity – are not occasions that we can slowly, consciously consider. Any branch of our evolutionary ancestors who couldn't react speedily to these sorts of events would have quickly died out.

So if you have more information rushing through your nervous system than your conscious mind can process, how

> " **Danger, arousal, genetic opportunity are not occasions that we can slowly, consciously, consider.** "

do you not freeze in the headlights? You have to act and you have to quickly reach an understanding of what's going on in order to know what to do.

In the same way that, when you are looking at a crowd, you start to deindividualize, you stop seeing each person and they all become a mass, so the structure of your brain in these extreme situations starts to generalize rather than deindividualize, you stop seeing each person and they all become a mass, so the structure of your brain in these extreme situations starts to generalize rather than attempt to react to each individual sensory message. The corpus callosum and thalamus have evolved to filter, synthesize, poll and reduce the millions of discrete impulses racing from every part of your body, to sort them into a less specific package which gives the gist of things but is not actually made up of any firm, singular bits of information. To your conscious, logical mind, what you end up perceiving seems to be imprecise, inexplicable, irrational, unfathomable, and yet you understand exactly what they mean. They're feelings.

The reason that we can still feel love, or hate, long after we have got used to the idea of our lovers or enemies, when the flood of data has abated, is because emotion is the basis of memory. When you see your lover, years after the first passion, and you feel a flutter, you may not actually be experiencing a moment of overwhelming sensation but the *memory* of one. As they defy rationality, the only way we may distinguish the emotion from the EmMemory is in their relative intensity. NS

Kate closed her eyes and let her body float on the emotional flood. She let her mind drift back to the last person who ever called her Catherine. It wasn't as if he could actually remember who she was. He just knew the name. She pictured the last time she had seen him: being frogmarched out of the apartment in New York. She opened her eyes again and looked over at the phone.

Dialling 9 for an outside line, Kate keyed in the numbers of her answering service.

'You have five messages.'

'Struggling to pay the mortgage? More than—' Beep.

'Message deleted.'

'Do not hang up, this is important information.' Beep.

'Message deleted.'

'Did you know that you could win a Green Card and work in the US—' Beep.

'Message deleted.'

'This is a message for Catherine Minola?' The voice was a gentle west country accent. 'This is Paula from Lotus House, just to say that your father arrived safely. He was picked up from Heathrow as arranged and is settling into his room nicely. Could you give us a call at your earliest convenience just to confirm the invoice address. Thank you.' Beep.

'Message saved.'

'Your girlfriend needs something bigger to really—' Beep.

'Message deleted.'

Kate hung up and stared at the ceiling, at the little blinking light in the smoke detector. A wisp of hair fell over her mouth and she blew it up gently to watch it eddying in the wind of her breath, like a kite straining to be free but forever grounded in the world of her own head.

It seemed the harder Kate strained to keep some purchase on Catherine's driftwood, the more numb she became, and however long she had kept herself afloat, her sense of who she was seemed forever to be drifting away. Most of the time it was like Catherine was little more than a concoction of distant, fleeting memories. Pictures from a book, scenes from a film she couldn't quite name.

Kate had been so many people. She had inhabited so many lives. She was tired. She really was tired.

Her vision began to blur as a couple of rare tears pooled in her eyes before running away across her cheeks. Maybe she was mourning Catherine, maybe Da, but after five years shilling the richest, most gullible nation on earth, Kate grieved, really grieved, for Kate. She knew what her recent promotion to the top of the FBI wanted lists meant. Her image was first on every Homeland Security computer check from El Paso to Poker Creek and it would be years before she slipped down the charts. In practical terms, Kate had no hope of getting back in under any disguise or name. She knew her life was changing again, now she was exiled to the poorer, more sceptical parts of the world and the ones that had no extradition treaties with the States. That meant she couldn't stay long in Mexico and that, however safe Da was back in England, she might never see him alive again.

TAC

<u>2. The Activating Condition (TAC)</u>
At some point, usually more recently, the
subject will have been placed in some emotional turmoil, often accompanied by hope
and generally a moment of positivity. This
is usually perceived as a make-or-break
moment. During TAC their life and their
past preconceptions are given a thorough
shake-up.

'The end,' I said, banging my pen down on the desk with a loud and definitive clap.

Peter leaned forward, finger raised, to object again.

'Finished,' I interjected. 'Nothing more. Once you go, there's no way back. End of story. You are, you will be, dead.' I swept my hands apart, tipping back in my chair and attempting a look of indisputable finality.

For a while we both took in the silent darkness. There were no ominous clocks to tick; I had banished time from my office. Neither of us had realized how thoroughly the autumnal gloaming had filled the study since we had started talking, but when I pulled the chain of the standard lamp Peter's polished magician's smile lit up.

'The end,' I repeated, just to make it clear that I was referring not only to his life, but the subject as well.

But Peter was just getting started.

'You see, if I'm going to be your guinea pig, doctor,' he insisted, tapping my desk, 'I want to make sure . . .'

'But that's it, Peter,' exasperation began to strangle my voice, 'you're not my guinea pig. Guinea pigs don't have a choice. And if they did, they probably wouldn't elect to have a needle inserted into their brain to prompt them to forget who they are, what they are and where they've hidden their bloody nuts.' I took a deep breath to regain my composure.

'It's squirrels,' Peter pointed out, 'who hide nuts.'

'You told me you wanted this.' My clinician's voice returned. 'This is everything we've been working towards for the last two months. Peter, you're a friend, not a guinea pig, and you know I'm doing this to help you.'

'To help me?' He seemed surprised. 'So you're not going to write this up? This isn't going to be your next book?'

'Well . . .' I shifted in my seat.

'Oh. So I'm not your guinea pig, but I'm still your rabbit. Something for you to pull out of a hat with a flourish and say to the world, "Look what I can do! Ta-daa!" You can tell me this is for me, but don't play the altruist.'

'Whatever happens after this, Peter, you won't know a thing.' I sat up straight and tried to measure my words. 'Let me paint the picture.' I held up a fist, spreading my fingers into a sun. 'It's morning. It's a morning that seems like every other morning in your life. Like every other morning, you begin to wake and your consciousness gradually returns. And like every other morning, for a moment you're a clean sheet, you're no one, nowhere, knowing nothing, you're in a limbo ready to be reinvented.'

'But usually dying for a pee.'

'Like every morning, before your eyes are ready to

open,' I continued, 'all within the space of milliseconds, you begin to retrieve memories buried within your eternally awake unconscious. You fish into your mind and pull out answers as you wonder where you are and who you are. You piece together the jigsaw that is you. And when you open your eyes and see where you are, you use what you see to confirm that those memories you retrieved were true. It all adds up. And maybe you're in bed with someone . . .'

'Or not,' he added, a touch sardonically.

'OK, maybe not, maybe you get up and you see someone familiar and they see you, and their recognition of you reinforces your assumption. Because that's all it is: an assumption that you are who you remember being before you lost consciousness the night before. It's only when these things all fit together that you feel absolutely sure that you are you.'

'But this particular morning isn't like every other morning?'

'I'm just saying that re-establishing your identity every time you regain consciousness is a delicate process of logical reinforcement; it's very vulnerable to false assumptions. So although you use it to persuade yourself that you really are the person you remember being the day before, maybe, this particular morning, you've been fooled. How would you know? Any one of us can be deluded and fall for an illusion.' I smiled. 'You, you're the conjuror, you know better than most.'

'So?' he urged.

'So if, with each dawning of consciousness, you reconstruct your identity again and again, who's to say you're right, that you really are the person who lost consciousness the night before? It could all be artificially constructed and, if it was, would you know a thing about it?

'That, in a nutshell, is what we're going to do. You will wake up and your brain will flood with memories, and everything – location, community, purpose – will correspond. The people around you will have all undergone informal hypnotic suggestion to believe you were always a part of their lives. Your occupation, your bank accounts, everything. This has taken years to formulate, months to set up, and in a few weeks everything will be ready. I will put you to sleep as Peter and you will wake up as—' I stopped myself before I scuppered everything. 'Well, I can't actually tell you as that would affect the present neural make-up of your memory patterns, but you'll wake up as someone else. A new life, knowing nothing of your old one, a totally new identity – like your own personal witness protection programme.'

Ever so slightly Peter cocked an ear towards me as if expecting something more.

'Sorry,' he grunted after a moment, 'just waiting for the bit when you say, "Then when I have power over men's minds, finally the whole world will be mine," and laugh maniacally.'

I didn't understand.

'Well come on,' Peter coaxed, 'it's all a bit Mad Scientist, bubbling testtubes and so on.'

'No, it's just a new way of seeing things, a matter of perception. It's not so different from what you do: create different perspectives, new senses of reality for people.'

'Doing card tricks?'

'Tricks for the young and the old; minds in the process of reshaping, generating or degenerating. And when, in an instant, you find their card that was hopelessly lost in the pack, do you see the wonder? In their brains, for a few seconds, the laws that govern the very universe are suspended. The mind is vulnerable and who we think we are can change entirely under all sorts of pressures: amnesia, fugues, false memory syndrome, alcohol, drugs, gods and even, for a split second, a pack of cards. Every day we see how susceptible the brain is to accepting false conclusions. How it can create connections and memories to explain the unexplained, in its insatiable eagerness to make sense of the world.'

Peter looked sceptical, though he knew he couldn't dismiss me easily. After all, he had actually helped me in that first experiment seven years before.

'Remember Sonia?' I said.

His eyes widened. 'How can I forget her? I still see her, grinning accusingly, whenever I do the show in the dementia wing.'

'She's not grinning accusingly, she's just grinning. She's happy. Isn't she?'

He nodded grudgingly.

'She's forgotten you, Peter. And you will forget her.'

'And Kate and Titus Black?'

I laid my hands flat on the desk. 'In just over three weeks' time Peter will be dead. Long live whoever you become. Nobody likes being who they are; we exist in a cult of reinvention, we all want to be someone different, thinner, brighter, taller. Every year around the world over three million people just disappear. OK, a small number are murdered and keep the DIY patio supplies business going, some are trafficked or washed out to sea, but most are just trying to start new lives without the debts or the guilt that's been hanging over them. But they always have their memories. What you're doing will herald a new world of choice for humanity.'

'It's not cold feet, doc, I'm not scared of the oblivion, I think it's just some deep-seated suspicion of optimism. I mean, what if, when I think I'm somebody else, I'm still plagued by the nightmares, the Peter nightmares, but I have no way of explaining them? And what if I find I do want to get back to being me, and I can't? Am I going to be stuck in some eternal purgatory?'

'Peter, honestly, I don't know yet. We experiment to find answers. I do know that it's impossible to really comprehend how completely different you will become, but once the dopamine flood is injected into your hippocampus it will disconnect all your neural pathways; you will remember nothing. The name Peter Ruchio might as well be Joe Bloggs.'

Peter stood up unsteadily, gripping the side of the chair. 'I'm sorry, doc. I know you've done a lot for me but if it's that final, if there's no going back, I might as well, I'd rather . . .' He hesitated. I knew where this was going.

'Look,' I barked, talking faster than a timeshare salesman who's just spotted an approaching tsunami, 'if you do end your life, there really will be no way back. But this way, not only do you live, but you help science and give succour to the hopeless, and you won't know a thing.' I spread my arms. 'This really is a chance of a lifetime.'

'Yes,' he shot back, suddenly angry, 'but I will be

alive, even if I'm not me, and what if I simply have the fuck-it-up gene? Have you considered that? What if this changing minds thing really does work, what if I just end up fucking it all up again, making myself and a whole bunch of new, innocent people around me as miserable as I did the first lot? This was a stupid idea. I'm sorry.' He turned to go.

'Peter, I know you.' I changed tack. 'You're a good man, you try your best; you can't walk out on this just like that. We've put too much work in. There's got to be a way we can do it.' My mind raced desperately. 'Just give me a moment, let me think.'

He was at the door, fingers cradling the handle. Leaning his head against a door panel, he exhaled. 'Doc, you're really persuasive. I mean I'm probably crazy – what other suicidal depressive would give up a chance like this? But it's not the finality, I can take the finality: it's the worry that it's not final enough. And then having no way back, that's the trouble. Life and death are simple, they're on or off, but this . . .'

I stood up, the chair squealing behind my straightening legs. 'Look, Peter, there is a way . . .'

He turned the handle and the latch clicked. 'Lots of ways, doc: noose, poison, asking for halal at the hotdog stand in a white supremacist meeting . . .'

'No, Peter. Hear me out. I have an idea.' And in that spell-like way, when just saying something aloud actually summons it, I really did have an idea.

But he had opened the door and was looking down the stairs and beyond. 'I'm sorry,' he said sadly, 'got to go.' He turned his head to me. 'I've just been indulging your scientific curiosity and fooling myself, yet another bloody illusion, delaying what I knew I had to do. There's only one sure way to end everything.'

'Really, Peter, stop. I know how we can do this. Listen. It starts like this . . .'

He stepped out on to the landing.

'Stop,' I shouted. 'Stop or I'll shoot!'

From: <u>*Draft Introduction – How to Forget,*</u> Tavasligh,
Unpublished

'Stop or I'll shoot!'
The next time you hear this shouted, perhaps you will
pause for a moment, if only to appreciate what a beautiful, well-rounded and articulate phrase it is. It is a
warning honed to perfection, it is how all warnings
should be: clear, concise and terrifying enough to scare
the bejeezus out of a bejesuit.

This book is a warning. I wish it could be as un-
ambiguous as 'Watch out' or 'Duck' or 'I'm going to
have to work late at the office again, dear.' I wish it
could be as brief as 'Stop', 'Danger', or that road sign
which simply says '!' and waits to accrue its meaning
after the event. But at nearly 400 pages, it is a little more
complicated – and not the sort of warning that requires
the same speedy attention as those made by a weak
bladder.

Unfortunately the same blinding ambition which pro-
pelled humanity forward in the exploration and
domination of the planet, sprinting ahead in the race to
evolve when other species couldn't be bothered, inclines
us to ignore most warnings in favour of learning from
experience. Despite having developed our primitive
guttural belching into speech, despite having created the
most fantastically complex warning system the planet
has ever seen, apparently 80 per cent of communication
is still non-verbal.

'Stop or I'll shoot!' is more than a warning, though.
It's a whole story in just four and a half words; with a
clear beginning, middle and end, conflict, drama, life,

death, action, resolution. Stories are warnings but somehow we're more amenable to them, more willing to go along with them. We don't just listen to a narrative; we 'suspend our disbelief', we put our natural scepticism on hold and experience it. We allow ourselves to learn because we're not being told.

Since long before Aesop, stories have been used as warnings when the clear threat was simply not enough. And we love stories because, with each one, we can forget everything for a while and be born again as wide-eyed children unwittingly ready to learn life's important lessons: not to talk to strange wolves in transvestites' clothing; how true toffs will know if you have a pea in the bed; or how you can sell beef for beans, thieve your way out of poverty, murder the victim of your robbery and still live happily ever after.

But the true power of stories, and why this warning comes as one, lies in your brain. More precisely, in a part of your frontal lobes which it took a hungry capuchin monkey to discover. He lived in a lab where, in a doomed attempt to bring a lighter side to vivisection, all the capuchins were given coffee-related names. Starbuck had teeth the colour of earwax and halitosis like mustard gas and on the day of his discovery he had been grabbing at snacks all morning. He'd been wired up to brain activity sensors, to study the components that register hunger before eating and pleasure in receiving food. Valuable research for the hunger-inhibiting diet pill trade. And not to forget the threat of an epidemic of obese monkeys.

At lunchtime, Starbuck's lab technician stopped for her break and happened to be absently watching the monitors as she reached for her sandwich. Which is when she noticed an amazing thing. As Starbuck watched her, she saw the same brain patterning light up on his monitors as when he had been reaching for food himself. She quickly realized that he was empathizing and she could see exactly the parts of the brain where this happened.

From that one sandwich, we not only found that monkeys were capable of empathy, and thus just how far men have evolved away from monkeys, but also that the brain's 'mirror neurons' extend into the premotor cortex, where we weigh intentions, and the parietal lobe, where we register sensation.

Now we know why we wince when we see another person punched. Empathy is hard-wired into our brains. We experience just by watching others' experiences. We tell stories to stimulate the mirror neurons. We watch a film and become the characters, we read someone's story and for the time we're in it, the connections within our own brains actually reshape, beginning to mirror the connections in the character's brain.

So this book, like every story you've ever read, heard or watched, will alter the shape of your brain. Whatever you think, this book is guaranteed to change your mind.

From: *Letters* Tavasligh mss. 14.8

DR C. TAVASLIGH MSc PhD
CHANGE IN MIND ORGANIZATION
CHRISTCHURCH
DORSET

So Peter. This is the way.

In just a few hours now you will be sitting here and finally we will end all your nightmares and anxieties, all those terrible memories, all your troubles. We will end your life.

And I really couldn't be more excited.

But this is the deal we made.

A life for 'A Life'.

And this is a way you might be able to become Peter again. If you read this you will relive your story. And while you're here, the network of neurons that encapsulates all the dreams and memories and hopes and feelings Peter had will again take the shape in your brain that it used to have. Maybe it will only be for the time it takes to

80

tell the story, or maybe it will all come back to you and take permanent form.

But I'll tell your story as well as I can. Please forgive me if, after a lifetime of looking into the brain, my craniocentric perspective leads me astray. When I see what people do I tend to see what makes them act rather than why they act. That may seem a subtle difference but as you read this, I'm sure it will become glaringly clear.

So I have your notes beside me now to shape into a story. It's all here. Well, not all, but everything we've needed to get to this point. Everything from our sessions that I have used to unpick the weft and warp that the fates have woven for you. As you read this you will see how carefully I have been unravelling the strands that stretch between the two edges of your loom; on

one side a moment in Barnet and, on
the other, an instance in Kent. Two
turning points, fifteen years apart, but
your very fibres have constantly
reached between and revolved about
them. Now, the strands disentangled, I
know precisely where to place the blade
when I cut your thread.

And that's the beauty of all this. I
even know how and where this yarn,
our story, your life – ends.

Peter, how many people get one of
these? This really is your big red book:
this is your life.

1

If there is a beginning to the end, if it is possible to start somewhere and say, 'This is it!' and ignore all the other tiny decisions that led to that moment – all the constant choices we make navigating life's innumerable diverging roads through its yellowing woods with the GPS still insisting that we need to go through Doncaster – if I have to pick out one time and place that made all the difference, locate the tipping point for all that happened after 'to follow', then I believe that the end of this story began fifteen years from the TIC, a year ago and a world away; on a road climbing through the foothills of the Southern Alps, winding through the sheep fields that border the dense forests of Fiordland.

In the key to the AA map of New Zealand there is no symbol for roads 'less travelled', nevertheless, that is exactly what this road was. No more than a rutted track of dried mud, it scratched a lonely route through gorse bushes and across stunted, windswept mountain grasses. Scattered with thousands of glistening black sheep's droppings and scored with heavy vehicle tracks, it bore a striking resemblance to the musical notation of

Karlheinz Stockhausen, only a little easier to play. Where the hillside became steeper the road twisted sharply around tussocks of sprouting yellow pampas. Every now and again a wandering sheep clattered across it, hoofs stumbling in the hard, pitted tracks, before deciding that the grass really wasn't any greener there and ambling back to the flock. Sitting, huddled against the August chill, most of the ewes just took turns moaning beneath the countless sullen rolls of heavy grey cloud which furrowed out across the dark Antarctic seas. The perpetual harmonics of wind and bleat were rarely disturbed except by the occasional strained whining of a motorbike engine and the barking of Border collies.

Henry Aloysius Colbert Rackham III, Harry to his muckers, kept his quad-bike accelerator on full twist even as he leaned into the road's sharpest corner. Millie and Molly found their paws scrabbling for purchase, surprised by the abrupt turn, despite having raced up this road beside Harry their entire working lives.

The Borderdales were all safely penned in the lower fields now, ready for their dipping in the morning, and Harry was on a promise – he'd promised his mother he'd be back at the farm for lunch. With his usual talent for punctuality he now found himself having to take every corner, lump and hump up the farm road at full pelt.

As he flew over the penultimate rise, a massive black object suddenly loomed. He grasped desperately for the brakes. Hitting the ground with the wheels locked, the quad skidded, sliding towards the back of the stationary Range Rover. Before the quad, and Harry, could actually stop, the front wheel hit an unexpected stone and the bike flipped. Harry leapt off as the quad rolled over and over, crashing into the rear of the car and bouncing off again. The quad landed back on its chunky wheels, much as a cat might land on its feet, and stopped. Harry's attempt to stop himself was considerably less graceful, involving his body and face smashing into the pitted tracks and then rattling for some distance over hardened sheep pellets as if they were ball-bearings.

Taking a moment to work out if he was alive, if anything was broken and what the terrible taste in his mouth was, Harry blinked up at the big black car. Slowly he sat up and spat out a sheep dropping, which pinged against the car door as if it was a cherry pip. He began to pick himself up and as a stream of blood coursed from his nose and bubbled over his lips the driver's door opened. A high-heeled foot slipped out, a leg, a black skirt, a waxed jacket, and there smiling at him was one of the most delicate, beautiful and out-of-place women he had ever seen. Admittedly it had been several months since he was last in town, and with only the sheep, the bitches Millie and Molly and his mother for company his aesthetic criteria were not very high.

'Oh my goodness,' the woman said, an upper-crust English accent sounding almost angelic. 'I'm so sorry, are you all right?'

'Fine, fine.' He smiled, squinting at her and wiping some of the fresher sheep excrement from his brow. 'What you doing up here? You lost?'

She looked around her. 'I was trying to get to the Fotherington estate? I was told it was up here.'

'Nah.' He pointed east. 'They're about thirty miles

85

that way. You must have taken a wrong turning about a mile back. This is Rackham's. If you head back down and take a left . . .'

'Oh, I would, only,' the vision gestured to the front wheels of her gleaming Range Rover, 'I think they've burst or something.' Harry walked round to have a look. The two front tyres had somehow eviscerated, maybe on the same stone that the quad had hit.

'That's pretty pukeroo.'

She pulled a phone out of her jacket. 'I tried calling the AA but,' she shrugged, 'no signal.'

'No, we're pretty remote up here. When do you need to get to Foths?'

'There's no real hurry,' she smiled, flashing a mesmerizing array of white teeth, 'they're not expecting me.'

'Right, let me take you up to the farm then, you can call from there. I'll send one of the hands down with the tractor to tow this. OK?'

The woman nodded. 'That's very kind of you. Oh, I have to get something.' She reached into the Range Rover and retrieved a briefcase. She patted it. 'Very important.'

Harry put two fingers in his mouth and let out a piercing whistle. 'Come to,' he shouted gruffly, 'come to, girls.' Millie and Molly raced to him and scampered around his legs. He walked the woman to the bike, holding out his still spittle-wettened hand. 'Harry Rackham. Pleased to meet you.'

'Felicity. Felicity de Vere. Charmed.' She eyed his fingers but didn't take them.

Harry looked down at his crap-and-saliva-coated hand before quickly withdrawing to wipe it on his trousers. He bowed as he gestured to the quad. 'Please.'

Felicity wobbled over the uneven ground to the bike and mounted it as modestly as possible, keeping the briefcase in one hand and her briefs from showing with the other.

Harry threw his leg over in front of her. 'Is that Miss de Vere or Mrs de Vere then?' The engine roared to life.

'Actually it's Lady. Lady Felicity de Vere,' she laughed as the two of them rocketed around the car and up the hill, 'quite unmarried.'

2

Curling through the Cosy Counties, the cream teas and Famous Five economy of the south-west of England, the river Stour is, for the most part, a model river: she looks lovely but, on closer inspection, she is shamefully shallow and painfully thin; she is a perfect size zero who ripples with temptation but you get the suspicion that, if you ever got the chance to strip off and plunge in, you'd quickly find yourself wondering why you bothered.

Most confounding of all, for anybody who has witnessed the tininess of the Stour's body, is just how immense her mouth is. In comparison it is vast, but then it is easy to forget that, like the mouth of any model, more tends to spew out of it than into it.

If there wasn't a danger in over-extending metaphors I'd also take the trouble to point out that the broadness of her mouth is actually enhanced by the Avon, and if you were to look for it on a map, you'd find it surrounded by groynes. It's true, but there is, so I won't.

Her mouth, though, is a wild place, a natural harbour pursed to kiss the sea with two opposing sandy spits lined with beach huts, like multi-coloured teeth biting the horizon. To the south lies the rocky outcrop of Hengistbury Head, gripped with orange gorse and lumpingly nudging the sky. It protects the bay from most of the English Channel's rougher elements. It closes the mouth into an altogether calmer place, a dark lagoon crisscrossed by treacherous quicksands and prehistoric water channels. Ochre walls of long earthy reeds stir and dip as they fringe the inlets and the wide rippling waters between the head and Mudeford. The reeds twist querulously between the surges of the current below and the urges of the wind above; hiding gulls' nests, gannet cries and the lapping border between sound and ground.

For as long as anyone can remember, the boggy land that curdles with mud and surrounds the harbour has been known as Stanpit Marsh, even though no one ever did find the pit – or, for that matter, Stan. But then perhaps that's what makes marshland so attractive to those who have a wish to disappear. It's the low-lying land for those needing to lie low, the hiding place of choice for artful dodgers: for Pip and Magwitch eluding the law, for the Duke of Monmouth running from the Battle of Sedgemoor, for the Venetians hiding from Attila the Hun, starting their own city state in the Po's swampy delta. To the hunter, this sodden *terra infirma*, this expanse of long grass, quick sands and slow sinking feelings, is perilous but, to the hunted, it is cover, breathing space and, if discovery is inevitable, it is a host of squelching escape routes.

Centuries old and perched on a small rise in the middle of the Stanpit marshes, at the northern end of the Stour's mouth, stands the priory of Christchurch. Surrounded by mudflats and washed in sea mists, its Gothic clock tower rises out of the quagmire and is visible far across the reaches. The town that has grown up around the priory has retained the marshes' peculiar attraction for anybody wanting to go to ground – and most of those who come are looking at six feet under it.

You see, just as Glastonbury is a magnet for those in their hippy phase, and Manchester attracts those in their gun-toting, clubbing phase, and even Swindon magically draws those in their hopelessly lost phase, so Christchurch seems to possess an almost supernatural fascination for those in their last phase. Its ability to attract pensioners has even earned it the dubious distinction of being the town with the oldest population in Britain and, consequently, containing the country's very own necropolis. In Christchurch, there is no such thing as an idle mortician, or a poor one.

It is a place you come to to bury yourself or be buried. Behind the twee façades of its thatched cottages, the picturesque marina and the gourmet pubs lies a world of pain, and aches, and catheters, and the terrible wait for the inevitable; of nursing homes and the forgotten, the lonely, the demented and the ghostly; of the old and the hunted.

And never have I met a man with a more hunted look than Peter.

Not at first. When he turned up in pale make-up and ridiculous moustache, applying to entertain the patients at the Lotus House Care Home, like everybody else I was misdirected. I couldn't see past the bewilderment of his illusions. I couldn't see him gaining the care home experience on his CV while serving a non-custodial one thousand hours' community service sentence. I got no glimmer of the despair that etched his young face as he signed the sex offenders' register, nor did I wonder how quickly he wiped his tears as he crept silently from his parents' house, taking his baggage, packed with disgrace, with him. I had no idea of the stony look he kept for travelling from one retirement town to the next seeking accommodation that met the required 'greater than a thousand yards from any school or gathering place for young people', nor did I know how it felt to wipe the duty sergeant's glistening spittle from his cheek during his fortnightly check-ins at the local police station and meet the utter disgust in the man's eyes.

Perhaps, if I could have torn my own eyes from the miracles that transpired in Peter's hands, I would have caught a hint of that hunted look, but by the time we met his mask was set hard and long established. Only his eyes could have given it away; they were pale, a blue drained to grey; filled with fear, looking to lie low, to find ground and ground down. But there were a million card tricks and sponge balls and twisted balloons, amid the snores and applause of the Lotus House day room, before I saw Peter without the make-up.

He was always Magicov the Magnificent, Magician to the Czars. In tall hat and long black cape Peter astonished the residents in the day room every Wednesday afternoon, with an élan more suited to performing spectaculars at Caesar's Palace than, as he put it, 'top-hat tricks for potty geriatrics'. And though many in his audience could barely distinguish their cups from their balls any more, or even cared to, Peter was always a patient performer, taking things slowly and getting the more agile involved. And I always made time to come and watch his transformations, vanishes, productions, and the reactions of those still sentient. Magicov, Peter, got me thinking about magic and memory as I never had done before.

If witnessing a story is 'the willing suspension of disbelief', isn't the watching of magic an 'unwilling' one? We know the magician will fool us, we look for it, with each effect we challenge the conjuror to defy our rational disbelief in metaphysics and fairy dust and yet still, under our cynical scrutiny, still he manages to amaze us. We know that what goes up must come down, that matter does not vanish, that rabbits don't live in hats, but for an instant, at the moment of astonishment, for a split second we forget all that, we forget everything we know about the material world, we don't give a fig for Newton's laws, and just watch open-mouthed. After a few moments order returns, we start asking ourselves how it was done, we see it as a puzzle: how did the illusion of magic really work in our logical universe? But, just in that instant we witnessed it, we forgot everything.

Peter gave me a funny look when I asked him if he would perform some magic for a patient simultaneously having her brain scanned in a magnetic resonance imaging machine. But considering he wore a waxed handlebar moustache that curled around to tickle his nostrils and thick false eyebrows in a similar arrangement, funny looks were about all he could manage.

The patient, Sonia, was a tall woman, loud in voice

and in her choice of Hermès scarves, a retired civil servant who had always prided herself on the acuity of her memory. She had once been a crossword champion but, by the time she was admitted to our care, her vocabulary rarely strayed from the angry, bitter and frustrated. Sonia had taken the news of her decaying memory, due to early onset Alzheimer's, particularly badly. In fact every time she woke in her room, filled with Post-it notes reminding her of the fact, she took it particularly badly again and again.

So as Sonia watched Magicov performing impossible feats on a monitor inside the machine, I watched the electrical patterns that sparked and undulated in her brain. It was only when I was reviewing each frame of the scan that I found one, just one, totally unlike all the others: an instant, lasting no more than a few milliseconds, a momentary flash that occurred at the split second of astonishment. The patterns of light in obscure parts of her cortex, the darkness in the otherwise ever active hippocampus and the brilliance around her amygdala made me realize, immediately, that I was looking at Sonia's own pattern of a neural reset; a moment when all her beliefs, logic and knowledge were forgotten in the shock of witnessing the world out of kilter when a bowling ball was brought out of a briefcase. I was looking at her brain rebooting. And if I could see it and measure the chemical balances in each critical area, I could, through reverse engineering, recreate it. And if I could recreate it, I could reboot Sonia's brain permanently. And that, that could bring her some happiness at last.

From: *Inducing Psychogenic Amnesia in Patient S.*,
C. Tavasligh, Southampton, 2002

PREFACE

EACH DAY THEY DIE

The happiest place in Lotus House is the dementia wing.

The saddest is the window where the early onset Alzheimer's patients sit. Each day they live through the trauma of discovering, for the first time, that they are suffering from a degenerative disease which will reduce their minds to mush. Each day they die all over again.

Whatever the morals, we need the humanity to at least ask the question: instead of spending millions on a series of ineffectual drugs that attempt to delay an inevitable onset of Alzheimer's, might it not be kinder to accelerate it, to quickly resolve the problem into the blissful oblivion of ignorance?

To visit a dementia unit is a disturbing experience because you cannot but be filled with unease even though you may be surrounded by the happiest, most carefree people you have ever met. The sadness comes from the contradiction of one of the key human ideas that we cherish: that memory is sacrosanct, the truth of identity and the bedrock of character. But then it is hard to deny that those who have, shall we say, 'gained' the nirvana of forgetfulness rather than 'lost' their memory are very often happy. As we are, usually, as babies, if our basic needs of food, warmth and entertainment/attention are met.

Is it a debasement of individuality to allow people happiness if the alternative is so devastatingly ghastly? Is it really better to insist that once-proud individuals must now sit with the hand of death on their shoulder and the dribble of decay falling into their lap?

If we are to have pity on the sufferers of Alzheimer's we must teach them how to forget rather than how to cling on to the continual disappointment of their ever-fading memories and identity.

I here publish the methods and successful findings of my experiments in using the combined processes of neuro-inhibitor amnesthetics, low-pulse electronic molecular induction and clinical hypnosis to create an apparently irreversible condition of psychogenic or dissociative amnesia in Patient S.

In order to save the layman going off to her computer at this point, this is what she will find:

Patient S., a long-term resident of Lotus House, a nursing home allied to my research lab, was suffering from mid-stage Alzheimer's disease when we began this experiment. She was fully cognizant of the dangers involved in the induction of a complete and total memory loss and she, and her family, consented to waive all rights of responsibility. Having suffered from severe melancholy related to her form of dementia, she was keen to cooperate. I am happy to say that Patient S. still lives at the home. She is robustly healthy and very cheerful. As far as any quality of life (QOL) tests can ascertain, she is happy and exists in blissful ignorance of a past, any emotional turbulence or, indeed, the present prime minister.

3

'No kidding? You work for the Queen? The Queen of England?'

Felicity laughed. 'No. Not quite. I work for the Commonwealth Royal Appointment Provisions Office. We're just commissioned by the royal family.'

'How cool is that, Ma?'

Clarissa Rackham sat at the end of the table, watching her son with palpable irritation. She found it all faintly embarrassing. He could, at least, have the dignity not to drool. She brought the post-prandial cigarette to her lips and pulled, keeping her two bony fingers straightened in a fuck-off sign directed at the posh English trollop who had invaded their lunch. She would have to warn him; the stupid tart evidently had at least ten years on him and of course, as soon as she said anything, he would accuse her of being jealous and ruining his life and say he'd never find a wife and live out the rest of his life rounding up sheep and catering to his sour-faced old mother . . .

Clarissa sighed and knocked the ash off her cigarette.

From: <u>*Project Notebook 23.1*</u> p51

What is so interesting to me is that, despite her obvious cleverness and ability to comprehend complex situations and bend them to her own will, Clarissa Rackham was a classic example of a faulty memory fixation. From her protruding cheekbones to her twinset's herringbones, everything about Clarissa was skeletal. She didn't like eating like a rabbit, she craved butter and cheese, but thinness for Clarissa was a way of life. On a rational level she knew that she was long past competing in the mating market where the young girls would kill for cheekbones like hers. Like many women who maintain a need to stay thin, Clarissa Rackham was a victim of a classic damaging EmMemory.

The peer pressure to be thin creates an EmMemory which defies reason later in life when, to all intents and purposes, the competition has gone, the skin sags from the bones and yet the diet continues. Like many women who retain the young girl's emotional memory of fat-fear into their later years, now everything about her was skeletal.

She put her head back, closed her eyes and listened to those pointless noises young people make when they're trying to disguise their racing hormones as genuine interest in each other.

'Have you ever met her? HRH?'

'Actually I have. Just once. She's very nice. She did a tour of the office.'

'And she sent you out here?'

'Not personally. It sort of works like this: my office

tries to foster links and encourage trade between the UK and the Commonwealth countries. We locate the sources of products used by the royal family and then offer royal commissions to the producers. You know, "By Appointment to Her Royal Highness", etc. The commission gives the manufacturer, merchant, producer, whatever, the right to carry the royal insignia on their products. I was sent here to find out who produces the New Zealand lamb chops that end up on the royal table and it turns out to be these . . . Fotheringtons. Look, look, I'll show you.'

As she stood up, Felicity's chair scraped the floor and Clarissa opened her eyes. She took a harder look at Felicity this time. There was something very familiar in the way she gestured and flirted; how she led the conversation without seeming to be doing anything but responding to questions. A memory, a unique pattern of charged neurons stimulated by a flood of associated data, something from an age before, suddenly reconnected. It streamed its way through a long-disused chain of synapses between Clarissa's amygdala and her cortex. Suddenly Clarissa saw what was going on in a whole new light.

Felicity fetched her briefcase and placed it on the table. Carefully rolling the combination lock dials, she flicked the catches open and looked solemnly at Harry and then at Clarissa.

'But you must promise you won't breathe a word of this. I'm really not supposed to tell anybody until the producer has accepted the commission.'

Mother and son nodded earnestly. Felicity opened the case and brought out a large gold-painted plaster shield emblazoned with a lion, a unicorn and a scroll bearing a Latin inscription. Underneath, a plate was inscribed '*By Appointment to HRH Queen Elizabeth II*'.

'This is the royal insignia, they can put it up on their gates or wherever.' She put it down on the table and started taking out other papers. 'This is the artwork, they can stamp it on all their chop packaging. But look, this is what I really wanted to show you, there at the end of this form, see? See who's signed it?'

'Good God! Is that really her?'

'Of course, she has to sign every appointee.'

'But this "By Appointment", what's the point? It's not like being knighted or being made a lord or something.'

Clarissa gave her son a withering look. 'It's much better than that, you ignoramus.' Her voice was husky; it growled like a sledge-dog and every word seemed to crunch like snow under paw, only much, much colder. 'It means that you can rack up your prices because customers will pay a premium to eat like the Queen.'

'Well,' Felicity laughed a little nervously, 'we're hoping that this scheme actually fosters good will and closer links with Great Britain and encourages higher standards and—'

'Lucky bastard.'

'Er, who?'

'Foth, Alistair Fotherington. His lambs are no better than ours. In fact, they don't treat their lambs half as well as we do.'

Clarissa interrupted before he turned it into a rant. 'Tell me, Felicity, just how do you know the lamb came from Fotherington?'

'I traced the lamb back to the exporters in

Christchurch. That's where I've just come from.'

'And that's South Seas Trading, down in Victoria Square?'

'Yes.'

'Well, they do ours too,' Harry butted in, 'and half the farms from here to Greymouth. All the carcasses get bundled together.'

'They were very insistent it was Fotherington's.'

'I bet they were.'

Clarissa smiled at Felicity as sweetly as she could. 'Fotherington is the biggest farm on the South Island. I think Harry is a little jealous. Alistair's very rich.'

'And South Seas know he's good for a tasty backhander.'

Felicity looked at the two with concern. 'I think I know what you're implying but I have to go with what they say. I'm so sorry, I don't want to cause any bitterness or rivalry.'

'You're not causing it, my dear.' Clarissa stood up and straightened her suit. 'It's been going on for generations.'

'I feel terrible, you've been so kind to me. As soon as I can get the AA to pick me up, I'll be out of your hair.'

'The AA?' Harry looked at her, somewhat surprised. 'Sorry, I thought you knew. I sent Nigel down to your car in the tractor but a garage had already turned up with a tow truck. I thought you had arranged it.'

Felicity frowned for a moment. 'That's a bit odd. I called the AA when I got here but I didn't think they could be that quick. Can I call them again? If you don't mind me using your phone.'

50,000 Milliseconds to Higham
(TEA *minus 11 months 19 days 8 hours*)

Peter

So who does want to be a millionaire?

You just make your friends envious, and the envious friendly. But then. I suppose millionaires can afford a certain amount of cynicism. In fact they can afford pretty much, well, everything.

And there it is. On the luggage rack right above me. Who'd guess what that tatty suitcase held? That it had all fitted in there. A million in fifties. Unmarked, untraceable, magic. Neatly bundled £10,000 packets jumping up and down with each jolt of the train.

And now what? A minute or so to go? We pull into Higham station. Then? Then it's just me and the case. No other way of doing this.

And when Kate wakes?

OK, reassure her. Let out a small snore. Now, if I open my eyelids just a touch.

And there you are. Well, the blur of your outline through this web of eyelashes. Asleep, yes. Pretty sure. You're slumped, too awkward to be faking. Fast asleep, lolling, mouth open, swaying with this lumbering rhythm. And look at your stretched-out, bare white neck. Out for the Count – as they say in Transylvania. You've got to be out cold. Who can blame you? This whole night's been more tiring than the Michelin Man, and any number of contorted similes.

Fuck. Kate. I'd do anything to stay. But then, you

get your hands on the case. Where would we be then? Once it's open?

Close eyes again, simulate that sleep I've longed for. The peaceful sleep of the blessed – the slumber beyond nightmare.

Right. Where are we? Woolwich Arsenal, Abbey Wood, Dartford, Greenhithe, Gravesend and, in a few moments, this train'll pull into Higham. And when it pulls out it will be without me and the case. Let her keep the dream.

4

'Are you next of kin?'

'Paula, it's me, Peter.'

Paula stared blankly at him.

'Mr Magicov.'

Suddenly Paula's face burst into a smile. 'Oh my God. Magicov. I didn't recognize you. I mean what without the make-up and the smile and the bald head and whatnot.' The Lotus House duty nurse stood to examine the new Peter. Soaring up from behind the reception desk like a tidal wave, her sea-blue nurse's outfit fitted her like a glove fits a double-decker bus, the short sleeves pinched at her bulging deltoids, crow's feet stretched from every button down her front and the face of the watch, pinned to her chest, rested horizontally so it could only be read by her and God. In spite of her six-foot frame, Paula was clearly determined to emphasize her femininity, with lipstick the colour of warning beacons, and, despite the Lotus House safety-at-work memo, she had elevated herself another six inches in stylish but colossal high heels manufactured solely for the transvestite market.

Peter smiled timidly under her gaze. The house was

always quiet at night and, after all the rush and fuss with the paramedics, the influx of the soundless dark had been, for Paula, a comforting return to normality.

'Paula,' Peter tried to keep the irritability out of his voice, 'is Cedric all right?'

'Oh, aren't you sweet. You really care . . .'

'Paula, please, just tell me what happened. You called me.'

'Well, you asked me to, if anything happened to him.'

'And?'

'It was a stroke,' she said, watching Peter's face fall, and quickly added, 'of luck he didn't die.' She smiled as brightly as she could.

'Paula, what happened to him?'

'Well, no, actually it was a stroke. I think he's OK though but, you know. It can make them a bit funny and all. The doctors came; they said he's probably going to be fine.'

'Can I see him?'

'I think he's asleep.'

'I'll go up anyway, if you don't mind.'

'OK.'

Peter turned towards the stairs and nearly made it to the first step.

'Hey,' Paula called after him, 'Mr Magicov.'

Peter turned back to Paula and forced a smile. Peter liked Paula. She was always bubbly, usually smiling at something but, at over six foot, she also seemed to embody an intangible air of menace, like a freshly spilt pint in a Southend pub. Peter tried to indulge her whenever he could, eager not to get on her wrong side, partly because it would be impolite and partly because it was likely to void any life insurance policies he might, in future, be interested in.

'Is there anything behind my ears?' she asked.

It was well known that Paula had very little between her ears, but behind her ears she seemed to keep a plethora of coins, computer mice, balls of rubber bands, paperclips or any other stationery items Peter could get his hands on.

Peter returned to the desk, looking up at the clock behind her.

'I don't know, Paula, I think it might be a bit too late. Behind your ears might be, I don't know, closed.'

Even as his eyes fixed on the clock Paula had involuntarily turned to glance at it; allowing Peter enough time to quietly swipe her stapler with his left hand and let it drop nonchalantly to his side.

'Oh, have a look anyway,' she giggled, 'you never know.'

At this point Peter would have flashed his most disarming smile but it was all he could do not to wince as the palmed stapler suddenly bit into his index finger, puncturing the soft pad at the end of his digit. He swallowed hard and tried to wriggle his finger free and delay his grand 'reveal' until he was liberated from the stapler's teeth.

'Do you think I could keep the – uh.' Peter realized he was about to give the trick away: if he said stapler she would look for hers. 'Keep whatever I find behind your ear?'

He tried to pull his finger free but, one-handed, he couldn't seem to loosen the stapler's grip.

'Naaah, it's my ear, my stuff. Go on,' she urged.

Peter found he was going slightly cross-eyed with the pain as Count Stapula sank its fangs in. What the hell, he thought. With his right hand he tapped the desk thoughtfully and the moment he saw Paula's eyes dart for the sound, he reached up with his left hand to pull the stapler out from behind her ear. He couldn't possibly have known that he had actually stapled his finger to his coat or that with this action he would pull his entire coat over Paula's head. How could he?

Having endured a string of monosyllabic and sense-lessly violent boyfriends, Paula had not only learned to endure what she called 'the four Fs' of blokishness – fight, feed, fuck, flop – she had also become more than competent in the basic arts of personal defence. Finding herself suddenly ensnared beneath a strange man's over-coat, she acted instinctively. She smashed her head forward, hoping to make contact with her assailant's nose. A loud crack and the lumpen crash of body to floor told her that she was right on target and, as Peter fell, the coat went with him. It slid smoothly off her head, revealing a bloody plain-clothes clown on the lobby floor.

Peter moaned as red bubbles gurgled and popped from his nose.

'What'd you do that for?' Paula glared at him.

He sat up and felt his nose, bleeding but not broken, and then prised his finger out of the stapler. 'Sorry, I didn't intend to.'

'Is that mine? From behind my ear?' She pointed at the stapler.

Peter nodded.

Paula suddenly looked apologetic. 'Oh I'm sorry, it's just I didn't expect . . .'

'No, neither did I.' Peter stood with some difficulty. 'No problem.' He handed her the stapler and grabbed a tissue from the box on her desk.

'I don't know how you do it.'

'With all my subtle powers of sleight of hand and magic.' Peter pressed the tissue to his bleeding nose. 'And I don't know if you spotted it but I used a little misdirection as well.'

'Personally,' said Paula, 'I prefer it when you just pull it out, none of the suffocating business.' She sat back down at her desk and quietly returned to her screen with another story to tell her Facebook friends, each on their own night shifts.

Peter loped back to the steps.

Upstairs, he softly opened Cedric's door and limped inside. The room was dark, save for a small lamp dangling a glowing sphere of light on the bedside table. A glistening drip bag hung ominously above the bed and an empty colostomy bag hung out to one side. Cedric slept peacefully, open-mouthed, with a tube snaking up his nose. Beside the lamp lay Cedric's precious 'bikes', his pack of fifty-two cardboard friends and the couple of jokers he kept with him at all times.

I watched Peter draw up a chair and it was only when he carelessly reached for the 'bikes' that I remembered that it was Mr Magicov who had found Cedric's mnemonic anchor, with that very deck of cards. Peter gave the cards a few riffle shuffles before running through a couple of one-handed cuts with the polished mastery of ingrained and well-practised expertise. It was only when I cleared my throat that the cards flew out of his hands and rained down about the room.

5

'All packed?'

Felicity smiled at Clarissa. 'Yes, I think so. You've been very kind . . .' She was wrapping the scam up a little faster than she was comfortable with but, when she had called her answering service and found Da had had a stroke, something strangely unfamiliar, a tiny inkling of sentiment, persuaded her that this might be a last chance and she should go back to England to see him, even if it was a quick in and out before the authorities worked out who and where she was. Haste is the enemy of any grift set-up, and she tried to read Clarissa's oddly imperious chin-up look.

'Park yourself a moment, it'll take Harry a while to load the truck.' Clarissa tried to smile.

Surveying the tatty sofa so covered in dog hairs, Felicity wondered if it might bite, or maybe even bark. Eventually, she lowered herself into a corner. 'I was just wanting to say thank you. You've been very kind to me, you and Harry, to let me stay.'

Clarissa tapped her cigarette against the ashtray that perched on her hand like a burnt offering. 'Do you think I'm a total idiot?' She sat in her armchair, levelling a blinkless stare at Felicity. The cigarette returned to the series of vertical lines that commemorated where her lips had once been, and it glowed brightly for a moment.

A little uncomfortably, Felicity started shaking her head. 'Mrs Rackham, I have—'

'Or maybe you think he's an idiot. To be fair, he is an idiot. Got it from his father. But at least he's got the sense not to try to pull the wool over my eyes.' Smoke tumbled out of her nose. 'There's not enough sheep in New Zealand for that, my dear. I see you. I see you.' The cigarette jabbed towards Felicity then returned to the ashtray as the stare continued.

Felicity straightened herself, flattened out the lap of her dress and met the stare with equal steel.

'This is how it goes,' Clarissa growled. 'A stranger turns up on a remote farm. She's had an inexplicable accident which has done no more damage to her very expensive car than the cost of a couple of tyres. She's . . . how can I say it? Alluring – in a rather slutty way – and she reveals a secret to the farmer: she is bearing a fabulous object, from a queen no less. An object which bestows the bearer with glamour and wealth and status; things that any farmer, stuck pandering to the whims of the most pathetic animals ever created on this wart on the backside of the planet, should find irresistible. But the object is destined for someone else, a rival in fact.'

Clarissa squinted as she took a long hard drag on her cigarette. 'So what do we have? Greed, envy, even a little lust. We've got some get-rich-quick sloth and status-raising pride. That's pretty impressive. Five of the Seven Ready Wins.'

Felicity said nothing. Her face was impassive, giving no sign of recognition or protest or admission.

'Oh. But how would you know? That's a grifting term. The things a con artist would use to tempt a mark to conspire in a little immorality, to collaborate in a crime, something illicit that'll stop the mark contacting the police after the sting. All in your one fabulous object.' Clarissa shook her head as she brushed some ash off her lap with the edge of her hand. 'Though I don't know what was wrong with good old snake-oil.'

The diminishing cigarette glowed again.

'Anyway, this stranger insists that she's far too good and moral to be bribed, the object's not for sale under any circum—'

'Not disturbing, am I?' Harry peered around the door, smiled amiably and ambled into the room. Both women turned to flash false grins at him.

'You haven't seen the truck keys, have you?' He lifted a magazine from the sideboard. 'Finished the feeds so we'll get off to town when you're ready.'

'I think they were in the hall, sweet,' Clarissa croaked, 'on the side.'

Felicity caught Harry's eye and she winked. Suddenly blushing, he fumbled with the door handle and slipped out, briefly leaving the fresh soapy scent of a pre-bank-manager shower. The door clicked shut and the competitors returned to their blocks.

'So aren't you dying to find out what happens next?' Clarissa widened her eyes to mirror the curiosity that steadfastly did not register on Felicity's face. 'Disaster! The stranger discovers that her hundred-and-fifty-thousand-dollar car didn't go to the garage, it was stolen, and there's no insurance because she'd "borrowed" it from the British High Commission without formal permission. Now, now she is compromised, now she is wretched and desperate and, in the circumstances, willing to sacrifice her moral posturing. Now, she waits for the greedy farmer to offer to help her, to pay for the car in exchange for the fabulous object which, let's face it, wouldn't have cost more than twenty dollars to mock up. And offer he duly does. Over the days it takes the bank to arrange the cash – it's cash of course because a deal like this, well, betraying a queen, it's nothing short of treasonous – she stays on the farm. She eats their food, enjoys their hospitality and then when the cash is ready she goes with the farmer to town to collect. You with me so far?'

'Bingo.' Harry's voice echoed from the hall.

Clarissa raised an eyebrow. 'So now, what do you think? The stranger reluctantly hands over the fabulous object, takes the farmer's cash and goes off to pay back the High Commission for the car? Or what about: she takes the cash, goes to collect the rental car she'd arranged to be "stolen", pays for the new tyres and drops it back with the rental firm one hundred and fifty thousand dollars richer?

'And the farmer? Heartbroken, he waits, in vain, for the stranger to return. But at least he owns the fabulous object. That is until he's visited by New Zealand Trading Standards, who tell him to desist from using the Queen's insignia and, when he shows them his official paperwork, from the Commonwealth Royal Appointment Provisions Office no less, they tell him that there is no royal department with the acronym CRAPO.'

Clarissa sighed. 'So which queen was it that

110

appointed you, my dear? Was it Sheba? Or Latifa? Or were you thinking more along the lines of Freddie Mercury?'

'All done, you ready?' Harry's face suddenly beamed around the door. He detected nothing of the frosty air that enveloped the two women, locked in their logomachy but momentarily frozen like the martial arts warriors who halt in mid-air between devastating kicks in those *Sleeping Dragon/Matrix* films so popular at the turn of the millennium.

'No,' the two women chimed in unison, surprised to find themselves sharing a single syllable and at least one of them making a mental note that that was all she would ever share.

'No, thank you, darling.'

'You two getting on then?' Henry pried.

Clarissa's eyes narrowed at Felicity and she mumbled, 'We're not getting off.'

Felicity fluttered her lashes. 'Like a house on fire, Harry.'

Harry nodded but then stopped, looking puzzled. 'Why do we say that? Why do you think being in-cinerated is the, um, you know, like something.'

'Simile?' Clarissa suggested.

'Yeah, why's that the simile for companionship?'

A silence smouldered as he thought about it and the women imagined each other's charred remains.

'Maybe it's something about starting with a good match?' Felicity suggested.

Harry laughed. 'Oh yes, that's pretty good. Don't be too long, it's about eight hours to Christchurch,' and he closed the door again.

' "Maybe it's something about starting with a good ma-aatch," ' Clarissa mocked Felicity's posh Pommy voice. 'Well, I suppose you'd know; you are, after all, completely burned.' She snorted smoke out of her thin little nostrils. 'I suppose there's a bit of irony in fleecing sheep farmers, but you see, Felicity . . . can I call you Felicity? I mean is that what you prefer to be called? Felicity? Rather than Catherine? Or maybe Kate?'

6

'Oh, it's you, doc, I didn't see you there.'

I moved out of the shadows beside Cedric's bed as Peter harvested the field of scattered playing cards. 'I was just checking on him when you came in. It took me a moment to work out who you were.'

'Without the make-up.' Peter nodded. 'Paula had the same trouble.'

It was strange though. And a little unsettling: to see an old friend with a completely new face.

Until that moment I'd never really thought about it but I suddenly realized that for years I had been having long conversations, tea and chatter, with someone wearing a false moustache, whitened face, cape and topper, filling the time between his Wednesday afternoon show at Lotus House and his evening performance at the Everest Nursing Home at the other end of Castle Street. It all seemed perfectly normal. Up to that moment Peter and Magicov were one and the same, but there, as he plucked up cards, looking up at me with sweet embarrassment, the tired, troubled, life-hardened man behind the astonishing Russian appeared as if in a puff of smoke.

I experienced that disorientation when something that has a huge impact but you didn't see coming suddenly presents itself, like a slap for a forgotten anniversary or a fist for an unseen spilt pint.

I suppose a neuropsychologist and an ersatz Romanov conjuror may seem strange bedfellows but Peter, Mr Magicov, really was as close a friend as I have ever had. And I do realize that that is not exactly saying much. In a life led between the lab and Lotus House, my only acquaintances were either peer reviewers, patients or rats; all of them equally loyal. Frankly, I needed Peter, my one outsider, my line to the world beyond my speciality, someone who was neither wanting something nor needing to have anything proved to him, except perhaps that I was human as well. A little cynical at times maybe; a flawed sense of the comic impact of a bad foreign accent; but he and I always found a mountain of common ground to talk about. I never asked about his secrets, his tricks, his past, and he never asked me about mine. But everything in between was there for us to pick at and gossip about. It was always relaxed and discursive, one moment trying to outwit each other, the next, outwitty.

That evening we fell into talking just as we had for years, and yet I think both of us realized that our relationship had changed in that moment, when the mask slipped, when we both had very real things to talk about. Even if most of them turned out to be about fish.

'It's the only way we've seen you, Peter. You've been coming for over a decade, and you always come with the smile plastered to your face.'

'Yes, I know. He going to be all right?'

'I think so.'

Peter got back on his chair and started to deftly reassemble the deck.

'You're pretty close to him, aren't you?'

'It, it's the common interest.'

'Magic.'

Peter nodded and looked over at Cedric's frail hands, pale blue veins fading into the white sheet. 'Have you told his family? Are they coming?'

'We've left a message.'

'He never talks about them.'

I put my hand on his shoulder and he turned to look up at me. 'He hasn't seen them for fifteen years. You, you're as close to family as he's got.'

He sighed. 'Oh dear, with family like me . . . I just can't believe he can be forgotten like this. You know, he was pretty famous when he was younger. World famous. A proper showman.'

'Yes, you told me. Golden age magician or something.'

Peter grinned. 'El Sid, the Supremo. I saw an old film of him. He's in a frilly matador's outfit and he struts on to the stage with his chest puffed out, a sword in his hand, and he's dragging his cape. Then, this is his opener, he lifts the cape and starts waving it like he's challenging a bull and then, bang, the cape falls to the ground and his assistant is standing there in a huge flamenco outfit, she walks forward to take a bow and

114

her massive skirt disappears and she's all, you know, legs. Classic.' Peter paused, trying to square the recorded memory with the grey, wizened old man asleep in front of him. 'And all he says in the whole act, after each astonishment, is "*Olé.*"' Peter snapped his fingers like castanets.

I noticed a tiny drip move quickly from his cheek to his jaw.

'Now look at him. How could those bastards just leave him here like this? For so long. If they were my fucking family I think I'd kill them. I really would.'

'Peter, didn't you once tell me you hadn't seen your own family for years?'

Peter quietened. 'If they needed me, I'd be there. It's just . . . they were better off without me.'

'How could you know that?'

'Oh, believe me, I know. The further I could get away from them, the safer, happier they'd be.'

'You know, Peter, I'm working on something that could help, something which . . .' I studied the red threads that laced his eyes. I knew exactly how to exorcize his phantoms, end whatever he believed chased him, and yet what I longed to propose was so extreme, so final, I knew I would have to plan my approach. Carefully. I had to wait. I shook my head. 'You know, when Cedric came here, he had an extreme form of transitory amnesia, he couldn't remember anything for longer than a couple of minutes. I spent months trying to find a way into his neural motives, but it took Mr Magicov, you, to find his mnemonic anchor. The one device that almost instantly gave him back a sense of continuity.' I pointed to the cards. 'When you first put

115

them into his hands, it was miraculous to watch. He suddenly came alive. You literally gave him back his life. With those in his hands he became an adult again. He remembered the art he had practised every day of his life. He asked me to pick a card.'

'El Sid again.' Peter chuckled. 'So who's the expert, eh, doc? Call yourself a world authority?'

'I don't.'

'But you are, aren't you? That's why he was sent here. Only the best. The expert on memory, Alzheimer's, fish oil and so on.'

I laughed. 'Well, maybe not the fish oil.'

'Don't knock it, it works. No, seriously. You know I've started taking fish oil to improve my memory.'

'Really?'

'Yes, trouble is, only type I can afford is goldfish oil. Now I . . .' Peter stopped. 'You know, I've started taking fish oil to improve my memory.'

I laughed again. It had the ring of material he was working up for his act. I sat down at the end of Cedric's bed. 'That's good. I'll have to use that in my lectures. Goldfish oil! You know, goldfish oil is exactly the sort of memory "improvement" I specialize in.'

Peter turned to look at me. 'A goldfish has something like a five-second memory. You know anybody that's an improvement for?'

'Yes. Everybody. No, really. I realize it may not be immediately apparent why having so little memory could be called an improvement but, you know, having a "better" memory isn't necessarily about having a greater quantity of retrievable data. What about the quality of the memories that are there? If, right now, you could take some goldfish oil, wouldn't your memories have some sort of improvement if they no longer had to harbour, say,' I pointed to Cedric, 'a sick friend, a phone bill, a weight problem or the imminent arrival of the in-laws?'

Peter smiled. 'You mean there are some things we're better off forgetting?'

'Or, at least, not remembering. Not having to think about.' Cedric mumbled slightly and we both looked at him.

'You mean all the fish oil I've been slipping Cedric hasn't done a thing?'

'It's baloney. The evidence for a fish-to-brain connection is all rather tenuous. Fish are high in protein but so are eggs and neither of them gets to go on *Mastermind*. Have you never thought, if fish are supposed to be so good for the brain, why are they so thick? It's like why do so many Chinese people think that ground-up parts of tigers are good for fertility when the species is very obviously dying out? Well, we say "dying", don't we, but, well, we mean something else. But fish really are stupid and if they don't possess any magic chemical which enhances their own brain capacity, I think the chances of anything piscatorial actually having a tangible effect on the human brain seem, well, slim.'

'You sure you're not a bit piscatorial yourself at the moment?' said Peter. 'I mean, I know that you can't exactly teach your pet fish to do tricks, or anything else for that matter, but how do you know that shoals of fish aren't swimming along quietly bubbling to each other about, I don't know, quantum mechanics and the cost of bringing up caviar nowadays?'

'Peter, they're pea-brained. In fact to a fish "pea-brained" would be a compliment, if it actually had a brain large enough to understand the concept of flattery. Which it doesn't. Whatever the housewives' tales, even if you were to wrap your cod 'n' chips in Wittgenstein's *Tractatus* you still couldn't call it brain food.'

'Maybe,' said Peter, still fiddling with the cards, 'something about being so low in the food chain has stopped fish brains from evolving. I mean, if you're only going to be eaten, why bother ruining your life by developing the ability to think about it? I imagine that they're blissfully free of self-doubt. Do you think a single one ever stops to ask, "Hang on, what's an earthworm doing floating about in the middle of a river with a great ruddy hook through it?"'

'I don't think it even occurs to them that they're breathing in the very same water they're defecating in. The hard fact is, your brain activity really can't be much above a vegetative state if there are even vegetarians who consider you edible.'

'So why are we all still thinking that fish is good for the brain?'

I shrugged. 'It's probably got more to do with the fact that from Omega-3 to Brain Training, Flash Cards to Sudoku, the "mind power" memory improvement industry, feeding on our terror of ageing and Alzheimer's, has become a multi-million-pound business. In this "information age" it is an accepted truth that a better memory leads to a happier life.'

'Not for me. This has all reminded me . . . God, there are things I'd do anything to forget.'

I peered at Peter. Without the make-up his face was alive with meaning. I could see he was absolutely sincere about what he was saying. I suddenly felt like Lucifer about to start haggling with Faust. Peter meant it, but would he, my prospective experimental subject, sign in blood? I was so tempted to say, 'Anything?' in a spooky way but stopped myself. It could wait. Softly softly.

Instead I said, 'We all have things we want to forget.'

From: _What The F*** Did I Do With My Keys_, Random House, London, 2006

What about that memory of your dad, when he used to tell you you were stupid and how worthless it made you feel? Years after the event you're still feeling it and, in your lower moments, blaming it for holding you back from pursuing your dreams or actually believing that you deserve success.

What about the memory of your first great love when they waltzed off with someone better-looking? Or the parent who walked out, leaving you with the psycho one, and all the hurt that went with it? Could that memory, that embedded fear, have anything to do with why, now, you seem to bugger up all your relationships before anyone has a chance to get too close?

Or what about those happy childhood memories of carefree roaming, endless summers and Enid Blyton? What happened when you grew up and real life turned out not to be full of magic, adventure and cream teas but stress, monotony and utter shit? Is there possibly some connection between your nostalgic memories and the disappointment, the resentment, that you won't admit to but which still drives you to infantilize yourself with Harry Potter, Friends Reunited or pretending that you're 'mates' with your own kids?

Maybe you find yourself inexplicably clinging on to relationships long past their sell-by date or in terror of asking your boss for a raise or relying on the blissful oblivion of drink or drugs – but if you ever get the sensation that something irrational is holding you back in life it is, usually, something from your past that is doing it.

But the past isn't really there, it doesn't exist, it's not another country. It is just one thing: a memory.

It seems incredible that the current 'brain training' racket, which seems almost to exist solely to justify the sales of hand-held gaming consoles to adults who should know better, is based on such a trivial gain. Being able to remember faces, or shopping lists, or the capital of Lithuania is, no doubt, helpful but it is nothing that the possession of a pen and piece of paper couldn't do equally well. On the other hand, we all have troubling and intangible things in our heads and, if we could only forget them completely, we could really improve the quality of our memories.

So many of us believe that we've buried our painful pasts but, with no knowledge of how to forget effectively, we've usually just stored their sleeping shadows in the deepest recesses of our minds, ready to surface again when they will be least helpful. The field of psychiatry is almost entirely based on the tyranny of inexpertly buried childhood memories rising from the grave, like zombies, to menace us in later life.

In this book I aim to give you the right spade and the best plot, so that you can bury your own no longer relevant zombie memories – to forget them completely, effectively and once and for all.

7

Kate strained to remain impassive. She was pretty sure she was caught but experience had taught her, as it does veterinarians, that you never put your hands up until it's absolutely necessary, or if they're in cuffs.

'Even your silence gives you away.' Clarissa leaned back. 'You're breaking the one basic rule: stay in character. No matter what. What happened to that eye-lash-fluttering, pouty, pathetic little rich wretch you were playing? Do you really think that sweet-as-pie girl would have suddenly sprouted the balls to sit and stare me out?'

Kate suppressed an urge to look away, or shrug, or even let an eyebrow twitch. Any sign, at this point, of agreement or disagreement would doom her to follow that path and, until Clarissa actually showed her how much she really knew, she had no way of knowing how to play it. The old woman could still just be guessing.

'No, of course not,' the lipless woman continued.

'"Felicity" would have been desperate to fill the silence with sound and noise and risible disingenuousness. "Oh, Mrs Rackham, what do you mean? How could you think such a thing, Mrs Rackham? I'm hurt, Mrs Rackham." And by now she would be in tears. But not you.'

Clarissa stood up awkwardly, unfolding herself from the chair in fits and starts like a badly made piece of origami undoing itself.

She looked down at Kate. 'No, because that's not your character. That's the act, the scam. You're an operator, a hardened nut. You're arrogant and you're tougher than your prey. I'd say you'd have all the pre-requisites of a grifter, or a gold-digger, if it wasn't so obvious that you're too thick to be the former and too old to be the latter.'

OK, so it was a bit more than a punt but the situation was not unsalvageable. Kate looked down at her knees and picked her words as cautiously as if she was snipping the coloured wires in a ticking bomb.

'You are so right to be suspicious' – always good to start with a compliment – 'it's so nice to meet someone who will speak up and is so sure in their convictions, but I—'

'Oh, I'm sure of my convictions, and I'm pretty sure you've had a fair few too. I've been watching you for a week now, I know how you think and right now all you're doing is trying to figure out if your Plan B will still work, the get-out, maybe with less cash but free at least.'

You spend millions of pounds on an FMRI brain-scanning machine to find that it will never even get close to the results achieved by just the slightest touch of human empathy. The old woman was absolutely right, that was exactly what was going through Kate's brain – along, of course, with a hundred million other impulses and calculations which Kate wasn't even conscious of, receiving data from nerves and telegraphing instructions to whatever vital organs and muscles were needed to keep her functioning.

Kate had no idea that from the moment she heard Clarissa utter her real name, her synapses were carrying orders from the medulla right in the deepest centre of her brain to her glands to flood her bloodstream with adrenalin; all she felt was a growing suspicion that she might have to make a run for it at any moment.

But now, as Clarissa loomed over her, Kate became all too aware of the urges that pulsed through her body and the sheer effort needed mentally to overrule the automatic effects of her adrenalin rush. She found herself having consciously to slow her breathing as her lungs tried to hyperventilate to keep up with the oxygen demands of her rising heart rate. As the air of menace intensified she found herself concentrating on telling her legs not to shake, entreating her brow not to sweat and begging her sphincter to hang on in there.

Clarissa leaned closer. She placed the ashtray on the arm next to Kate and twisted her cigarette hard into it. Her knees were practically touching Kate's. 'Maybe you've got a whole alphabet of alternative plans but you, and I, know none of them will work. You've been burned far too late in the game, you're flying solo, you've got no partners to pull you out and now you're in big, big, big . . .' Clarissa bent so close to Kate there was only the smell of old Marlboros between them. She whispered in a growl that shook, 'Shit.'

This was ridiculous. Kate was a fit young woman, at the height of her powers, all her wits about her, so how come this spindly septuagenarian was making her feel so intimidated?

Kate grabbed hold of the heavy ashtray and, knuckle white, gripped it hard. There was nothing to stop her from jumping up, knocking out the old lady and making a run for it. She could get Harry to take her straight to the airport. She could be out of the country before anybody was any the wiser, and yet she felt almost incapacitated with fear. A fear absolute and chronic and way out of all proportion to the actual threat.

She felt sick, not throw-up sick but disconnected, unbalanced nausea.

The feeling was not from the effects of the cocktail of neuro-chemicals that gushes through the bloodstream in times of stress, it was from memory. It was an emotional pattern of synaptic connections in the amygdala long buried, thought to have been disconnected an age ago, which suddenly, through a mirror event, became live again, as stomach-churning as the moment that made it. It was a restimulated long-forgotten feeling of extreme anxiety, a pattern that had lain dormant from the time she first experienced the tension and fear of being close to capture fifteen years before on Fifth Avenue.

Because EmMemories have no conscious signifiers, no visual data to clue you in, Kate had no idea of which specific event she was being reminded. She had no flashes of all this happening before. She had learned this emotion in extreme circumstances, committed it to heart, and now it was returning, even though she was older and somewhat wiser. She was rooted in a girlish fear out of all proportion to what the experienced woman she now was should feel in the same pitifully unthreatening situation she was now in.

Kate desperately controlled a shiver she could feel working its way down through her shoulder bones, embellishing the feeling that everything was hanging on a knife-edge with a cold sensation of terror.

'You've got a vivid imagination, Mrs Rackham, and to construct such an elaborate story about being ripped off, I can only think that there might be just a touch of paranoia or—'

'Oh, paranoia? Oh yes, Dr Freud. Do tell me.' Clarissa bared her teeth in the sort of smile which nature gives to her deadliest predators: the sharks, the crocodiles, the democratically elected leaders of western societies. 'You know that someone is scraping the quarrel barrel when all she can come up with is that the opposition is mad. Psychology is the last refuge of the failed argument.'

'Actually I think you'll find that stepping out of the argument to question the methods used to conduct it might be an even further last refuge.' Kate hung her shoulders. 'But that doesn't sound quite as catchy. Look, I wasn't saying you are paranoid. Maybe your fear of being ripped off is justified. You seem to know an awful lot about conmen though, so either you've learned because you've been the victim of some unscrupulous hustler, for which my sympathies are completely with you, or,' Kate looked Clarissa straight in her stony eyes, 'that hustler was you.'

A flash in Clarissa's eyes was all that Kate needed. As Henry had said: bingo.

Clarissa slammed her fist down on the table beside Kate's chair and brought her face within inches of Kate's. This time there was none of the confidential air, the lowering of the voice. 'Oh yes,' she jeered, 'yes. You're quite right. And I'll tell you, forty years ago I went up the aisle with that disgusting man.' Her finger pointed to a lurid painting of Mr Rackham dressed as a shepherd. 'But he was a millionaire and you know what I was singing in my head? "Heigh ho, heigh ho, it's off to work we go." I might as well have had the spade on my shoulder, all I was thinking was, Yee haw, my prospecting days are over, there be gold in them there wills and I've hit the mother lode.

'Then. Then I dutifully gave him Harry.' Clarissa put one hand on her hip and stretched backwards. 'And he really was the bloody mother-load. But that was the idea, you know, one kid, only heir, primogeniture and all that. Give it a few months then I'd skip out and sting him for visitation rights, or maybe a buyout, whatever.

'Then, picture this, Harry's six months old, I've engineered the big row with Evan and my bags are packed, the taxi's at the gate and you know what?' Clarissa stopped and ground her jaw. 'Then I look in the mirror, on the way out, just to check myself. One look in the bloody mirror. That's all it took.'

Kate examined Clarissa and imagined what the mirror saw in that pinched face.

'I was younger than you are, girl, but you should see what having a baby does to you. Even with the help.

One look in the mirror and I took my hat off, I put my bag down, and I cried. Real, real tears. Suddenly I was feeling again. And you know what I felt? I felt shit. The game was up. I was too old. Sell-by date passed. I knew if I left then it would only get harder. I'd lost it.' Clarissa pointed at the Persian carpet. 'One look in the mirror and the fuck stopped here.'

The silence that followed really was unendurable and Kate brought a stammer on, 'I, I, I . . .', buying time and hoping beyond hope that she could follow the revelation with some guiltless guile.

'Oh, save it,' Clarissa snorted. 'Who do you think you are? Oh no. I know who you think you are. And I know who you want us to think you are. But who you actually are? Now that's something I doubt even you have a clear handle on.'

In some unfathomable way, Clarissa's ever-tightening targeting finally hit Kate's button. She could no longer resist the urge to come out fighting.

'Don't you worry, I know exactly who I am,' Kate lied.

'Were,' Clarissa corrected her, reaching into the pocket of her tweed skirt and pulling a photo out. 'We both know exactly who you were.'

She gave the photo to Kate.

It was a printout of the same cropped wedding photo she had been asked to identify fifteen years before in the apartment on Fifth Avenue.

'We live in an internet age now. What can't we find with Google and a little know-how? Beware the silver surfers: far too much time on their hands. It's all about knowing the right places to look. Like the rather pitiful

FBI Most Wanted site. Seems you earned yourself a little reputation some time ago, Catherine.'

Kate swallowed hard, transfixed by the photo. It was the same bloody picture that she had hoped would eventually drop off the US Homeland Security database and allow her to take America again. Instead she had been stuck fleecing the greedy marks of the distant colonies. It all seemed a lifetime ago. She couldn't even remember the mark who had been cropped from the picture.

Clarissa picked up a silver box on the side table and took out a cigarette. 'You were quite good-looking when you were younger. But I think it's your turn to look in the mirror, girl. Someone needs to tell you. I don't suppose you have friends who will. Or parents, for that matter. You've chosen a lonely road. It's not like you can trust anyone like you because, well, because only a fool would trust you. Right?'

'OK,' Kate said quietly, 'yes, that's me.'

'No. No. That isn't you,' Clarissa snapped the box shut and turned to Kate, 'that's you a long time ago. Not now. I mean, look at her, she's a stunner. I mean, what a man wouldn't do for a girl so easy on the eye. But, my God, look at you now! In case you haven't noticed, everybody is more than ready to forgive the young. The older you get, the more suspicion you're treated with.'

'Maybe I should go and pack my bags.'

'Oh no, Catherine Minola. You're going to have to do more than that. You see, a smart little worker like you, I reckon, is just the right person finally to get me out of here.'

'You want me to help you?'

128

'There's money in it, for you.'

'Not a chance.'

'Trouble is, Catherine, I was talking to a gentleman the other day, I think you might know him, a Special Agent Brown. He seemed very eager to catch up with you.'

'He's still working?'

'Oh yes, and it turns out that in his illustrious career you were the only one that got away. He has a yen to make things right, to feel the only collar he missed. He seemed very interested in finding out where you were.'

'You told him?'

'Not exactly. But he seemed to think that he'd have no problem arranging a trip to come and work with his colleagues in the South Island Police.'

'I don't believe you.'

Clarissa snarled, 'Really? So you want to try me?'

Kate thought for a while, looking into those cold eyes, and decided that maybe she would be best off just rolling with this one. 'What do you want me to do?'

'Nothing, my dear, except what you do best. Lie, cheat. Oh, and marry my son.'

8

'You see, Dick. One fifteen. He's right on time,' smiled Jacob Wissenschaft, a man who looked as Father Christmas would if he had gone over to the dark side. An Anti-Claus; the same large portly body but all in black: beard, ringleted hair, suit, and black fur ringing his black hat. 'Every day,' he continued, 'the same place, a beef and horseradish sandwich. Pays with a Visa card.' Wissenschaft didn't look at his companion as he narrated but kept his eyes fixed on their mark crossing Islington High Street.

Haim Verstehung sat next to him on the bench, carefully logging John Ogilvy's movements in his spiral-bound notebook. He too bore an uncanny resemblance to an iconic figure, and though no impressionist, he mirrored the painter Toulouse-Lautrec with uncanny accuracy: pince-nez, voluminous beard and legs like flower pots. 'He's a creature of habit, Dick,' he noted. 'I knew it just from the look of him.'

'This again?' said Wissenschaft. 'No, Dick, you didn't, at best you thought he might be *like* that, but you can't *know* something unless you've actually witnessed it.'

Verstehung smiled at the taller detective. 'Witnessed it? So by your logic, Dick, I can't know, say, right or evil or love because I can't witness anything more than their effects, but I can know that you're a narrow-minded twat because I witness it every day?'

'A twat? A vagina?' Wissenschaft looked horrified, and would have shown it if it weren't for the beard, moustache and *samet hoicher* hat covering most of the expression centres of the face. 'You call me a vagina, Dick? Then you do the world a favour: if you can't tell the difference there's small chance you'll be muddying the gene pool.'

'I? Muddy the gene pool? The only reason I sit next to someone as ugly as you, Dick, is because I look like

130

Adonis in comparison. Just being in your vicinity increases my chances of a *shtup* by a hundred.'

'You need a *shtup*. You think my brain is narrower than anybody else's?'

'Dick, I said narrow-minded. Not narrow-brained. But, for you, you can't know that there's such a thing as a mind, because you can't witness a mind. So by your empirical logic, wouldn't it be fair to call you mindless, my friend?'

'Maybe, but it wouldn't make me brainless, *bubbeleh*.' Wissenschaft pointed down the road towards WHSmith. 'Dick, suspect's left the sandwich shop, he's off to the newsagent already.'

Verstehung slipped off the bench, standing ready to go. 'All right already?'

The two Hasidim moved from the bench in unison and walked towards the pelican crossing. Outside the Earl of Sandwich they looked both ways along the street and entered, setting a little bell ringing above the door.

Verstehung hung back, keeping an eye on the street. Wissenschaft went up to the counter and flashed an official-looking identity card at the owner.

'CID. We're pursuing a suspect who just bought an item here. My colleague and I would like to see your PIN device.'

'Hang on.' The owner stopped ladling Flora from a catering tub, put his knife down and leaned over the chopping board. 'Can I see that card again?'

'Sir, the man we're after is very dangerous and every second you withhold the information that we need puts a life in danger. Do you want that on your conscience?'

'No, but—'

'So you think it's OK not to cooperate?'

'I just wanted to see your badge thing again . . .'

In an instant, Wissenschaft picked up the bread knife and plunged it straight through the owner's hand. The knife embedded itself in the chopping board, neatly severing the second and third metacarpals and pinning the hand firmly down.

Verstehung winced as the owner screamed. He checked the street again. Wissenschaft calmly walked round to the till, pressed the recall on the credit card reader and memorized the account number he was looking for.

The initial stages of shock were quickly over and the sandwich maker started shouting. 'What sort of fucking madmen are you? You're not the fucking police. I'm calling them straight away, you fucking loonies. They'll get you.' He tugged at the knife, which just tore more of his tendon, inspiring further screaming.

Verstehung held the door open for Wissenschaft, who, adjusting his hat to a jauntier angle, strode out with a nonchalant '*Shalom.*' Verstehung smiled apologetically to the owner and shrugged. 'What are you to do? Always the problem with these Jews, they all look alike, *shalom.*' The little bell tinkled again as the men left and the owner fainted.

Outside the two men strolled back to the Lexus. Verstehung drove as Wissenschaft keyed the account details into his mobile phone and started a credit check.

'Did you have to do that, Dick?' Verstehung glanced at the big man. 'Really? Did you have to do the stabbing? You don't think there was another way?'

132

'We needed the information, didn't we? Was there a more efficient way?'

Verstehung braked to let an old woman inch a Zimmer frame over a pedestrian crossing. 'Haven't I heard something like that before? Wasn't there another bunch of people obsessed with efficiency?'

'What? So I'm a Nazi now?'

'I'm just asking: when you're dealing with people, is efficiency always the most rewarding route?'

'We got the numbers, didn't we?'

'Sure. You know what else we got? Another supporter for Hamas.'

Wissenschaft swivelled his head, looking all about him in surprise. 'What? You mean we weren't in Islington?'

'You know we were.'

'So you don't think he was a *Gazardian* reader already?'

Verstehung tutted and nodded.

'You know,' said Wissenschaft, 'all I did was make one more person a bit less dismissive, a bit more cautious, a bit more aware that we're not all wimpy four-eyed Woody fucking Allen.'

Verstehung laughed. '*Oy*. You made him a bit less handy, at that.'

The Lexus decelerated into silent running as it was waved through the barrier at Ealing Studios. The electric motor noiselessly pulled up in front of Sound Stage Five, surprising a number of the people standing in line by the door and making those still old-fashioned enough to expect cars to make noise when they moved jump.

Wissenschaft prodded his phone with his great fat

133

fingers. 'John Ogilvy. He gets paid by PM and T Advertising, groceries from the Angel Waitrose, Tesco in Peebles on the weekends. Our friend Mr Warner had him in Barbados this summer.' He scrolled down. 'Pet-a-Lot Veterinarians, Mothercare, Rymans, the Earl of Sandwich of course and – uh-oh,' he paused as he continued to scroll, 'several payments at the Hendon Health Club.' Wissenschaft winked at Verstehung. 'You think he keeps fit, our man? Long way from home for a gym. That's a lot of horizontal jogging going on.'

'So he gets a bit of exercise. He's a man, isn't he? We're out of the blackmail game, Dick, we're legit, we're working for the Magician now.'

'What? We going to pass up an opportunity?'

'You don't think Titus Black pays us enough? Just to get information about his audience? We get the low-down and he spews it out like he's mind-reading. Everybody's happy. We need to break the law too?'

'Too? You blind? You didn't see me stab that man?'

'Blind? Dick. You too deaf to hear what I'm saying? We're in a different game now, it's not the old days. We don't need to be so . . . you know.'

'Violent?'

'Efficient. He's not paying us to go that far.'

Wissenschaft and Verstehung got out and walked along the queue to the sign: 'Sharing Thoughts – Audience'. Verstehung pushed the studio door open.

'Oi, curly,' a man close to the front shouted at them, 'don't you know what a queue is?'

Halfway through the door Wissenschaft stopped and turned. His knuckledusters had already dropped from the straightened sleeve of his jacket into his hand and his fingers were slipping through the holes as he strode towards the heckler.

Verstehung caught his sleeve. 'No, Dick, they're the audience. Black needs them.'

9

The pick-up growled over the rise of yet another hill peppered with gorse, keeping to a steady seventy as it crossed the rolling tundra towards hazy cerulean mountains which never seemed to get any closer. Strapped into the passenger seat, Kate felt everything around her race or shake or bump, and yet she found herself in an anomalous oasis of calm.

When you no longer hear the engine for the persistence of its roar, when you no longer see the road for the inevitability of its stretch, when you no longer feel the vibrations running through your body for the constant tremor of the entire chassis, there is a stillness. It's one of those odd paradoxes like Zeno's arrow that never hits its target or how the Acme Company managed to continue trading when all its Road Runner-catching equipment was so lethally crap.

From: _NeuroScientific – The Journal of Neuroscience_,
Vol. XI, Issue 34, London, 2010

NEUROPERSPECTIVE

The Paradoxical Mind

As scientists we search for answers, but are our brains too reductionist to really find all of them?

I FEEL sorry for Zeno, a philosopher plagued by paradoxes and the limits of logic, but if you will irrefutably argue that your arrow will never hit its target, you're just asking for trouble. Half the bag snatchers in Athens, delinquents playing truant from the Epicurean School looking for their next fix of amoral self-gratification, would have had him marked as easy prey, a defenceless mug with defective weaponry. Perhaps, having logically proven that a tortoise could outpace Achilles, Zeno felt he could always get away from any anti-ascetic muggers. Of course he was in trouble if they turned out to be one of the Zenophobic smart-arses from the School of Cynics, hanging out at the _agora_, giving him the finger. There was no convincing them.

I like to think he took it all philosophically.

It's probably best not to take paradoxes as literally as quantum physicists seem to, but to look at them as the guards that patrol the borders of our minds. They are the danger signs, the 'Here be dragons', the no-man's-land between the workings of this neurological patterning device which sits between our ears and the inconceivably immense operations of the universe outside it, between the conceit and the concrete.

The brain is hard-wired to reduce everything to its own manageable dimensions, to condense the cosmos into patterns and algorithms, rules and laws, numbers and words. Quick, just try to think of anything that isn't defined in those ways.

Even if you thought of something as indefinable as a feeling you once had, your brain was immediately trying to find words, metaphors, signs or even symbols to define, summarize, demarcate, reduce, explain. It's what it does, that's its job.

So whenever we try to reach beyond our mind's limits, to impose its regulated methodologies on the world, we soon start tripping over paradoxes, things that shouldn't be but are, warnings that our propensity for *reductio* is, quite frankly, *absurdum*; whether it is an arrow that mathematically never hits its target or a universal 'Maker' who, by definition, has no 'Maker' himself.

Wherever we find a limit to what we, and the machines our brains construct to help us, can conceive, there is a paradox warning us that shoehorning the universe into the brain's own egotistical rules and formulas and patterns is doomed to failure. So for all its atoms and quarks and electrons and Newtonian laws the universe still fails to conform to any neat mathematical formula that the human brain has yet conceived. And we may be eternally stuck making the sums longer and more complex and never getting any closer to an answer, unless we can embrace the message of the paradox and admit the limitations of our own perspective.

Maybe it's fear and vulnerability that drives us to crave a universe as neat as a theory or holy book. Perhaps that is why we want Einstein and his relatives to be right even though the numbers, however big, however they are crunched, just keep getting bigger; so we don't feel that we are just victims in the face of the unpredictable actions of an immeasurable universe.

Or are we just power crazy? Do we think that somehow, if we can comprehend and re-create the workings of the universe, then we can become gods? If that's so, should we really be trying to shrink the universe to our size? Or should we be going the junk food route and finding ways to expand ourselves to its proportions?

Is it really so hard to accept that the 'chaos' caused by the butterfly that creates a hurricane may not simply be a mathematical formula just waiting to be solved but actual real chaos? Or that the banking systems, based on innumerable different investment variants, from liars to the weather, can't be defined absolutely within

137

some algebra? Even if we recognized the irreconcilability of our paradoxes, and accepted the limitations of human understanding, it wouldn't be a surrender; it wouldn't necessitate a 'spiritual', a god or a higher power. It might just open us to new possibilities, undreamed-of scientific horizons, ways of experimentation that are not limited by always having to be recreated on a human scale.

The brain is hard-wired to reduce everything to its own manageable dimensions, to condense the cosmos into patterns and algorithms, rules and laws, numbers and words. Just try to think of anything that isn't defined in those ways.

Even if Zeno was getting his toga in a twist, it took his chum Socrates to point out the paradox that underlies all paradoxes. Had he been one of the later, beardless philosophical pin-up boys, a Wittgenstein or Heidegger, say, he'd have no doubt called it something like 'the subjective awareness of the unattainability of objectivity', and then had the title lifted by a fashionable artist to adorn an expensive pickled fish. As it was, he just said, 'All I know is that I know nothing.'

And he was right, because as close as we may think we are to discovering how the mind, or the universe, works, we will really only ever be guessing while we're stuck observing either of them from the inside.

Dr C. Tavasligh

Inside the vehicle inside the constant thundering motion, shaking and rumbling, inside the head inside all that, there is a paradoxically sublime peace, far beyond the usual paradigms; past the quietude of any bird-thronged lakeland idylls, or breeze-swept, insect-humming picnic meadows or cough-echoing, sandal-shuffling temples, chapels and churches, from Tiber to Tibet. Inside the wall of sound and motion, within the music and vibration of the aeroplane, the Walkman, the train, the nightclub, the Floyd, the acid house, the trip hop or, in this case, the Toyota pick-up truck, when you are deafened and numbed beyond sensory prioritization, when the outside world is deadened, and the mind released from its eternal waking vigilance to its immediate environment, it is the hypnotic trance state, the end result of the aural trip, that turns to an inner peace. It finally finds its own world to wander in and ruminate.

Which was exactly where Kate was. It was another five hours before they got to Christchurch but Kate was thoroughly in her own world. She stared straight ahead but everything she saw was in her head. Replaying recent memories.

Kate wasn't sure which she resented more, being caught by Clarissa or being used by her. For Kate's entire grifting life she had worked alone, always the one who was in control, pulling the strings, writing the script. Now, apart from anything else, there didn't seem a hope in hell that the old bat would keep her end of the bargain. If she was anything like Kate she wouldn't. But then if she was anything like Kate she would already have worked out how Kate was going to try to turn the situation to her own advantage. Kate had to think beyond Clarissa's horizons, beyond her game. First she had to assume that Brown was already on his way to New Zealand. She ran through the deal again, looking for Clarissa's tells, the unconscious giveaway behaviour, the clues to how she was playing her cards.

'I know it's not nice to talk ill of the dead, my dear,' Clarissa had said, sticking her chin out to raise her nose into the air, 'but that deceitful little fucker, my bastard husband, screwed me over. He left the whole bloody lot in trust for darling Henry. A million dollars, not including the value of this place. It's inconceivable! Did he really think I put all that effort into him, stuck with him, for love? My God, I was way out of his league. The arrogance. It was all a tax avoidance "next generation" thing. Did the selfish git think about me? I put in all the hard work, all the nicey wifey, lie-down-and-think-of-the-Bank-of-England stuff. And what did I get out of it? A management fee, for running the trust! Management, for God's sake!'

'Henry'll look after you. You're his mother.'

'Oh yes, he's very well intentioned. A little flat in Wellington and a fuck-all allowance. Very nice. This isn't what I dreamed about. I should be in Paris, swathed in couture, courted by gigolos. Not traipsing round a sheep farm in galoshes. Henry's never going to do right by me, he can't even get his hands on the cash until he's married, which is where you come in.'

Kate laughed. 'Look, I'm sure there's plenty of girls who . . .'

'Oh yes, yes there are. He's an attractive man, an attractive package. Trouble is, I wouldn't be able to . . .' Clarissa looked up in search of the right word.

'Blackmail them?'

'Trust them. To do right by me.' Clarissa shrugged. 'Best I can expect is a stipend for the mother-in-law. Not quite the Rive Gauche. It's my money, I bloody earned it and I'm going to get it. You, you're a greedy little operator, I can see you won't let emotions get in the way of the job.' Clarissa watched Kate carefully before the kicker. 'Don't worry, you'll get a fee.'

Kate's chin pulled sharply back towards her neck. 'If I do this I don't get a fee, I get a split.'

'You think you're in a position to negotiate?'

'Do you think you are?'

'I'd consider one per cent. Think of it as a commission. An incentive. You can buy a lot of face cream with that, and, my dear, it's not like you don't need it.'

'One per cent? You're joking. Let me just work this out.' Kate retrieved her mobile phone and pretended to tap at its calculator, surreptitiously switching it to 'Memo Record'. Blackmail being a game for two players. 'So you're going to give me ten thousand dollars to marry your son? Is that right?' Was that entrapment? Kate had used the ploy a thousand times but she had never bothered to find out. The marks were all too ready to pay out when they heard their own voices.

Clarissa nodded. 'As soon as he's married, the funds will clear into a joint account that needs both your signatures. You simply transfer the money to me, minus your commission, and you can say goodbye to Henry, me and Agent Brown.'

'So somehow, on the way to town, you're expecting me to propose to him?'

'Save yourself the trouble. You may be getting past it, my dear, but you're not that far gone. He'll propose before you're halfway there. He always does. I can't tell you how many silly little girls I have had to prise this back from.' Clarissa waved her bony fingers at Kate as if she didn't know that, the very moment they had met, Kate had already clocked and priced the enormous diamond ring now glittering in front of her.

'It doesn't seem fair,' Clarissa continued drily, 'that men only get dogs as their best friends, does it?' She pulled her hand away and with her fingers spread looked down for a moment to admire it. 'Henry will be asking for this before you leave, I guarantee it. But you can stop drooling. It's not part of the deal. This comes back to me. Clear?'

'As Daytona Beach after *Jaws* was released.'

'And don't think about doing a bunk. You really won't get very far. I've already locked away all the stuff from your bags, your cards, your money. I've cancelled the cash transfer at the bank. You're going to Christchurch for one reason. Henry would never have the courage to ask you here, with his mother around. So you're going with nothing but the clothes you're in, girl, and that's how you'll come back. We'll call it collateral.'

Clarissa pulled her blouse straight and craned her neck to relieve a crick brought on by her intense stare. But she never took her eyes off Kate. 'After this is over, take my advice: you're getting too old to be still playing this tune. It's not for you any more. Get out of it. While you still can.'

'What, I should settle as happily as you did?'

Clarissa raised one of her string-thin eyebrows. 'If you'd been at the top of your game, would I have even spotted you coming? It's too easy when you've got the looks to keep other people's eyes off the ball. But what are you now? Late thirties? How much longer do you think you can trade on your looks? People are not so forgiving, not so eager to assist, not so keen to buy the story from someone who looks like their mother.'

'I'm not looking at retirement quite yet.'

'It's looking at you, my dear.' Clarissa swivelled and began to strut away from Kate, each step screwing her heels into the carpet as if walking over kittens she had tired of. 'In case you're wondering, the recording you made is inadmissible. Really, if you're not going to quit you're going to have to up your game, learn some new skills. You can't keep peddling the same dreams. Work on some new strategies, change your tactics,' she got to the door and glanced over her shoulder, 'or can an old dog not learn any new tricks?'

Kate broke her trance, and suddenly the shapes and sounds flooded back, the car, the engine, Henry. She turned to him as he clutched the wheel and stared down the road to Oblivion, population 325, last restrooms before the motorway.

She smiled at him. 'OK,' she said, 'OK, I will. Let's do it.'

Henry looked over to her, and flashed a beautiful white-toothed smile. 'That's fantastic. You've made me the happiest man on South Island.'

'I just want to ask one thing.' Kate looked hesitant. 'Before we do it, I want to get my father's blessing.'

10

'Oh my giddy aunt, you gave me a fright. Oh my heart.' Ethel Ogilvy clutched her chest dramatically and stared at the familiar stranger in her kitchen. 'I know you.'

'Of course you knnn-nn-know me, Ethel. I am Titus B-Black and I've come to talk to you about your grandson John.' He sat at the end of her kitchen table, carelessly pushing back a stray lock of his white-blond hair. His trademark ankle-length leather Driza-Bone squeaked as his hand returned to lace fingers with the other on the table.

'You're that man off the telly.'

'To be more accurate, dear,' Titus replied peevishly, 'I'm that m-m-man *on* the telly. Every night this week at nine o'clock it's *Sharing Thoughts Week*.'

'Yes, well, our John thinks you're the bee's knees. Watches all your shows. Even booked to be audience in one next week.'

'Yes. I kn-n-know,' Titus said briskly, winking one of his famed pale-blue hypnotic eyes at her, 'I saw his name on the bookings sheet, which is why I'm here.'

'In my kitchen?'

'Ah, but Ethel – you don't mind if I call you Ethel? – I'm n-n-not in your kitchen. And neither are you.'

Ethel looked about her. It definitely was her kitchen but at her age it was always best to check twice. Young people often accused her of being slow, but Ethel knew she was as fast as she ever was. What slowed her down was all the double-checking that she had to do. After all the hype about the onslaught of dodderiness she did twice as much 'making sure', letting her conscious and unconscious processes check in with each other, as she had always done as a young woman. She checked as if, were she extra-vigilant, she might spot dementia before it sneaked up, whacked her on the head and sent her doolally; not realizing that that sort of personifying of mental illness is a sign that the damage has probably already begun. 'I'm definitely in my kitchen, and so are you,' Ethel insisted.

'Think about it,' Titus continued, confidently gesturing to the seat opposite, which Ethel drew out without even asking herself what right a total stranger in her house had to offer it in the first place. 'Just a m-m-moment ago, you were sitting on your settee in the lounge. Yes? You were watching that show, *The Nation's Got Talent But It's More Fun to Laugh at These Pathetic Losers*. Yes? Your room's warm and comfortable and you've had a long day and you're f-f-feeling tired and your bones have been throbbing and the tiredness just runs through every part of you and your eyelids ache.'

As Ethel listened to Titus's monotonous voice her shoulders visibly drooped. The wrinkles in her face began to smooth.

'Then, you're feeling so tired, you could just do with a little shut-eye but you promised yourself a cup of tea and swore you'd go make one in the next ad break. But can you even be sure the ads came on before you found yourself standing in the kitchen? And you can't be completely certain whether you walked to the kitchen at all because you can't actually remember it, can you? So maybe you're suffering some sort of amnesia or . . .' Titus let the preferred option dangle for Ethel to persuade herself.

She nodded hesitantly. He was right. Without any evidence one way or the other, she had a limited choice of perspectives: either she was asleep right now on the settee and dreaming the weird little celebrity in her kitchen, or the dreaded senility had finally struck and she really was losing her memory.

Titus had come a long way from that eight-year-old terror who had debagged Mr Noodles. He was now, at the very least, a twenty-three-year-old terror. Among the many talents he had acquired was an uncanny mastery of the functioning tricks behind neuro-linguistic programming, the pseudo-scientific discipline for those low in empathy and chronically disempowered that exploits the art of boring people into hypnotic stupors to aid the sale of trinkets, used cars or 'game', balding, middle-aged men's own bodies to gullible women with more alcohol than sensation.

This, though, gave Titus enough insight to know that if we're forced to choose between possible beliefs we will pick the one that is least disturbing to our image of ourselves and what we perceive as our 'identity'. For Ethel, choosing between accepting she was in a dream

146

or that she was losing her marbles was a no-brainer, which pretty much describes the state of mind that Titus was taking advantage of.

Yes, Ethel had amnesia. But it was exactly the same forgetfulness that every one of us experiences several times every hour. We spend our waking lives lapsing into and out of autoamnesia and we only find it puzzling when its discrepancies are pointed out to us.

From: _An Autoamnesia of My Own_, *NUTTA Quarterly*, London, Spring 2008

Since Plato described the two different horses that drove the chariot of his mind, one wild, one tame, we have been dividing the brain into the simplistic binary of conscious and unconscious: in other words the bits we're awake for and the bits we're not; the bits we can feel responsible for and the bits that seem to bubble up from nowhere and tend, like wind, to get covered with 'Blimey, I don't know where that one came from'; the bits that we can work through rationally and the mistakes we try to elevate by calling them things like 'passion'; the bits that know right from wrong and the bits that don't even bother to find an excuse for the third cream bun.

This, though, is so simplistic it has as much relevance to the classification of brain function as noting that the only two types of people in the world are those who divide people into two different types and those who don't. Freud was even less help, not in two but in three minds about identity; as if his ego wasn't enough, he had to have a superego. Even the basics of neuroforensics try to divide the brain into four broad categories, moving from the outer, rational 'cortical areas' down through the more emotional 'limbic' and 'mid-brain' areas to the 'primitive' core functions of the brainstem.

The term 'unconscious' is far too blanket, covering everything from the excitement of dreams to the tasks that we perform under autoamnesia, which are just too mundane for words.

Let me imagine, since facts are so hard to come by, what would have happened had Virginia Woolf's wonderfully gifted brother Thoby been a writer too. In post-Victorian England, the suffragette movement and the general emancipation of women was the big news. It put literate women in the public eye; they were the 'sexy' of the day and enjoyed more privileged, publicity-enabling star opportunities than their male counterparts, who were emasculating themselves in the wake of Austen, Brontë and Eliot. But when Virginia wrote *To the Lighthouse* she chose to narrate it as a 'stream of consciousness', to follow the ranging thoughts of a woman as she, for instance, performed the routine task of preparing dinner. But what if Virginia's brother had had her opportunities? What if he had been the more experimental sibling and he had written *To the Lighthouse* instead as a 'stream of unconsciousnesss'? You cannot doubt how extremely dull the text would have been, crack six eggs into bowl, whisk, rest, etc. The lack of excitement may well be why the brain chooses to forget autoamnesiacally, and though he might not have become a great literary scion, Thoby might have been able to beat Mrs Beeton and pre-date the mind-numbing metric-brackets-imperial measurements and hob-setting magniloquence of the supermarket bestseller *Delia's Edwardian Tesco Feast* by a hundred years.

By delegating our often repeated or humdrum tasks to the unconscious, the conscious brain progresses through its own narrative like a *tuk-tuk* rushing through the busy streets of Bangkok, blind to the everyday common beggars and even the pingpong-shooting showgirls of our unthreatened automatic lives. It's the stepping stones I mentioned earlier, where life may seem an analogue 'stream of consciousness' but is in fact a series of digital moments where the automatic unconscious mind and the peripatetic conscious mind check in with each other to make sure that they agree they're in the same place, reading off the same page and that all is right with the world, before going off in their multi-tasking different directions.

Indeed, without our autoamnesia we would probably drive ourselves mad in an unending constant awareness of the now. It's why, no matter what the gurus say, we keep forgetting to 'live in the now', to 'appreciate every moment' or why, at school, I got sent to the head for translating as 'fish of the day', *carpe diem*.

The fact that we can often recognize our own mental abnormalities stems directly from these two parts checking in with each other and finding they don't agree. One of them, for instance, hears a voice and the other can see that there's no one around but the dead prostitute with her entrails laid out in a pattern resembling the Sigma of the Illuminati. We have a sort of myhabitopia, a blindness to the intermoments that carry us from one moment to the next; whether it is driving up the motorway and realizing that you have no recollection of travelling the last thirty miles, or getting from the sofa to the kitchen to make a cup of tea.

Ethel smiled and wagged her finger at Titus. 'You're trying to say I'm asleep. That I'm dreaming I came in here for a cup of tea.' Ethel gripped the flesh on her forearm and pinched. 'Well, how come I'm not waking up?'

'Because we've got things to talk about.'

'Why don't I just check on myself in the living room?'

'You won't be there, Ethel, because it breaks the first law of lucid dreaming. You cannot occupy two different locations and be aware of that fact at the same time. You might see yourself in a dream but you won't question it saying, "How odd, I'm looking at myself, but that's impossible." You'll just accept it as completely natural, without question.'

'This is nutty,' Ethel said crossly.

'I understand you're cross . . .'

'I'm not cross, I'm discombobulated,' she said with all the steady rhythm of a well-worn catchphrase.

'But somewhere in the back of your head, Ethel,' Titus continued, 'you must know the alternative is nuttier still. TV celebrities don't just break into and lurk about in people's kitchens.'

Ethel pondered this for a moment and clicked her tongue. 'They might,' she said slowly. 'In fact that's very much the sort of thing they do do when their careers need a boost and they agree to perform some publicity-creating hidden camera stunt of dubious ethical relevance, like convince an old lady she's going bonkers.' Ethel's eyes started roaming the room, hunting for hidden cameras.

Titus was dumbstruck. 'You're quite c-c-cynical for a woman of your age.'

'I'll tell you, laddie, for a woman of my age it's not cynicism, it's experience.' Ethel stopped searching for hidden cameras and looked at Titus. 'The end result may be the same, it's just I've taken the more painful route.'

Titus sighed. 'Really I don't have a lot of time. It's very power-sapping visiting people over the astral plane. I need to talk to you about your grandson. About John. He's coming to my show and I'd like to find out a little about him.'

Ethel hummed to herself as she suddenly decided to peer about the dresser looking for cameras.

'OK. What can I do to convince you that you're not being filmed?'

'Strip.' Ethel smiled.

'What?'

'Strip. If you want to know anything from me and I want to know you're not going to use this footage, take your clothes off. It's not as if I've never seen anything like it before and it's not as if I could do anything about it even if I wanted to.'

Titus grinned. 'You dirty old woman.'

'That's the deal. It's my dream, it's only a dream, so what do you care?'

'So I sit here in my underpants and you . . .'

'No, dear. Stark naked or I'm not saying a thing.'

'You promise you'll tell me what I need to know about you and John if I do it naked?'

'Yes, dear. I promise.'

Titus stood slowly and began to take his clothes off, placing them very neatly on the chair. He made sure that his trusty stiletto knife, which lurked in his sleeve, didn't pierce the lining as he folded his jacket. Well, why not give the old girl a thrill? It was the last thing she was going to see anyway.

11

'OK, you most luke at your card and you most not say a thing.' Mr Magicov's faux Russian accent might have been more Rasp than Putin, but he fixed the woman with a hypnotic stare worthy of any mad monk. Lotus House was always his biggest crowd of the week and he knew how to get them eating out of his hand, serving it up with extra cheese and ham. He twisted the ends of his waxed Dalí moustache and then touched the tips of his white-gloved fingers to his top hat. 'Mr Magicov will demonstrate the power of his mind. His extrasensory perception. He will read your very thoughts. Look, look now, Beryl, and remember, think about the card, try and send Mr Magicov your thoughts. Help him. Think hard. But of course. Yes. Yes. Magicov, he already sees something. He sees, he sees a colour. It is the colour of the card, he sees a cherry colour. Yes?'

Beryl looked at the card a little more closely and shook her head. 'No, dear, it's—'

'No, no, don't tell him. Look harder at the card, it is like the cherry in my country, the black cherry. It is a black card. Yes?'

'Yes, dear.'

'Yes, yes, he can see it clearly. Now concentrate on trying to send him the suit. Hmm. It is spades . . .'

Mr Magicov let the word dangle for less than half a second but that was all he needed to gauge the reaction. No micro-tell, no beginning of a smile, so he continued as if it was no more than a dramatic pause. '. . . or clubs. It is one of these two. But. In the mind of Mr Magicov he sees a clover shape, it is clubs. Yes?'

'Yes, dear. That's right.'

Mr Magicov now looked slowly around the room. A few of the residents had already closed their eyes. It was too soon after lunch. But five or possibly six were still awake. 'Now, now is the hardest part. It could be one of thirteen cards. Yes? There are ten cards with numbers, the pip cards . . .' Another pause to fish for a reaction. He always had to make sure that he picked one of the more conscious residents, usually Beryl, who was always volunteering but none of the others seemed to mind. '. . . and three picture cards, called the court cards. But Mr Magicov sees that it is a number card, isn't it?'

Beryl had another look at the card. 'Oh yes, dear. You're doing very well.'

'No, no, miss. It is miss, yes? You are not old enough to be married.'

Beryl laughed. 'I could be your grandmother, dear.'

'Miss, it is you who are doing all the hard work, sending the thoughts. Mr Magicov merely receives. Mr Magicov thinks that he sees your number and it is odd . . .'

Beryl let the slightest of grimaces pass across her face.

'. . . it is odd that he is getting more than one number. Is there someone else here thinking of a number?' Magicov scanned the room again but if any of the audience were thinking of a number it was wondering when their own one might be up. 'Now, miss, concentrate a little harder. Oh yes. That's much better. Ten . . . Ten cards to choose from and it is not two . . . hard to see that eight . . .' Magicov mangled his pronunciation, neatly making the number sound like 'it', '. . . it has got to be four . . . all this hard concentration the number . . . sssssix. Miss. Magicov sees clearly. You are thinking of the six of clubs. Am I right?'

Beryl held the card up for everyone to see and everybody in the room still conscious burst into an enthusiastic applause. A noise not entirely unlike the sound of one hand clapping.

Magicov made a florid bow and, whisking his cape around him, as only magicians and evil landlords should, he dashed from the day room and was gone. This wasn't quite the exit he'd done for his first shows at the homes. He used to do this with a flash and some smoke but after one minor seizure, an overenthusiastic sprinkler system and a lengthy lecture about health and safety the dash was about as dramatic an exit as he was allowed.

For Mr Magicov what usually happened next had been repeated for so long it had become a ritual: after the performance, Cedric would follow him out and invite him to tea. If it was a Wednesday, when Magicov had no more performances that day, the two men would go up together to Cedric's room and Mr Magicov would perform his last trick, peeling off his moustache, wiping away the mascara, folding up his cape and vanishing, transformed into inconspicuous Peter again.

But for Cedric, no amount of repetition ever made the event anything but a first time each time. He would watch the show, puzzle out the solutions and, as is customary in the Brotherhood, he would invite the performer for an after-show tea.

'Peter, you say? How very nice to meet you. Wonderful show. Are you here for the season?'

But then, when the door was closed, each man would take up a deck of 'bikes' and the real magic would begin. For Cedric, the muscle memories in his hands and gestures, ingrained through years of practice and habit, the perfect faro shuffle, the false cut, the immaculate fan, the force, the nimble working of the fingers, the sleights and misdirection so entrenched as to be automatic; they would bring his world back. Not in snatches of memory but a reliving, as if he was back there all over again, down the Bowery working a monte box or at the Egyptian Hall catching bullets in his teeth. Peter and Cedric would riff together, work up card tricks, improvise little illusions, propose the impossible and find ways to solve it, the conjuring equivalent of a musician's jam or an actor's improv. And Cedric would tell Peter about the 'golden age' of magic; about his nights in New York showing off with Downs, Cardini, Vernon, and the other upstarts who saw a need to invent a more intimate magic than the grand illusionists before them, vanishing elephants and sawing women. Cedric and the men he remembered were pioneers of the new close-up, a world of cards and coins, cups and balls, rings and cigarettes, pocket-sized illusions that were portable from war fronts to back yards. And however many times he heard the same stories, Peter would never tire of listening: the time Cedric bet no less a man than Al Capone that he could cut to the four aces from a newly opened and shuffled pack. And how Houdini was fooled by a double lift, a trick so simple a child could do it.

Since the stroke Cedric had been confined to his room upstairs, and not wanting to encounter anybody else while still in costume Peter bounded up and burst through his friend's door.

'Sid, you're going to have to get better, I don't think I can do it without you there at least . . .'

Peter stopped. Cedric was sitting up in bed, clean-shaven, a cup of tea in his hand, a biscuit filling his mouth. A man and a woman Peter had never seen before stared at him suspiciously.

Peter lapsed back into Russian. 'Gud afternoon. Mr Magicov, he greets you. In his country people give hug. *Da?*'

The couple turned to Cedric but he shrugged innocently.

'Are you one of Daddy's friends?'

Peter stared harder at the woman. Finally! This was the toerag who had hung her father out for so many years. This was the bitch who had abandoned her old man to the vagaries of care homes. She was a slimeball, a shit, a repugnant unforgivable scoundrel and perhaps most indefensible, worst of all, she was bloody beautiful.

'So you are famous Kate, daughter of Cedric and rrrrravishing beauty, *da?*'

She laughed coquettishly. 'Is that what he told you? Well, he got it completely wrong apart from the daughter bit. He can't remember a thing. I'm Felicity. This is Harry, my fiancé.'

The man stood up, tall and muscular, tanned, with a handshake that gripped Magicov's hand in the same friendly way a pitbull's jaw grips a baby's skull.

'How are ya?' he said. Australian. It figured. Dump your dad and head off to the other side of the world just in case you're asked to visit or take some responsibility.

'Mr Magicov, he is well. He apologizes to Sid, he did not know he had company.'

'It's OK, we'll be going soon.'

Mr Magicov backed out of the room. 'No. It is long time since he see you. Magicov, he go first. Goodbye.' Closing the door he scooted downstairs again and gathered his prop case.

'Oh, Mr Magicov,' Paula called to him, 'is there anything behind my ears?'

'Charming lady. Mr Magicov is late for Trans-Siberian Express. Molotov.'

And he disappeared into my office.

12

Titus Black swept his hand downwards in front of Rebecca's eyes and she obediently closed them. He put a hand on her shoulder.

'Now, as you listen to your breathing and relax into

this comfortable trance state, you will find your ability to remember, and focus, sharpens. You picked the Childhood card so you need to focus on a childhood memory. I'm sure there's quite a bit that you could choose from, but I want you to see if you can concentrate on a happy memory. I want you to take a moment to see if you can remember the details. Try and really visualize it, make a picture of it big and bright. Pretend that you're there.'

As Rebecca's eyelids fluttered in avid concentration, Titus slithered away towards a whiteboard. Camera Three glided along with him, stopping exactly at the little cross on the studio floor. He picked up a marker and wrote the word 'GARDEN'. Then he drew some trees and flowers.

'So you've chosen a memory. Is it clear in your mind? Let's see what you can remember. First off, can you describe where you are?'

'In a garden.'

The audience applauded warmly and Titus smiled his trademark smirk which always gave the impression that he was supremely confident, a master of the universe, a god capable of anything except, however hard he seemed to try, modesty.

Next he scrawled the word 'DOG'.

'Now you're not alone. There's something else there in your memory.'

'A dog.'

A gasp of amazement rippled through the studio audience.

'Your dog. That's excellent.' Titus wrote 'BIFFER' and then stepped back to look at it. He stepped forward again, rubbed out the 'IFF' then put 'UST' in instead, as if stage mind-reading was a process of concentration rather than a foregone conclusion. He replaced the pen's cap, smirking again. 'I'm sure you can remember his name.'

'Yes,' she smiled, 'it's Buster.'

This time the audience clapped enthusiastically and Titus paused to let the cameras rove across the astonished faces in the audience.

'You're doing good, that's great. Now,' Titus slowed his voice and wrote the word 'FRISBEE', 'as you imagine yourself there again, I want you to try and remember what you're doing. I think, I think you're playing a game with Buster, aren't you?'

Rebecca nodded. 'Yes.'

'What are you playing?'

Rebecca thought for a moment. 'Catch.'

Titus looked over to Rebecca and the trademark smirk momentarily turned into a sneer. It was at these adrenalin-filled instants, when an illusion faced collapse in the hands of an incompetent spectator, that Titus prided himself on being able to improvise and turn disaster into opportunity. This was his real skill, the real power he possessed: influence, persuasion and manipulation. It was this opportunistic instinct that had helped him leapfrog the hordes of eager young magicians at the Blackpool conventions and made him a household name by the time he was twenty, a byword for uncanny prescience and a magical sixth sense.

'Catch, yes,' he nodded, 'and what are you throwing for Buster to catch?'

Rebecca hesitated and her brow wrinkled. Titus had

picked the word 'frisbee' precisely because it looked odd and memorable, but this dozy bint had completely forgotten.

'A ball?'

'A ball.' Titus shrugged to the audience and knew that he should leave the trick now with its one imperfection. But he looked straight at Rebecca, still with her willing eyelids tight shut. 'I don't know, it's just a hunch, but I wonder if you can remember a frisbee in any of this?'

'Oh yes, a frisbee. It's just I couldn't really imagine a frisbee. A stick or a ball. I mean I'm not the sort of person who would throw a frisbee to a dog.'

If nervousness told on Titus's face it was for the barest fraction of a second, the sort of micro-tell that MI5 agents are trained to look out for.

'You've done magnificently, Rebecca. Now in a moment I will wake you up again. You will feel wide awake and full of energy. When you wake, people might ask you what you remember from all of this, and you'll find that you've forgotten pretty much everything, and that anything that remains is very hazy – but don't be alarmed, it's perfectly normal. Normal and comfortable to forget all the stuff that we did up here – to remember to forget everything on awakening. I just want to tell you that now, so that when people try and make you talk about it, you understand why you've forgotten. Now, ready . . .'

After he had returned a rather dazed-looking Rebecca to her seat, Titus heard his theme tune begin: time for him to look straight into Camera Two. 'I'm Titus Black and we've been sharing thoughts. Goodnight.'

The audience applauded and Titus gave a small it-was-nothing, I'm-just-a-god sort of bow and scuttled back to make-up.

Ronnie Newlyn, a stocky man with narrow glasses and a wide tie, whose long wavy hair bounced off his shoulders as he walked, moved forward from the back of the studio, clapping loudly. 'Titus Black, everybody,' he threw his arm out in the direction of Titus's exit, 'Titus Black. Titus Black. Come on, everybody, please give another round of applause for the mikes.' He never tired of hearing the applause for his inventions, which, in fact, included most of the illusions that Titus performed. The only ones he wasn't responsible for were the psychic readings and speaking to the dead that Titus spooked people with in the second half of the show. But as Titus's friend, his colleague, his producer and his sternest critic, Ronnie always felt very much part of the show, of the Titus Black machine.

The audience needed no hypnosis to induce them to follow his command, just good will, a desire for compliance with Rousseau's social contract, a need to fulfil the requirements of mutual benefit and a herd mentality, to applaud just as enthusiastically the second time.

'That's great.' Ronnie smiled as he walked to the front. 'OK, we've got about twenty minutes' interval now while the crew sets up, so go stretch your legs. When you come back it's the mediumship part of the show where Titus will be communicating with the dead. Things get a bit disturbing from here on in so anybody who has a nervous disposition or feels uneasy about necroration should leave now, but please remember to tell one of the researchers before you do. Now give yourselves a great big clap and see you all back here in twenty minutes.'

♣

Titus lay back pensively for his touch-up.

'Good show so far?' Lara asked.

'I don't know, what d-d-did you think?'

'I didn't actually see—'

'No, just another shhhh-shhow to you.'

Lara had been with Titus Black since the first series and, if he wasn't such a twat, being his make-up artist would have been a pretty cushy number. He was only in his early twenties and didn't need the sheets of powder and foundation that the generally elderly chat show hosts did. She had to get them in the chair an hour earlier than Titus. They'd sit there and learn their lines, and she'd stand there removing them.

But then they had their compensations. They were generally genial and genuinely grateful. Black, on the other hand, seemed to think her a witch determined to emasculate him. 'No bloody lipstick. Eyeliner, what for? My nose isn't sh-shh-shiny.' Lara wiped the hot make-up off. Ronnie strolled in.

'Hey, Titus. I think that went well.'

'She didn't remember to see a frisbee.'

'No, well, the mistakes are what convinces the audience that it's genuine.'

'Next time I'm picking the spec.'

'You know, Titus, you really are a wanker.'

'It's not you up there on the screen, I don't see you on the posters. I carry this, Ronnie. I carry you.'

Titus ripped off his make-up bib and pushed Lara out of the way.

'And maybe,' Ronnie smiled in his usual affable way, 'if your dad didn't happen to be a major fat cat at the BBC and maybe if the world was meritocratic rather than based on nepotistic dynasties, then maybe some people who had genuine talent would be up there. Carrying it.'

'I can't help it if it's in my genes, to be the front, the focus.' Titus stomped off towards his dressing room.

Lara flung her brushes at the mirror, dropped herself into Titus's chair and gawped at Ronnie. 'How do you stand him?'

'I don't know,' Ronnie shrugged, 'I just push him up and he seems to stay balancing there all on his own.'

It is hard to tell whether Peter's impact on the child Titus was what drew him closer to the art of conjuring or if it was an interest that he already had when he ruined Peter's handcuff routine and, of course, the rest of his life.

♥

Titus shoved the door of his dressing room open to find two men already there.

'We've been waiting for you, Mr Black.'

'What? You think he sees us sitting here in his dressing room and he doesn't know we've been waiting for him?'

'*Oy vey*, Dick. Perhaps we've just arrived. Then I would say, "Ah, Mr Black, just in time, we've just got here too."'

Titus opened his arms. 'Gentlemen. Good evening. I hope you bring me good news.'

13

Late dining in Christchurch is something that only happens when the Meals-on-Wheels van breaks down. So, to find a restaurant still serving after nine o'clock, those residents who are still mobile have to travel to the neighbouring bright lights of Bournemouth.

To the English Tourist Board this seaside resort is known as 'England's St Tropez', with innocent obliviousness to any irony in the comparison. Visitors taken in by the term soon realize that the only similarity is that it is possible to drown in both places – but only one of them could actually inspire you to do it. For most of the Bournemouth year, the sea and the sky are the same endless grey, an irritated wind blows continuously, clanking the fairy lights slung between lamp-posts and scraping the paint from the terraced neoclassical Victorian town houses which seem to rise up, a shock of dainty white, affronted by the presence of an end to England. When it rains, which it seems to more often than not, the downpour is so thick and heavy the only way you can tell that you've not been struck by Bournemouth's famous 'gull glue' is how sticky it is when you try to wipe it from your face. Then, on the few days when a chilly sun does shine, the whole town becomes swamped with bickering families and chip papers and discordant ice-cream-van chimes and red sunburned children with their cacophony of shouting, crying, whining, squabbling, and their parents screaming that they've had enough and one or two even swimming out into the cold sea and purposely not waving but . . .

Kate and Henry walked quickly away from the night-black seafront, swept along by a force four gale. They stopped at the first open restaurant they found.

Sellotaped to the glass door of La Esplanade, above the peeling credit card stickers, there is an ochre blow-up of a cutting from the *Bournemouth Chronicle*. 'There is no doubt that La Esplanade is the finest Italian restaurant to be found in Bournemouth . . .' The rest of the review is neatly torn away here so as not to delay eager diners with the original's details: '. . . if you enjoy sea views. If, however, you enjoy food, I recommend you seek out any other restaurant, café or hospital in town, all of which will provide you with higher quality cuisine. If you have any respect for your palate, your stomach or your bowels you will avoid this place like a hoodie with the words 'DIAR' and 'RHOEA' tattooed on his knuckles.'

Though there was some truth in the proposition that most of La Esplanade's 'repeat business' tended to be food coming back from where it had gone in, during the summer season its location near the pier assured a steady flow of visitors. Off season, the restaurant's deeply tanned manager, Signor Bert Molloy, enthusiastically invented incentives and promotions to attract food lovers: Karaoke Fridays; monthly Dine with Your Dog nights; Magic Malcolm; Laughing Allowed – Open

165

Mike on Monday Night; Sunday Cabaret; Kids Eat Free.*

Although that night the restaurant harboured a few intrepid customers, when the good-looking couple came in Bert immediately homed in on them.

'*Signor*, *signorina*, a table, I get you best table in house. Here.' He ushered them to the window so they could tempt other passers-by blown along the front. He pulled the chair out for Kate and patted a stiff serviette a little too enthusiastically into her lap.

'Tonight's specials are dishes inspired by writers from Bournemouth. You see on the board we have Pizza alla *Hobbit*, Linguini alla *Frankenstein* and Ravioli alla *Vindication of the Rights of Woman*. Our entertainer this evening is Magic Malcolm. *Buon appetito*.'

As Bert left Henry looked around, following the contours of the flock wallpaper that still showed through after seventeen coats of paint, gazing at the black-and-white signed photographs of film stars who all had suspiciously similar pens and handwriting, the couple eating pasta and huddling in their bright yellow anoraks, the shiny red-and-white checked plastic table-cloths and of course the beautiful Pommy aristo in front of him. He laughed loudly and banged the table. 'You know? If you'd told me two days ago that in forty-eight hours I'd be sitting in a restaurant in England, eating with the girl I was going to marry, I'd have thought you were mental.'

*Offer limited to one child per table, available only on weekdays (excluding Friday) after 10.30pm. Kitchen closes promptly at 11pm.

'What did your mother say when you called her?'

'She was OK when I told her we were in Christchurch. But then I said in England and she took a bit of um, convincing.'

'You told her about the engagement?'

'Oh yes, I clean forgot, she told me to say something to you. Something about brown Asians.'

'Agent Brown.'

'Could have been.'

'You ready?' A toothy waitress stood at their table, artfully moulded into a shirt two sizes too small for her but which encouraged big tips. The strategy had worked wonders. Before the sartorial change her service charge was more on a par with the Light Brigade's, disastrous.

'Sure,' Henry said, quickly scanning the menu and then turning to her, 'actually, what I'd like is a quickie.'

Kate and the waitress stared at him.

'Yeah, I'd definitely like a quickie. Please.'

'You can have a bunch of fucking fives, mate.'

'Er no, I just fancy a quickie.'

The waitress craned her neck towards him and peered a bit harder. Realizing he was pretty gorgeous and it was a slow night, she shrugged. 'Fine by me.' She nodded at Kate. 'What does your girlfriend think?'

Kate rapidly looked down the menu and then at Henry. 'I think, Henry, that it's pronounced *keesh*.'

Henry's ears were the first to go, followed by his nose, cheeks and then his neck, all flushed and inflamed. 'Oh. Sorry. I'm not really up with my Italian.'

The waitress crossed something out at the top of her pad. 'It's all mouth and no trousers with these Aussies. What you having?'

Later, as Henry jabbed his knife through his quiche crust, turning it as if executing a difficult work of calligraphy, he said, 'You know, Fliss, when I first met you I thought your father was a nob. I mean, you know, a lord. I didn't expect . . .'

'Oh God, you mean the title? No, no, I got that from my previous marriage.'

'You've been married already?'

'Quentin, Lord de Vere of Strathclyde.' Felicity looked guilty. She was pretty good at it for someone who spent her life trying not to look guilty because she actually was. 'Oh Henry, I'm so sorry. I should have told you. It's just this has been such a whirlwind. We know so little about each other.'

Felicity's eyes started to film with tears.

'It's OK, hon. If you don't want to talk about it, that's cool. In fact . . .' Henry reached into his breast pocket and pulled something out.

Felicity didn't need to see it to know what it was.

'Fliss, I want to make this official. Will you accept this?' He held in his fingers Clarissa's ring.

Felicity choked back a tear and smiled. 'It's beautiful, Henry. Of course.' She held out her engagement finger and let him slip it on.

Game over.

Kate had everything she needed and from now on it was all exit strategy. Not one to let a moment go, she held out her fingers, admiring the ring, gave it a few seconds and then let her face drop as if a thought had just clouded the moment. 'But. Is that what you see in me? Is that what you really wanted? My title?'

'No. I just – no, you're great, Fliss. I—'

'So. Would you have been so interested if you didn't know I had blue blood?'

'Of course. I mean, I think I would.'

'You think? You absolute tosser. This is the biggest moment of my life and you're not fucking sure what you see in me?'

With the consummate timing of a man who makes a habit of being in the wrong place at the wrong time, Magic Malcolm strolled up to their table. A thin man in his early forties, he wore a tweed suit and woollen tie.

'Good evening, I hope you're enjoying your meal. I'm Malcolm. Would you like to see some magic?'

'No,' Henry said with a touch of irritation, 'we wouldn't.'

'We? Well, I would. Actually. In fact,' Kate pointed at Henry, 'can you make him vanish?'

Magic Malcolm smiled and backed off a little. 'Perhaps later.'

'No,' Kate insisted, 'I'd like to see some magic.'

Malcolm looked nervously at Henry, who leaned back and shrugged.

'You don't need his permission.'

'Well, for starters,' Malcolm pulled up the sleeves of his jacket to expose his forearms, 'I want you to look at my hands, nothing front or back.'

'Is this how you're going to be? Making the decisions for us? The big macho man?'

'But don't trust your eyes, they can be deceived.'

'Sometimes. Yes. I can't help who I am. I know you're a big girl, you can look—'

'Big? Big? Thanks. You've just put me back twenty years of weight-confidence-building.'

169

Malcolm opened his hands again to reveal a flower cupped between them.

'Why are you being like this?'

'For the lady.' Malcolm gave the flower to Kate. She smiled at him.

'Thank you. A gentleman.'

'Sir. I sense that you have an aptitude for extrasensory perception.'

Kate laughed. 'Can you read my thoughts, Henry?'

'I would like to see if I can read some information, straight out of your head.'

Henry sighed. 'OK.'

'I want you to think of something significant. Something I couldn't possibly know. Your birthday. I will try to divine your birthday just by asking you to think hard about it. Now, do you know your star sign? I'd like you to picture your star sign as if you've written it on a blackboard. Now, in your mind, imagine writing the name of the sign underneath. Ah. Yes. Concentrate on the letters. I think I can already see them. A. There's an A.'

Henry shook his head.

'I can definitely see a vowel. Oh no. It's an I. I see an I.'

'Yup.'

'And an S.'

'Yes.'

'And then an R?'

Henry laughed, shaking his head. 'You're not very good at this.'

But just from those answers Malcolm had everything that he needed. 'OK. Maybe you're right. Maybe you should just concentrate on the date.'

'OK, mate.'

'Now I can tell you weren't born in the summer. It was some time in the spring. Not May or April. But March . . .' Malcolm paused and Henry nodded.

'Yes, March, and it's the beginning of the month.'

Henry nodded again but a little slowly, as if he couldn't quite agree.

'Fairly close to the beginning, like, like the seventh or eighth of March.'

Henry suddenly coughed. 'Jeez. March seventh. How the hell did you know that?'

Malcolm smiled. 'I didn't, but you did. You just sent it to me. Thank you for thinking so hard about it. Now, would you like to see one more trick before I leave you in peace?'

The two nodded.

'For this I need something metallic.' Malcolm searched his pockets but didn't have anything. He then pointed at Kate's new ring, courtesy of Clarissa. 'That would work wonderfully.'

Kate took it off and passed it to Malcolm.

Henry suddenly looked very uncomfortable. 'Hang on. Be careful with it. That's my family's—'

'You know what,' Kate narrowed her eyes at Henry, 'I think I'm finally starting to see the real Henry Rackham. The narrow-minded, tight-fisted, gold-digging twat.'

Malcolm looked uneasily between the two of them. He put the ring on his little finger and began to admire it. 'It's a lovely ring. I'll make sure that nothing happens to it. Oops.' Malcolm had curled his fingers in as you might to inspect your nails. For less than a second the ring was out of sight but when he opened his hand again the ring had vanished.

Henry looked at Malcolm. 'Very clever. Now where's my ring going to appear?'

'You gave that fucking ring to me, you himbo. It's mine.'

'Actually I'm not sure where it is. Sometimes the magic is so strong.'

'Fliss.'

'Don't call me that. I never said you could call me that.'

'Felicity, I flew halfway round the world for you, bought you the air tickets just so you could see your dad. I left my farm and—'

'Actually, I'm serious, I'm not sure where it is.' Malcolm was patting all his pockets and then ducked down to have a look under the table.

'So in the end it's all about the money, isn't it? That's all you think about. Your true colours finally come out.'

'I tell you what,' Malcolm tried. 'I realize that the ring is pretty valuable. I really don't have that sort of cash. Look. What about I give you my car in exchange?' He reached into his back pocket and pulled out a small leather key case. When he unzipped it the keys jangled out, all of them dangling from hooks. 'Oh look.'

The couple stopped to see what Malcolm was looking at. In among the dangling keys, locked to a key hook, was the ring. Malcolm unhooked it and offered it back to Kate.

'You know what. The ring is mine now and I can do what I want with it.' Kate looked straight at Henry.

172

'Malcolm, you keep it, as a thank you for showing me this bastard's true colours.'

'You know what, you're a fucking bitch.'

'It doesn't take long for a man to start showing what he's really like.'

'Thank you but I couldn't, it's very kind but it's yours.'

'I said keep it. And you, Henry, can swivel if you think I'm ever going to marry you.'

'Listen, I don't want to be the cause of any—'

Henry and Kate were both standing and all Henry seemed to be able to say was 'Oh really? Is that right? You're a snake.'

'You're a cock.' Kate grabbed her coat from the back of the chair and stormed out of the restaurant.

'Felicity,' Henry shouted after her, grabbing his own coat. Throwing a twenty-pound note on the table, he headed out after her. 'Stop. Fliss.'

Suddenly La Esplanade was silent. Malcolm and the entire staff stared at the door in bewilderment. Malcolm looked at the ring and then put it into his waistcoat pocket. 'Thanks,' he muttered quietly to himself. 'Thanks, Kate.'

He ambled off to the next table. 'Hi, my name is Malcolm,' which, of course, it wasn't.

40,000 Milliseconds to Higham
(TEA minus 11 months 19 days 8 hours)

Kate

. . . *thirty-eight elephants, two hundred and thirty-nine elephants, two hundred and forty elephants. Four minutes. He's asleep. Got to be.*

Really?

Relax the eyelids, no quivering, open slightly and . . . bingo. Thank God for mascara. Totally inert, unconscious, gone. Schmuck.

He's asleep, opposite a known moral reprobate, a compulsive grifter, and he's leaving a million pounds in used notes on the rack above his head. Can he be that much of an idiot?

Doesn't he know me at all?

Has he learned nothing over the past two weeks? Fools. Money. Parted. Shit. It'll serve him right when he wakes and finds what he's lost. Train's slowing. That'll be Higham. Timetable said four twenty-seven. It's a parkway. There'll be plenty of hot-wireable cars, commuting lawyers staying in their pieds-à-terre in town. Nab a motor and head north. Charter another boat. Heard the fjords are quite nice this time of year.

A million quid. Long time since I had a haul that big. We were good. We really were pretty good.

Did he shift? Hard to make out, his breathing's shallow. Is he as fast awake as I am? Is he lash-spying too? Crafty bugger.

Wouldn't put it past him.

He's been fast to catch on so far, but. Got to give it a go whatever, make a grab for the case, I'll soon know if he's awake. We'll play it from there.

14

It was different this time. This time, along with the kids dancing around him and chanting about his 'wonky willy', there were other kids behind, stamping their feet in an urgent rhythm. Peter pleaded for them to stop but they were oblivious, pointing, laughing and stamping. They were still thudding hard when he sat up, eyes wide open. It took him a moment to realize that the banging was not in his dream but on his door.

He rolled over the bed, grabbed a pair of boxers and, half pulling them up, half tripping over them, he stumbled to the door.

'Hold on,' he shouted.

'Does Malcolm live here?'

'No,' Peter said as he undid the bolt.

'Or Pitter?'

'No.' He pulled the door open and the sudden bright light that streamed in off the fire escape momentarily blinded him. Even in the few seconds before he was fully focused he realized who it was.

'Remember me?' said Kate. 'Why did you say you didn't live here?'

Peter stopped rubbing his eyes and pointed into his tiny studio flat. 'Call this living?'

Not waiting for any clearer invitation, Kate strode into the room. It was barely five paces to the bed, which seemed about the only place to sit, apart from a chair by a dressing table used as a workbench, neatly lined with boxes of coins, corks, sponge balls, ropes, billiard balls, thread reels, silks and takeaway coffee cups. Kate opted for the bed and perched on the least messy corner.

'Sorry to get you up like this, but I've had a change of heart since last night. I want the ring back.'

Peter started dragging the rest of his clothes on. 'How did you get my address?'

'Your boss, Molloy, was pretty cooperative when I explained you'd nicked my ring.'

'Shit. I didn't. You gave it—'

Kate smiled. 'I'm sure I can straighten it out with him, if you just hand it back.'

Peter went over to his 'Malcolm' jacket and started rooting through the pockets.

'Did you make it up with your boyfriend then?'

'You're kidding. He'll be long gone by now.'

Peter located the ring, pulled it out and studied it. It was a nice piece. Big glittery thing. A bit too bling for his liking.

Kate was looking at the old magic posters he had pinned to his wall. One of them had caught her eye. 'El Sid, El Niño Diablo'. Bristol Hippodrome, 1948. 'What are you doing working in a crummy restaurant like that anyway?' She looked back at Peter. 'You're pretty good.'

'From you, that's a compliment.'

'What do you mean?'

'You should know. About magic, magicians.'

Kate stood up and narrowed her eyes menacingly. 'What do you know?'

Peter skirted around Kate and nodded at the poster. 'Why did you leave him?'

Kate looked back at the proud magic matador, swathed in a red cape, his sword drawn with its tip at the throat of a red, horned gentleman with goatee and hooves. She looked back at Peter. 'Oh, I get it. You're Magicov. You're Mr Magicov. You're the one who's been helping Da.' She smiled. 'Good luck to you, mate.' She reached over to take the ring but Peter was too fast, closing his fist around it.

'You didn't answer my question.'

'Oh come on. You've seen the state of him. He didn't know who I was. He was a burden, a ball and chain. He needed proper help.'

'So you don't see him for fifteen years. And when you do decide to turn up you tell him you're someone called Felicity. It's a pretty mean trick.'

'Not that it's any of your business but I had my own things to do. I wasn't going to play nursemaid. At least he's with people who know what they're doing. People like you. People who want to help. I had my own life to get on with.'

'Yeah? How's that going for you? Have you made yourself a great life? A roaring success? Is that why you're roping him into some two-bit scam on some poor bloke for some shitty little ring?'

'That shitty little ring, Mr Magicov, is worth in the region of fifty thousand pounds, and I'd like it back please.'

Peter stopped and looked down at the ring in his hand. Fifty thousand pounds? Fuck. Like most people, Peter believed he'd always tried to do the right thing, navigate his life with a 'moral compass', the one with the arrow that pointed to the 'Right Thing' in one direction and 'Success' in the opposite one. After 'the incident', it was that moral compass which had led him away from his family, to break all connections and spare them the shame. It was what brought him to Christchurch, a town where defibrillators outnumber children, and where his sex-offender-register status would worry as few people as possible. In this mecca for retired gentlefolk he was far more likely to bump into a major than a minor. Peter's two hundred hours of community service had been spent in nursing homes but there he had seen a meagre opportunity, that a living could be made from his skills as a floating entertainer around the horde of nursing homes that clustered about the town. But, right then and there, knowing that he had enough sitting in the palm of his hand to set himself up again, in a new country with a new beginning; to buy himself a green card and go to the land of Blaine and Criss Angel, and realizing what a shit the thieving owner was, someone who left her own father to rot, for the first time in his life he found himself in a moral quandary. Should he give it back, or keep it for himself? Was giving it back even the 'Right Thing' to do? It would only encourage her. She gave it to him fair and square.

'Fifty thousand pounds? Why?'

'You seen the central diamond?'

'You know, you did give this to me.'

'Yes, and now I'm taking it back.'

'Listen, Kate. I don't think I like you. I certainly don't like what you did to your dad. I don't like what you did to the bloke who gave you this ring and I don't like you in my flat.'

'Flat?'

'Studio, bedsit, room . . . whatever. If you want this shitty ring . . . here.' Peter dropped the ring into one of the empty Starbucks cups on his dressing table and slammed the lid on. He rattled it once then lobbed it out of the door. The cup flew over the edge of the fire escape and arced down into the parking lot below. 'You can take your shitty ring and get out of my fucking house.'

Kate scrambled past him, managing to stick an elbow in Peter's stomach as she went. She was out of the door before she could even finish the single word she was uttering. 'Cun.'

She dashed down the ironwork steps, clattering as fast as she could before coming to a standstill in the car park. She looked back at the door and tried to work out the trajectory. Men! Useless petty gestures! She dashed in a straight line over the pitted asphalt and spotted the cup nestled next to an upturned family fried chicken bucket. She grabbed hold of it and ripped the top off. But even as she did so, she started feeling sick. Even in the second it took her to prise the plastic lid off she knew the ring wasn't inside. The gypsy switch. Oldest trick in the book. A ten-pence piece lay at the bottom of the cup. She spun round to look back up the fire escape. The door was closed and she knew that Mr Magoo would have already made his way out of the front of the house. She hadn't a chance of catching him. Maybe

Clarissa was right. Maybe she was getting too old for this game.

15

First things first.

Kate prised open the door using her pre-kinked Woolamaloo Tesco Club Card, a little nous and a fair bit of shoulder muscle.

The latch flipped and she found herself back in the Magic Kingdom of Malcolm or Magicov or, as the manager of La Esplanade insisted on calling him, Pitter.

'See where they sleep, know your enemy,' Kate muttered, misquoting Sun Tzu's *Art of War*, 'or at the very least find out where not to buy your curtains.'

Kate knew that if she could just read the room right, she could find everything she needed to know: is he settled here or would he dump the lot for fifty grand? Would he even know how to get that sort of money for the ring? Was he emotionally attached to Da? Was he a grifter or a grafter, a huckster or a shyster? Was she a mark? Could he have organized all this from the moment he bumped into them in Da's room? Could she find him before he could dispose of the ring? She picked carefully through Peter's room. Much of it was as her first impression. The walls were dark womb red, the surfaces mostly green baize. It resembled the foyer of a cinema from the fifties with all the old posters that lined it: Houdini,

Maskelyne, Thurston, Carter and, of course, El Sid.

Standing in a corner was a set of three boxes which Kate recognized as the 'Zig Zag Woman'. She paused to look inside. It was a staple visual illusion from the misogynistic era of magic in which women would be regularly sawn, quartered, caged and made to vanish. Kate was convinced it was a fantasy attempt to stem the growing autonomy of women's lib and somehow pop Pandora right back in her box. The Zig Zag Woman was one of the more benign examples, no buzz saws, just a couple of razor-sharp steel plates used to separate the boxes. The centre box could then be slid to the side to demonstrate that really it's OK to dismember women: like the Terminator, they would always come back.

Apart from the tossed duvet and a few piled books, Pitter was evidently a little obsessive-compulsive. She had chased him out of bed unexpectedly but now as she looked closer she realized that the room was bizarrely tidy for a man living on his own. Everything clean and swept. The only thing Kate ever swept a room with was a glance.

The underwear in the drawer was clean and even folded. Ditto the shirts and trousers in the other drawers. Apart from the essentials of hygiene, dress and reading, everything else was packed in three old over-sized travelling trunks plastered with yellowed liner stickers: Cunard, Blue Riband, *Queen Mary*, antique signs from a more innocent age. Way too ancient for him. It certainly looked like he was about to take off. Perhaps Kate had just got to him sooner than he expected.

One of the trunks had a green silk hanky hanging from it, and something about it brought an indefinable soft murmur to Kate's heart; an organ, like those belonging to churches and men, that rarely touched her. But there was something dreadfully familiar about the old trunk which drew her attention as clearly as an odd sock in a murder mystery. A memory that hadn't been fully formed, or fully lost, a vague sense of recognition.

Opening it, she felt a rush of dizziness, her vague memory becoming a solid object so suddenly it was like that distant meteorite, no more than a bright star one moment and within seconds shaking the entire planet and putting the dinosaurs off their eggs. She knew the box, it was her box. It was Da's. It was the very trunk she used to call her 'box o'sins'; trying to imitate, in her toddler tongue, what Da called his 'box of illusions'. Suddenly a particular array of neural impulses that hadn't cascaded in this specific balance of chemicals and routes for over three decades flashed a meaning, a value, into Kate's consciousness, then again and again, faster and faster, finding the old routes more easily now that the first was established, all stimulated by a co-incidence of visual, olfactory, kinaesthetic and auditory sensations reconfigured; Kate was left almost breathless by the surge of emotion and nostalgia that flooded through her at that moment.

It was this box that, as a child, she would endlessly search through, fascinated by its contents. Not because they were 'magic' but confounded as to why they weren't. She would pick over each object, expecting at any moment to find the enchantment or mojo that they became in her father's hands. She would examine the

182

'gimmicked' object, the trick apparatus, as much enthralled by their simplicity as their potential, each article benignly made to look like one thing but fashioned to operate in an unexpected way so that, in the right hands, it could help effect miracles. But how could a simple hollow plastic thumb be responsible for the appearance and disappearance of hankies or coins? Yet in the right hands, it did. But, look as hard as she did, she never found any magic in her box o'sins. It was only when they were in Da's hands, harnessed to the right looks and gestures, patter and timing, that he would create astonishments and challenge the very rules that keep us stuck to this planet and this planet revolving around a sun that almost mechanically drives out into the expanding universe. All between his two hands.

Now, as Kate sat cross-legged, as she had done as a kid, pulling the strange and colourful objects out of the trunk, the silks that interchanged, the magic wand that collapsed and re-formed, the countless decks of cards, she finally and most unexpectedly found what she had missed for all those years. She stumbled upon it when she no longer thought she was looking for it: magic.

There are a couple of laws of physics which we are pretty far from breaking: apart from bad meals and love-children, the past does not come back and, except at some bizarre quantum level, using machines the size of mountains, objects don't exist in two places at the same time. And yet, through no sleight of hand, no gadget, Hadron Collider or even iPhone app, there, in the bottom of the box, magically, there was Da.

Perhaps Kate's childhood search for magic had just been a little premature. If we're to believe all the Peter Potter Pan hype, magic is something for gullible children and the autoretards who buy kids' books in adult covers. Something to be grown out of. But this is an over-promoted Disneyesque misunderstanding of early perception. As small children our brain's right, emotional hemisphere overwhelms our perception. We are impressed by magic because it is unexpected but not because it demonstrates something outside the realms of possibility. At that age, we're still learning the rules and, just as the make-up of our brains is reorientable, our view of reality is equally elastic.

As we get older and our logical left brains begin to dominate our development, we start to miss the sense of wonder and infinite possibility we had before. We're tempted to indulge in *Dr Who*, fantasy fiction or computer games (some of us much longer than others) before submitting to our teen and twenties left-brain world, our own age of reason. Then magic becomes a puzzle to be worked out ... How did you do that? we ask, knowing that there must be an answer even if we can't see it.

But then as our enlightenment starts to dim again and we're approaching forty, our two hemispheres begin to gain equilibrium from that early rocking to and fro. We realize that we have become more reliant on our emotions to understand the world around us. We notice that when the orchestra of violins swells at the end of the movie we actually feel a little bit teary, charity ads fill us with despair and each wrinkle we find is not just one of the seven signs of ageing (there are, of course, a damn sight more than that), it is a bloody affront, an assault, a tragedy.

On the plus side, the memory of how to deal with situations has become so commonplace it has embedded itself as emotion. You go by your hunches; hard-earned observation now pays off and feels instinctual. Younger people look at you and wonder how you do whatever you do without apparently thinking about it. And all you can tell them is 'It will come, it will come.'

The dark side of thirty-five: it is the best of times, it is the worst of times.

Kate – who prided herself on possessing a blood temperature equivalent to the mid-July ambient heat levels on Kenai Beach, Alaska – was suddenly wrapped in the box's enchantment. The man who, for as long as she could or would care to remember, had been a dementing codger unable to recall even her name, the man who was right now sitting in Lotus House with a mind as thoroughly shuffled as the cards in his hands – he was here and sane and remembering, and big and strong and cuddling her. So strong was the trigger, Kate's neurons had effectively reverse-engineered her senses: she was there, she could smell it, hear it, taste, touch and see. Emotional memories of the most complete order occur like this when, instead of the senses informing the neural networks that create conscious awareness, the senses are the receivers and the brain the sender.

Kate glanced at her hand resting on the box. It was trembling; this alien rush of love ached in her as if it was tearing something within, needling her ribs, pushing against her stomach and back. It was pain as unfamiliar as single-star hotels, paying taxes or working for a living, and equally unwelcome. For twenty years this marvellous marbleless man has had no idea who she is. So why, when she touched this inanimate box, should she just feel so, so desperate? Had she allowed some crack in her carefully hewn carapace? With that thought, another remembered moment, from somewhere else entirely, caught her: a country singer rasping a ballad on the radio as one of her 'husbands' drove her into town so she could 'just pop into the bank', withdraw the entire contents of his bank account, slip out of the back and drive off to Reno in a hire car. 'Every face has a flaw,' the radio had croaked, 'every room has a door. That's how the truth gets in.'

The box, the sight, smell, touch, the sensation, triggered connections between past and present, here and there, as tangibly as one synapse links to another, drawing each line of that complete sensory picture that we call reality. Kate began to recognize the magic of the box; in that moment of wonder she realized that this box, which had prompted some sort of unexplainable, magical connection between them, was exactly the sort of magic and wonder and astonishment that had connected El Sid to his audience. They connected in a common suspension of belief in the restrictions of nature, where things could vanish and float and appear from nowhere. E. M. Forster said, 'Only connect,' which is sage advice unless you're sitting in a bath with the toaster.

Kate closed the lid of the box o'sins. She realized that nothing had moved from it. Pitter wasn't an exploiter, he was a collector, he functioned in a realm of respect and conventional moral patterning. He was no fly-by-night con artist. Maybe he didn't take the ring for the money. She was starting to like the idea of Pitter. He had skills she wished Da had taught her and, more than any-body – blame Freud if you like, guilt was his game after all – but Pitter could conjure up Da for her. He did from the moment she met him.

And if Kate hadn't opened the door next to the bed she might still have been feeling positively chipper about someone like Pitter entering her life. Unfortunately, in her pursuit of clues, she did. What she saw there changed her mind completely: one moment a comfy nostalgic warmth, the next a terrifying skin-crawling creepiness. What she found when she opened the door could lead her to only one conclusion: Pitter was no innocent jobbing magician trying to make his way in the world, he wasn't a cute obsessive-compulsive, he was an obsessive-obsessive, a bloody psychopath.

Since the release of the movie *Se7en*, it has become an almost obligatory cinematic meme for thrillers; if you're a serial killer or even just a red herring loony, along with a painfully slow gait when you're about to kill the heroine you must own an OR, an Obsession Room. The house rules for the Obsession Room are that you cannot use a normal photo album to put the photos of the object of your obsession in. You must plaster them on every wall or piece of furniture in a dark grungy room, preferably behind a hidden door. And then you mustn't show any respect for the pictures – after all they're only showing the person you're infatuated with. No, you are obliged to draw odd satanic symbols or write, hopefully in blood or an ink resembling blood, all over them. And stick them with pins and sharp objects, running threads or beads or human hairs between them. And you have an absolute duty to light your room with Gothic wax candles. And then on a sort of altar at the far end of the room you place an extra-big picture of the person you are crazy about. But this shot is just that little bit closer, something which could only have been taken by someone intimate, perhaps the object's wife, husband, kids or bunny rabbit.

You can forget the fact that that would mean serial killers had to rent places with extra rooms to house their obsessions, making them a lot easier for the police to find, and causing all the problems that making an OR creates for sprinkler systems or unexpected visits from the landlord. Apart from anything else, there is hardly a single incident in real life of anyone making a room like this who wasn't called Tracey and didn't belong to the Hoxtonic BritArt movement, which was popular before the turn of the millennium.

The reality of obsessives and stalkers is that they keep their precious photos very carefully. They store them in boxes or albums, or even scan them on to their computer hard drives, especially if the sociopath in question is prominent and suspects that there might be a visit to PC World in the offing.

So, this being not cinema but real life, the door that Kate opened was not into an OR even though the way it made her feel was somewhat similar. It was just a cupboard door. But what she found in the cupboard disturbed her deeply. Neatly catalogued by date, a dozen or so photo albums were stacked on the shelves, and some shoeboxes were also filled with photos. She took them down and sat on the bed. But as she began to leaf through them, Kate grew increasingly nauseous. Hundreds upon hundreds of photographs all of just one person. The photos had notes, annotations and phrases neatly written around them. But more often than not there would just be some foul word scribbled hard by it. 'FUCK,' it said above one photo. 'FUCKING CUNT. DIE!' it said beside the next. 'Remember to get shoelaces,' it said above the next.

She closed the books and listened to her shallow breathing. Perhaps he was coming back. How could she have read him so wrong? Even for a moment. Should she just give up on the ring? Was he dangerous? Was he just luring her into his room to murder her? She listened, acutely aware of every noise beyond. Was it footsteps?

She had thought that she could read his room and work out who he was, what made him tick, and so through a process of empathy discover his next move. But these piles of sick photos stacked high in albums showed he was well beyond any normal psychological frame. A shiver ran through her. How close had she come to being murdered by an absolute nutter? She looked around the room again. She had been relying on her cold-reading skills to work out where he would be now, though, of course, a Post-it note stuck to the side of his computer screen with a pawnshop address scribbled on it would work just as well.

16

'Cold reading is the secret discipline behind the art of phoney fortune telling, of faking talking to the dead, of voicing the impossible and convincing the gullible.'

A titter worked its way around the studio audience.

'It works by making a little knowledge go a long, long way. But, my friends, a little knowledge is a dangerous thing. And I'll show you how.' Titus looked up over the camera, trying to convince it, and himself, that there were hundreds of his acolytes present, rising through the tiers to the rafters. Rather than the fifteen ticket holders, the ten creepy obsessive fans who were still tweeting him on their phones even as he was standing in front of them, and the twenty 'padders' who turned up to be studio audience regardless of the programme being recorded and were only there because they had been turned away from the opening of that day's paper bag.

'If I could really talk to the dead, obviously I would be able to consult your dead granny, sir.' He gestured casually to a man in the front row, smiling to show this was merely by way of illustration. 'And she might just tell me all sorts of interesting things about you and your family, proof of the fact that she really has communicated from another plane. She might tell me stuff which I would feel justified in revealing on national television, to the entertainment of the many and the distress of the few who actually loved her.'

Titus was now interrupted by uncontrolled sobs issuing from the man he had just indicated. 'I did love her,' he wailed at Titus. 'I did.' Tears streamed down his cheeks before he nursed his shaking head in his hands. In the control room Ronnie was screaming into the headsets for Cameras Two and Four to focus in on the tears.

'I only saw her last week,' the man wailed.

Titus strode back to comfort him. 'I'm so sorry, sir.' He patted him with more condescension than condolence. 'But,' and now Titus fixed the camera with his famous blue-eyed stare, 'though it may have looked like it, this was no accident. I had already spotted this gentleman, seen just from the way he was sitting, his shoulders sunken, a tired pallor to his skin, that he was likely to have been recently bereaved. That is cold reading: bold, chancy statements informed by empathy, statistical savvy, knowledge of psychology and physiology, experience and the fact that we are not as unalike as we like to think, to convince another person that you have more intimate knowledge of them, or their loved ones than you actually do have.

'Even when we meet a total stranger we have an enormous amount of knowledge about them; all we need is to know what we're looking for. How, for example, how did I know that John . . .' Titus looked at John Ogilvy, 'I'm guessing from the way you're dressed and your age that you are called John. Close to twenty per cent of boys born around nineteen seventy-two were called John and so I'm taking another punt . . .'

John Ogilvy nodded. 'Yes, it's John.' Warm applause rippled through the studio.

'Nineteen seventy-two?'

'Seventy-one.'

Titus shrugged. 'Not bad, but how did I know that John was grieving for his granny and not someone else?' Titus spread his arms. 'Consider where we are. Ask yourself, would you come to a show in which the performer demonstrates talking to the dead for the titillation of a telly audience, would you have turned up here if you were still grief-stricken by the loss of anybody as close as a sibling, wife or child?'

As Titus continued towards his peroration he increased the speed of his delivery until his voice approached an almost constant rhythmic hum. 'So, without saying a word, this gentleman was telling me that it was possibly a more anticipated death; a parent maybe, but probably a grandparent or favourite uncle. So I've arrived at the generation, but then, understanding our psychological make-up – that boys tend to bond closer with their female progenitors – I assumed the gender of the lost one, a mother or grandmother. I simply suggested his granny because not only was it a kinder thing to suggest, if it turned out that it was his mother I could then have asked, "But someone calls her Granny, or Grandma or Nanny or something?" Again, working on norms, someone who is old enough to be John's mother, they are likely to be a grandmother as well.'

At which point a new round of sobbing was caught by Camera Four.

'But the truly skilled practitioner of the art of cold reading can go beyond a few chancy guesses by reading micro-tells, the tiniest tics and gestures that we unconsciously send out all the time. Even though I tell you here and now that I cannot really cross to the other side or talk to the dead, that I don't even believe in an afterlife of any sort, using my years of training to mimic the techniques used by fraudulent mediums and pyschics I will convince you that the dead still whisper to me.'

Titus gently took John's forearm and helped him up. He guided him towards the deep red velvet-covered table in the middle of the stage floor. 'Come with me to my spirit table and we'll see if we can find you some closure. John, ladies and gentlemen, help me get in touch with her because I have already heard a voice calling.'

John looked suitably sceptical but carried on towards the table with Titus.

Suddenly Titus seemed to be talking to himself or some invisible presence. 'No,' he said forcefully. 'No, we're coming. Don't go. He's coming. Your John is coming, Ethel.'

At the sound of her name, John stopped as if he had just smacked into a gravestone. 'How, how did you know her name?'

Titus didn't reply. He didn't need to. He looked directly at Camera Three and let the smug smile-that-begs-to-be-wiped creep across his face, as satisfied as a milk-drunk cat pawing in circles before a lie-down to sleep it off.

17

Despite the patchwork of myriad fields and gardens that covers east Dorset, you will struggle to find a fence – not one anyway who could get you anywhere near fifty grand for a diamond ring.

The closest that Christchurch can offer is the KashKonvertors and TrinketTransformers-style pawn-shops that seem to swarm near pound shop and retirement home hotspots, usually run by men to whom middle age has not been kind but who seem to find an affirming comfort in the irony of their job title as almost everybody entering their establishment is 'broker' than they are. The 'broker' behind the counter at ValuablezVampirez was no exception, offering Peter a sobering 'fifty quid to take it off your hands'.

Peter's eyebrows jumped towards his hairline. 'Fifty quid? I thought you'd have some sort of assessor, you know, someone with a magnifying optic wedged into their eye socket. Someone who'd turn the ring over a few times, actually examine it and talk about carats and facets, and . . . and other . . .' Peter had just exhausted the totality of his knowledge on the subject, based entirely on scenes from heist movies, '. . . stuff.'

'Not much call for that sort of specialist really,' said the pawnbroker, taking the ring off his tiny digital scales and passing it back before turning over a new leaf of his Buffy graphic novel. 'You only get that sort of thing in Hatton Garden up in London.'

'You just asset-strip by weight then?' said Peter. 'No consideration of the actual value of things.'

Not that any nerve needs to be cooked, but Peter seemed to touch a raw one. The pawnbroker growled. 'Asset-strip? Bloody hell, there's no appreciation, is there? There's not a week goes by without some geriatric git accusing me of being a "pawn of the devil" and that's not even like a proper pun. I'll tell you what I am, I'm the liberation, mate, I'm the bloody angel of mercy.' He waved a hand around the shop. 'All the stuff we have, it completely stresses us.' He pointed to the plaque on the wall behind him, the one you expect to carry a witty observation about the world of employment starting with the phrase 'You don't have to be crazy to work here but . . .' But this one just said 'Stuff Is Stress'. 'If it's not stress from earning enough to buy the stuff, it's stress from owning it. Every bit of technology chains you, me, everybody to more responsibility. You got a camera, you got to take a picture, you got email, you got to check it and write to people, got a mobile phone, you got to charge it, answer it, not forget it. But me, I am the bloody liberation, mate. We gather stuff all through our lives and half the time we don't know what to do with it and then we start worrying that when we die our children will fight over it, and although it's all just posturing and substitution for the love they feel they always deserved and never got from us, we worry that we'll be leaving a legacy of hurt, all because of stuff. I, my friend, am the ruddy dove of peace for all those who want to truly rest in it.'

The pawnbroker clocked Peter's incredulity.

'All right, maybe not a dove.'

'Vulture?'

'Oh. Right. Yes, for you, I'm carrion picking at the as yet undead carcasses of the elderly and vulnerable, ripping the heirlooms from their withered arms, their prized possessions which survived hidden under skirts when the Gestapo stomped through, rescued from the Luftwaffe, saved through rationing, breadlines, market crashes, depressions, kept for that rainy day. They've all got stories. But guess what? The sun's shining and we're not suffering the fascist yoke, poverty, sickness, plague or pestilence. No, nobody's prising the treasures from their bony fingers, they're giving it away because they're suffering a much more terrible fate than all that, something they never saw coming: a long life, relatively painless and comprehensive healthcare, more time with the family, friends, hobbies and online second lives. I weep for them, I really do, poor sods. Look at this.' He pointed at a delicate opal brooch. 'The money they get for this stuff is financing the distractions and the pleasures, not the needs, of their longevity. It's not the landlord at the door this paid for; it's rarely for pills to alleviate a painful disease or fund the basics of food or shelter. This is the welfare state, this is the science fiction future. No, this, this is for custard creams, a tot of rum, an eBay bid on some nostalgia stuff or something else to bring some pleasure or distraction to the apparently endless life they're leading. I enable, I help. If I'm a vulture, you're a small-minded cock.'

Peter started polishing the ring on his sleeve before giving it a closer look. 'Maybe I have a small mind . . .'

'And cock,' the pawnbroker added.

'I've probably got all sorts of small things but I've still got a huge wodge in this ring. The last time it was valued it was worth over fifty thousand pounds.'

This time it was the pawnbroker who looked incredulous. He took the ring from Peter's fingers, peered closely at the hallmark and shook his head. 'Really, mate, you should be paying me. Seen it all before. Your girlfriend's thrown this back at you and fucked off, hasn't she? Only legal reason blokes come in with women's rings, and they always say what you said, mate. They've always paid way over the odds when they still thought their girlfriends were keepers. And now you feel bad because it was you who cuffed her one so you know it's your own fault your relationship went down the pan, like it always does, and this ring you forked out way too much for is just staring at you, driving you crazy with guilt. And I'm your man. I'm the freedom. The liberator. I'm in your corner. The guilt grinder. The angel of mercy. I'm the bloke who'll take the pressure, take the bloody weight off you, no, I'll take it for you, and you're out of here guilt-free.' He dinged open the till and pulled out a couple of fifty-pound notes. 'I'm doing this for you, chum, because I like you and you deserve a break. I'll take this horrible needling symbol of your inability to get a decent girlfriend and won't charge you a thing. And this dosh.' He laid the two fifties squarely on the counter. 'I know you're proud, I know you don't want charity but I . . . I feel sorry for you. Buy yourself something nice, cheer yourself up and I'll —' he held up the ring and sighed, 'I'll shoulder this terrible burden for you.'

Peter wasn't going to lose sight of the ring again; he snatched it back and, passing it from one hand to the other, promptly vanished it.

From: _Sessions Transcripts 03.09_ p68

Transcript - 3 September.

Present: Dr C. Tavasligh, Patient P.

CT: Just going back a bit. You vanished the ring? Why?

P: I honestly don't know. He was a bit of a toad, an eloquent toad but the sort that no amount of kissing was going to make a prince. And he was kind of showing off.

CT: Weren't you?

P: Yeah. You know he was pretty convincing and I almost felt he was doing me a favour. Kate calls it my . . . Kate called it my innate gullibility. It's something you're born with. I call it morals.

CT: But you didn't act morally when you took the ring. Or with this man. Why did you change?

P: I don't know. Maybe I was just sick of it. Maybe I was jealous that he had that gift of being convincing.

CT: You don't?

P: I never thought I did but . . . What happened with Kate. Maybe it changed that a little. But you know, poor social skills is what gets most

boys into magic in the first place. It's a mask
of competency. A way to show off for those
least equipped to do it. So maybe I wanted to
show off what I could do. I couldn't persuade
like that but I could vanish things. I just
took the ring out of his hand and did it. You
don't really think about it when you do it.
Force of habit, habitual practice. A French Drop
and False Transfer. Like this. (Demonstrates
with coin.) I've done it thousands of times. It
looks like I'm passing the ring from my right
to my left hand. But I'm actually just letting
it drop into the palm of my right. As long as I
keep my eyes on where the coin is supposed to
be going, the vanish is clean. Especially if
there's no expectation of a trick.

I didn't say, 'Now I'm going to vanish the
ring.' I guess I only really thought about it
when I saw the pawnbroker's eyes follow the
false path of the ring from right to left. Then
you just do things instinctually. I started
prattling, it buys time: misdirection. You put a
long enough stretch between the move and the
reveal and they'll swear that one hand never
went near the other. It's all impossible. I was
fooling with the guy. I wouldn't really have
taken him like that but, I don't know, he was -
hitting my buttons.
CT: But you knew it would be wrong to cheat
this man.
P: Yes but. Well. After pulling that trick on
Kate and, you know, having the ring, I think I

was reassessing what I considered wrong. Is it wrong to steal from a con artist and a leech?

CT: Do two wrongs make a right?

P: Actually, I think most of our rights were born out of huge numbers of wrongs being done, creating the will to prevent them happening again by codifying them in bills of rights. And our judicial system couldn't be based on precedence if there weren't hundreds of wrongs informing us how to judge what is right. You know, if you think about it, the whole experimental system that underlies scientific discovery relies on thousands of wrong answers before a right one is found. In fact, if you look at it like that, two wrongs making a right is pretty good going.

CT: You know what I mean. You're just deflecting.

P: Maybe. All I can tell you is, at the time, it just didn't actually feel wrong.

NOTE: P unable to recognize secondary gain in acts that contradict his own moral code. Post-justification.

'You know,' Peter said, 'I'm not sure when this land of stiff upper lips and fair play in pricing became a souk where everything gets bartered and persuasion rules. It's as simple as this. If you can't offer anything near the price this is worth,' he pointed to the fingers of his left hand, 'I go elsewhere. And if this is charity, I'll take it.' With his right hand Peter started picking up the notes.

The pawnbroker held out his own hand for the ring and after pocketing the notes Peter pushed his empty left fingers into the pawnbroker's hand, pretending to place the non-existent ring in it. Immediately he folded the man's hand into a closed fist as if to say, 'Keep tight hold.'

When we are confused, we act on instinct and the major instinct for herd humans is social compliance. In short, when we don't know what to do but we know that we must do something, we do what we're told. The act of having one's hand touched and curled into a fist is confusing and Peter knew it, he knew that the pawnbroker would simply comply and allow his fist to be closed. Had it been a friend or someone he was used to, the man might have elbowed him away, but a lot of magic, as well as a lot of medicine, relies on our compliance with strangers.

'You hold on tight.' Peter smiled.

Peter was also exploiting another strange physical misapprehension, used by conjurors, that the over-abundance of nerves in the tips of our fingers often makes us assume that we have just as many sensory inputs in their lengths. We don't, in fact, when we hold a small object tightly in our fists; we just fool ourselves that we can feel the object.

Usually, a magician will prevent the 'spec' from looking in their hand with some distracting business elsewhere. Unfortunately the pawnbroker did not just stand in dumb amazement, watching Peter leave. Peter got an almost three-second start before the man opened his hand to look. As soon as he saw it was empty he grabbed one of the hocked pool cues and sprinted around the counter.

Peter was just about to push the door when the blue chalk end of the cue sliced the air in front of his nose and stopped him. The pawnbroker pulled Peter around by the collar and held the blunt end of the cue to his chin.

'You think you're fucking Raffles? You can give me the money *and* the ring if you want to leave here alive.'

The thing about even the most disarming of smiles is that you can't really expect it to disarm anyone who is actually carrying arms. To give Peter his due, he did try, but his own disarming smile had always been so pathetic it wouldn't even convince his granny to put down her knitting needles – let alone a crazed pawnbroker with a big stick.

The pawnbroker pulled the cue back to pot at least a couple of teeth into the pocket.

'Peter Smith?' a voice behind Peter interrupted. Peter nodded slowly. 'I thought it was. And up to your old tricks again? I always told you it would end with someone kicking the shit out of you.'

There was a pause as Peter tried to pick out the interlocutor reflected in the pawnbroker's eye.

'Don't mind me,' the voice continued, 'I'll do the arresting when you're through beating the crap out of that thieving little low life.'

18

'Would you mind if I just spread out a little on to this seat?' The wiry man with thick glasses pointed at the empty seat between him and the incredible bulk who sat in the aisle seat.

'Would I mind? Of course I wouldn't mind . . .'

The smaller man smiled and started lifting the armrest. It was, after all, going to be a long flight.

'. . . had the goddamn airline,' continued the man mountain, 'not made me pay for that goddamn seat. "Fat premium," they said. Ignorant assholes. Twenty years working on this body and they call me fat? This, my friend, is three fifty pounds of muscle. My body's more ripped than a Whitechapel whore and those stringy little airline staff have the nerve to call me fat? Should have just got my Glock out and given them some excess weight, excess lead wei—' An unpleasant odour made him look abruptly at the man by the window, who was clenching his knees together and seemed to be trembling. 'Cold?'

The man shook his head. 'You, you have a gun?'

'Sure I do, but not here. You crazy?' He smiled. 'Is that why you look like you just found Madonna's got no kettle after she invited you up for coffee? Man, you don't need to be scared of guns. Guns don't kill people.' He reached over and patted the man comfortingly on the shoulder. 'People like me do.'

The smaller man gulped but pointed back to the empty seat in the hope that this bonding session had brought them closer.

'Oh yeah. Short answer, buddy, I've paid for the seat, we split it, we split the cost.'

The lesser man put the armrest down and looked out at the trembling wing of the plane. It really was going to be a long flight.

♠

Somewhere between Nova Scotia and Iceland, after a near miss involving a rock of ice, turbulence and the fifth Jack Daniel's, the giant in the aisle seat was talking again, oblivious to the fact that his wingman was fast asleep.

'So, I say to him, "Do you know how many years I've been tracking her? And now, now she's made the mistake we've been waiting for. This is the best lead I've had in years. She's finally gone back to the old country and they're such a bunch of toadying assholes, they're so desperate to be our buddies, they set the gold standard for extradition. We just tell'em we got a person of interest and they'll lick'em, stick'em and ship'em before you can say, "Guantanamo!" Carte blanche. So now. We know what town she's in. The ol' Bill are happy to cooperate, I just got to get out there and we'll pick her up. She'll be in state pen within the week. And

204

you know what, he okays it, even organizes the tickets. He knows I've not got long on the street so either it's my boat on the Florida Keys or a desk. Between you, me and these steel aerodynamic curvature walls, I'll never do the desk but he knows, if I go for it, the only desk I'm getting is his. I'm the best the Bureau's got. Came top in observation . . .' Agent Brown continued in this vein for the next three hours until, twenty minutes before landing, he fell into a deep, dribbling sleep.

Brown's body was a testament to a life less orderly. It might have been fifteen years since the young, sleek special agent last encountered Kate Minola, but after two thousand seven hundred and fifty-four doughnuts, five hundred and six on-foot pursuits, one thousand eight hundred and twenty-two Big Mackenfries, five hundred thousand bench presses, three commendations, a hundred and one hookers, thirty-seven internet dates, six bar pick-ups, four second dates, one unsubstantiated accusation of date rape and no commitments, Brown was still in the game. Even if his girth had gathered a few strata over the millennia, with a little assistance from regular top-ups of 'Boytox', his muscle-paralysing poison of choice, at fifty Agent Brown had the face he preserved.

Unfortunately even observational experts can be tricked by the mirror. Whatever Brown saw when he looked at himself, he was unable to see the corruption and the accustomed hard-set threatening stare. What he saw was more akin to the very old photo of the smiling recruit that he emailed to the cool-sounding 'Scotland Yard chick' who was picking him up at Heathrow.

DI Madeline Brightly was a handsome woman, not

beautiful, nor pretty, but undeniably handsome in a most masculine sense. She was tall and wore her long mousy hair tied up in a bun pulled tighter than an anorexic's belt. She was muscular, with a large chest and small breasts. DI Brightly's jaw protruded like a comic book hero's. She used it mercilessly to intimidate suspects or interrupt unwanted conversationalists by just jerking it forward, causing anyone to recoil for fear an eye might be taken out.

In line for promotion, DI Brightly was intensely keen to avoid doing anything that might make her look stupid. She refused to hold up one of those daft signs, as she stood in arrivals at the airport, like all the tired limo drivers looking shrunken in their creased suits and the kids who find it funny to scrawl 'Mr Fucov' or 'Ellie Gal, Emmy Grant' on bits of cardboard.

I'm not convinced that all is vanity but since Brown was convinced he looked younger and Brightly was too proud to carry a sign, it certainly was the reason why they completely missed each other and Brown, rather than travelling into town in an unmarked police car, found himself yawning on the Heathrow Express train to Paddington.

Pulling his wheeled case behind him as he stepped into the early evening commotion on the platform, Agent Brown checked his phone signal and tried to ring Brightly again. This time it rang and Brightly answered.

'Hello?' Brown said as he tried to inch past a couple having an argument. Brightly's voice was drowned in the hollering.

'Oh ha ha,' the girl wearing the man's jacket was shouting at the tall guy, 'funny, is it?'

'Is that you, Brightly?' Brown could hear some faint noises.

'My skirt's gone and maybe you think I can wear your "ha ha"?'

'I'm in Paddington. You're where?'

'Perhaps I'll go to work in a "ha ha" from now on, because right now that's all I've bloody got.'

'I can't hear you. Let me find somewhere quieter and call you back.' Brown flipped his phone closed and was about to say something about selfish behaviour in social situations when the girl gave him such a filthy look he decided it might be best just to trundle on. Maybe a Limey being told by a Yank that they're being too loud was an irony too far.

'Maybe the invisible bloody "ha ha" skirt will start a fashion. That'll thrill them on the catwalks. So fucking brief you can shove it up your arse . . .'

Agent Brown found himself a quieter spot, standing by the still-chugging engine of the D370 diesel on platform four. He dialled Brightly's number again.

19

'Arresting?' The pawnbroker's grip on Peter's neck loosened.

'Well,' said Kate, 'I am off duty at the moment.' It tightened again. 'But I am still honour bound to arrest a felon whenever I encounter one. This nasty piece of work will be getting at least six months for this sort of con. And I'll put in a word with the Super to drop you from Grievous to Aggravated. First offence, you'll be out before he is.'

The fist unknotted and Peter fell to the floor. He spun to look at Kate and wobbled to his feet.

'Remember me?' Kate said, and then to the pawn-broker, 'Good choice.'

Peter's instinct was to run. He grabbed for the door handle but Kate pounded her fist against the door.

'Naughty naughty, Mr Smith, where do you think you're going?' She flashed a suspicious-looking identity card at him. 'You know the rote. Up against the wall. Legs apart.' Kate proceeded to frisk him. If he hadn't known better, he would have sworn that there was some unnecessary extra play around his genitals, sizing him up – or threatening him. Peter swallowed hard.

There are always a number of tricks in any magician's pockets: gimmicked coins, false thumbtips and the like, ready for an awkward moment and an impromptu illusion when someone says, 'So you're a magician, show me some magic,' as, apparently, people did all the time according to the ads Peter saw for magic tricks. This particular scenario had never happened to him. It was always him approaching people asking if they would like to see some magic, or could he show them some magic. And though never utilized, these tricks gave him confidence, being prepared, just in case. Kate obviously felt these but delicately retrieved only the two fifties and the ring.

OK, Peter realized, now she had what she wanted, game over. He turned to the door.

'Not so fast,' Kate barked fiercely then produced one

of her own pocket tricks, a sandwich bag, for those awkward moments when you just might need to impersonate an officer of the law. She placed the three items in the bag and then said solemnly to the pawnbroker, 'This will need to be borrowed in evidence. If you could just sign the bag.'

The pawnbroker took the marker she offered him and signed her evidence bag.

'Now, Peter Smith,' Kate looked at him sternly, 'I am arresting you on suspicion of an act to defraud. You do not have to say anything, but it may harm your defence if you do not mention when questioned something which you may later rely on in court. Do you understand?'

Peter nodded.

'If you understand you must say, "I understand." '

'I understand.'

Kate looked at the pawnbroker. 'OK. Now, Mr . . .' she looked at the signature on the bag, 'Ladro. As I am currently off duty and not carrying any restraints for the perp I'm going to have to call a car, but it would mean other officers coming who would have the right to search these premises as a felony has taken place on them. I realize that this is something you may not wish . . .'

The pawnbroker looked aghast, his mouth opening and closing as if powered by a piston.

'But,' Kate continued, 'I wouldn't have to call them if you happened to have any restraints, handcuffs or the like, here. I could just walk him up now to the station and we wouldn't need to bother you any more.'

'Right. I think I may have just what you need.' The

pawnbroker darted off to the back of the shop and let himself into the armament room, ubiquitous to all good pawnshops. Kate started pocketing various items of jewellery, a watch, a camera, an mp3 player, a mobile phone. And when her pockets were full, she started shoving things into Peter's.

By the time the pawnbroker returned, bearing some police-issue Hiatt Rigid double-lock handcuffs, the two stood there bulging with booty.

Kate took the cuffs with a knowing smile. 'Now, now, I do hope these were legally procured.'

The pawnbroker smiled weakly and Peter felt the too familiar cuffs gripping his wrists again. Anxiety seized him and he felt a distinct déjà vu, but then had the unsettling feeling that he had seen the déjà vu some-where before. He turned to leave. Kate had the keys so, surely, she had all she needed now. But she stopped him again and looked sternly back at the pawnbroker. 'One more thing. I'll need the footage from your security camera up there.'

The pawnbroker looked up at the Ozzie Dalek dome on the ceiling. 'It's a dummy, doesn't actually work.'

'Pity. What about those?' Kate pointed at an array of video cameras lined up on a shelf, each screen and lens pointing towards them.

'None of them have tapes in them, they're just on to show they're working, what they look like.'

'Oh well,' said Peter. 'It's a fair cop. Shall we just go then?'

But Kate wasn't finished yet. 'You. Shut it. If you want to do a job you've got to do it thoroughly. Now, Mr Ladro, you seem to be a man with quite a sound knowledge of law enforcement equipment so I'm sure I don't need to tell you about the TGB.'

The pawnbroker had obviously never heard of it. 'Yes. Of course. The TGB. I just can't quite remember . . .'

'The two gig black box is the two-gigabyte ram memory that all video camera manufacturers are required by law to include in consumer video equipment in order to sell in Europe or the United States.'

'Oh yes. It's coming back to me.'

'Obviously most normal people know nothing about it but it is an encrypted crime evidence feature which is only accessible to certified law enforcement agencies. It continuously stores the last twenty minutes of camera feed whether the camera is recording to tape or not.'

Peter couldn't stop himself raising his eyes. But the pawnbroker nodded seriously. 'Yes. Yes, of course. I knew there was something like that.'

'Right, so we'll just need to get the evidence off your cameras. If you switch them off now they'll still have the footage in memory. I'll take them up to the station, we'll offload the footage and I'll have a car drop them back by end of play today. OK?'

Peter's eyes grew as big as the balls Kate obviously possessed, as he stared at her in total disbelief. But the pawnbroker hurriedly went around the shop, picking up all the video cameras on sale and putting them in a ValuablezVampirez plastic bag.

There being evidently no point of swag without swagger, Kate boldly gave the bag to Peter to hold.

'Thank you,' she said curtly to the pawnbroker. Turning to push Peter, and some of the shop's most expensive items, out of the door, she told him, 'Move it: your next stop is up against the bench.'

20

'Do we really still need these?' Peter rattled his Hiatt Rigid Speedcuffs.

Kate nodded. 'I have reason to believe you're still a flight risk.'

'Well, you're quite right. I am. And I wonder why that is? Could it have anything to do with the fact that I've been fitted up like Patty Hearst and have just become implicated in a major robbery? Oh, and I'm sitting just three hundred yards from the shop we've ripped off. Yes, I'm a flight risk, like the Middle Eastern gentleman in the aisle seat whose shoe has just started to smoke.'

'You were already robbing the man and, might I add, making a complete fist of it.'

'If I could get my hand out of here I'd show you a fist.'

'Oh yes. No, I saw your fighting skills. Very impressive. Remind me what your moves are. Did you do the uncontrollable whimpering before or after you soiled yourself? I turned what was going to be a sorry fiasco into a victory. You should thank me.'

Peter and Kate sat on one of the ornate ironwork benches which South Dorset Council had bolted to Christchurch Quay in a vain, underfunded effort to give the town a 'focal point', something which, up to then, had been provided by the opticians on the high street.

'You are absolutely right. Thank you. You turned what was a minor misunderstanding into a major heist. And now I'm going to have to leave this place, my jobs, everything. Really, I mean it, thank you. I mean I was just thinking I needed a bit of a change of scenery but couldn't think where to go. Now it's so much easier. I'll go on the bloody run. Why on earth didn't I think of that earlier?'

'Oh bite me.' Kate lapsed into the joyful directness of Americanism. 'You've got no right, no right to pour your scorn and sarcasm on me.' Her voice was starting to rise – all on its own. She realized just how pissed off this plonker was making her. Twenty years grifting and not a jot of an emotion ever interfered in the act; a thousand marks and none of them had ever got to her like this tosser had done in barely twenty minutes of knowing him. The last time her feelings had got in the way of her composure she joined an ashram, fasted for forty days and nights and then took her guru for two of his Rolls and an Aston Martin. Kate concentrated and pulled her voice into a more measured delivery. 'Didn't anyone tell you, you do bad things, bad things can happen to you?'

'Karma?'

'No. I'm still fucking seething.'

Kate began to realize that it must have been something to do with the box o'sins. Like she hadn't just opened the box, the box had somehow opened her, and now emotions and feelings seemed to be bubbling up in her like molten lava seeping through the cracking solid rocks of the long-extinct volcano.

213

'You nick my ring, you fuck off and try to pawn it and, when I come along and save your head from almost certain brain injury you think you've got the right to whine at me. You don't want to get into trouble, don't fucking start it.'

'First off, I didn't steal it. You gave it to me.'

'And when I asked for it back, you stole it.'

'I don't think that not giving back a gift is technically stealing. Or illegal.'

'No, but that doesn't make it right or good either. And for sure taking a hundred quid for a ring that you kept was.'

'Right. Well, perhaps you should have just gone off and reported it to the police. The real police,' Peter added.

'There's still time. Doesn't look like you're going anywhere.'

'I have my doubts. You're probably wanted in several different countries.' Peter was joking. Kate was not.

'Fuck. What do you know? My dad couldn't remember th—' Kate stopped herself fast as she realized that she had been caught in the 'accidental truth' paradigm. An artless part of dramatic exposition also known as 'out of the mouth of babes', despite the reality being, on the whole, shrill cries and vomit. He didn't know that. He was just trying to be funny.

'Oh bloody hell. Don't tell me I'm right.'

Kate shook her head and watched the gulls weaving through the dinghy masts. The gulls, in turn, watched Kate and Peter and, assuming the presence of food, glided closer.

'You know,' said Peter, 'I find it hard to watch a sea-gull glide through the air without a feeling of awe, a

214

sense that if you could only find it, perfect freedom would be as easy as they make it look.' He pointed at a gull homing in on them, scudding over the surface of the water. 'Look at that. Honed through millions of years of evolution, easy, elegant, like an incontrovertible proof of the perfection of nature.'

Kate watched and had to agree, though she was careful not to show it.

'It's just a shame they never got round to putting the same care and attention into their landing skills.'

Kate clapped her hands to her mouth but couldn't stop herself laughing. It was true. Each gull approached in a graceful swoop across the water with barely a flap of a wing or alteration in course but, when they tried to stop, it was as if it had come as a complete surprise. Suddenly they became a desperate flurry of flapping, squawking and jerking motions, completely ruining the entire effect and simultaneously countering any arguments for either evolution or creationism.

'That sounded like a real laugh,' Peter said.

'What do you mean?'

'Most of the time you're very convincing,' Peter said. 'Maybe not as the "concerned daughter" but when you're CID I start thinking you really might be a detective, and when you're the "flirty fiancée" I'm convinced you're passionate for the guy, but when I've heard you laugh . . .' Peter shook his head.

Kate kicked out at one of the bolder seagulls. 'So my only relative's had a stroke and is in a home, I've broken up with my fiancé and I'm being one-upped on morality by a man who not only makes his living by deception but in the,' Kate checked her watch, 'eighteen hours since I first met him has turned over a pawnshop, and robbed, cheated and lied to me. Remind me again what I'm supposed to find so hilarious?'

'You can try and deflect it but you're too much of a perfectionist. When you're pretending, you want to get every detail right. You're good at what you do. You know you are. You treat it very seriously. Which is why laughter's your Achilles heel, your giveaway.'

First Clarissa, now this chancer. Had she really just slipped over the edge where no one would give her the benefit of the doubt any more? Had she been so reliant on her looks to carry her through her grifts? She had prided herself on her skills. And now, now, had she finally become so transparent? Kate examined him. He clearly wasn't stupid but could he have really sussed her?

'You're brilliant at showing the world how indomitable you are,' Peter carried on, 'but I know that there's something inside you telling you it's just bravado, that's not the real you, you're as vulnerable as the next person and there are times, when you're on your own, you just feel so tired of having to sustain the tough exterior. And more recently you've started asking yourself whether this is actually what you want to be doing with your life.'

It was true, she was feeling that exactly, it was like he was seeing right into her and . . . but no. Had Kate been less controlled in her gestures this would have been the moment she slapped her forehead saying, 'Of course.' It was so bleeding obvious what he was doing. Kate immediately stood up and gathered the plastic bags full of booty. 'You. You're a fucking amateur.'

'Hang on,' Peter said, rattling the cuffs that held him to the bench, 'what about these?'

Kate walked off, shaking her head. 'They'll be selling ice cream in hell when the likes of you can cold-read the likes of me.'

21

'Dr Tavasligh, I really really need you here, the police, a couple, a man and a woman from the police, they're in the lobby and the manager is at a conference, his phone's off, and I didn't know who else to call and there's a policewoman and an American man and they're asking—'

'Paula, slow down.' I cradled the phone between my ear and shoulder as I peeled off my latex gloves. 'Let me get this clear. The police are at Lotus House, and they want to speak to somebody?'

'Well, they want to see Mr Minola.'

'Cedric?'

'But I said I couldn't authorize it, it would need to be one of the Lotus House management. But Mr de Myers is off and you're a director so . . .'

'Paula, you did just the right thing. Now ask them to take a seat and tell them I'll be right over. I shouldn't be longer than five minutes or so.'

I hung up my phone, my testtube rack and my lab coat. I presume. Of course I have no actual memory of this because my automotive unconscious was taking care of all that. My conscious brain had taken over the majority of my cognitive processes in responding to Paula's call. It was channelling most of my neuronaline energy through my synaptic circuitry, which processed an array of creative possible outcome patterns, manufacturing numerous scenarios using all the similar data patterns it had gathered throughout my life . . . or, if you prefer, experience told me that there could be a number of reasons for this visit from the constabulary but the most likely was probably the one I should prepare for. From the spits and spots of information I had gathered about Cedric's daughter over the years, and having met her for the first time only the day before, I was fairly certain that she was at the heart of this.

I was right.

The man who stood in the Lotus House reception dwarfed the entire room. He was built like the famous brick shithouse, but without any of the Houses of Parliament's crazy Gothic crenellations.

Paula saw me and pointed to the man mountain, as if I might not have noticed him or the seventeen climbers and twelve sherpas gingerly making their way up the frozen North Face.

'Dr Tavasligh, that's them.'

I smiled up at him but before he could say a word, or even get the ski lifts going, a mousy woman in a dark trouser suit appeared from behind him holding an identity card.

'DI Brightly, Flying Squad, this is Special Agent Brown of the United States Federal Bureau of Investigation. You are?'

'Dr Tavasligh, one of the directors here.'

218

'We believe you have a resident here called Cedric Minola.'

I nodded.

'We would like to talk to him.'

'That may be a little difficult. He suffers from severe amnesia and regressive dementia.'

'We believe he has information that may lead to the arrest of a fugitive.'

'If he did, he'll have forgotten a long time ago.'

'Nevertheless we would like to see for ourselves.'

I shrugged. 'OK. I'll take you to him.' I led the way up the stairs. 'But I warn you his mental state is that of a small child, which makes him emotionally very vulnerable. Please just ask facts. I will terminate the interview if at any time I think you are putting pressure on him.'

Cedric was sitting by the window when we came in. I had to say his name twice before he remembered that that was him and he turned to look at us.

'Cedric, this is the police. They want to ask you a few questions.'

Cedric looked around nervously and located his 'bikes'. I saw them catch his eye and without thinking – no, no, of course I was thinking but when I look back at it I seemed to be acting automatically without any clear motivation – I blustered forward as he reached for the cards and clumsily knocked them to the ground. If Cedric had his 'bikes' there was a good chance that he would be cogent enough to answer questions. Something within me wanted to protect Cedric – from what? Losing his daughter and any chance of connecting to his long-term memories again? I can't recall being aware of that reason, but that in itself must have a reason. Maybe I felt guilty about trying to mislead the law, maybe there was something about Brown and Brightly I didn't trust, maybe I thought I was protecting Cedric. Whatever it was, my brain has stored it in the same place that the regrets from a drunken night before are stored in the hungover morning after.

'Sorry, sorry.' I looked back at the officers. 'He likes to play cards. Cedric, they're here to ask questions. They're not here for a game.' I started gathering the cards up as Agent Brown squeezed in the door.

'Hey Sid, long time no see.' Brown grinned at him, hitched up the back of his trench coat and sat down heavily on the opposite armchair. 'I don't mind playing a hand while we talk. Five-card draw?' Brown took the cards from me and gave them a showy riffle shuffle before cupping them into an arch and ending in a ratcheting waterfall. He leaned over the coffee table and dealt out five cards to both of them. Cedric picked up.

'We were wondering how your daughter, Kate, is.'

Cedric pursed his lips tightly until the area between his nose and chin resembled a walnut. 'You haven't placed your ante,' he said tetchily.

'Oh, pardon me.' Brown drew out a ten-dollar bill and laid it on the table. 'We heard she came to see you.'

'Dear heart,' Cedric looked at me, 'could you spot me?'

I went up behind Cedric. 'Spot you?'

'This gentleman has placed a tenner. Do you think you could match it for me?'

'I'm not sure.' I checked my pockets.

'I'm good for it.' Cedric showed me his cards.

'Cedric, Lotus House does not allow gambling and,' I caught sight of his cards then lowered my voice, 'Cedric, you can only pick up a hand that rotten in a leper colony.'

Cedric looked over to Brightly. 'What about you, girlie?'

Brightly stiffened. 'Can't gamble on duty, sir.'

'Tell you what, Sid.' Brown smiled amiably. 'You tell me about Kate and I'll lend you the money.'

'Sir,' I implored, 'I really would ask you not to gamble on these premises.'

But Cedric was determined. 'Better see what you're investing in.' He fanned his hand in front of Brown's face. 'Can't lose . . .' Cedric's voice tailed off as he looked at Brown, looked back at his hand and slowly seemed to realize that he was showing his entire hand to his opponent. He threw down his cards and gathered up the pack quickly. 'Let's start again. You, sir, win, I tell you everything I know. I win, you sod off out of here.'

Brown laid his cards down. 'We just want to know if she said she's coming back.'

'And that I'll tell you.' Cedric gathered Brown's hand and began to shuffle suspiciously awkwardly before dealing again. 'I'll tell you everything I know when you win.'

The crafty old fox. Now the cards were in his slightly trembling hands. And when the cards were in Cedric's hands they only ever did exactly what he wanted them to do.

22

'Remember me?'

'You took your time.' Kate didn't bother to look up as Peter let himself into his room. She was sitting on his bed reading *Divining Man*, Titus Black's Christmas TV tie-in book of cobbled-together half-truths about human psychology and how to tell what people are really thinking from their behaviour, sponsored by *Burn!*, the magazine for connoisseurs of the exclamation mark:

WANNA KNOW IF HE'S INTO YOU?!

Look into his eyes! If his pupils are getting bigger, he thinks you're hot!!!

Wanna MAKE his eyes grow bigger when he looks at you?!

Wear black or dark clothes because pupils get bigger in the dark!! The bigger his pupils, the more scorching he's thinking you are! In fact why not go superhot and wear the full burka!!! Now you're sizzling, gal!

She was surrounded by the albums of photos and the carefully collated magazines, papers and magic 'lecture notes' that formed the bulk of Peter's 'collection'.

'I was a bit tied up,' Peter said hesitantly, trying to figure out why, now she had the ring, Kate was still in the country, let alone his room. 'I didn't know that I was expected.'

'Considering those, I reckoned you'd have no trouble.' Kate pointed to a cascade of silver chains that hung from the coat hooks on the back of his door. It was Peter's collection of handcuffs, gimmicked and real, all clipped together in a jailer's fantasy of enough shackles to make Marley's Ghost seem an unfettered free spirit. 'Unless you're just very, very kinky.'

'Used to think I might specialize in escapology,' Peter said. 'I made a promise to myself, I'd learn how to escape from any handcuffs. I've sourced these from all over the world. I've practised, found their flaws, their weaknesses, and what it needs, picks or pressure, to get out of them.'

'Have a nasty experience with a pair?'

'You could say that.'

'And then you thought you'd be like Houdini.'

'Yes. The great park bench escape was one of his classics. Headline news.'

'Da, my dad. Ced . . .'

'Sid. He likes "Sid".'

'He used to say the magicians who became escapologists, they're working out a terror of being caught. What do you think? That you?'

Peter sat down heavily on the corner of the bed.

Kate tried again. 'I've a theory about Houdini: had

223

some trauma *in utero*. Then, like any Jewish kid, invents all those escapes to try to get away from his mother; all that hanging upside down from umbilical cord chains, trussed up in tiny womb crates and drowning in amniotic fluid. But then she died and managed to escape him. The loon.'

Peter closed his eyes to enjoy the moment fully. He hadn't had a two-way conversation about magic since before 'the party' and, even if it was a suspicious bit of 'bonding' chat, it brought back nostalgic memories of his youth magic club and sweaty demonstrations of faro shuffles. 'That's your theory?'

Kate smiled.

'If he simply wanted to escape his mother, how come he didn't just go the normal route, years of bickering, scathing sarcasm and disenfranchisement leading to a newspaper on a park bench being the preferable option.'

'That was your escape?'

'No. I was lucky. Six-month suspended sentence and a lynch mob organized by the Neighbourhood Watch complete with pitchforks and burning torches. That did it for me.'

'Well, Da's theory holds then.'

'Da?'

Kate gave a goofy smile. 'Short for Dada.'

'The anarchic art movement?'

Kate sighed. 'I always thought they were more annoyingly facetious, but it turns out that was actually just you all along.'

Now Peter threw Kate a smile. It's hard not to admire the personal skills in others which you hanker after in yourself. Kate was forthright, and she would clearly insist on being third, second and first right as well. She evidently got what she wanted through charm, guile or thievery and even if she had left him chained to a bench it had forced Peter to finally put his long-practised skills to use. For all his training, Peter had never dared to don the cuffs of destiny or sit in the chair of doom again. The bench of disagreeableness was a start.

Feeling his stare might have stayed a fraction too long, Peter quickly turned away from Kate, but her look burned in his mind like the last firework that gets etched into the irises long after the black night returns. She was pretty, no doubt about it, maybe a little quirky-looking; a little shorter, a little wider in places than life's lanky paper-thin cover girls; but then she didn't have full-colour ads on her back either. Kate paid few dues to classical beauty; she figured life was too short for the sort of nail filing it takes to be the Venus de Milo. But she had learned early the first rule of beguilement: wrong-foot the inevitable criticism, flaunt your imperfections, use your flaws. So she was a bit fuller on the lips and hips? They just served to give her a sway and pout that, in Peter's mind, put her in a league he had only ever watched from the sidelines. There was something in the heady concoction of street-smarts, wisecracks and the confidence of the big-eyed, knowing grin that tipped 'pretty' into 'stunning' and was very hard to dislike.

Peter knew he would just have to try harder.

The alternative was far too painful to consider. What if he allowed himself to have feelings for her? Right now he'd give himself the same odds as a Shetland in the

Grand National. Over the years Peter had become aware that his appeal to women rivalled that of cleaning the hair out of the plughole. They kind of knew that he was there but never wanted to go near him until their plumbing had completely seized up.

Lucky at cards, unlucky in . . . ? Well, Peter was superb at cards.

'Sorry.' Peter kept his back to Kate but could still see a partial reflection in the dresser mirror. 'I don't actually remember inviting you here, in fact, I can't remember giving you keys to my place. So I have to ask, Why are you here? What do you want with me?'

'Well, for starters,' Kate threw down her book and gesticulated across the piles of Titus Black merchandise, memorabilia and annotated candid photographs, 'I want to know what's up with your obsession with this guy. He seems a total arse. You got the hots for this Titus Black, or what?'

Peter tried not to flinch when he heard the name. He turned to her. 'He's a magician I admire . . .'

But Kate had spotted it and zeroed in. 'Oh, oh, oh, I see. That's your little raw nerve, is it? There's a little dead thing in the corner of your eye, I saw the same look when you were talking about "specializing" with handcuffs. We have a little lie going on. So what? You got into a little S and M with this midget mind-reader?'

'Is that the time? I think you really must be going.'

'Peter and Titus sitting in a tree?'

Peter pointed to the door.

Kate studied his face harder. 'OK, I can see it, it's not that you love him, is it?'

Peter knew she hadn't seen a thing, she was still

fishing. He knew because he had used the confused 'questment' a million times. You say, 'It's not a red card, is it?' with enough ambiguity of intonation and the punter with a black card hears a statement, the punter with a red card hears a question which seems to pre-suppose the outcome. The black-card holder agrees, 'No,' the red-card holder agrees, 'Yes.' Either way it's an agreement, a win–win piece of verbal conjuring. But here, Peter's silence spoke volumes while Kate's gut instinct divined the appendices.

'No,' Kate seamlessly continued, 'it's not a stalkery, lovey thing, is it? It's hate. It's bitterness. It's resentment.'

'What? Now you're cold-reading me? After your huff down at the quay?'

'You ought to use it.'

'Use your huff? To huff and puff you out of here?'

'Your anger. Your passion.'

'Yes, well, I am, I'm passionately, angrily pointing at the bloody door and trying to get you to sod off out of it.'

'It's what drives people to do great things, passion. Big things.'

'It's going to make me do something I regret if you don't get out of here.'

'Oh yes, yes, regret. You've got a lot of that.'

Jesus, wouldn't she just shut up?

Kate looked at him. 'My problem, Peter, I lost contact with my emotions so long ago I don't even get visitation rights. But you know that feeling inside you? That knot of despair and hate and anger and passion? It's what drives humanity, it's what forces our evolution. It's the money.'

'What are you getting at?'

'Peter, I'm going to give you a gift.'

'What, like you gave me the ring?'

'No. No. I wouldn't, couldn't, take this one back if you paid me.'

'It doesn't exactly sound like something I'm going to want either.'

'You've already got it. It's as obvious as acne in McDonald's. You've got something that causes you such pain it's driven you into this little shithole of a life. But I've seen your skills. You've got real ability. I've watched some of the best dippers and pickpockets in the world, I've known operators from the Stock Exchange to the telephone exchange, and if you weren't so very scared of whatever it is, you could have made your prestidigitation into an art form. But you're running from something and it's something to do with that Titus bloke. And you know what my gift is?'

She pointed to the back of Titus's book, which sported a publicity shot of him staring mysteriously out as he held his fingers to his temples, as if pointing to his brain could somehow get it to function better. 'Him, at the point of a sword made of all the hate and jealousy and envy and resentment and regret and anger you have seething inside you.'

Peter stared at the picture. She was a good sell. 'Why?' Peter looked back at her. 'Why would you give me this . . . this gift?'

'Oh, don't worry, I'll get what I want out of this too.'

'Why am I not surprised?'

Kate got up and looked at her dad's box o'sins.

228

'Dr Tavasligh, at the home, told me a lot about you. What you did for Da.'

Peter looked down at the trunk. 'Oh, I think I'm just looking after it for him. He said I should have it but, well, it's hard to tell if he's in his right mind when he says anything. I think he just didn't want some of the other inmates rummaging through it. If you want it . . .'

'No,' said Kate, 'no, he meant it for you. He meant it to go to another magician.' Kate's voice tailed off but she stood staring at it.

'Did he want you to follow in his footsteps?'

Kate nodded wistfully as she stood there.

'But you decided maybe life as a . . . what? A sort of scammer, a thief, a consummate liar, a police impersonator? I'm not quite sure what it is you do.'

'I make plans. I change lives. I exploit people's passions, their desires, to squeeze cold cash out of their dreams.'

'So, all of the above, but giving it some sort of positive spin to make you feel less guilty about it.'

Kate nodded again and turned to him.

'OK. And now we do it to him.' She pointed to one of the bundles of Black publicity photos. 'What do you reckon? We take him and squeeze him. What do you think he's good for? A million?'

Peter smiled. 'You mean I help you do some sort of sting. A con. Scam Titus Black? For a million quid?'

'Considering your behaviour this morning you've ethically crossed the line. Now let's just go and get some bigger game. Fifty-fifty share. What d'ya say?'

'I don't know, I need time to think abou— Yes. Of course. Of course I'll do it.' Peter looked at Kate's hand, already extended towards him to shake on the deal. 'But if you can extract that sort of money out of him why not go it alone? Why do you need me?'

'It's what I was trying to explain. To do something like this, things will get tough, and if you don't have the passion, the drive, the anger to finish it off, it can all fall down around your ears. I've got the plan if you've got the emotion.'

'You're going to want to know, aren't you?'

'Why you've been obsessing about him? Yes.'

'I've never told anybody.'

'Peter. Two weeks from now you'll have half a million quid in your pocket, and you will look at every single note and say, "That's Titus Black's, that is."'

Peter grabbed her warm, soft hand and he shook, he couldn't help himself, his whole body shook like a leaf that had spent its life lashed to a tree that drained it of all the sunlight and nourishment it gathered but finally it could feel the wind that would liberate it, free it from the tethering branch. He shook. To float free. To fall.

Kate felt the tremble. 'It's all yours and it starts with you telling me why. Why Titus Black is your *bête noire*.'

Peter hid his face in his hands to begin his story. If he wanted to relieve it he would have to relive it, one more time.

30,000 Milliseconds to Higham
(TEA minus 11 months 19 days 8 hours)

Peter

But then what?

I sneak off the train; and what if I did have a million quid? What would happen next?

Get a yacht, a fancy pad somewhere without an extradition treaty? Get leathery and brown in the sun, pottering about my villa?

Was that the point of all this? Is it just the money?
No.

No, when this started it was all about the dish served cold. It was about Titus. It was about . . .

It was about Kate.

If I squint a little I can just make out her pale face against the velveteen seat. It's her. She changes everything. It's been Kate all along.

Then, just looking at her, everything aches. It's like a despair, torn between opposing truths: knowing the transience of our lives and yet longing for the for ever. Each time I look at her I can't see the woman any more. Yes, I see the shape, the eyes, the form, but at the same time, there's this agonizing array of memories she triggers. That moment I looked down at her soft hand, surprised to feel its hot grip on mine, leaning on the cold stones of the Pont Neuf. That sliver of orange streetlight coming up through the slatted shutters of that tiny hotel room, catching her pearl camisole and shimmering up from the loose cloth that fell about her waist to the hard, dark shadow of a nipple pressing against the silk. That almost smile, so slight only I could see it, because she wanted only me to see it.

I can't go, I must go. I have to. She's only going to find out what a fucking fraud I am and then she'll be gone anyway.

It's better this way.

23

'And she only died a week ago.' Titus shook his head sadly. He held John Ogilvy's hand. 'Was she,' he coughed to show some reticence about the indelicacy, 'aware that it was coming?'

'She had had a few strokes but no, not really. She haemorrhaged. Side effect of the drugs she's taking.'

'I understand. And I understand why she's so cross. What's that?' Titus looked at the empty space next to him and disagreed with it. 'Oh Ethel, you are cross. Oh. OK, you're not cross, you're "discombobulated".'

John sobbed again. 'That was her word, that's how she used to say she was angry.'

A small burst of applause rattled around the audience but Titus, keeping to his Peter Brook performance method, seemed more interested in the empty space. 'It's because you didn't get a chance to say goodbye? And you missed him. John and the kids, especially the little one when they left you to look after the cat and went where?' Titus looked back at John with a raised eyebrow. 'Barbados, John? You're certainly someone who doesn't mind forking out for a holiday.'

John Ogilvy looked dumbstruck. 'How, how could you possibly know?'

Kate turned away from the television to look at Peter. 'He's a stooge. He's got to be.'

'I know it looks like it but Black couldn't risk it.' Peter shook his head. 'He'd be having to find new stooges all the time and all he would need is just one of them to blab to the papers and his whole career would be buggered.'

By this time John Ogilvy was talking directly to the empty space as well.

'No. No, I know they're bad for me. I know they'll kill me.'

'Well,' Titus intoned haughtily, 'Ethel just wants to know why she found a packet of Marlboros at the back of her antimacassar drawer.'

Some of the audience squealed with delight to watch a grown man squirm as he was told off by his dead grandmother. Titus smirked, and the face that the *Sunday Times* television reviewer had called 'a mug doomed to be preceded by the letter S,' beamed out of twenty screens up in the producer's control room. Ronnie hugged himself. This was classic TV, this would make all the clip shows. This was always the part of the show when Titus baffled even him and it was a pleasure to watch. It reminded him of the earliest unfathomable magic he ever witnessed, the slightly tipsy uncle who pulled coins from Ronnie's ears. Ronnie had followed Titus from their first days in Junior Magic Circle; he was proud of the tricks he devised for the earlier parts of the show but not even he could work out how Titus could read people so accurately and get hit after hit. It made

Ronnie feel comfortable, justified in being behind the camera while Titus was in front of it. This was something that put Titus up there with the gods of magic.

After Titus had revealed another twenty-two impossible-to-divine facts about Ethel and John, after the funky credit music had played as Titus raised his arms into a messianic cruciform outlined with a back-lighting spotlight, Peter hit the remote and the TV clicked off.

'That was the one I just recorded.'

Kate sat silently awestruck, her mouth still open. 'He can't be that good, can he?' she asked.

Each of them sat cross-legged on Peter's bed, still staring at the blank screen. It was a brain-boggling crescendo at the end of a mind-messing day.

Peter's story of the birthday party was behind them – he had cried and she had laughed – followed by the more serious business of watching every single record-ing of Titus Black that Peter owned. They found themselves unable to tear their eyes away from the blank screen as their brains raced with possibilities.

'So how? How does he do it?'

Peter shrugged. 'Well, first can we agree that there's no afterlife and there was no dead granny there talking to either of them?'

Kate nodded.

'Also,' Peter carried on methodically, 'that it is im-possible to tell that someone goes on holiday to Barbados from the way they sit, or what they wear. I mean you could make a good guess but Titus didn't exactly use any ambiguity in his language. It was stated as unarguable fact.'

Kate nodded again.

'So we're going to have to assume that it's pre-show work. Information gathered before the show which he's then pretending to "discover" during the show.'

'But what about the hidden packet of ciggies?'

'Very confident guess?'

Kate cocked her head at him.

'OK, well, he must have spoken to his granny.'

'But she's dead.'

Peter sighed, 'I know. It's a teensy-weensy flaw. But it's the first thing you discover when you learn about magic: you buy your first trick and you open it up and you realize how stupidly simple it is; you start to understand that most conjuring secrets are banal, nothing like the sophistication of watching the trick in action. They work on the improbable. I mean, why would someone go to all the bother of printing a playing card with different index numbers at the two corners? That would render the card unplayable and every card you've ever seen always fits into the expected pattern. The question is so stupid that the brain never even asks it, but that, that is where the trick lies. All the conjuror has done to magically change the card is turn it around. But it's Occam's razor: the simplest solution is the most likely one.'

Kate raised her eyes. 'Any other products in the Occam shaving range? Something to deal with Occam's razorburn: the most likely solution is invariably the most disappointing one. Or worse, Occam's pimple cut, which says that the simplest person is the one most likely to try patronizing you by suggesting you don't know what Occam's razor is.'

Peter bowed. 'Yes, of course, madam. You could try

Occam's aftershave, which smells of trite aphorisms with a suggestion that neat solutions are overly tempting and may well obscure messier solutions which could still be true. Or indeed Occam's cleansing balm, which lets blasé assumptions of simplicity soothe any logic snags that get in the way of a neat premise.'

Kate smiled. He was keeping up. Good.

'I don't know how,' Peter said, 'but if the most obvious answer is that he talked to the granny, even if the granny is dead, then all you've really got to work out is how.'

Kate pointed at the TV. 'You know, I don't think it matters how he does it. If we're going to scam him, we just need to know why he does it.'

'Why he does what?'

'Why he talks to the dead. Why he wants to perform, why he wants public recognition, why he wants people to believe he reads minds. Why he wants people to believe that he can control their minds.'

'Well, they're all quite cool things to do.'

'If you're, like, twelve they might be.'

'Why do we need to know these things?'

'Because whatever it is that he wants, that's what we're going to sell to him. The confidence trick, the grift, the scam, is just selling, Peter. The only thing that's different is that the product is a dream. It's the worst sort of product, it's intangible, but that also makes it the best one ever as well.'

'Like you're selling me revenge? Who's conning who here?'

Kate laughed and punched him in the shoulder. 'You've got to trust me, my man.'

'I was afraid you would say that. You do realize that you have made a career of making people trust you so that you could then rip them off?'

'First of all, Peter, you live in the shit end of Shitville in the county of Shitshire. What can I rip you off for?'

'Some class A manure?'

'Secondly, it's not like you haven't made your entire career doing exactly the same thing. This is the ace of hearts, you flip it over and shove it into their hand. "So that's the ace of hearts you've got there," but of course it isn't. But they trust you and you reveal what idiots they were to trust you and then you elicit money from them for the pleasure.'

'But I'm not selling the ace of hearts pretending it's a Maserati. They buy what they see, a moment of wonder, distraction, astonishment. It may not earn big bucks but it's honest.'

'Really? You'd call pointing at a card and saying it's something that you know full well it isn't is honest?'

'Maybe not, but then I don't charge the earth or ruin people's lives doing it.'

'We're in the same job, Peter, we're selling illusions.'

'I perform illusions, you sell delusions.'

'We're both dishonest, the only difference is scale.'

'But that's like saying an actor is dishonest because he is not the person he's playing.'

'So you know any actors you can trust?'

Peter stopped and thought about this. 'Point taken,' he nodded. Ever since the Witchfinder General started rounding up some of the uglier crones in the Ipswich area in the seventeenth century, magical entertainers had not improved their reputation for moral rectitude. 'And we're going to try to sell Titus a dream?'

'Not a dream. His dream.'

'So this is where actually reading minds would come in handy.'

'No. No, it's all here.' Kate gestured to the stack of books and videos that they had ploughed through. 'We've just got to find it. The thing that he would break laws to obtain.'

'Three inches more in height? To walk down the street without someone shouting, "Hey, Titus, what am I thinking?" An Emmy?'

'Peter, think. He's someone who's driven to risk exposure at any moment, who wants us to see that . . . Hang on.' Kate looked hard at Peter. 'We've only seen what he wants us to see. We've only seen him performing. Have you got anything more candid?'

'Like, caught off guard?'

'Yes, interviews or fan videos.'

Peter grabbed his laptop. 'Google is your friend.'

Kate looked at him. 'You won't believe how many times I've been shafted up the arse by that thing. Seriously, with friends like Google, who needs enemas?'

Peter considered this and realized that for a scam artist on the run, the sharing of information on a global scale was probably not good for business. The two started trawling through the blocky video clips on the internet, interrupted only by the rumble of Kate's stomach.

'Hungry?' asked Peter. 'The chippie downstairs is open.'

Kate was unwilling to break her concentration but shook her head. 'No, couldn't do fish and chips. Have you got the number for a pizza? Something spicy. Americano. Something like that.'

Peter grabbed the phone to order. He was halfway through repeating that he knew his address was a chip shop but the entrance to the flat above was a fire escape around the back, when he noticed that Kate had been scrubbing backwards and forwards through the same clip of Titus for some time.

'What is it?' he asked, finally hanging up.

'It's a fan trying to talk to him at the stage door. Listen.'

The location of the scene was barely discernible, a bright door, a lot of shifting heads. 'Titus, you were great, I love you, can I have your autograph?' A hand reached forward with a pen and pad, which Titus took. He started writing as various other faces seemed to be jostling. 'You l-l-liked the sssshow. That's great.' Titus handed back the book and smirked towards the camera.

'See?'

'No.'

'Watch again but really listen.' Kate ran the clip again but any significance eluded Peter. 'He's stuttering. He's got a stutter. He does it on some other clips as well. The impromptu stuff.'

'But he never stutters on stage.'

'Exactly. That's the clue. He's showing us his inner-most desire.'

'He is?' Peter said, baffled.

'He is.'

'What exactly?'

Kate shook her head.

240

24

'A man, tall, with a New Zealand accent. He was with a shorter woman with blonde hair.'

'Last night?' Bert Molloy, manager of La Esplanade, eyed the giant American suspiciously. 'And you're sure you're not from the health inspectors?'

Brightly interjected. 'Mr Molloy, we are definitely not from the health inspectors but if you continue to be so evasive I assure you I have their number.'

The three sat in what Molloy liked to call his 'office', although the transient décor of coats, hats, scarves and bags hanging in the tiny space suggested 'cloakroom' might have been a little more accurate. Molloy wiped his brow with the sleeve of the nearest coat; he had been playing for time but the temperature was getting intense. Between Agent Brown and the coats there was only trysting room for Brightly and Molloy, an idea that filled Brightly, as her knees rubbed Molloy's, with revulsion. She knew there was something suspicious – why couldn't they have just stood in the dining room or even outside? – but she had doomed herself to the claustrophobic office the moment she had flashed her ID at Molloy. In passing, he had nonchalantly reminded a waiter to 'Redo the napkins,' the code red signal to be taken to the kitchen. The chef needed at least ten minutes to give the three illegal Moroccan cooks the rest of the night off, whip the zebra 'beef' out of the fridge and into the dumpsters standing by at the back, and hide the rat traps that had been placed strategically around the skirting boards of the kitchen and dining room.

Brown passed Kate's infamous America's Most Wanted picture to Molloy. 'This might jog your memory.'

Molloy looked at the picture of the pretty girl. 'I think I know who you mean. She's a bit older. They sat in the window bay.'

'Our information tells us that you have a magician working here?'

Molloy beamed. 'Magic Malcolm, weekends and Wednesday nights. He's very good, you know.'

'Our witness says he took a ring from this woman.'

Molloy looked surprised. 'No. Not Pitter.'

'Pitter?'

'Yes, Pitter.'

'Is that like, Italian?'

'Maybe Italish,' Brightly offered, having already picked up the Irish accent but still trying to hold her breath so that the smell of the cloakroom didn't make her retch.

'Pitter, loik Sellers, Ustinov, Mandelson, Rabbit, Pan. Pitter's very professional. He might have made the ring disappear but he always returns what he vanishes.'

Brown smiled. 'Ah, Peter. Peter who?'

'Pitter Ruchio. Magic Malcolm is his stage na— His table name.'

'Apparently this woman,' Brown emphasized by

242

pointing to the picture again, 'Kate Minola, she insisted that Peter, Malcolm, she insisted that he kept the ring.'

'You think he stole it?'

Brown was treading gently. 'Well, they might be in league. Old friends or something. Do you remember if Peter was acting any differently last night, especially when he saw that couple come in?'

'No. He is always very professional.' Molloy looked at his watch. Chef had had plenty of time.

Brightly interrupted, 'Well, we'd like to ask him a few questions to help us with our inquiry.'

'He'll be in on Saturday.'

'Do you happen to have an address for him?'

Molloy looked at Brightly, then at Brown. If it was Peter's problem, it was Peter's problem. He reached into the pocket of one of his filing coats and pulled out a stack of business cards. He found the one with a star drawn on the back, a remnant of the prediction trick that Peter had played on him when he had applied for the job.

Molloy handed the card to Brightly, who sprang up faster than a teen stiffy and burst out of the closet gasping for breath. The diners all turned.

Molloy followed her, looked around quickly, raced to the kitchen and stormed back again. Brown was squeezing out of the office.

'They've all bloody scarpered,' Molloy screamed. 'Where's my fecking staff?'

◆

Brown pulled the door of La Esplanade closed and crossed over to the beginning of the pier, where Brightly was clutching the rail above the beach. She was braced against the elements, her loosened mousy tresses dancing about in the wind as she took deep breaths of air and hair.

'Sorry, sir,' she said as he approached, 'confined spaces, not good with them.' She handed Magic Malcolm's card to Brown.

He looked at it. 'Whadaya know. We're heading back to Christchurch.'

Brightly checked her watch again. 'Sorry, sir, not feeling the full ticket and technically I was off duty from about half an hour ago. Going to head back to the hotel if you don't mind.'

'Aw c'mon,' said Brown, 'yes, I do mind. Of course I mind. If we act like now, we may get her before she skips town or the country.'

Brightly bit her lip as she tried to hide a knowing smile by glancing at the floor. She took another big gulp of air. 'Look,' she fixed him with her pallid brown eyes, 'we've done everything we can to make this happen for you. We've got her description posted at all ports, with all police patrols. If she's as smart as you say, she's not going to be hanging out anywhere near her last sighting. If she's such a clever piece of work, right now she'll be on her way up north and trying to sneak away out of Aberdeen on a fishing trawler. And, apart from anything else, as far as we know she's not even committed a crime on English soil. If you think she's got a reason to stick it out here, she's as likely to be here tomorrow as today and if you think she's going to go back to see her old man, with all due respect, you head back to the home and stake it out. I, sir, am going to the Happy

244

Sleeper Hotel, getting myself some dinner and some shut-eye, and I'll be reporting back for duty at eight o'clock tomorrow morning. As you chaps say in your country . . . "Chill." '

Agent Brown stiffened. 'Brightly. I've waited fifteen years, I've travelled five thousand miles on the red eye, all for this moment. You think I'm going to let her slip through my fingers because some Limey cop chick needs her beauty sleep?'

'If we had even the slightest of leads I'd be with you. But going to interview a magician who entertained her for ten minutes must be a world record for tenuous. This cop chick is going back to her chicken hut, mate.' She turned and strode back towards the pier entrance where they had left the car.

The big man followed the minimal woman. 'You know I've got no authority to question suspects without you. C'mon.'

Brightly got into the car and lowered the window. 'I'll give you a lift to Christchurch, then you're on your own, chum.'

Agent Brown looked out to sea and then back again. 'OK. Drop me off near the magician's place. And pop the trunk for me, I need to get something out of my bag.'

The boot popped open and Brown rummaged deep in his suitcase. He pulled out a few metal boxes which looked like spare mobile phone batteries that had been rolled up in his underpants; he unscrewed the black metal tube that acted as a bulky handle for the safety razor in his washbag and retrieved an odd-shaped carbon fibre handle that detached from a portable travel

245

fan. In under a minute a familiar object had been reconstituted, primed, and slipped into his jacket pocket.

Brown slapped the lid of the boot down again and Brightly watched him in the mirror as he lumbered to the passenger side. After awkwardly pushing his massive frame into his seat and struggling to find enough slack in the seatbelt, he grinned at her. 'Let's hit it.'

25

Colonel Harris eyed the emergency alarm pendant which sat on his chest of drawers. Never wore the damn thing. It was an impertinence. Symbolized defeat. A big daft button worn on a DayGlo sash that called for help when pressed. How could his niece expect him to wear it? He who had five times bowed his head to accept sashes hung with medals for valour, courage and bravery. He who had seen action in Dunkirk and Arnhem, not to mention a particularly raucous holiday in Blackpool. He who had sat under a burned-out tank for three days with only a sniper rifle for company, waiting for the passing, literally and figuratively, of the third in command of the Waffen SS. That he who never asked for artillery cover should be so reduced as to wear at all times a big button that summoned help was too pathetic, too humiliating, and yet now, now he was looking at it and his only thought was, How? How do I get to it and press the damn thing to buggery?

If he made a lunge for it he might just make it but, if not, there was no way he would get back into his wheel-chair. It was a do-or-die but, if he succeeded, it might shut up the weaselly, blond-haired mental case who was standing at his sideboard.

'You see, Colonel, I'm a bit of a fraud.' Titus was mixing the drinks. Gin and lime for the old warhorse, a splash of tonic for himself. There was no reason why this couldn't all be conducted in a civilized manner. 'You know, I think that there are people who can really do it. They can look at somebody else and take in the way they're walking or the way they've buckled their belt and they can deduce the sorts of things that that person is thinking about. And I've tried, I've really tried. I've read all the books, I've studied the tells but still I just look at people and think, Oooh, you can't do that handbag with those shoes, or Bad hair alert. Which, on the whole, doesn't qualify as mind-reading. You're a military man, I bet you're pretty good at sizing someone up, friend or foe, hero or cannon fodder.'

'Is this something to do with why you wanted to know so much about Sandra?'

'You see? You're pretty astute for somebody who's, what, in your nineties? Yes. Sandra. I told you that she's booked to come and see my show.'

'And now,' Colonel Harris intoned in the pacifying calm that he had used as a prisoner of war in Burma when humouring the natives, 'if I understand you correctly, you're telling me that you are in fact some sort of charlatan. I'm sorry to say, sir, that that's hardly big

247

news. No one really thinks you or anyone else can actually read minds.'

'Oh I know. I'm not trying to convince the audience that I'm reading minds. It's more to do with being a bit like Sherlock Holmes, that I can read the tiny human clues that no one knows they're giving off to create an accurate portrait of them, and of course their connection with someone close who's dead. I demonstrate how psychics do what they do, not through the ether but through a certain bit of nous. Only,' Titus shook his head and looked into his glass, 'I seem to lack the nous, or maybe the will. Other people, well, they just bore me with their snivelling, pathetic lives. I don't seem to be able to bring myself to care about anybody else and so I lack empathy, to be honest. So I just gather my information in different ways. I mean you seem a nice chap, probably seen all sorts of things, led an interesting life, but I have as much interest in it as a vegan has in the hygiene standards of an abattoir.'

'So you're going to use things I've told you to make Sandra believe you have uncanny powers of observation,' the colonel summarized. 'I see. So I shouldn't have said a word then. Should have just given you rank and number.'

'Yes. But then that would have made my life really difficult and I'd have had to make your life really difficult. As it is you've been really helpful, I now feel I know your niece very well indeed. And you, sir. It really has been a great privilege.'

'You can't stop me telling her when I see her though,' the colonel said, holding his neck up proudly, 'about you pretending to be a reporter and getting all that intelligence out of me. You can't stop me.'

'That's the funny thing,' Titus said in a jovial manner, 'not only can I stop you, but because the act involves talking to the dead, I'm committed to—'

That was it. He had to lunge for the button. Colonel Harris launched himself from his wheelchair and grabbed for the sash. The tips of his fingers curled inside and as he fell to the floor the sash came with him. He pressed the button so hard his thumb clicked.

Titus cocked his head sideways to look at the prone colonel.

'I don't think it works without these.' He opened his hand to show he had the button's batteries.

Colonel Harris looked up at him with a steely eye, his stare flashing with defiance, his lips tightly pursed in long habit of military tongue-holding.

'That's a nasty fall you've had there. You could be lying there for days, no one finding you. And what with your broken neck, quite tragic.'

'I haven't broken my neck, man. Help me up.'

Titus walked forward but didn't lean down. He quietly stepped on the spluttering colonel's throat and as the full weight of the foot descended on the Windsor-knotted regimental tie, a cracking noise suddenly quietened the army man and Titus succeeded where so many of the twentieth century's bogeymen had failed.

26

'All right, I'm coming,' Peter shouted to the door. 'It's the pizzas.' He turned to Kate. 'I'll just . . .' He started patting his pockets.

Kate dipped into her bag and passed him a twenty-pound note. Peter looked at her a little pathetically.

'It's all coming back. With interest,' she reassured him.

Peter passed through the four-foot-square area that the estate agent had called the entrance hall and opened the door, to look up at the biggest man he'd ever seen.

'Hello?'

The accent was a thick, gravelly American. 'You Peter,' Agent Brown squinted at the card again, 'Ruchio?'

'Yes.' Peter held out the twenty-pound note. 'It's one Fiorentina, one Pepperoni.'

'Wise guy, huh?'

'Um.' Peter felt his heart plummet into his stomach; he remembered Kate's story, peopled with vicious Americans. What if this was one of them? He spluttered slightly, 'Well, I was . . .'

'Can I come in?'

'Well no, not real—'

'Thanks.' Brown pushed past Peter and swept into the room. He quickly scoped it with his ex-obs mental checklist. It was all pretty much what he'd expect of a jobbing magician: the boxes of tricks, the nostalgic posters, the chains of handcuffs. He noted the piles of DVDs, he noted the laptop with a freeze-frame of Titus Black. He didn't note Kate.

Kate had vanished.

'You here alone?'

'I,' Peter looked around for Kate but couldn't spot her, 'am, yes. Is that any of your business?'

'I smell perfume.'

Peter sniffed hard. It was true. In the conjuring business the impromptu lie, the adlib save when a trick goes wrong or is in danger of being spotted, is called an 'out'. Adding a slight lisp, Peter improvised his 'out'. 'What of it, dear?'

'You some kinda fag?'

A positive affirmation at this point looked likely to stop this line of questioning. 'Well, if you must know, I prefer "queer"; more empowering.' That didn't seem quite enough. Peter put a hand on his hip, pouted and added for effect, 'Ducky.'

Brown didn't look too convinced.

'So I was asking you what you're doing here, um, big boy.'

'Jeez, you coming on to me?'

'Well, my dear, I thought it might be a bit too much of a cliché to ask if that's a gun in your pocket or . . .'

'Yeah, it's a gun. OK?' Brown opened his jacket to show the butt of his reconstituted Glock peeking out of his inside pocket.

Peter suddenly realized that he was playing with fire or, more specifically, gunfire. His bravado at playing the camping game suddenly lost its ging gang goolie goolie wotsits. 'I see,' he put his head down, 'well, if you would be so kind as to make your way out of here.' Peter flapped the back of his hand as if shooing cattle.

Brown, however, remained bullish. 'Sure I'll go, when you've answered a couple of questions.'

'Do you have any right to be here? Are you the police?' Peter tried to keep his eyes from roaming around the room, just in case he spotted Kate and gave her away, but every time he did glance about there was no sign of her. And if she wasn't in the room, and there were so many boxes of magic paraphernalia under his bed she wouldn't fit, the only place it seemed she could be was in the, as she had called it, OR.

'Police? I'm a federal agent. Special Agent Brown.' He extended his hand. 'FBI.'

The very name that he had heard Kate rage about. It had seemed comfortably distant, years and years and thousands of miles away, but now, suddenly, here he was. The man himself.

Peter flaccidly laid his own hand in Brown's and promptly got it crushed. 'Have we just become the fifty-first state?' he asked. 'I mean I know there was talk and everything. Or aren't you a bit out of your jurisdiction?'

'Were you working at the Esplanade yesterday? Doing your magic?'

'Yes,' Peter said cautiously as he let a sweep of his eyes brush over the door to the OR. It was slightly ajar. She was in there.

'And did you take a ring from a woman you entertained there?'

Peter chose his words carefully. 'I didn't actually take it.' He edged closer to the door of the OR to see if, in an off moment, he could casually close it with his foot. 'It was given to me, she said I could keep it. Honestly. I think it was to piss off her fiancé. It wasn't even my colour.'

Unfortunately Brown not only kept his eye fixed on him, he followed and got closer. 'Can I see it?'

Peter shook his head. 'There's a slight problem with that.'

'She came and took it back off ya, didn't she?'

'No. It's just I pawned it this morning. You know, late on the rent.'

'You have to pay rent for this dump?' Brown looked doubtful.

They were disturbed by an urgent knocking at the door. Brown looked round for a second and Peter took the opportunity to push the OR door closed.

'Pizza Slut!' a voice shouted.

Peter didn't want to leave Brown alone but not answering would look even more suspicious. Brown looked over his shoulder at the handcuff cascade. 'Is that a real Hiappage 2000 TuffCuff?'

Peter craned around. 'Yes.'

Brown whistled and nodded. 'Nice.'

The knocking started again, louder. 'Pizza Slut!'

'Excuse me,' Peter said. He could delay no longer. He walked backwards to the hall and reached over to the door-latch without taking his eyes off Brown.

'Pepperoni and Fiorentina, mate,' the voice from the motorcycle helmet said.

'Thanks.' Peter barely looked at him but reached across the hall to give him the twenty-pound note. The hot boxes were shoved into his hands.

Brown watched Peter's contortions with bemusement. 'Sir?' he said when the door had closed again, 'do you have issues with me being in your place?'

'To be quite frank, Agent Brown, I do.'

'OK, well, I'll get out of here as soon as—' Brown spun round and yanked open the OR door. Peter squealed. That afternoon Kate had taken every picture of Titus down and bagged the lot. Brown was now staring into an empty closet.

'Excuse me,' he murmured to Peter, 'thought I heard something.'

Peter was as surprised as Brown. If Kate wasn't there, where was she? He looked around the room but there was nowhere else to hide. The only thing she could have done was go out of the window. It was quite a jump but then she'd proved how resourceful she could be. She didn't seem to need keys to get into a place, so she probably had no problem leaving. Peter felt both the relief and the pain. She wouldn't be so daft as to return and he had no idea where she might go. This brief chapter of optimism in his life had drawn to a close spectacularly quickly. Now he just had to wait for the crushing grief to begin.

'OK,' Brown said, 'as I was saying, just tell me where you pawned the ring, I'll be out of here.'

'ValuablezVampirez,' Peter said, 'it's on the high street.' On reflection that was, of course, the very worst one to name. When Brown checked it in the morning, discovery of a link between him and Kate would be inevitable. In the heat of the moment the desire to keep the tangled web of deceit as knot-free as possible persuaded him to lace his lies with as much truth as he could.

It is in fact the switching between fact and fiction that gives rise to the behavioural 'tells' that reveal liars: the sweaty palms, the dry throat, the shifting eye contact. The brain utilizes different parts to remember and to create; so to mix and match, to switch between the realities of empiricism and convenience, is processor-heavy and, as we've already witnessed, at moments of high cognitive activity, more physical processes are consigned to the automotive unconscious. So we show the signs that we cannot control, not because we are lying but because we are trying to fit the lie into an empirically true framework.

In order to make a lie convincing, and if Kate had still been there she could have told Peter this, the best thing is to plunge right in and submerse yourself completely, then you are much less likely to give yourself away. This is why the fantasist serial killers, the really dangerous nutters who live their entire lives in the realms of their own fictions, stay out of the arms of the law far longer than the motivated criminals who can still distinguish between their lies and their alibis. If your brain is busy trying to switch between your story and the facts, you're far more vulnerable to the old one-two: 'But, Mrs Peacock, I never said that it was a lead pipe that was used to bludgeon him in the conservatory. How could you possibly know? Unless . . .'

Brown wrote the name in his notebook, snapped it shut and smiled at Peter. 'Thank you for your assistance. I'll leave you to your own,' he took one more look around the room, taking in the trunks, the magic tricks, the cuffs, 'devices. You know she's made a career of getting gullible men to do what she wants and hand over money?'

'I'll bear that in mind.'

'She'll do the same to you, friend.'

'I doubt it,' Peter cocked his head at his room, 'I'm not exactly Bill Gates.'

'There's a reason she's on America's Most Wanted. You'd be even more of a total dumb ass than you look if you try to help her, or protect her. She'll just rip you off and rip your heart out. You deal with her, you're guaranteed to come out bottom.'

'Is that what happened to you?'

Brown looked thoughtful. He reached into his jacket and pulled out a card. It said 'FBI' in large, serious, serif-less letters. 'That's my cell number. If she turns up again, I suggest you call it. Save you a whole world of pain and heartache.'

Peter took the card and forced a grateful, nervous smile.

Brown crushed Peter's hand one more time and strode out of the moonlit door. Peter heard his foot upon the fire escape, the sound of shoe on iron, and how the silence surged softly backward when Brown's plunging hooves were gone. He waited for all the sounds to fade into the night, and then, almost without warning, his entire body began to convulse. It was uncontrollable, he gasped for air and then choked out each breath with a sob. He tried to pull himself upright but found himself folding and falling heavily to the floor. Struggling to sit leaning against the foot of the bed, he rocked his head and tried to stifle the scared little moan that had been so desperate to come out all the time Brown had been there.

27

'So you understand what we're asking?' one of them shouted.

'Aye,' Kenesis screamed into the wind, 'yes.'

The Great Kenesis, or Kenneth as his mother called him, didn't want to look up – he was terrified of what he would see – and yet felt a terrible compulsion to do just that. As he was currently suspended upside down off the edge of the Tyne Bridge, looking up involved staring into the dark, churning waters of the Tyne fifty feet below him. Driven by a gale-force wind, the rain pelted hard, lashing him horizontally and working the waves beneath into an angry frenzy. His dripping punkish-pink shock of hair pointed to the maelstrom below and Kenesis felt his lunch retreating back to where it came from.

'Do you see what I mean, Dick?' The smaller man who held Kenesis' left foot looked down at rainswept Newcastle. 'This bridge is the most recognizable symbol of this town, and why? Because it's the exit. You don't think every Geordie dreams of crossing it and getting out of this shithole? The one thing that everyone in this city agrees on is that they all want to get out of here. You see why this bridge is the town's greatest prospect?'

The larger of the Hasidim, whose wet grip was slipping along Kenesis' right ankle, looked at his partner. 'What are you now, Dick? Samuel Johnson? You think we should get on with the interrogation before we drop him? Do I look waterproof?' The two men looked back down at the Great Kenesis. He had already given them everything Titus had asked for; all the secrets behind the spectacular 'mind control' effect that the Geordie magician had devised and had used as the grand finale to his act for the last two months.

'Please, please. Ya divint have teh do this, I'll tell yas anything,' the twice Blackpool Young Mentalist of the Year award winner shouted up, his mouth instantly filling with rain.

'You think we don't know you'll tell us?' shouted Verstehung.

'Isn't it what you won't say that we're more interested in?' Wissenschaft called down. 'You going to try to take credit for the effect?'

'No. No. I promise.'

'If you say anything you think we won't be back?'

'I swear. It's his. He can do what he likes with it. I'll be wisht.'

'And just so we're clear.'

Kenesis felt his legs slithering from the men's grasp. He realized that his previous opinion, that certain effects were priceless, was a particularly daft way to think. Everything has a price when your own life can be included on the bill.

'All the business of the cross-eyes and the hemispheres disconnecting, that's all bullshit? All patter?'

'Aye, aye.'

'It's just another dual reality trick?'

'Er, aye.'

'*Oy vey*, that's a pity, Dick,' said Verstehung. 'He's not going to be too pleased with that.'

Wissenschaft grimaced. 'Isn't he always barking up the wrong lamp-post?'

'Please, just pull me up.'

'It's "tree",' said Verstehung, 'the expression is "barking up the wrong tree". Must you always get your expressions wrong, Dick?'

'My leg, you're letting it go. Pull me up.'

'I get them wrong because I don't see the point of them. Isn't there something about dogs and lamp-posts?'

'Please. Oh God, please.'

'No, Dick. I think the one you're thinking of is about "peeing into the wind". Or is it "on your own doorstep"?'

'But why use the expression at all? Instead of dogs barking and trees. Why not just say, "Titus goes looking for things in the wrong place"? Why does the clichéd metaphor get preferred?'

'Can you not get it into your head, Dick?' Verstehung tapped Wissenschaft's forehead with both his index fingers, which Wissenschaft quickly batted away. 'Are we not poorer if everything is just as it is said?'

'Poorer? No. Clearer.'

'Can we deny our imagination the chance to imprint the importance of things in our head by using the bigger, better images that the metaphor offers?'

'It's your head, Dick,' Wissenschaft countered, 'that needs examining. When it becomes a cliché, you think we still imagine a dog and a tree or a lamp-post or whatever? No. Do you not see that it loses all its colour and impact from overuse? It's not an image, it just becomes a dull substitute phrase. It doesn't even have the clarity of the straightforward, non-metaphoric phrase.'

Both men stood on the bridge gesticulating in the rain.

Above the sound of the rain and the wind and the passing of the 22.40 to Durham rattling across the neighbouring rail bridge, local boy the Great Kenesis performed his very last vanishing act, slipping silently into the turbulent waters.

'The metaphor is still . . .' Verstehung paused. 'You're not holding the guy, Dick?'

Wissenschaft looked at Verstehung's hands. 'Aren't you, Dick?'

The two men peered over the edge into the murky, swirling waters.

'You see,' said Wissenschaft, 'there's no bucket for him to kick.'

Verstehung sighed. 'No, Dick, but he does swim with the fishes.'

'He doesn't swim. He told us he couldn't swim and you think fishes would survive in that?'

'But you still can imagine it. Can't you see the image is clear, the body floating under water, the fishes curiously darting around it?'

'But that,' Wissenschaft began to shout, 'is because that's a gangster movie phrase and hasn't been demoted to the level of cliché yet. People kick buckets or push up daisies or pass over to the other side and you hear it being said but you don't see daisies or buckets, all you hear is the person saying someone's died but being too scared of death to use the actual word.'

Verstehung nodded. 'All right already. You don't think that's the exception that proves the rule?'

'No,' Wissenschaft shook his head, 'do you?'

Verstehung pulled his hat harder on to his head and turned his collar to the wind. 'You may be right. Come on, Dick, we better go tell Black.'

The two men strolled back over the bridge to find their Lexus on bricks and the wheels nicked.

Verstehung shook his head. 'It may be a cliché, Dick, and I'm sorry that the metaphor has lost its visual impact because I was right from the start. This really is a shithole.'

28

'You going to do that all night or are you going to help me out of here?'

Peter pulled himself up. It was Kate's voice but where was she?

'I'd get myself out only I think I zigged when I should have zagged.'

Peter rushed to the Zig Zag Woman and aligned the three boxes to let Kate out.

'Remember me?' Kate smiled and rubbed her waist. 'Wow. Those beautiful assistants were skinny little tarts in those days.'

'Fuck,' said Peter, rather overcome with everything, 'fuck. Fuck. You were here all that time. I thought . . . he had a gun. Who is he?'

Kate smirked. 'He's exactly who he said he was. He's the FBI. Well, the FBI agent who's been dogging me for what, twenty years? And, don't tell him, but this is the closest he's got for the last fifteen.' Kate sat heavily on the bed and lay down looking at the ceiling. 'Agent Brown. He's the bloody reason I can never risk trying to get back into the States again.'

'One bloke? A country with one of the longest borders in the world? How does that work?'

'He keeps me on Homeland Security's Most Wanted visual roster.' Kate made a square with her fingers, looking through it at the ceiling like a director framing her shot. 'On the screen of every border official are the top twenty photos of America's most *un*wanted fugitive outlanders and, you know, I've never been convicted of anything over there, but he keeps me up on it like it's some personal vendetta. So whatever passport I use, whatever disguise, the odds are stacked way too high against me.'

'What did you do?' Peter leaned round to look at Kate. 'I mean to make him so pissed off?'

Kate shrugged. 'I don't know. Just eluded him, I guess. Never gave him the satisfaction. Maybe I scammed a friend or relative of his. It's all so long ago.'

Peter looked silently at his desk littered with half-finished homemade magic gimmicks. 'But so what, Kate? Why would you want to go back? What's so great about America?'

'Oh, what isn't, Peter?' Kate sat up and Peter caught a glint of some ancient, still unbridled enthusiasm in her eye. 'In my business it—'

'Your business,' Peter interrupted, 'which is exactly?'

'You know, when Martin Luther King wanted to get America's attention he started his speech with four little words. I just peddle the same thing.'

'What's that? Emancipation, civil rights, non-violent resistance, racial harmony? Is that why they don't want you in their country?'

Kate ignored him. 'In my business America really is the land of milk and honey, land of the brave, home of the free lunch. Streets paved with gold; well, fools, but same difference. Life on the grift is just easy. Never was a nation so wealthy, so cocksure, so deficient in even the basics of cynicism and consequently so utterly, utterly gullible. It's like it's almost in their genes; lardy arses, linguistic lethargy, an overfondness for trite rhymes and saturated fats and zero, absolutely nil, nada, zip, jack, *niente* incredulity.'

Kate rolled off the bed as if her subject needed her to take the stand. 'Scepticism is so rare there they can't even spell it, it's so alien to their culture they even have a registered society to promote it. Scepticism!' Kate shook her head as if she could still hardly credit it. 'I've been around the world and everywhere it's almost second nature, something slipped into the breakfast cereal of every child alongside the crappy toy that's never as good as it looked on the box, but in America it actually needs to be taught! Disappointment seems to leave no trace. There's just a will there: to believe. You barely have to convince anybody of anything.'

Kate cupped her hands as if carrying one of her dreams. 'You're selling something, you start talking about how fantastic it is and, anywhere else in the entire world, the first thing people do, before they even know what you're saying, is ask themselves: why? Why are you saying it? "Is this true? What's the evidence? Can I trust you?" In America, they hear a statement and it's,' she spread her arms out wide and slipped into a broad nasal Midwestern accent, ' "Heck, yeah. Right on. OK. Ain't that the truth. I'm hearing ya." Their default is: if you say it, it must be true.'

Kate knelt down to get closer to Peter, clenched her fist and held it to her heart. 'They want to believe. They need to believe . . . that there's such a thing as big money for no work, or you can get the perfect wife, or you can be successful if you just vibrate the right way, or there are people who can really see the future, or read minds or have a direct line to God.' She stood again, her knees cracking slightly, spun round and sat back down on the bed. 'The idea you might actually be lying for profit barely computes.' Kate laughed. 'Well, after all, in a God-fearing country, if you're just guaranteeing yourself eternal damnation, why would you lie? Maybe that's how they think. I don't know. But that hokey, clichéd, folksy, pioneering spirit that they built their country on, the belief that anything's possible, it pervades everything.' Still smiling, Kate shook her head. 'My God, and aren't they proud of it. You call anyone on any other continent a "dreamer" and they know you're calling them a lazy good-for-nothing who'll never get anywhere. Say the same to an American and they see a visionary. So the same people who can touch the moon are the same credulous innocents who believe that the world was created in a hundred and forty-four hours. They are the dreamers.

'Only they could have created a vastly profitable industry out of stories and shadows on celluloid.' Kate closed one eye and mimed the operation of a hand-cranked camera which hasn't existed for almost a century but still represents the making of movies. 'They can't get enough dreams, which is lucky, because that's exactly what I'm selling. They can be racked with poverty and no health-care and cockroach-infested lives and never graduate from the school of hard knocks. They're like the romantic idiot who would rather have loved and lost than never have loved. My God, they are infected by the Romantic movement. The world moved on but not America. They are still there, the legacy of Wordsworth and Byron and the other backlashers to the Industrial Revolution who insisted on the supremacy of art and the imagination over science and fact.'

'Are you talking about that period like in the nineteenth century?'

'Maybe it started then, but who said it ever finished? Maybe future historians will look back at the nine-teenth, twentieth and twenty-first centuries and say that was the Romantic period. While there are still idiots who believe the stories above the facts, the illusion will persist. You take advantage of that wonder and so do I. It's home.'

'A dream home.'

Kate smiled and nodded. 'Brown'll be back, you know. As soon as the pawnshop opens in the morning. Maybe sooner. Could be any moment. We might have minutes, at best maybe hours. We're going to have to decamp, fast.'

'What?'

Kate had already gathered some bags and was frenetically stuffing them with food cans, the Titus material, jumpers and socks. 'Leave. Pack your bags. We'll drop your big stuff off at Lotus House. Dr Tavasligh's pretty amenable, I'm sure they'll look after this stuff while we go get Titus Black.'

Peter stood open-mouthed. 'You're crazy. We can't do that now. You've got to go. Yes. You've got some madman with a gun after you. It's you he's after. You've got to get far, far away from here.'

Kate stopped to wonder at Peter's naivety. 'Yeah? And what do you think they're going to do to you when they discover that not only have you been harbouring a criminal, you assisted her in a robbery? You're looking at prison time, matey, and I tell you what: prison ain't a great place for a nonce like you.'

'Nonce? I'm not a nonce, I told you.'

'Peter, I understand, but when you're inside and they get wind of your previous conviction and you're walking to your cell with an entire bunch of bruisers chanting, "Short Eyes, Short Eyes," at you, you can explain the mistake all you like.'

Peter's eyes grew wide. 'Shit.'

'Why do you think,' Kate pressed her point, 'they don't put more nonces like you away? It costs way too much to protect them. Community orders, relocating. Much cheaper.'

'What? What do I do?'

Kate took his hand. 'Peter, this is a godsend. You start

266

your life now. You stop running away, start running towards a goal. Who you want to be. What you want to get done. Now's your chance.'

Peter shook his head. It was all great fun imagining that they might swindle the odious Black but now, now there were real people, massive, strongarm people with real guns. Now it was officially way beyond the quiet, hidden life he'd made for himself. 'I can't, I can't. You need to go. I'll stick it out. If I have to go to prison I'll, I'll survive.'

'No you won't.' Kate was bagging the Titus DVDs. She shut the laptop and stuck it into a bag. 'You'll be dead within a week, or castrated. They like to do that. And you won't go to a special prison because the offence they're going to charge you with is category A boring straight robbery.'

'I'll say you forced me.'

Kate shrugged. 'Whatever. I hope you enjoy what's left of your life and thanks for the tip on Titus.' She looked at the box o'sins and suddenly her tough criminal façade melted and softened into a smile; she touched it and it seemed to cast a spell of serenity over her. For the first time since he met her, Peter saw a softer, more vulnerable side to Kate. It lasted for just a moment but he suddenly felt this overwhelming desire to hold her, as if she were a little girl. He moved towards her and just this slight gesture woke her from whichever of her marketable dreams she had been in. She tapped the box with more efficiency. 'Will you get that back to Da? Before they come for you?' She took one of the silk hankies from the box and smelled it. She closed her eyes.

'Kate, if you need . . .'

'Thanks,' she said abruptly, her eyes snapping open again. 'You know, you have a lot of potential. I'm sorry this is ending like this, I think we could have—'

'What is it? What did you really want from me?'

'Honestly?' Kate sighed. 'I was hoping you'd teach me. You know. Tricks. Magic. How you do all that stuff.'

'You grew up with a magician. You know how to do all this "stuff".'

'He always told me he would teach me, that when I grew up I could be his glamorous assistant like Mum was. But then . . . Then he, you know.'

Peter nodded.

'It's like there are a million secrets that used to make me cry in wonder and they're all locked up in there and I know you've helped him remember some things but it's such a very tiny part of . . . of what, of who he was.'

'You wanted me to teach you what your father didn't get round to?'

Kate looked at him hard. Evidently, in even the most strained of situations a massage for the ego pushes its way to the front of cognitive needs.

'You think I'm that good? As good as El Sid?'

'Yes. When you first told Henry his birthday. I knew. The way you did it. Like you were looking right into his head. You had an earnestness, it was just like Da.'

Peter grinned. 'Well, it's all in how you show it, the trick behind it is the smallest part, all I—'

The front door crashed open, hinges splintering in a giant crack. 'Two pizzas, one guy, how dumb do you think I am?' Three hundred pounds of American muscle

268

stormed into Peter's room wielding a gun which he pressed right between Kate's eyes.

'Miss Kate Minola, as I live and breathe,' said Agent Brown. 'It's been way too long.'

29

Agent Brown gripped Kate tightly by the arm as he marched her down the fire escape. He looked back at Peter. 'Thanks for the keys and cuffs, kid.' He leered at him as if to challenge him to do something about it.

With her hands chained in front of her, Kate twisted back to look at Peter. He was standing there like a lost puppy. Really, what was the point of men having balls if they never used them?

Just as they reached the bottom step, Peter found his voice. 'Wait, hold on,' he shouted, scampering down the fire escape. He grasped Kate's hands. 'I,' he muttered, 'wanted to say goodbye.' Then he did something extraordinary. He leaned forward and kissed Kate, passionately, pressing his mouth hard against hers. Kate was no less surprised than Brown by this passion but then she was a somewhat captive audience, it wasn't like she could slap him. As they kissed she felt him pass something small and metallic to her.

'OK, Houdini. Break it up. I know that story too.' Brown pushed them apart. 'Spit it out, Minola.'

'What?' Kate mumbled.

'Spit it out or swallow it. I know what he just did.

You got a key in your mouth. Houdini's *Daily Sketch* challenge. His wife did the same thing.'

'Swallow?'

'Or spit.'

Faced with the classic 'girlfriend's choice', Kate raised a defiant eyebrow and swallowed hard.

Brown shook his head. 'Jeez. Now open.'

Kate opened her mouth and in the half-darkness of the moon and orange phosphorescent streetlight he shoved a stubby index finger in and rolled it around. 'Shit, man, you did as well.' He whipped the gun around to Peter. 'That's the last of your funny stuff, Magic. Now get back up into your little room and disappear. If I see you again, asshole, I won't hesitate to kill you.'

With his hands raised, Peter retreated back up the fire escape. Kate had wondered why he hadn't passed the key in his mouth instead of just putting it in her hand, it would have been much more sensational – but then the scam, like the magic trick, was all about managing the expectations of your audience, and Peter had anticipated Brown perfectly. She had the key. Now all she had to do was unlock herself, get away from a very determined armed man, evade the British police force and skip the country.

Brown was on his mobile phone. 'Brightly? Yeah, sorry about that but I've got what I came for. Yes. At the magician's. Yes. Check her in. Yes, I know. How long you think you gonna be? OK. No. I'll meet you there. No. No, I'll wait outside. Twenty minutes. OK. No. Sure. See you then.' He flipped his phone closed and looked at Kate. 'Let's go.'

As she was hustled down Bargates, Kate was kept in front of Brown with the occasional shove. These buffets slowed her progress as she tried to track the key into the handcuffs' lock. With the key held by the very tips of her fingers she risked losing it at each nudge. It felt like she needed to dislocate her wrist just to get the key into the hole, and then how was she going to turn it? She didn't have the fingers of an escapologist or gynaecologist. She had Hobbesian fingers: nasty, brutish and short. She hated them. They were like chipolatas, dumpy, chubby, stubby things best for gnawing on or dipping in gravy. She gripped the key as tightly as she could and took another glance down to her wrists, a move which invited one more jolt between the shoulder blades from Brown.

'You ran and you ran, Kate, but you could never hide,' he taunted. 'I personally cannot wait until you're back Stateside and we can show you what real American justice is. They're going to throw away the key.'

'Really, Agent Brown, have you not had anything better to do in the last fifteen years?' Kate had realized she was thinking about the cuffs the wrong way round. Counter-intuitively she needed to push her wrists further into the cuffs even though every instinct was telling her to pull harder away. Stumpy though her fingers might be, she did have wrists to die for, thin and delicate. They had room to manoeuvre and she pushed her arm further in until the steel band was halfway up her forearm. By the time they had turned into Barracks Road she had the first cuff off. She locked it loose enough to pull her left hand out and set to work on the right hand.

As they approached the police station Brown began to slow. Kate realized that he couldn't take her in himself, he had no jurisdiction. It wasn't like she was wanted for a crime in England. He needed an English copper with his formal extradition request to get the process started. That must have been the bloke Brown had phoned, someone from the yard.

Though there's no attempt to make it look at all sweet, Christchurch police station does seem to be built like a cake. Three layers of corrugated concrete are separated by filling strips of glass, designed in a period of public architecture when, it seems, these were the only two materials permitted or perhaps available, somewhere around the mid-1950s. It does, however, retain a little of Christchurch's gentility, being set back from the road. A path running up to its doors skirts between grey concrete planters across a neatly kept lawn.

'OK, stop here.' Brown placed Kate in front of the closest lamp-post to the station and, keeping hold of her wrist, went round to the other side. With a rough jerk he pulled her hands either side of the lamp-post. This was where he intended to keep her until his English friend turned up. He was about to go to his pocket for the key when Kate slipped out of the cuffs, whipped them around her side of the lamp-post and quickly slapped first one and then the other on to Brown's thick wrists. In a moment captor became captive but in the same moment the quick reactions that were the result of years of Bureau training allowed Brown to snap his giant fingers around Kate's slender wrists. His enormous hands began crushing them until she buckled at the knees, wincing with the pain.

'Wrong place, wrong guy,' he snarled. 'Unlock me.'

Kate was in the middle of saying no but it turned into a loud 'Now.'

'OK,' Brown said, 'have it your way.' He started shouting at the top of his voice. 'Officer down. Help, emergency.'

Duty officer Sergeant Trenchant heard the shouting in loud American tones but assumed it was coming from the small TV on the duty desk that was disguised to look like a security monitor. He figured that the screaming heralded some further complication arising during the denouement of *CSI*. A woman's voice joined the man's, but she was shouting, 'Rape, attack, help.' Then all went quiet. Trenchant concentrated on the screen but not even Grissom seemed to have noticed the shouting. Had Trenchant shifted his line of sight just fifteen inches to the right he would have witnessed a far more exciting drama taking place on the front-door CCTV. But the story held him transfixed.

Brown roared at Kate, who was now on her knees, all feeling in her hands ebbing away with the pain throbbing in her wrists. 'What the fuck you think you're doing? They going to believe you? They come out here, they're going to take you and me together.'

'Maybe,' Kate panted, 'but first they'll make you let go of me.'

'Like fuck they will. I've waited too long to let something like this get in the way.'

'Maybe,' Kate continued, almost whimpering with the agony, 'when I . . . point out . . . the gun in your jacket . . . they may . . . have a moment of clarity . . . about just who's the victim here.'

273

'I'm not giving you up, Minola, not in a blue moon, not if I have to kill you here myself.'

The pressure on her wrists increased and she cried out, 'Please stop.' Through the tears that were bubbling up in her eyes, Kate saw a flash of something charging down the road towards them and realized that she had only moments.

Brown's blood was boiling. 'Minola, they'll have to prise you from my goddamn dead hands before I let you g—'

There is a frightening sound when metal and bone meet with just a thin layer of flesh sandwiched in between. It's not a clang but then neither is it a thud. A loud bass crack is perhaps the best way to describe the noise a skull makes when it connects with a frying pan travelling at full pelt.

Brown crumpled to the floor, taking Kate with him. She twisted her body to try to break her fall with her arm and looked up to see Peter.

30

'Remember me?'

'A frying pan, for God's sake? You haven't a bloody clue, have you.'

Peter looked at the pan smeared with red and waved it at her. 'Apart from this one of course.' He then looked down at the unconscious Brown, the side of his head bubbling blood through his matted hair. 'Oh fuckity fuck. Is he? Is he dead?'

As if in answer, Brown began to groan.

'Help me, you idiot,' Kate barked.

Peter bent down and prised the stony grip of the semi-conscious federal agent apart. Kate stood up unsteadily, massaging her wrists.

Peter couldn't take his eyes off Brown. 'Do you think he's going to be all right?'

'Him? What about me? You took your fucking time.'

Peter carefully checked Kate's expression. 'You didn't think I would come, did you.'

'We've got to get out of here. He's got some mate due to arrive in the next couple of minutes.'

'Look, I've never done anything like—'

'No time. Did you bring the backpacks?'

'No. I just grabbed the pan and—'

'Fastest way back to your place?'

Peter pointed to the lane that led up to the police station car park. 'Through there. You can get through round the back, past the magistrates' court. You guys went the long—'

Kate started sprinting. 'Thanks.'

Peter watched her go for a moment and then realized that if anybody wanted to keep up with anyone as fast as Kate they would have to learn to run. And quick. He ran.

Even as they burst through the door of his room, they could hear the first distant siren. Kate jumped to the backpacks that she had been filling before.

'They'll be here in a couple of minutes.' She hoisted her bag on her back. 'Well done, you're officially a fugitive, now where do you keep your tinfoil?'

'Are those two things related?'

275

'Oh, you better believe it.'

Peter pointed to the kitchen utensil drawer and Kate lunged for it. She pulled out the roll of tinfoil and plunged it into the other backpack. She slung the bag at Peter. 'Stick your fucking bag on and let's go, Short Eyes.'

Peter pulled the bag on to his back. 'I told you not to call me that!'

'Oh yeah . . . that'll work,' she called back, disappearing out of the door. Peter hesitated. This was it. He looked around the cocoon that he'd built over all these years, the drawers full of tricks, the three-foot shelf of magic books, the vintage magic memorabilia, the OR, everything that he had always thought had significance, but now that he looked at them with the sound of Kate's feet clicking down the fire escape, they seemed to mean nothing. He looked at the glinting collection of handcuffs that testified to his years of practice and realized that it was now or never, it was either all within him, in his memory, or not. He couldn't keep practising at life. He had to trust that it would be there when he needed it. It was muscle memory, practical memory, and it was meaningless, unemotional, repetitive rote-learned memory. Now. Now was the time to give everything he'd learned meaning, context, life. He knew he had to follow his heart or, more specifically, the woman who had just yelled from the bottom of the steps, and leave all this behind. He could do it. He knew he could. But he also felt that sickening pre-show panic: what if he was caught short without a trick? His trousers and jacket were stuffed with apparatus to astound and amaze but even as the

276

police siren was howling closer he dithered; he had to find something, some security, something he could always use to astonish anyone with. To be the man he wanted to be seen as. It was his credentials, his identity, his memory, the years of practice. Then he spotted them on his desk and, like Sid, found himself reaching for his 'bikes'.

'Now, you stupid bugger,' Kate screamed. Peter could see the flashing light through the front window that faced on to Bargates. It would take less than a minute for the squad car to negotiate a route into the alleys and find the back parking space. Peter slammed the door and skittered down the steps. 'Where now?' he shouted to Kate.

'Somewhere dark.'

Together they ran to the opposite side of the parking space and just as the squad car screeched in they pushed through a hole in the fence. Policemen piled out of the passenger doors before the car had even stopped. They ran up the fire escape and started hammering on the door.

Peter took the lead; they ran down the narrow, silent streets and back alleys until they got to the meadows that mark the flood plain of the meandering Avon. Under a willow tree they stopped to catch their breath.

'Where do we go from here?' Peter panted, leaning forward, his hands on his knees.

'This isn't my town,' Kate gasped back. 'What's the quickest way out?'

'From here? The station.' Peter pointed.

'OK, so they're going to cover that first. Next?'

'If we had a car . . .'

'Right, we nick a car, where would we go?'

277

'Out there.' Peter pointed to a string of lights that marked the bypass cutting through the darkness of the swampy meadowland they were standing in.

'OK, so considering you've nearly killed a bloke and you're with me, we'll have to presume that they'll go to the effort of setting up roadblocks. Which would be the best way to get out of here on foot?'

Peter pointed north. They could see the railway track and where the river passed under it. 'Once we were under the bridge we could probably make our way anywhere.'

'Right, then we can assume that that is where the police will start coming from. What's that way?' She pointed south.

'The marshes, the harbour, the sea.'

'And that would be the most stupid place to go, right?'

'We would be pincered, trapped between the marshes and the harbour. You need a boat to—'

'Let's go.' Kate grabbed Peter's hand and they started lolloping in that direction.

They picked their way through the inky darkness along the sticky, muddy path, frequently stopping to listen; to check their proximity to the invisible rippling river waters. Every now and then they would glimpse the moonlight dancing off the foaming rapids and have to alter their course but always keeping ahead of them the bright strip of light that was the bypass. In eerie quiet it bisected the dark meadows like a golden saw-blade, its sequence of orange streetlights casting a row of teeth along the serrated causeway. As they drew to within a few hundred yards, the orange began to throb purple as the blue flashing lights of three squad cars raced silently to the far end of the causeway, their tyres crackling along the tarmac. Now that the streetlights were closer, they could see the river running deep and fast beside them.

Peter crouched down and scrambled up the small bank to the road, close to where it bridged the river. It was empty, well lit and he could clearly see the three police cars at the end by the roundabout. Their lights were still flashing and they had parked across the width of the dual carriageway, all ready to stop and check any who came their way. He knew, from his numerous solitary walks, that if he and Kate carried on under the bypass they would end up circling back before they found anywhere shallow enough to wade across.

Kate came up behind him.

'If we continue on this side of the river it's a dead end,' Peter said. 'We'd be forced back into town by the ducking stool.'

'Ducking stool!' Kate was aghast. 'They've got a ducking stool? Like for witches? No wonder they're looking for you, Magic Malcolm. How good are you at holding your breath?'

'Actually it was put there for nags and scolds,' Peter eyed Kate, 'to cool them off.'

'I knew this was a backward bit of the country but . . .'

'Listen, we've got to cross the bridge to get over the river.' Peter pointed diagonally over the road and then at the police cars. 'We'll be crossing their direct line of sight.'

'So what we need is some sort of distraction.' Kate

rummaged in her bag. 'Maybe I can use this flare gun to make them look elsewhere.'

'You've got a flare gun?'

Kate came up empty-handed. 'No, of course I don't have a sodding flare gun. It was irony, not the movies.'

'I wouldn't put anything past you.'

'Why would you want to put something past me?' She started down the bank again. 'Come on, we'll get under the bridge on this side of the river, at least it will save us having to cross the road.'

With clearance of just a couple of feet they crawled on their hands and knees. Their backpacks scraping the black underbelly of the bridge, they were just able to get under the low span without falling in the water. Now, looking at the road bridge from the other side, Kate studied the railings before grabbing hold of one of the lowest horizontal crossbars and swinging herself out over the river. 'Still with me?' she gasped. She shuffled herself hand over hand along the bar, her feet dangling above the heaving current.

Peter wasn't sure. He was sure that he was at the trough of his physical fitness. The last time he was challenged to do the monkey bars he'd argued that it was counter-evolutionary and against the basic tenets of Darwinism. He got the feeling that none of the other kids in reception really understood or, for that matter, liked him.

Kate was almost across. Peter gripped the same bar and leaned as far as he could over the river before swinging his feet off. He was heavier than he imagined and his leading hand slipped. He desperately tried to pull himself up with his left, grasping for the bar with his right. Contact. With long pauses he grunted and groaned his way along the rail, listening to the rumbling water beneath him. At last he was close enough to swing and get a foot purchase on the opposite bank. Kate grabbed him and helped him find his balance again.

'All those hours down the gym pay off, hey?' she winked.

He looked at his poor swollen hands and wondered if he would ever be able to back-palm a card again.

Kate was already trekking along the bank. 'Come on,' she hissed, 'no time to hang about.'

31

'Cup of tea?'

'You're kidding me?'

'You're in shock,' said Sergeant Trenchant, dipping into his first aid kit.

Brown scowled. 'I thought tea twenty-four seven was just a Limey myth like London fog, bowler hats and paralysis during sex.'

'Well, I don't know about the fog and the hats, but the tea bit's true.'

Brown sat at the table in the staff room as various officers strode in and out with their radios screeching updates. He peeled away the sticky cloth he'd been holding to the side of his head. It was darker red now, the blood congealing. Brightly watched him.

'Did she do that then?' Brightly pointed to his head and Brown shook it.

'Magic Malcolm. Peter Ruchio.'

'Blimey. Did you see him?'

'If I'd seen him coming I would have done something about it before I ended up like this.'

'It'll be on the CCTV anyway. I've posted an All Points Warning for the two of them and the ambulance is on its way.'

'I don't need a goddamn ambulance. I need to get Minola back before she disappears again.'

Sergeant Trenchant tried to pacify him. 'We're going to catch them, there really is no way out of here. We've called in units from Bournemouth. We've got one at the station. We've got six cars patrolling and a dog team's on the way, they're going to comb down through the meadows. We've got the coastguard on standby, set up roadblocks on all the roads out of here. There's a limited number of ways in and out of this town. It was made for sieges. They're trapped.'

Brown stood up, winced and quickly sat down again.

'You've twisted your ankle, or broken it. You need to just sit tight.'

'Show me a map of this place.'

Brightly moved forward. 'Listen, you're injured. We've got this covered, they'll be back in custody before—'

Brown brought his fist down on the table, making the cups of cold tea jump. 'Show me the map. Now,' he bellowed.

32

Peter caught up with Kate. The meadow grass was shorter, more firm, this side of the river and with the light from the bypass behind them, they could see the shapes of horses night-grazing. They could also now see the houses on Christchurch's ancient Bridge Street ahead of them.

'We going through there?' Kate nodded forward without breaking pace.

'Yes, once we've crossed Bridge Street there's a lot of cover, we can sneak past the gasworks and the baths then we're out on to the marshes and then . . . then we'll be utterly trapped. Isn't this where you tell me you have a cunning plan?'

'I have a cunning plan.'

'Which is?'

'. . . not quite made up yet. At the moment I'm still trying to concentrate on outguessing Plod. You know, Magic, you can be a bit trying.'

Peter stopped as Kate kept marching. 'Oh, oh, excuse me. Doesn't the fact that I came and found you and saved you from a homicidal maniac who makes Mr T. look like Mr Tea Cosy, doesn't that warrant a little bit of respect?'

Kate's shoulders sank and she turned back to him. 'I'm sorry, Peter, of course I respect anybody who makes a courageous choice.'

'Yeah?' Peter instantly smiled. 'Well, it was nothing; I couldn't exactly leave you at his mercy.'

'I know. Which is why you haven't earned my respect.'

'What? Come on . . . it's not as if I had to whack that guy, risk my life.'

'You think that was a courageous choice?'

'Yes.'

'Look at it this way.' Kate sauntered back to him until she was barely a skin's thickness away, then spoke slowly, lowly, deeply. 'Almost all the choices you will ever make, especially the split-second ones, are not really choices at all.' She looked up with her large hypnotic eyes, the bypass lights glinting gold in them as they widened. 'They're just inevitable actions, Peter, impelled by a combination of just three things. The weight of circumstance, the universal human imperative to believe that you're doing the right thing and,' her mouth glistened for a moment as she put it so close to his it was like she was stealing his breath, 'desire,' she whispered. She held him there, just with her eyes, for an infinite second and then fell away.

Peter was deafened by his heart pounding as suddenly he could breathe again. She was right, he had had no choice; she knew exactly how he felt and exactly what he would do for her. He felt played and yet felt there was nothing better than being her plaything. In magic it's called 'audience management', in life it's called 'a many-splendored thing', but in the world of the scam, it's just 'the game'.

284

Kate was heading off again. 'You actually get to make a courageous decision, Peter, then you'll earn my respect.' And under her breath she murmured, 'Then you can find out just how worthless that is.' Kate had always observed a strict fiscal apartheid: there were the marks; and then there was everybody else, generally poorer, smarter or more principled, all of whom she tended to ignore. She had always reserved her charm plays for the fools who needed to be parted from their money, and yet there she was padlocking the Reluctant Escapologist into something more confining than his handcuffs or his legacy of nightmares. And if all it takes to captivate someone is a few tricks, are you ever going to respect them? Was that what she was looking for? Someone she could respect? Someone who could outsmart her, get there before her, put her in her place? God, that was a depressing thought. Can you only respect the people you're willing to surrender to?

Peter trudged behind Kate in silence, partly to recover from the pounding in his ears and from the one that his ego had just received. He felt like he'd metamorphosed into a puppy yapping at his mistress's ankles with his tongue hanging out. At once both powerless and strangely empowered, invigorated by being chosen to be in her company, all at the same time.

Peter caught up with Kate only when they got to the back garden walls of the Bridge Street houses. The last obstacle before the open marshes. A path led along the backs and then through an arch. Peter put his finger to his lips. Kate raised her eyes. 'What is this? Black oops . . .' Kate suddenly darted into a shadow, pushing Peter back as she watched the street.

An unmarked police car was pulling up on the apex of the bridge. Of course the whole point of an unmarked police car is that you're not supposed to be able to spot it, but its unmarkedness completely defeats its purpose by making it the only type of car that lacks a dealer back-window sticker, or any other decal, making it easier to spot than Wally in *Wally Alone in the World of White Walls*.

A plain-clothes policewoman with brown hair tightly wound in a bun got out of the driver's side. Kate and Peter watched silently as the passenger door opened and Agent Brown eased himself out of his seat.

'If this woman is so smart, why would she walk into the lion's jaws?' Brightly said.

'Because,' Brown grunted, 'it's the last thing we would suspect. That's how she keeps out of our grasp.'

Kate raised an eyebrow. OK, so there was a guy who was one step ahead of her, and outsmarted her, but surrender? You've got to be kidding.

Brown leaned against the bonnet. 'I'll keep a lookout here. You check the other side of the bridge.'

'You'll give me a shout if you see anything?'

'Sure.' Brown smiled easily.

'So you won't be using this.' Brightly pulled the gun out of Brown's jacket. 'Found it when you were still on the floor. This is England. We catch our villains with our wits and we expect our visitors to do the same.' She emptied the clip into her hand and gave him back the gun.

Brown looked at her like she had just laughed at his penis.

'I'll go keep an eye on the towpath by the mill, it's the

only other way through to here from the meadows.' Brightly strode off over the bridge and disappeared near the castle mound.

Brown waited until he could no longer see her, then undid his belt where he had hidden his second clip.

'Shit,' said Kate, 'now.' She ran as fast as she could straight at Brown and knocked the new clip and gun out of his hands. He launched himself forward at her, forgetting his injured leg, and immediately fell to the ground clutching his ankle. Kate stopped as he scrabbled and winced. 'Now now, no guns here, didn't you hear your friend?' She gestured for Peter to follow her.

Brown pulled himself back to the car and leaned against a wheel. 'You a double act now, Minola?' he grunted. 'Not like you to trust anyone else.' He spotted Peter coming timidly out from the archway. 'Ah, there's the chef. You coming back to griddle the other side of my head? You got yourself a saucepan or something?'

Peter, being English, immediately fell to abject apology. 'I'm really sorry, I really hope you're not too hurt. I'm so sorry, it was the only thing I could think of doing, I just really . . .'

Brown pointed his thumb at Peter. 'This guy for real?'

Kate smiled. 'I think so. Aren't you going to call your friend?'

'Brightly? Sure. You heading down to the marshes?'

'I guess you'll be finding out.'

'Listen. I'll do you a deal.' Brown looked up at her. 'You give yourself up to me now. I tell the judge to go easy on your time, ten years max.'

'Oh, Agent Brown. You certainly know how to tempt a girl, don't you.'

'You've had your run, Minola, you've had a good time, you've spent a lot of other people's hard-earned dough. Now c'mon, do the right thing. Do the time. You take the deal now, you'll still be a looker by the time you're out.'

'It's the same as it's always been, Agent Brown. You want me, you come find me.'

'You know if you run right now, they're going to throw away the key.' He pointed at Peter. 'And lord knows what will happen to the paedo.'

'I'm not a bloody paedo.'

'I seen your file, man. Boy, they love your sort in jail.'

Peter looked at Kate imploringly.

Kate went over to the gun and kicked it skittering down the road. 'OK, *señor*,' suddenly there was the voice of Lola de Sanchez, '*hasta la vista*.' She pulled at Peter's sleeve and they ran.

They were past the gasworks and the swimming pool, past the marina and were just being swallowed by the Stygian darkness of the marshes when they heard the dogs barking.

33

Kate stumbled over one of the springy hummocks that dotted the Stanpit marshland and Peter caught her arm. She could feel his hand trembling.

'Dogs,' he said. 'This is hopeless, we can't hide from them. Can we give this up now? We'll be at the furthest point of the promontory in a couple of minutes. The shore of the marshes. Then we're as far south as we can go.'

'What? Is there like a wall in the way?'

'No. Just a lot of water.'

'And you can't swim?'

'That's the plan? We just swim away? Kate, it's a very, very big bit of water, I've got the laptop in my backpack and I believe the police have got boats.'

Kate laughed and the baying dogs grew louder.

Suddenly they found themselves splashing in the reeds, feet pulled into the slurping mud. The moonlight that had been so useless at showing them anything on dry land now glittered on the water ahead of them, and to the left, to the right and behind them a congealment of bloodhounds strained at their leads. Peter could see the distant lights of Mudeford and Christchurch coruscating over the dark water and the lines of moored dinghies that spent their weekdays rotating with the tides, anchored midstream in the current. This was it, this was where they would swim or the dogs would sink their teeth into them.

Kate turned to Peter. 'Right. Take this.' She pulled her top off and Peter's mouth fell open. The emotional impact of what his visual senses were taking in caused his synapses to flood, their signals to block out the dogs, the chase, the gunman, the trap, as they focused on trying to store every glorious part of that single moment and how the moonlight lit Kate's body in a pale shadowless glow. She handed him her shirt, pulled her jeans off and passed them to him too and then waded into the water, her white ankles and then her legs and waist seeming to quiver and fall apart. 'Should be back before the dogs find you,' she whispered to him before disappearing beneath the dark and glittering waters. For a second Peter wondered whether she had been there at all, whether this was all imagined. His reality anchors, the places or things of habit, were far away and his grip on the difference between what was real and fantasy was far less solid.

The dogs' barking became suddenly louder and disturbed his solipsism, bringing the danger he was in right back to the forefront of his cranial activity.

Even if all the empirical evidence shows that time on earth barely fluctuates, in the brain, where eight hours' sleep can seem no more than a minute, it's like a yoyo on the trembling finger of a cold-turkeying coke addict. Perception may not be everything but it's everything you know and in it time, like in-flight movies, can simultaneously fly and seem to go on for ever. The next ten were the longest minutes of Peter's life. By the time he saw the beams of the approaching torches swinging about and could hear the policemen shouting to each other, he had developed cramp in his knees from years of crouching on his haunches, his buttocks dipping in the cold water.

Where was Kate? Had she just left him there? Had she just used him to find the best way out of town and now buggered off? Why was it so hard for him to have any faith in her? Could it have anything to do with the fact that she was a scam artist, someone who lived by gaining people's trust and confidence and then ripping them off like so much clothing in a Swedish porn movie? Never letting anything touch her, or anyone get close. But then, Peter thought, that was probably not a bad summation of his own life. And would he come back for her, listening to the hounds and the shouting and the thudding of boots? He wasn't sure. As he clutched her clothes in one hand and pushed the reeds apart with the other, he reasoned that standing up and surrendering might just be the smartest thing to do. If the dogs found him down there they'd rip his throat out before he had a chance to give himself up.

Stand up. That was the only thing. Stand up. Put your hands up. Apologize. Say you were led astray. Stand or die.

Peter tried to stand but the cramp had set in and he groaned with the pain, immediately squatting down again. He started bouncing on his haunches to try to get the blood circulating. Twenty bounces and he'd try to stand again. The pain shot through his thighs and calves. He couldn't stand and the dogs were metres away, so close he could hear them sniffing between their growls and their barking. Stand, you fool, stand before their teeth are in you. Stand here.

'Here.' He heard a hiss. 'Wade out, keep low.' Peter turned back to the waters; it was her voice, like a siren, a harpy, a silkie calling him to the deep. 'Keep your head down and wade out. You'll see me.'

Peter began rocking from side to side, lifting his feet and swinging his shoulders, angling forward like the wobble walk a child gives a toy figurine that lacks the movement of limbs. As he got deeper into the cold water, his legs began to unfreeze. As the water got deeper, he felt himself able to rise and hold the bags and clothes above his head.

Peter followed her voice, his feet sticking in the slimy mud, the shifting floor of the bay slowing his move- ment. As the water reached his shoulders he broke through the reeds to find the clear moonlit waters glittering around the dark shape of a small dinghy, barely a few feet away. Keeping his packages high he lunged forward with them, and his feet left the bottom as his empty hands swung down into a swim. Kate grabbed the bags before they hit the water and placed them carefully on the floor of the boat. She turned back and reached for him.

Behind him Peter could hear the dogs splashing in shallower water. Even as Kate took hold of his belt and helped him flip over the side, he could hear the voices clearly. 'It's a dead end here.' 'Sure the hounds got the right scent?' 'What's that out there?' Peter lay on the deck holding his breath as Kate noiselessly paddled out and away from the marshes. 'Goddamnit, no wonder you hicks lost the War of Independence . . .'

Slowly the voices, the yapping, the barking and recrim- inations faded and only the lapping of the water and the sound of Kate's dipping paddle could be heard. Peter sat up and peered over the edge. They were in the middle of the vast lagoon that makes Christchurch harbour. They floated past some of the other dinghies that bobbed and swayed patiently in wait for their weekend captains.

'Ahoy,' Kate smiled, 'now just who was it who thought who wouldn't come?'

Peter smiled back and nodded. 'OK.'

'These are nice boats, I can't believe people just leave

them out here and no one nicks them. Just because they might get a little wet in the process.'

Peter looked at Kate. She had found a fisherman's boiler suit and she sat in the stern, paddling. Her wet hair was tangled and curling around her moon-pale face. Peter found his breathing becoming easier and more even as he drank in the scene, her, the world, the bright star on the western horizon.

The star was intensely bright and constant and rising over Bournemouth.

Kate followed his line of sight and looked out towards the star, which was fast becoming bigger and more blinding. Kate stood up and Peter rose in his heavy, wet clothes.

'It's a helicopter,' Peter said, stating the plainly obvious.

'Yup. And I'd say we have less than sixty seconds.'

34

'Alpha One, this is Echo Golf Zero, fifty seconds to visual, do you copy?'

'Copy that, Echo Golf Zero, looking for suspects on boat within harbour. Sweep requested. Over.'

'Roger that, Alpha One, sweeping from north-west above Tuckton Bridge. The TIC will pick them up, no trouble. Over.'

'That's the thermal imaging camera,' Brightly said helpfully.

'I know what a TIC is,' Brown snapped back as he watched the approaching lights of the helicopter.

Brightly held the crackling radio to her lips. 'Wilco, Echo Golf Zero, we're on stand-by, over and out.' She turned back to Brown as he limped along the jetty. 'There are over a hundred dinghies and small boats moored in this estuary. Most of them are lined up along the deep-water channels; it won't take air too long to spot bodies on board one of them.' Brightly nodded to the skipper as they boarded the police boat. 'We'll pick them up when air give us the location.'

As the motor launch grumbled slowly out into the harbour, Brightly and Brown sat at the back, above the engine's churning waters, with a path of white foam fizzing in the moonlight behind them. They watched the blinking lights of the helicopter swing round above Tuckton Bridge and start hovering as it primed the cameras. Then, slowly, it began to move forward above the chinking masts disturbed by the sudden wind from the blades. It cruised carefully, putting every yacht, dinghy, rowboat and motorboat under thermal scrutiny.

Brightly looked at Brown quizzically. 'You say you saw her. Definitely. A positive ID?'

'I spoke to her, for Chrissakes. If you'd left me my bullet clip, you'd be looking at her right now.'

'Dead or alive?'

'Does that matter?'

'Yes, it matters. She's only wanted for extradition, Brown. You kill her, it's murder.'

'Look at this.' He pointed to his head. 'I'd call it self-defence.'

'Or revenge. Just consider yourself warned, Brown. Know the law here. Obey the law here.'

Brown nodded and turned back to observe the police helicopter now whirring loudly over the darkening area that marked the beginning of the marshlands.

'What I don't understand,' continued Brightly, 'is why, if you had time to have a chat with her, you didn't shout for me?'

'I did.'

'Agent Brown, I was only a few seconds away. I came as soon as you shouted, I didn't see anything.'

Brown shrugged. 'She's a fast runner.' He chose not to explain how he had to crawl over to retrieve his gun and spare clip before he shouted.

'And Ruchio was definitely with her?'

'Yeah. What can I say?'

'Well,' said Brightly, starting to sound a little tetchy, 'if you look at it from my perspective, I'm here to escort you, trying to find someone who only you seem to know is even in our country. This is someone for whom the only evidence I have is a couple of spurious witness statements. But despite that, it's someone you claim to have seen repeatedly tonight, someone who seems to get past roadblocks and patrols and dog teams like a ghost; dog teams who appear to have done nothing more than take their dogs for a jolly good walk tonight. All this, the helicopter, the launch, the sniffer team, the squad cars, the overtime, this is all on your word. Nobody else has seen a thing and, well, I'm starting to wonder, in fact I've been wondering since you got here and insisted on interviewing a bloke who had evidently left his marbles with Lord Elgin, I've been wondering. Well.

Can you see, as you chaps say, where I'm coming from?'

'Sure,' Brown looked back at her, 'you're calling me a lying motherfucker. I see where you're coming from. So how do you account for being handcuffed to the lamp-post and,' he pointed to his ear, 'the head injury?'

'Are you sure the lamp-post incident came before the head injury?'

'Oh right, uh-huh uh-huh, that's like funny because you're referring to the fact I might be mentally defective and I like made this whole thing up.'

'Well?'

'Listen,' Brown poked one of his fat fingers at Brightly, 'you'll be eating every single one of those words when we pick her up. She's in one of those boats, I know it. I know her.'

'I was just wondering, Agent Brown. If the British police were chasing a criminal in the States, do you think you would put so much time, manpower and equipment at our disposal?'

'No. No. And I'll tell you why, Brightly. We would have already caught the guy.'

'You never caught Kate Minola.'

The name echoed in the night as Brown looked down into the tumbling water and the launch slowly drifted in the direction of the helicopter, the Mudeford flats and the open sea.

It was another ten minutes before the radio crackled to life again.

'Alpha One, this is Echo Golf Zero, do you copy?'

Brightly grabbed the radio. 'Echo Golf Zero, this is Alpha One, have you got contact? Over.'

'Alpha One, that's a negative. We've scanned every

296

boat in this harbour, there's nothing coming up on the TIC. We sure the suspects are here? Over.'

Brightly gave Brown a somewhat smug look.

'You know what I would do,' Brown said, 'if I was expecting a helicopter with a thermal camera to come looking for me? I would lie down in the bottom of the boat and cover myself with something that blocks infrared radiation.'

'Alpha One, this is Echo Golf Zero,' the radio spat, 'awaiting further instructions. Over.'

'Like what?' Brightly asked Brown.

'I don't know. Something like a metal plate or tinfoil.'

Brightly looked thoughtfully at the helicopter hovering downstream. If she continued this search any longer than necessary and came up with nothing, she would be hung, drawn and quartered by her division head. On the other hand, if they captured two felons in this co-ordinated high-tech operation she would be another couple of cap feathers closer to the DCI job she was gunning for. That is, if the perps even existed. But then, if they didn't, maybe the evening still wouldn't be a total waste, she could at least bring in the nutter in the boat who was carrying an unsanctioned weapon, and had purposefully wasted police time and resources. International incident or not, she wouldn't leave empty-handed. She clicked the call button on the radio.

'Echo Golf Zero, this is Alpha One. Come in. Over.'

'Alpha One, this is Echo Golf Zero, we copy. We going home? Over.'

'That's a negative, Echo Golf Zero. Want you to do another sweep. This time visual. Turn off the TIC, use your spot. We're looking for anything glinting, metal or silver that could be shielding suspects. Do you copy? Over.'

'Alpha One, we copy that. Over and out.'

Brightly and Brown watched the helicopter switch its blindingly bright vertical spotlight on and sweep back down the rows of boats.

After a couple of minutes the helicopter seemed to stop and hover, its light wavering over a small dinghy.

Even before the radio had started chattering again, the captain had eased the launch forward and the engines were thrusting it towards the spotlit dinghy.

'Alpha One, this is Echo Golf Zero. We've got a dinghy here with strips of, what looks like tinfoil, covering some body shapes. Over.'

'We're on our way, Echo Golf Zero. Over and out.' Brightly put down the radio and felt the sea air blow through her hair again.

It took the police boat less than a minute to arrive at the dinghy. Brown and Brightly stood at the edge as they came alongside. Brown was smiling from ear to sneer. 'So they don't exist, Brightly? Huh?'

There, indeed, were the unsubtle shapes of two people lying as still as possible under a number of strips of tinfoil, hoping beyond hope that the voices above were not referring to them.

'Now that's a nice try, Minola.' Brown chuckled. 'You can do the honours, Brightly.'

Brightly took hold of the side of the dinghy and leapt aboard. She immediately grabbed the edge of one of the tinfoil strips and pulled it back. She revealed a number of fishing tackle bags, four gathered fishing nets, two lobster pots and a series of curled ropes. She looked back up at Brown. He was glaring at the pile, his lips mouthing an unutterable 'no'.

'Agent Brown?' Brightly said sternly. 'I think we need to talk.'

♣

'The chopper's gone.'

'Yes.'

'I'm freezing.'

'Be grateful, that's exactly what's saved you.'

Peter couldn't see Kate, who was swimming on the other side of the yacht's bow, but he could feel her warm hand next to his, holding on to the keel. Under instructions from Kate he had pushed his head under the cold water every time the helicopter hovered over them. It had successfully masked their heat beneath the water and the body of the boat. For the last half-hour they had been slowly swimming, guiding the bobbing yacht that they had quickly exchanged for the first little dinghy towards the sea. It really was very cold and Peter wondered if his feet were even still attached to his legs.

'You think they found your tinfoil?'

Kate hummed. 'I don't know. I hope so.'

'You really did have a plan then. All that time.'

'No. No. Not completely. Just prepared.'

'Can we get in the boat yet?'

Kate ignored him. 'What are those things sticking up straight ahead of us? They look like teeth.'

Peter squinted into the night. Moonlight picked out the jumble of rooftops of the Hengistbury Head beach huts. They stretched across the sands of the spit, the breakwater that prevented the south-eastern sea waters from crashing straight into the harbour.

'Beach huts,' Peter said.

'Beach huts?' Kate repeated. 'That's nice. I could do with a holiday.'

20,000 Milliseconds to Higham
(TEA *minus 11 months 19 days 8 hours*)

Kate

Straight, I promised to go straight. Promised him, promised myself.

But a million quid? Just jumping around in the suitcase up there?

C'mon. Let's face it. Bread before cred. It's the cash first, then the going straight. It's got to be. I mean I've worked this right from the start. What the hell has old Magic done to deserve half of it? It was my game, my play, he was just along for the ride. Give it all up now? What the hell am I thinking? I really must be getting a bit weak in the head. The money's always the endgame.

So, maybe he'll be upset, cry for a bit. Poor loyal sucker. That's the price of being a mark. It's an expensive lesson but he'll have learned something. Every mark does.

Anyway this is the last one, a million quid and that's it. Got the rest of my life to go straight.

But then, haven't I said that before? Aren't they always the last one? Until the next. No. This was different. It feels different. It was different because . . . well, shit, because of Peter, I suppose.

I mean he's not really a mark is he? It's not like he's being turned over by his own greed. What's going on? I've always walked away with no compunction. Maybe I've been kidding myself but I've always felt I

301

was at least teaching a moral lesson about avarice or pride or whatever. But what's Peter going to learn? Don't be a schmuck? Don't trust? Don't fall in love . . .

Hey, if I need people I can buy them. It's a million bloody quid. What makes him so special? There's a billion sweet loyal innocent idiots like him in the world, but . . . a million quid!

Do the maths.

The train's starting to slow. I just stand up, take the case, open the door and I'm home free, girl. Biggest, easiest single haul in my life. Thanks, Magic.

35

'OK, so what's the line again?' Titus squeezed his worry ball and looked at Ronnie. 'How does "the Great" Kenesis work it?'

'The late Great Kenesis,' Verstehung whispered under his breath to his colleague.

Ronnie brushed off his thighs, stood up and crossed over to Wissenschaft and Verstehung who had both, in an act of perfect synchronization, removed their hats to reveal pale beige yarmulkes beneath. Ronnie put his finger on Wissenschaft's forehead. 'Just demonstrating, do you mind?'

'It is my mind,' Wissenschaft shrugged, 'but you play with it as you will.'

'It's pretty convincing.' Ronnie looked to Titus.

There was just enough room to stand next to the considerable bulk of Wissenschaft but the cramped dimensions of the subsiding Georgian office in London's 'TV land' of lower Fitzrovia offered little more than the last resting place of many a swung cat, and made large gestures impossible without grazed knuckles. Verstehung shifted to Ronnie's chair and, shoulder to shoulder with Titus, they watched Ronnie run through the effect.

'OK, Titus,' Ronnie tapped again, 'from what I can gather, you start by saying you're going to influence the volunteer's mind. You touch their forehead around here. Then you draw your finger down their nose and explain that, as they look at your finger, their eyes will cross and they will feel a little dizzy. Obviously this is just the unusual muscle strain on the eyes opposing each other but your line is that the dizziness is because the left and right hemispheres of their brain are seeing different things but knowing it's the same object and becoming confused over which image to prioritize, and the conscious mind is becoming disconnected from rational understanding as each hemisphere tries to achieve dominance over interpretation.'

'That's the bit that turns out to be a load of bollocks,' Verstehung added helpfully.

'Not necessarily bollocks.' Titus nudged him. 'The brain does do that, it's just not proven that it does it when you go cross-eyed.'

'But it sounds brilliantly convincing,' continued Ronnie insistently. 'You carry on saying that: while their brain tries to achieve stability again they are susceptible to suggestion.'

'Now that bit is true,' Titus said haughtily. 'I did a lot of that confusional technique in Series Two.'

Wissenschaft let his crossed eyes focus again on Titus. 'Confusional technique?'

'You mean you never used it in your line of work?' Titus was surprised, he had seen how these detectives worked, they were pretty hard core. Influencing a witness would, he had always imagined, be one of their staples. 'When you purposefully confuse someone, as

304

their brain's trying to create order from whatever confusion has arisen, they are hyper-susceptible to suggestion.' Titus grinned with pride when he thought of the BAFTA he had got for this. 'In Series Two I convinced a man to think that his hat was his wife. He was really talking to it, telling it to be quiet. I was holding his hat while he tried to work out the Christmas cancellation railway timetable for First Great Western. We stood in the station and I just pointed to his hat and said to him, "Why don't you ask your wife?" It took him a few minutes to realize that the rather awful grey homburg wasn't actually his wife.'

'It's great when we find real nutters for the show.' Ronnie beamed. 'Great TV.'

Titus glared at Ronnie. 'He wasn't a nutter, dear heart, he was just very vulnerable to a skilful practitioner monkeying with his mind.'

'Of course,' Ronnie said pacifically, 'of course, you mind-zapped him, didn't you, Titus. Yeah.'

'Yeah.' Titus grinned, unaware of the irony in Ronnie's voice. Titus got nuance in the same way Attila the Hun got a quiet home life.

'Yeah,' the two Hasidic detectives enthused.

'Anyway,' continued Ron, 'you tell them that while their mind is disconnected or confused or whatever, you will "Carry ot" the implanting of a subliminal image in their brain.'

Titus laughed. '"Carry ot", that's really g-g-good. So at the end we can replay the VT, we can show that I actually s-s-said "Carry ot", that's a real convincer. Audiences love that stuff, the slurred words as a s-s-subliminal suggestion. They'll buy it.'

'And the rest of the thing,' Ronnie said brightly, 'is the usual Kentonesque dual reality you've been doing for years.'

Titus looked around at Verstehung. 'And Kenesis okayed this? Said we can use the trick on the shows?'

'It's one of the last things he said. Should we look a gift horse?'

'Well, it's not exactly a gift horse,' Ronnie responded. 'You say he charged you three thousand pounds?'

The two detectives nodded sadly. 'Cash,' said Verstehung.

Ronnie ticked something in his notes. 'OK, well, you'll have to see Sandra for the reimbursement.'

'And the fee?' Wissenschaft reminded him.

'That too.'

Titus rewarded the members of his star chamber with his trademark smug smile. 'Thank you. We're doing well.'

The two detectives rose, bowed and left in unison but, getting stuck for a moment in the narrow door, proceeded to hit each other with their hats until the bigger beat the smaller into submission and led the way out.

Ronnie finished crossing an I and dotting a T that surrounded the word 'dio' on his executive leather 'magic' clipboard, one of the items that he marketed on the back of being 'The Man Behind Titus Black', his unofficial title within magic circles. Indeed within the Magic Circle. The clipboard was a gimmicked piece of apparatus with carefully hidden carbon papers and various pockets that afforded a magician a peek at information that had been written on it by unsuspecting spectators before a show, a move that was far too obvious for the likes of Titus Black to use. The original clipboard cost in the region of five pounds to buy and another five to get altered in a sweatshop in Delhi but, in the rarefied market of aspiring magicians enticed by the promise of 'secrets' revealed and endorsed by Titus Black himself, the 'magic' executive clipboard sold for closer to two hundred pounds. This price also explained why their Charlotte Street office was even more cramped than previously, due to its being stacked high with unsold boxes full of the things. Thankfully, the clipboards also worked as ordinary clipboards for taking notes and Ronnie slammed his personal one down.

'Right.' Ronnie stood. 'I'll put something up on the Black Blog about disorientated hemispheres of the brain. That should get the tweeters and responders going and nicely anticipate the effect in tomorrow's show. We can use it as the first effect. What's the matter?'

Titus sighed and looked down at his worry ball. 'It's the old thing.'

'It's getting worse, isn't it. Listen, Tite, even in Junior Magic Circle you never seemed to get overwhelmed by the disappointment like the rest of us.'

'Which disappointment?'

'That all we ever do is fake the magic, simulate it. It's just cons and tricks. But, you know, I think that's what makes you so good for telly. You look into most magicians' eyes and you see cynicism has just hardened them. They may smile on stage but I never saw a magician who didn't look weary. You, Titus, you think that you're just faking all this mind-control stuff until you actually find a way to do it for real.'

'But the confusional technique thing works, we're not far off.'

'Tite, we're playing around the edges of mind shit, little scratches. Maybe there's some neuroscientist working on the mind-control machine of your dreams but, let's face it, it's probably decades before anything usable comes about, before one person can control another person's mind. You know that when you do your hypnosis shows it's just social compliance. Nobody's going to do anything that they don't want to, we're a long way off *The Manchurian Candidate*. If ever.'

Titus crossed to the window and stared down at the Soholics sitting on steps and pub tables, enjoying the early spring sunshine. Smoke pouring from nostrils, laughter.

'What makes all the difference,' Ronnie continued behind him, 'is that you're an optimist, and that makes you a believer and maybe that's the real secret behind your telegenicness. They love you because you appear to think like they do, that magic is really out there. You know you're faking it but for you it's only until you find the real thing. You've even got Laurelstein and Hardyberg there on a permanent retainer looking for it and I wish I could believe too. I really do. I envy you that.'

'But you think it's a fool's errand, don't you.'

'Not if it's what keeps the ratings up.'

Titus laughed and turned back to Ronnie. 'Thanks,' he said, making his way to the door, kissing Ronnie as he passed. 'Thanks.'

'Shakespeare wrote about that, you know,' said Ronnie.

Titus turned back to look quizzically at Ronnie.

'Titus and Ronnie kiss.' He smiled.

36

Shadows flickered. Those limitless dark horizons behind the eyelids lit up with syncopated flashes like the windows of a train passing in the night. They pulsed quickly then slowed and sped again. Kate floated. Disconnected from the world. Disengaged from her limbs, even her eyelids. It felt as if just trying to regain control over them, moving them, might be impossible and it was best to wait a little before seeking to confirm such an unfortunate condition. But even with her eyes closed she felt completely aware of everything around her. The hushed, rhythmic crashing of a calm sea beating the sand and the hissing of the waves rushing back across the shale. *Wish hiss*. The sound of a hundred holidays. The shouts of children, the occasional zinging ding of a beachball and somewhere, far away, the drone of a motorboat. Closer, something tinkled like a spoon in a glass. She could smell the sea, the sides of her tongue swelled to the roof of her mouth with the tang of the salt and on top of it was that thin whiff of butane that lingers in the proximity of a camping stove.

In my business it's known as the hypnopompic state. The hyper-awareness of everything around you as you waken but before you are fully awake. The brain, alert before the body stirs, is unencumbered by the automotive responsi-bilities of moving your anatomical parts around or gathering visual information. It sequesters this spare capacity for problem solving or analytical processing just as it does in its sister condition the hypnogogic state, the place the brain finds itself as you close your eyes at night but before sleep has overwhelmed it.

It is at these times that problems are most often solved or that creative solutions are dreamed up, often seeming to come as if out of nowhere. The brain is lucid, liberated from the drudgery of everyday tasks, even of an aware-ness of time, and can harness its full creative potential to exploring all the different possible avenues a new idea might lead to. They say Archimedes was observing the water in his bath, but I say he was nodding off: if we are going to have a Eureka moment it is most likely to occur just as we fall asleep or just as we wake up. If necessity is the mother of invention, the borders of sleep are her deliv-ery room.

The breathing is slow, the brain waves are still in a lan-guorous theta pattern, what we might call a trance state, and from cortex to amygdala the brain is free to simulate the multiple outcomes of new directions and pay little attention to the things that so often hold us back: our inhibitions or our physical shortcomings.

This also makes this state highly suggestible. A sugges-tion from a third party will often be acted out in this playground of the mind and chased through its possibilities.

For this reason it is this state that the successful hypnotist encourages her client to enter. All the counting down and the stepping stones and relaxing places, the sunny gardens and the sandy beaches.

Kate listened to her sandy beach and felt the warmth of the sun on her arms and let her mind run naked through the night before. She watched it in rewind. The endearing fear in Peter's face. The delight at the frying pan rescue. She had never been rescued before. It was an odd feeling. She made her own plans in life. Made her own escapes. She didn't need anyone else. She didn't want rescuing. Did she? It was probably dangerous to confuse need and want. Kate flitted through what she could have done to escape. Where she would have made the move, had the knight with his shining frying pan not come to vanquish the giant. But that just opened up a flood of questions. Kate really was not used to questioning herself because, well, she was always right. Even at times when she was utterly wrong. Attempting to scam Clarissa, for instance. Kate tended to find a way to justify things to herself, to convince herself, that she had been right. Look at Clarissa's warning, she did need to change her game. But to go so far as to let herself be rescued? The questions, the questions. Was it disempowering to allow someone else to do something for her? Was that an erosion of her own abilities, an insult to her own skills, to her autonomy, that she allowed herself to be rescued? Allowed him to rescue her? Did that make her like every other eye-fluttering bimbo the world over? Had she just taken the first step into the yoke of dependency? Would it make her more complacent if she thought she had back-up? Would it make her rely on it? That way danger surely lay.

Kate was used to getting answers in this space before she opened her eyes. Not questions. She rewound again, Peter and her sitting on the bed watching the ridiculous Titus Black. The beginnings of her delayed induction into the conjuring world, the one she had yearned for her father to give her. Their laughter together. Had she been connected to her muscles, she would have smiled.

And there. There was a warmth in having no expect-ations of the person you're with and them having no expectations of you. When was the last time she had experienced that? Not having to keep up a character, play a part, just be plain old Catherine again. She felt like a schoolgirl. These feelings were new and exciting and scary. But. Hang on. She had blocked 'scary' from her emotional vocabulary. In fact, come to think of it, she had blocked 'emotional' as well. So why was she thinking in those terms? She had decided a long time ago that she wouldn't be limited by any of those things. But this now? Think positive. This now was the game change Clarissa had warned her about, and she had known deep within her she had to make it. Years on the road, always a shape-changer but, within, the same ruthless girl.

She retraced the Titus Black shows in her head. This was safer territory, the pre-scam research. She watched Black stammering in the crowd. Here, she knew, was the answer to finding what Titus most desired. What he would do anything to achieve. She listened to the stuck repetitive sound, saw the slight fear in his eyes. This was a moment he could do nothing about. This, unlike anything that happened on stage, was out of his control and he didn't like it. All his shows were about controlling minds, even the afterlife.

Kate opened her eyes. She stared straight up at a twisting glass mobile that spun and unspun above her, sending prisms of sunlight around the room and flashing into her eyes, the crystals tinkling against each other. The beach hut had the dusty comfort of age. The beds covered with old throws and worn cushions, a chipped camping cooker and fridge, a few shelves with damp curled books on nautical themes. Everything was painted a faded blue or decorated with shells or crystals. She had chosen it last night exactly because it looked the least visited. The sound of the sea and the children and boats all seemed much further away now that she had her eyes open and her visual sense had taken over again. Even the smell of the sea had receded. Exhausted, she and Peter had fallen asleep in the towels they had been drying themselves with and now she peeled herself off her dried, rigid bedding.

Kate dragged a long red T-shirt from her bag and pulled it on. She ran her fingers through her hair in lieu of a comb and pared her towel from the bed. Stepping out into the bright sunlight of a spring day, she blinked for a moment and looked out at the endless plain of the calm blue sea. The beach was almost empty, too early for day-trippers to come by ferry or walk over from the Head. On either side beach huts of every colour lined up along the sand bar to face the sea. Further down some children were throwing a ball at each other. Peter, in a pair of shorts, was lying on his own towel by the water's edge, his eyes closed.

Kate crept up to him. She could see his baggy clothes had hidden a fairly muscular frame, a little bony, a little scrawny perhaps, but he looked like he could handle himself. With which little phrase she unwittingly summed up the last fifteen years of his love life. She walked around him until her shadow fell over his face. He opened his eyes and blinked up at her.

'You're a little exposed, aren't you?' Kate said.

Peter quickly covered his crotch. 'Am I?'

'Out here, I mean. You're a wanted man, remember.'

'I had my suspicions but you never put it in so many words.'

Kate looked around at the dark green vegetation climbing up the steep sides of Hengistbury Head to the fringe of windswept grasses that fluttered at the top. She scanned the horizon and the wave-white streaks that flashed in the teal sea until her gaze met the beach again and the long line of beach huts that stretched across the pale yellow sands to the mouth of the sound. She sat down next to Peter in the sand still cool from the night. 'They may come looking for us again. We need to be careful.'

Peter sat up. 'I thought you might say that. Which is exactly why I came out here early. To enjoy myself before you scared me shitless and I'd have to cower inside again.'

Kate laughed. 'You don't cower. You did good last night. It'll take them a while to regroup anyway. Relax.' She lay down next to him and absorbed the hot sun on her face and the cool sand on her back. As the conflicting nerve messages attempted to regulate her body temperature she had the most curious feeling of being a battery energized between the polarities.

The two lay silently alone on the long expanse of beach, waves skittering along the side of the rotten wooden breakwaters and the misshapen boulders that helped them. It was a few minutes before Kate spoke again. 'You know what Titus Black wants?'

'A good kicking, a pleasing manner, a new name, modesty . . .'

'A remote control.'

'What? He wants to change channels?'

'No. The thing he wants most in the world. He wants to control everything, the people around him, his own body, everything.'

'Well, there's a surprise.'

'It's the stutter. He can't control himself, never could, so he has an urge to control those around him. That was why magic, maybe even Mr Noodles' magic, appealed to him. From controlling an audience to being this sort of mind guru, ghost whisperer, cold reader.'

'But if that's true,' Peter sat up, 'everything he does must be one disappointment after another. Because it's all tricks. He knows it and most of his audience know it.' Peter looked out at the sea and the distant Needles, the pointy outcrops of rock that darned the north and south coasts of the Isle of Wight together. 'Poor bastard. I think you're right. What a deluded fool. Oh shit,' Peter looked down at Kate lying next to him, 'you've just made me feel sorry for him.'

'Not too sorry, I hope.'

'No. No. Fifteen years of shit because of him will not be wiped out by a little sympathy.'

'So that's what we're going to sell him.'

Peter leaned back on his angle-locked arms and

laughed. 'Well, that's going to be easy, we just invent something that controls men's minds and flog it to him.'

'It doesn't have to work. He just has to think it does.'

Peter lay back and closed his eyes again. 'That's a relief. For a while last night I started to think you were actually sane.'

37

'To be honest,' DI Brightly slid the Zig Zag Woman boxes with idle curiosity, 'I was all ready to throw in the towel last night. Wasn't sure your perps even existed.' She turned to look at Brown, who was examining the handcuff cascade. 'It was only when they showed me the CCTV of you and the girl and then the bloke coming and whacking you that I changed my mind. Can't see either of them clearly though and we don't have unlimited pockets. Got the boss to give us another forty-eight hours. But then you're heading back with or without her.'

Brown was looking at the less faded squares of wallpaper that commemorated the positions of the Titus Black photos in the OR. 'I'm very grateful, Brightly. You're a dame.' He sat heavily on the bed and started sifting through the boxes of Titus stuff. 'Who is this guy?' He flashed a photo of Titus holding a gun from his infamous bank-robbery show, in which he had apparently convinced a bunch of dodgy-looking people to rob a bank.

'Titus Black. He's a TV magician. Reads minds. Talks to the dead. That sort of thing.'

'Ruchio's a real fan. I mean major like bordering on weird.'

Brightly had crouched down and, with her latex gloves, was carefully sifting through the box o'sins. 'The guy's a magician. It's probably research.'

'Oh, this is way more than research. This is,' Brown tried to think of the most appropriate word but all he could come up with was 'emotional. It's like personal.' Brown got his phone out and started taking photos. 'You know, if Ruchio's not involved, where is he now? I know it was him and I'm sure your CSI team will find forensics that put Minola here.'

'We don't have CSI. You do know that we are a separate country and not one of your dependent colonies? I don't think we need forensics though.' She pointed at one of the labels on the trunk.

Brown looked. ' "C. Minola". This is her dad's?'

'If Ruchio stole it, then we've got a crime, but considering the magic connection I've got a feeling that's a dead end.'

'There's a bunch of cameras and video equipment. In the cupboard. Stolen?'

'I saw,' Brightly said. 'They don't exactly look brand new. It's not really a smoking gun. Face it, Brown, without the frying pan we've got no evidence to link him to a crime.'

'You checked his kitchen? No frying pan, right?'

'Not owning a frying pan is, as yet, not a crime in this country.'

'How the hell would you know?' Brown muttered under his breath.

'Sorry?'

Brown shrugged at her. 'Oh come on. It's not like it's written in your constitution.'

'That's because we don't have a written constitution.'

'Exactly, so you can make it up as you go along.'

'We still have statute books and an ancient system of precedence which goes back a lot further than your precious American written constitution.'

'At least we had the guts to decide once and for all what is right and what is wrong and write it down in stone.'

Brightly stared at him as if he had just taken a dump in front of the Queen. 'In stone? OK, what's your eighteenth amendment? Written in stone?'

Brown could see where this was going but was helpless to avoid it. 'That it's illegal to sell or make alcohol anywhere in the United States,' he mumbled.

'And the twenty-first amendment? Written in stone?'

'Yes but that—'

'Which is?' Brightly insisted, putting her hands on her hips. Trust him to be teamed up with a constitutional expert.

'That everything stipulated in the eighteenth amendment is null and void but—'

'In stone!' huffed Brightly before turning on her heel and heading back down the fire escape. 'When it suits you.'

38

'Neuroscience. The science of the brain. It's the cutting edge of today's greatest breakthroughs. It is taking us in extraordinary new directions and many of my skills have been garnered from utilizing these neuroscientific discoveries.'

Titus stood next to Maurice, his volunteer, and basked in the spotlight. He could have continued in this strain of neurobollocks for hours. It had become an almost ritualistic credo. He knew his modern young audience. He knew they were sceptical of religion and worshipped at the altar of science. Just as the Victorians' longing to believe in their last unconquered territory, death and a life after it, made them vulnerable to the trickery of 'spiritualists' and psychics, so today's believers in science left themselves open to the self-help charlatans peddling our new metaphysics: psychology, whether as neuro-linguistic programming, subliminal mind control, brain training, hypnosis, pinpoint accurate psychological profiling or any of the other numerous indisciplines based on a few observed tics of human behaviour. You dropped enough names of brain parts, prefixed almost any verb with 'neuro' and the mouths of the modern undereducated fell open in awe. Of course Titus's tricks were no more sophisticated than those of the Victorian psychics, but when he claimed his effects were achieved through psychology, rather than ghosts, he fitted into today's longing to believe that it is possible to have dominion over the mind, our own twenty-first-century frontier. In another hundred years the cyberhumans of the future will look back and wonder how the public were so easily fooled by something so blatantly bogus. And yet they flocked. His stage shows were sell-outs, his ratings enormous, his smug grin was widescreen and in high definition.

'Tonight I will be demonstrating to you one of the human brain's most frightening vulnerabilities. What's known as stress obligation. I've picked Maurice here to show how we can hack into the mind and im*plant* thoughts.' Titus stressed the syllable 'plant' a little oddly. By no means a tall man, he liked to make sure that his volunteers were seated whenever possible. Maurice giggled nervously and Titus put a hand on his shoulder.

'Not nervous are you, Maurice? We can *orrange* for someone else to volunteer if you prefer.'

Maurice shook his head and smiled willingly.

Titus looked back to camera, holding his hands out as if carrying an imaginary brain. 'Now, it's been known for some time that the two hemispheres of our brains control different parts of our personality and even our bodies. Left-handed people tend to have dominant right brains which absorb information from the left eye and ear and tend to be more creative; right-handed people have dominant left brains which gather information from the right eye and ear and tend to be more logical and organized. But new neuroscientific research has shown that our two cooperating hemispheres can sometimes act quite independently of each other, even compete for dominance, and at moments when we are confused it is often due to a war raging in our minds, with each hemisphere insisting that their interpretation is the correct one. It is at these moments that the mind has been found to be at its most suggestible. Now, Maurice, I'm just going to touch your forehead if you don't mind.'

Maurice nodded his head and smiled.

'Now try to keep your eyes on my finger if you can.'

Maurice had to cross his eyes to try and focus on Titus's finger. Titus drew a line down from the middle of Maurice's forehead to the tip of his nose and Maurice's eyes dutifully followed.

'Now you might find it slightly uncomfortable but as you look at my finger and your eyes cross you will feel a little dizzy. This is the left and right hemispheres disconnecting as they try to achieve dominance. One sees the finger one way, the other sees it the other way and while the brain tries to achieve stability again I will *carry ot* the implanting of a subliminal image in your brain.'

Titus lifted a small dry-wipe whiteboard off the back of the chair. 'So, Maurice, I want you to look at the board and right away it's saying something to you, it wants you to draw something, so you go right ahead and draw it.'

A couple of pens were clipped to the board and Maurice quietly went about drawing. Titus moved to the camera and started drawing something himself on his hand. He winked at the camera and, keeping his hand close in shot, looked back at Maurice. 'Finished?'

Maurice nodded.

'Now there's no way I could know what you've drawn.'

Maurice smiled and clutched the board to his chest. 'No.'

'But I know you've gone for something which comes from under the ground.'

Maurice giggled.

'I'm seeing rabbits, but you couldn't have drawn a rabbit. It's something a rabbit likes, right? It's. Um. "What's up, doc?" That mean anything to you?'

At this point Titus turned his palm to the camera, to show a carrot. 'It's rather bizarre but have you drawn a carrot, Maurice?'

Maurice turned his board to show, indeed, a carrot.

Titus capitalized on the similarity of their two drawings even though, if you're not Albrecht Dürer, there are only so many ways you can draw a carrot.

'But I've been playing with you, Maurice. I knew you would draw a carrot because I told you to. Take a look at the VT.' The cross-eyed moment was replayed and the audio was amplified on Titus's strange pronunciations of 'im*plant*', '*orrange*' and '*carry ot*'.

Maurice's mouth dropped open, the audience applauded enthusiastically and Kate leaned over the laptop to pause the clip from that evening's show. It had been posted on Titus's Black Blog, the internet meeting place for all things Titus Black-related. Ronnie kept the blog focused on reinforcing Titus's scientific credentials rather than his tricksy sleight-of-hand abilities. It mainly featured articles by atheists and sceptics and almost any whisper from the world of neuroscience.

'He likes his neuroscience, doesn't he.' Kate scrolled through the posts. 'So how does he do that carrot thing? The cross-eyed thing doesn't really work, does it?'

'I doubt it.' Peter had been watching over her shoulder. 'It's probably just a du-re trick.'

'Du-re?' Kate turned to him.

'Dual reality. It's a favourite of Black's. He's very good at it. It's when you do a small trick for a volunteer which they show some astonishment at, but for the audience watching the trick it seems much bigger. Then if the volunteer and the audience compare notes, they both agree that they experienced a great trick, and the difference between the impressive but possible one that the volunteer experienced and the incredible but impossible one that the audience experienced gets lost.'

Kate stared at Peter. 'Explain.'

'OK, so what if, on that whiteboard, there was something written very lightly. Maurice saw it but the audience didn't. So when Titus said, "It's saying something to you," Maurice took it as a direction whereas the audience thought he was just psyching Maurice up. It probably said, "Draw the very first vegetable that comes into your mind." Nine times out of ten, people think of a carrot. And I bet the only pens clipped to the board were green and orange. But the audience think that Maurice could draw absolutely anything.' Peter spread his arms to encompass the world. 'Everything Titus said after that could apply equally well to the trick of guessing the first vegetable that comes into your mind as guessing a totally random thing garnered from an entire universe of potential objects.'

'And what if he had drawn, I don't know, broccoli?'

'Black'd have an "out".'

'A Plan B.'

Peter nodded. 'He'd still get credit from the audience for knowing it was a vegetable. The odds are massively in his favour though. And it's telly. They can always drop it or reshoot or edit or whatever.'

'So all that stuff about implanting subliminal messages?'

'There is some science about it,' Peter said. 'When we are confused we often carry out suggestions without realizing it. But Black's just using it as a "convincer". He knows that people will believe in the effect and stop thinking that they're watching a plain old trick if there's a scientific explanation, however retarded. Mentioning science somehow makes it more true.' Peter sat heavily down on one of the beach hut's dusty beds and was quiet for a minute.

'Doesn't it piss you off,' Kate went to sit next to him, 'seeing him so successful?'

'No, no, I don't think it's his success.' Peter shook his head. 'That's just a little irritating. No, what's worse, what really hurts, is seeing that he's doing something that is actually new in magic, that he is doing it brilliantly well and it's something that I would never have thought of myself.'

Kate lay back against the faded patterned curtain of the little hut. 'So we need to sell him a remote control that's got the stamp of neuroscience on it. And don't we just happen to know a neuroscientist?'

'Tavasligh? You think we'd get the doctor to go along with it?'

'Don't need to. You know Tavasligh's been low profile to the point of incognito since the Patient S. scandal. Won't even know what's happening.' Kate closed her eyes. 'Tavasligh's work's all about memory, isn't it?'

'Actually it's forgetting.'

'And,' Kate continued musing, 'if you forgot everything, like Da, if you lost your memory, you'd be pretty confused, right?'

'I suppose so.'

Kate nodded to herself and a smile slowly snaked between her lips. 'And that would make you pretty suggestible.' She opened her eyes and sat up. 'Do you think Black reads the stuff posted on his blog?'

'An ego-booster like that? What do you think?'

Kate smiled at Peter. 'Grab the video camera, my friend, we're going to be posting something Titus Black won't be able to refuse.'

39

Ronnie entered sideways, pushing the door open with his shoulder, and wandered into the office yawning. He set down the cardboard tray with tall cardboard coffee cups from the café downstairs.

Titus was already stationed at his computer. He peered cautiously into the cup Ronnie gave him.

'Beware of geeks bearing gifts,' Ronnie said, collapsing into his chair.

'Actually it's your inner geek I need to consult.' Titus waved at the computer with his cup. 'I need you to see something.'

Ronnie pushed himself up again resignedly and circled Titus's desk to look at the screen.

'Do we know who posted this?'

'Paul11?' Ronnie said. He tapped a few keys and clicked the mouse about. 'An IP address in France, though that may be through some sort of proxy connections. Could be anywhere.'

'Ever hear of a neuroscientist called Tavasligh?'

Ronnie thought for a moment. 'Yes. Yes. Writes stuff about memory and forgetfulness, that sort of thing.'

'Some of the bloggers have been posting a link to this video, look.' Titus pointed at a video headed 'Momentary Memory Wipe – Tavasligh Up to Mischief Again – Leaked Video'. He clicked the play triangle and something resembling a clinical trials video started playing. It was a tripod shot, a clock visible in one corner, a watermark saying 'Tavasligh Laboratory, ChangeInMind.org' in the other. It was too obscure to make out much, it looked like it might be a hospital bed. For all they could tell, the whole thing could have been shot in a beach hut. A woman lay on the bed, her head pixelated, and there was a man next to her holding what looked like a little radio with wires wrapped around it.

'OK, just some preliminary questions,' the man said. 'What's your name, just your first name?'

'Fiona,' said the blur of pixelated squares in a distinct Welsh valleys accent.

'And how old are you?'

'Twenty-four.'

'And where were you born?'

'Cardiff.'

'Have you got a boyfriend?'

'Yes. His name's Carl and . . .'

'OK, thank you. Now I'm just going to place this Alpha Wave Disrupter near your ear again. Just as we did before. You won't feel a thing. Is that OK?'

The pixels nodded. The man placed a small box near her ear and the pixelated girl suddenly started casting her head around. 'Hold on,' she said, 'I'm—'

The man interjected. 'Could you just quickly answer some questions, please? Can you tell me your name?'

The girl's head stopped moving; for a few moments she seemed to be thinking. 'I'm not quite sure.'

'And where were you born?'

'I . . . I don't know.'

'Have you got a boyfriend?'

'No, yes, no, I can't.'

The pixels stopped moving. The clock ticked forward for about ten seconds and then the man started speaking again.

'Sorry? What was your name again?'

'Fiona, I told you.'

The video finished and Titus looked at Ronnie. 'I've watched it twenty times this morning. Do you think it's true?'

'Could be.' Ronnie moved away, wary of going on another Titus goose chase. 'You'd need to contact them. Might be difficult. From what I remember, Tavasligh was involved in a scandal, put on a sort of witness protection programme after threats to blow up the lab. Difficult to contact, I should imagine.'

'We could put the boys on it.'

Ronnie returned to his desk. 'Is it worth it? What's the big deal?'

'Ron Ron. You know what happens when you have a temporary memory loss. You do Ron Ron, you do Ron Ron.'

Ronnie hated that joke and habitually ignored it. 'You going to tell me about suggestibility?'

Titus smiled. 'I'm emailing this Paul11.'

40

'It's not here,' I looked at Agent Brown and then at Brightly, 'and it's got nothing to do with anything that I'm working on.' Brown stared at me steadily as Brightly made her way around the lab, looking in drawers and cupboards as if Kate or Peter might be hiding in there.

'So you don't recognize these people?'

'No,' I said, even if I could make a pretty good guess.

'It's a hoax?'

'Yes,' I said, 'and it's probably just going to stir up more trouble for me. I dread it.'

'It's just that Peter Ruchio had a real Titus Black thing going.'

'Thing?'

'Obsession. Interest.'

I nodded.

'And he knew you too. Mr Magicov, I believe.'

I nodded again.

'Then within twenty-four hours of him disappearing there's a direct link made between you and Titus Black on Black's Blog with this video, so . . .' Brown pointed at the laptop screen.

'It really has nothing to do with me. It doesn't even look like this place.'

'But you do experiment with memory, don't you?'

'Research. Yes.'

'Do you mind,' Brown shifted his considerable weight on the lab stool, 'explaining exactly why this lab is so secret? You had some trouble, I hear.'

I stood and walked to my bookshelf to retrieve one of my last copies of *Inducing Psychogenic Amnesia in Patient S*. It's not that it had sold well but it had proved remarkably popular with hordes of journalists from across the world. Brightly was examining a spectro-scope. I gave the book to Brown, who held it between finger and thumb as if it was evidential knickers from a syphilitic rock star. 'It was this experiment. When it went public, I . . . I got a bit of a lambasting about it.'

'Experiment went wrong?'

'No. No. Everything went fine. It's just some people had a problem with it. Felt it crossed a line. An ethical line.'

Brown looked at the book with what seemed a little more respect. 'Go on.'

'It was part of my work with the dementia unit at Lotus House. I noticed that the patients with the best QOL were—'

'QOL?'

'Sorry, quality of life. The ones who seemed to be enjoying their lives were the ones for whom Alzheimer's was full blown; they saw the world from a generally happy oblivion. The ones in the early stages though, their quality of life was frankly crap. They wake up only to be reminded for the first time, as far as they're concerned, that they're suffering from a disease which will rob them of their memories, their loved ones, their lives. And every day the same trauma repeats until finally dementia relieves them of knowing or caring. I had been working with certain psychogens and therapies but it's like rust in metal, you might be able to slow the corrosion but you'll never get back the shiny metal that once was there. If you work with these people day in day out you might well start thinking like me: that if I couldn't actually stop the Alzheimer's, if it's inevitable, I could accelerate it, fast-track them through the hardest part.'

'You did it. With this Patient S.?'

I nodded. 'As soon as this was published all the gossips and generalists in the press started chattering away, calling me the new Dr Mengele. That it was identity theft, that I had robbed the patient of her memories, therefore her life. There were threats made against my life. The readers of my self-help books were very supportive but I didn't want this kind of attention, always looking over my shoulder, always having to defend myself. The whole thing turned into a terrible mess. The police helped me set up a new lab here and generally I've been keeping a low profile. Nothing with the address, everything kept low key. And I've been working on how we can establish new memories to replace the ones we've lost. It's very interesting and I—'

'Well listen, doctor, this video is going to dredge it all up again. You sure you've got no connection to Titus Black?'

I shook my head. 'No. None.'

It was only when Brown and Brightly had gone and I had a cup of tea in my hand that I felt able to think about it rationally.

From: *Project Notebook 17.6* p12

Why did I lie about recognizing Peter? I'm still not completely sure. There was something about the aggression in Agent Brown's demeanour that made me feel protective. Peter and Kate were clearly using my identity, my background, my name, to do something dodgy. I had no idea what though. Since the Patient S. saga, the death threats and the police-assisted relocation, I had assiduously kept a low profile. This threatened to bring the whole nightmare up again: I dreaded that hunted feeling: the bricks through the window, the suspicious packets with wires hanging out of them, the shouting outside the lab, that ridiculous mirror stick I had to use to check for bombs under the car. And yet, when I watched the video clip, I found the idea of my identity being stolen an incredible relief. As if there was a way of no longer being responsible for myself. As if all the pain of my life was being taken over by someone else. That I could be unburdened and someone else could carry around the weight of being me. I let myself fantasize about disappearing completely, about a life so completely different from my own that all the pain and worry and stress and

shittiness would be totally erased. Maybe that was when I
started thinking about creating a totally new identity.
Started this whole project going. Later, I knew I would envy
Peter the obliteration of his past life and the opportunity to
start as newborn, fresh, someone else, somewhere else,
with no knowledge of ever having been him.

'Paula?'

Paula's voice sounded reassuringly familiar. 'Oh hi,
doc.'

'Listen, I think the old trouble might be kicking off
again.'

'Oh doc, no. I'm really sorry. Anything to do with the
American policeman?'

'Sort of. Anyway, I might need to close the lab for a
little while. Just until things blow over. Lotus House
doesn't need the bad publicity and I don't either. So . . .'

'If anyone asks for you, I don't know nothing, right?'

'That'll be it.'

'Don't be too long, the patients will miss you.'

'I won't. Oh, and Paula?'

'Yeah?'

'Thanks.'

'No probs, doc.'

10,000 Milliseconds to Higham
(TEA minus 11 months 19 days 8 hours)

Peter

What if she goes for it? The train's practically stopped. What if she's planning to make a grab for the case and I've gone and grabbed it first? Maybe that's what she's planning but if I go for it, I'll never know. I'll give it like thirty seconds after we've stopped. Just to see.

Oh bugger. I'm supposed to trust her, why am I thinking like this? What chance have we got, would we have had, if I couldn't trust her?

So she goes for the case, just hypothetically. What do I do? I've got to stop her. I'll just wake up and stop her and we'll laugh and she'll say something like, 'Just testing you.' And she'll sit down again and that will be that.

But. But that won't be that will it? If she does make a move, if she does go for the cash, what exactly have we got? Not love, not a relationship. If she is willing to rip me off now, however long it took, the moment when she took the money and ran would always hang over us. I'd be constantly worrying that she'd be off again, maybe not today, maybe not tomorrow, but this wouldn't be quite the beginning of the beautiful friendship I had hoped for.

Why am I even testing her like this? The only way to make sure someone doesn't fail a test is not to set it in the first place. If I'm testing it, the trust has already gone hasn't it? So fuck the thirty seconds. As soon as the

333

train stops I just take the case and go. Go now or . . .

Maybe just a few seconds. But if she even stirs, all I have to do is open my eyes, she'll make no move and we're done. But then, then I'll never know. Please, Kate, please just lie there and sleep. Trust me. Please.

41

Subject: Tavasligh Memory Wiper Video
From: iam@titusblack.com
Date: 08 May: 09.27
To: paul11@gmail.com
Hi Paul

Saw your video on YouTube. Fascinating. I'd be very interested in discussing this with you and/or Dr Tavasligh. As you probably know, the work I do is very close to this field. Please reply as soon as possible, it would be good to meet you.
Best – Titus Black

Subject: Re: Tavasligh Memory Wiper Video
From: paul11@gmail.com
Date: 08 May: 12.42
To: iam@titusblack.com
Hi Titus

Wow, wow. I can't believe it. I am such a big fan. Unfortunately, I'm in serious trouble for putting that trial video up. It was supposed to be a bit of leverage to get a pay rise but Tavasligh called my bluff and now I'm not even sure if I'm going to be in a job this afternoon. Never expected things to go so far.

I assist Dr Tavasligh and I can tell you categorically that this is a **MAJOR** project and it's more than my life's worth if I'm caught discussing it with anyone. Thank you for your interest and if there's ever a chance of a ticket to your show, I'd be thrilled!!!! Paul

Kate tapped 'Send' with a flourish. 'There, he's hooked. It's like taking sweets from a baby. Next step, Pareee.' She happily kissed Peter on both cheeks in a fit of Frenchness and pulled the towel from her head to return to rubbing her hair dry.

'Are you condoning taking sweets from babies?' Peter didn't look up from his exercises, an assortment of false shuffles, strip-outs and culls, laying the bright red 'bikes' in patterns on the faded blue bedcovers.

Kate leaned over, massaging her tangle of damp tresses, and watched him. She was fairly sure that his indifference was affected. That air of worldly nonchalance.

They had spent all morning jumping about in the freezing Channel waters or lying in the sand beneath the brilliant sky and the not-so-clever dregs from a left-over bottle of sunblock that had rendered the two of them lobsterized – which may not be a word but you can just take it as red. As they rolled around and laughed and talked and touched in passing, they twisted about 'the move' like a tarantella, neither of them making it until any chance of a pass did exactly that.

Kate dropped her head towel and clutched the one she was wrapped in, knuckle to chest. Maybe Clarissa's wake-up call had come too late, maybe Kate was past the time when she could rely on her looks to do all the

336

work. Maybe they were just going to be friends, or maybe any kind of relationship was beyond the reach of two such habitual deceivers. But their soaking underwear had told another story. Having doubled for bathing suits, sodden, transparent and clinging, it only emphasized their unruly parts hardening in the wet, the cold and the warmth.

Kate pulled her fingers through a fierce knot of hair. 'I'm not condoning taking the sweets. I'm condemning the sort of idiots who give sweets to toothless babies in the first place.'

If this had been a grift, if Peter had been a mark, Kate knew she'd have no inhibitions; it would just be a job. The towel would drop to the floor and, as he was rendered speechless, she would curl her naked body around his, like a python.

But as Kate stared at Peter's rhythmic dealing, she found herself short of breath, her stomach and shoulders aching as they tensed. It was that same rising panic she had experienced at Clarissa's career appraisal and Brown's interrogation. Fearless for so long, she now felt paralysed with the terror of being irredeemable. What if she couldn't even be honest enough to connect in one genuine relationship with someone she was attracted to without trick or artifice? Had she become something less than human? A succubus perhaps, deriving nourishment by drawing all that was vital from her victims. If she couldn't distinguish between her life of pretend, her *femme fatality*, where every move was hers or directed by her, and this strange uncontrolled 'reality', was there any hope that she might grow old gracefully rather than turn into the empty husk that was

Clarissa Rackham? Kate looked around the hut desperately. She eyed the corner of the table; she felt an urge to smash her head into it and keep smashing it just to remind herself that there was a real solid world there, something authentic.

Kate took a huge breath to try and calm herself and turned back to Peter. She followed the gentle curves of his arms as they delivered cards to the bed. And why him? How did she end up relying on a virtually hermitic sociophobic sex offender to take the lead and guide her into the world of the genuine? A man so cowed by the real world he had buried himself in Gerontaville Central for nearly a third of his life? But then, there was something in that. At least he'd be careful. Maybe that was what she saw in him when he first approached her table in the restaurant. She knew he'd be gentle, let her take her own time.

Bollocks. He was an opportunity and she was an opportunist: she had seen a weak man to spirit the ring away who could then be bullied into returning it when she had disposed of Harry. But Peter hadn't returned it. He showed some of what the Americans call 'spunk'. He clearly had it, but then where was it now?

Each card clicking as it hit the bed, Peter had moved on to a casual but invisible bottom deal, serving cards from the bottom of the deck but making them look like they were from the top. 'Babies aren't all toothless,' he said, his eye on the cards. 'Some of them will be nearly toddlers. Just try and take a sweet off one of them.' He stopped to look up at Kate in her towel, still staring. 'Not that that's something I've done, you understand. Not the nature of my offence. But I know they'd

338

scream the bloody place down.' He went back to examine the hands he had dealt, turning over a neat series of royal flushes. 'Maybe the phrase should be "easy as taking sweets from a tranquillized baby".'

Kate brushed the 'bikes' off the bed and sat down next to Peter, futilely trying to pull the towel over her thighs. Without even thinking, she had dropped her head slightly forward so she could be looking up when she caught his eyes. It was an ancient, subtle seduction trick, as old as fuck-me heels. Make him feel powerful, you look submissive, tap into his inborn paternalism and fragile ego. A trick! A play! She had to stop it now. Kate shook her head as if her habit could be disposed of as easily. 'Let's face it,' she smiled, 'if you're going to use a tranquillizer then the baby's irrelevant. It might as well be as easy as taking sweets from a tranquillized . . . I don't know . . . gorilla.'

'Ah but then,' Peter put the rest of the deck down, 'it would be bananas.'

'Yup,' Kate sighed, 'absolutely crazy.'

Peter laughed, holding his hands up, conceding the last word to her, even if he had had the last laugh.

And just as suddenly he stopped. Kate found herself looking into serious eyes darting back and forth between hers, as if one of them might be saying something different from the other. In the cinema people seem to just look at each other and know, in a mutual drawing close, that it's time to kiss, and that's not even the back row. But, through the lens of Kate's habitually mendacious perspective, this whole new landscape of mutual honesty, unconditional friendship and un-affected courtship was fraught with strange dangers; to her it was as bizarre and uncharted as those parts on old maps that were evidently terrorized by giant, swollen-cheeked puffing heads.

Here, back behind the lace curtains of their borrowed beach hut and breathing in the musty sawdust of a thousand woodworms slowly consuming their second home, could Peter really not have noticed that the comfort of their banter was no more than a feeble mask for the discomfort of their frustrated intimacy?

Their heads were close. Kate blinked slowly, her lips parted and she gently lifted her mouth towards him, willing him to do the same. Peter twisted, shifting his weight to look at her more directly.

Quickly Kate feigned a cough and looked down at her hands curled around the bottom of the towel. How could she expect him to trust her, she couldn't even trust herself. 'Peter. There's stuff I need to tell you, stuff you need to know before we go on. You see, I'm . . .' Kate floundered. How do you tell someone you're a virgin at genuine emotion?

'A man?'

Kate smiled. 'No.'

'Scared of clowns?' Peter suggested.

'No.'

'Working undercover for the Magic Circle, investigating me for revealing secrets?'

'No.'

'A hardened con artist trying to turn over a new leaf because forty's steaming towards you but you're struggling to communicate with me because you can't remember the last time you spoke to anyone who wasn't part of a scam . . .'

340

'NO!' Kate shouted. 'I'm, well, yes. But no, I'm . . .'

'Kate, you're you.' Peter's voice began to soften. 'That's really all I need, all I want, to know.'

'I'm not me, Peter, I've got no idea what that even means.'

'I'm just saying, you don't need to explain anything. In fact, whatever it is you want to tell me, I'm pretty sure I'd rather not hear it. You see, Kate, I'm having such a brilliant time I don't want it to stop, and when people start explaining things it's usually to justify something that the person they're explaining to won't like.'

'I think,' Kate said, 'you're confusing explanations with confessions, or possibly school semolina.'

Peter's leg was suddenly afflicted with frustrated-teen knee spasm and he placed a hand on his thigh to stop himself. 'You know, in magic books, when they explain a trick, it always comes in two parts: the effect and then the method. First they describe what the spectator sees and then they explain how the illusionist achieves it. Effect and method. But the two are worlds apart. The effect is everything, the promise of the impossible. The method? A guaranteed anticlimax. The Statue of Liberty disappeared! Oh, you just revolved the bank of seats we were sitting on. Wow, that lady's sawn in half! Bugger, she's just curled up in one box with some false legs sticking out the other. First it's the poetry, then it's the terminally prosaic. You know, Kate, I've lived more in the last forty-eight hours than I have my entire life. I'm right in the "effect", I'm enjoying the magic, I'm begging you, please don't explain it. I don't want to know.'

'Peter, you think this is a trick? That's exactly what I'm trying to explain. This isn't a trick, I don't want it to be tricks or fakery or lies any more. I've been working that sort of thing since I was in short skirts. Now, now I've got this terrible feeling that I must do something real before it's too late, I want things to be true before I lose my grasp and, you know, I don't think I know how to do it and I just want to tell you what's going . . .'

Peter gently held Kate by the shoulders and looked hard into her eyes. 'Look. I know that there must be some reason why we're here, why you've changed your life to . . . to allow someone like me in; why you've lowered your sights, if just for a moment, to take in a low life like me but . . .'

'Peter, you couldn't possibly imagine a lower life than the one that's in your hands.'

Peter let go and spread his arms. 'Now we're going to compete for who's got the feeblest life? You mean to tell me that finally a competition comes along where I could be a real contender and I'm even beaten there? Kate, I'm just trying to say, if you explain things, that will be a beginning, it will define the first margin of our . . . whatever this is, and beginnings, they imply endings.'

'You're saying you wouldn't start something, however great, just because you might not enjoy it ending? That's almost the definition of inertia.'

Peter nodded. 'I suppose so. Fear does shitty things to you.' He smiled. 'When I was a kid I used to think that that was an English county. You know: Wiltshire, Berkshire, Inertia.'

'Oh,' Kate raised her eyebrows, 'you didn't realize it was the whole country.'

342

Quietly Peter tried to push home his point. 'These past couple of days, I know we've recited our histories but we've had no need to explain anything, we've just been. And that, that has felt infinite. Indefinable. And without definition, whatever this is, it's not a "thing". A thing has limits, it has edges, it starts, it stops. But if I don't think about the why or the how, if I ignore that there must be a method beneath it, suspend my disbelief, then I can just immerse myself in the wonder, enjoy the magic of right now as if it's here always now, for ever.'

'Pardon me?' Kate's voice was suddenly acerbic as she turned her ear to Peter. 'I'm having a little difficulty understanding what you're saying. Maybe if you took your head out of the fucking sand I'd be able to hear you properly.'

Peter's shoulders slumped and he turned away. For a minute only their breathing and the wheezing sea pervaded the hut.

'Come on.' Kate talked softly to his back. 'I know what you're saying. Really I do. You've been creating miracles for people all your life, you're probably due a few yourself, but I can't offer you miracles. Just plain old-fashioned revenge, a wodge of cash and . . .' but she couldn't quite bring herself to say 'me'. 'You want the sky, Peter, I want the solid earth and I've just been trying so hard to be honest and straight with you. Clearly I'm a rank amateur. You're right, I'm here because I'm trying to change things but it's not a leaf I've got to turn over, it's a whole sodding forest, and if I do it, that's not an end, it's just another new beginning. I just . . . I can't do it on my own.'

'I'll lend you an axe.'

'Listen. I have an unfortunate tendency to try and control things, everything, and now I'm not sure I know how to let go. I've been sitting here right next to you and . . . you know? I just wanted to kiss you.'

Peter looked back over his shoulder at her.

'But I haven't dared make a move in case that's being manipulative, in case that's what Kate the player would do. I'm not even sure if telling you this now is playing you or being straight. Seriously, I can't even honestly ask for a kiss any more. It's pathet—'

Peter's lips were on her mouth and whatever 'beginnings' he had feared he was suddenly embracing them with passionate urgency. And when their mouths at last parted again, the beginning of the end sealed, even Kate realized it would be wrong to utter the last syllable of the word he had interrupted.

As they held each other, skin hot against skin, on the faded blue bed inside the tiny hut, nestled in the rank of tiny huts, on the dark sands embraced on either side by the inky waters, Kate felt every muscle drop, relief flood through her; she could even hear the unfamiliar sound of her heart beating. And though she longed for this blessed relief to be the result of real emotion, she couldn't help suspecting it might just be the fact that she was clearly back in the driver's seat.

42

The baby wasn't quite as ready to give up his sweets as Kate had anticipated. Titus tipped back in his black faux-leather office chair and read the reply from Paul11 for the fiftieth time. Unfortunately he found it just as frustrating as the first.

Paul11's reluctance to engage in dialogue piqued Titus's curiosity but also his suspicions. The video could well have been, as Paul11 said, some in-lab power play that went wrong, but his loathness to elaborate and be caught up in a bigger lie meant it could just as easily be a hoax. Had Titus only been better at reading between the lines he was sure that it would all have been much clearer.

Was such a gizmo even possible? A machine that could wipe minds for a second? Titus had applied himself to research over the last couple of days. He had sent one of the production runners to buy my self-help books and surreptitiously scan my academic publications in the British Library. Titus read the lot – poor boy – but he at least realized that inducing amnesia was a tangible reality, which backed up the possibility of such a device. It all seemed quite credible yet he remained wary. If he chased this down and it turned out to be a prank, it might not just be a massive waste of time, it could be an awful publicity own goal. Like all celebrities, he had to keep one eye on how anything he did would look to the paying public. He had an image of savviness and uncanny foresight to protect.

Ronnie had reckoned the video might be a wind-up and he was pretty good at reading these things, but he lacked what Titus called his 'vision'. If it was true, if you could really cause a twenty-second fit of amnesia so easily, in Titus's hands it could be the ultimate hypnotic induction device, the mechanism that could influence anybody to do anything. If Tavasligh was only interested in the memory-loss aspect, he probably didn't even know the significance of such a device in terms of suggestion and persuasion.

For forty-eight hours Titus's indecision had fuelled his inaction. He had left things as they were but the idea that the Alpha Wave Disrupter could be genuine and he might be missing a golden opportunity haunted him.

Every scam or trick needs a 'convincer'. Something that appears to independently verify the story being spun. The three-card-trick find-the-lady monte teams use 'shills' – other gang members posing as random punters and appearing to win – to draw genuine punters into the 'game'. The magician might 'accidentally' turn the deck, giving you a glimpse that your card is exactly where it should be. The hypnotist might suggest that one hand is heavier than the other while your eyes are closed, claiming any disparity in their heights when you open them as proof positive of hypnotic suggestion and not just the imbalance we all suffer when deprived of our visual sense. Kate had presumed that the brush-off email was her convincer. It wasn't. The real 'convincer' came up the narrow Georgian staircase of Titus's Fitzrovia production offices just as Titus descended for lunch.

Blocking the entire staircase was the burliest man Titus had ever seen, who clocked him immediately.

'Mr Black?' he asked in a nasal American drawl. 'We'd like to have a word.'

'I only do autographs after g-g-gigs.'

Brightly's voice circumnavigated Brown's bulk from below. 'We're the police, Mr Black, and we'd appreciate some assistance with our inquiries.'

Titus froze. He had always known that this moment would come. He'd been anticipating it for years. He was surprised by its suddenness. He cupped his hand around the back of his neck to check he wasn't sweating. He must have slipped up. Left a clue at one of the old dead fuckers' houses. It was bound to happen, however careful he was. Could he run? Make it to the roof. There was bound to be some sort of way down a fire escape. The big guy was probably slow. Whoever was behind would have to get him out the way. But would they have come alone? What if the place was surrounded? Keep calm. There's still the plan. Titus did indeed have a plan for this eventuality. He wouldn't need to run. He had been spiriting away money specifically to post his bail. He had the beautiful Villa Rosa outside Tangier just waiting for him, where he could surround himself with beautiful boys or his own harem, he really wasn't fussy. And his psychic acolytes would flock as the newspapers bid for his exclusive story. In this dream of fragrant frangipani nestling about the white walls of the villa, Titus led the police back upstairs.

By the time they were sitting in the office, Titus was much more relaxed, especially when Brown produced Kate's seventeen-year-old wedding photo and it became abundantly clear that this visit was not about his fact-finding missions to the pre-dead.

'Do you know this woman?'

Titus looked. She seemed nice, but unfamiliar.

'Her name is Kate Minola.'

Titus shook his head. 'Did she come to one of my shows?'

'We're here because we think she posted a hoax video on the internet which featured in your blog.'

'There are a lot of videos, I can't vet them all.'

'It's about a memory-wiping device.'

Brown had Black's full attention.

'And it's a hoax, you say?'

'Sure.' Brown leaned back. 'The alleged originator, Dr Tavasligh, told us that the lab didn't produce the clip.'

Titus nodded with an indifferent shrug. That fitted Paul11's story. 'The video was posted on YouTube, it's probably featured on loads of blogs. Why did you think I'd be able to help you?'

'We believe Minola has an associate, another magician, a Peter Ruchio?' Brown showed Titus a still from the CCTV footage, too grainy and blurred to tell anything from it. 'He seems to be quite a fan of yours.'

Now if Titus hadn't been quite as cosseted by his parents as he was, he might have recognized that name. Mind you, if he hadn't been as cosseted he might never have become the spoilt brat that caused such misery in

Peter's life in the first place. But Mr and Mrs Black, following advice from Hampstead friends in the child psychology racket, had done everything they could to stop the trauma of that 'attack' at his eighth birthday party from affecting him. After the court case, it was never mentioned again. They held another birthday party, this time without a clown. Peter's name was never spoken, the event never referred to. So while Peter could never forget what happened that day, Titus couldn't help but forget. It had been a prank. There had been no emotional impact at the time. All he had was a vague memory of talking to a video screen showing a woman whom others addressed as 'your honour'.

Equally, in Peter's police records, as a minor, Titus was referred to only as 'Child A'. Brown had no idea that he was talking to the victim of Peter's only recorded offence.

'I'm sure you know,' Titus said earnestly, 'that I'm really not responsible for my fans' actions.'

'Oh no,' Brown put his hands up, 'we know that, but he really seemed such a big fan we thought you might know him.' He pulled some of the photo albums from a bag and passed them to Titus.

Where Brown had seen an obsessive, Titus was vain enough to see only adoration. Page after page of photos of himself. Even the derogatory comments scrawled on some of them seemed no more than the jealousy of one of his many imitators. Titus smiled smugly and handed the albums back. 'I really can't help you.'

'OK, well thank you.' Brown rose and Brightly nodded.

Titus waited for the door to close and their footsteps

to descend before laughing out loud. 'Hoax? My arse.'
Now he was convinced. The police don't come calling
just because a hoax video gets posted. Somebody badly
wanted to protect the existence of the memory wiper.
But Titus was ahead of them. He had a fan on the inside
at the lab; it was time to use him.

Titus logged back on to his computer and pressed
'Reply' to the email. 'Dear Paul11,' he wrote.

43

The police launch chuffed through the moonlit waves,
sending a widening spume of luminous froth in its
wake. Agent Brown stood at the bow, not quite believing he was back in the dead-end delta that was
Christchurch harbour. Surely Minola would have
moved on by now, but then the double, triple, quadruple bluff were all standards in Kate's repertoire. He
turned to take in the elderly cyborg standing next to
him on the foredeck. 'Do you mind telling me all that
again,' he said, 'but this time without the TLAs?'

The mandroid, his silver hair pulsating blue, lit by the
phone headset clipped to his ear, looked puzzled.
'TLAs?'

'Three-letter acronyms, buddy. No jargon, just plain
English.'

'Right. Put simply, we traced the Proxy Server
Address for the Media File Upload, the video clip you
asked about, and logged the pattern of all the Discreet

Packet Switches that were made. We then looked for corresponding Data Packet Burst patterns on the South Dorset Area Internet Service Providers' servers and the mobile networks. We found the same pattern chunking through the V-Mobile network from a Pay-as-You-Go data stick with a Subscriber Identity Module card. We then triangulated the computer from the Aerial Data Logs to find out exactly where the card was at the time the data was sent.' He peered up at Brown's dark features. 'Was that clearer?'

Brown suppressed his urge to send Inspector Gadget flying off the boat with a jab to his solar-panelled plexus. He laced his large fingers together and exhaled loudly; a calming technique he had learned on a psych evaluation following an unfortunate 'undue force' indictment. If the complainant had been a suspect nobody would have batted an eyelid but, apparently, witnesses bleed more easily. He was told that the finger weaving and breathing would help. It did nothing to help his feelings of utter frustration, but it did help the people he wanted to hit remain conscious.

♥

'So. First things first. We'll start with the basics. Like, what is magic?' Peter tucked his thumbs into his imaginary professorial sub-fusc as he strode in front of the little table. Kate was sitting on the opposite side, exercise book open, pencil at the ready, and had already concentrated for longer than she had ever done at school. Before writing 'What is Magic?' she licked the tip of the pencil but as soon as the sour graphite bit her tongue she regretted it. She wondered why reporters in old films always seemed to be doing it.

'Focus, Minola,' Peter barked.

Kate sat up straighter.

'Every magic trick revolves around one simple principle: illusion. Convincing people to believe one thing is happening when what is going on is quite another.'

Kate scribbled, looked at it and shook her head. 'But that's just deceit. You could say the same about any scam plan.'

'Scam plan?'

'The blueprint for a con, a grift, a play.'

Peter sat down wearily. 'Kate, do you really want me to do this? I keep telling you: finding out about making magic is an exercise in accumulating disappointment. If the simplicity of the basic premise frustrates you, you really won't like what else there is to conjuring. Look at the Magic Circle. It all seems very mysterious, very glamorous. But really? It's more like a support group for the terminally disappointed. For the jaded and wonder-less. They're all there trying to find some value for the heavy price they paid for their disillusionment. They guard entry to the circle judiciously, not to protect them and their secrets from the outside world but to protect the outside world from their morbid disenchantment. Outside it's all smiles and "pick a card". But inside, they can't stop asking themselves, "What's the bloody point? Maybe if my sordid puzzles can astonish and entertain enough people it will give me some sodding purpose in life." Maybe that's why it's a circle, they just go round and round.'

'I'm not that easily dissuaded, Peter.'

'OK, well how about this? Not only is performing magic just about one basic principle, guess how many physically different magic effects there are?'

Kate raised her shoulders and spread her fingers. 'I don't know. Thousands? Millions? Tell me.'

'Six.'

'OK,' said Kate cautiously, 'I'm pretty sure I've seen more than that.'

'What you've seen are just variations on the six themes. I'll show you.' Peter took a pound coin from his pocket and started throwing it from hand to hand. 'First effect, think glamorous assistant disappearing from locked box or a card from a pack.' He caught the coin in his right hand, clenched his fist, and then his fingers opened one by one like the petals of a blossoming flower. The hand was empty. 'Number one.' Peter smiled. 'The vanish.'

♠

Beyond the low throbbing of the boat's motor Brown could hear Brightly talking quietly behind him. She was giving last instructions to a huddle of police officers. Just from how the moon shone in their eyes, blacked in kohl, swathed in balaclavas, he was pretty sure that they represented the less-hinged, gung-ho, hooligan element of the Wessex police force. They appeared to have volunteered for this bit of overtime on the condition that they could dress in full Black Ops gear and pretend that they were members of special forces. Organizations which had, in all likelihood, already rejected them on the grounds that their proximity to lethal weapons would present a clear and constantly present danger. It was probably a mistake to have even issued them with tasers but Brightly said it had been a 'deal breaker'.

Brown sighed. He was starting to get homesick for the straightforward world of bullets and busts. Somewhere that didn't hold armaments in the googly-eyed awe of a forbidden sensation, worshipping the gun with the fear and thrill of a cargo cult. Somewhere you're not having to watch your back all the time because you're as likely to be gunned down by jumpy friendly fire as by hostile. His gaze returned to the incomprehensible Cyber Crimes detective festooned with so much gadgetry it looked like he was turning into something bionic, a sort of steampunk electronic automaton. 'So,' Brown managed to breathe, 'in short?'

'In short,' said DC 'w00t' Williams, pulling out his hi-def GPS tracker device displaying a satellite picture of the beach with a large X on one of the huts, 'the computer was located in the fifteenth hut from the north end, facing the sea.'

'You can be that accurate?'

'Video files are big. We had a large data footprint to follow.'

◆

Peter waited patiently for Kate to write '1.' and 'Vanish' in her notebook.

'Next,' he said, lifting the notebook and pulling the

vanished pound coin out from under it, 'there's the effect of something materializing from nowhere. That's the wizard arriving in a puff of smoke or maybe the ball appearing under the unexpected cup.'

'2. Materialization,' Kate scribbled.

Peter started throwing the coin from hand to hand again. 'You get magicians arguing that the ball disappearing under one cup and appearing under another is a transposition, something travelling invisibly from one place . . .' he caught the coin in his right fist again and then opened it to reveal it had gone once more, 'to another.' Peter opened his left hand to show the coin there. 'But, let's face it, that's just a vanish, then a materialization.'

Kate sat at the table scribbling more notes. 'So that's just two effects?'

'I think so. The coin's invisible journey is just an explanation for the two effects to follow each other. Which is a bit like transformations. You know, when one object . . .' he closed his fingers around the coin, rolled up his sleeve and then, inserting the fingers of his left hand into his right fist, pulled a five-pound note very slowly from the closed hand, 'becomes another. But really that's just one object vanishing and a different one materializing. The metamorphosis, like the invisible journey, is just a bogus explanation, a bit of misdirection.'

Kate thought about this. 'But some things transform in front of your eyes, without disappearing. You know, when a hanky becomes a dove, or a candle.'

'It might just be faster than the eye can see but really that's just a vanish instantly followed by a materialization. Sometimes something can seem to grow unnaturally, but I think that's just the materialization of parts that were invisible before.'

Kate snatched the five-pound note from Peter's fingers but, unlike the schoolgirl who would examine the objects for their hidden magical properties, now she just eyed the delicate fingertips that had performed the feat. Now, at last, she knew she was looking in the right direction.

♣

In the pallid moonlight, the captain cut the engine and let the launch drift silently into the shallows on the bay side of the beach. One by one the ninja nutters slipped quietly into the water and lolloped to the shore in strange monkey-like crouches, not unlike the movements of those prevolutionary homoreptilians that first lurched on to dry land.

'They do know we're arresting a con artist, not invading Cuba?' Brown asked.

Brightly shook her head. 'Trouble is, you give them a taser and it just goes to their heads.'

Brown, Brightly and w00t waited for the boat to moor at the little jetty twenty feet beyond, before disembarking in a more evolved manner.

♥

'Even an escape is a vanish of sorts,' Peter began to fold the fiver carefully, 'from the locked box and chains and cuffs. And then a materialization outside of those chains and things. But that brings us to the third effect, the visible penetration.'

Taking the pen from Kate's hand, Peter pushed it through the note so it appeared poking out the other side. 'Where one solid object goes through another, a coin through a table, a cigarette through a coin.' He looked at the pen and the note. 'OK, I know that any-body can push a pen through a piece of paper, but that leads us to the fourth effect . . .'

♠

The two senior officers and the huge American agent stopped again, at the end of the row of huts, waiting for the all-clear. The rise and fall of each neat peaked roof in a line stretching along the margin of the bay appeared to merge into a single silhouette, to cut the moonlight with a serrated edge. The sea slowly climbed up and down the pale sand in easy-breathing sweeps. Nothing disturbed the calm except the occasional flitting of dark shadows among the huts as the various tasered-up squad officers darted in and out, taking up position to block all possible flight paths for the fugitives.

W00t's radio crackled quietly. 'Officers in place,' it whispered. He tapped Brightly on the shoulder and she twisted round to smile at the techominid. 'Thanks,' she murmured. By the time she had turned back, Brown was twenty yards away, striding towards the hut.

♦

'. . . restoration.' Peter ripped Kate's pen straight through the fiver and passed it back to her but when he opened the note it was completely intact. 'Think of all the women getting sawn in half and emerging unscathed, the torn and restored playing cards, the Zig Zag women and so on.'

Kate wrote down more in her list. 'So what are the other two?'

Peter scrunched the fiver up and placed it on the table in front of him. 'They're both to do with impossible motion. The fifth effect they call telekinesis: an object is moved independently, just by thinking about it. Like this five-pound ball.'

Kate looked at the paper ball and then at Peter. Suddenly the ball started to quiver, then jerk, and then roll around on the spot ever so slightly.

'Which,' Peter whispered, watching the ball intently as if he were controlling it with his mind – or perhaps surreptitiously blowing it – 'obviously contravenes Newton's first law of motion, but what's even more impressive is that the last of the six magic tricks defies his fundamental law of gravity.'

Right before Kate's eyes the paper ball rose sharply into the air. Peter put his hands up and moved away a little, as if to emphasize that he wasn't in control of the ball that danced and hovered in the air before dropping suddenly to the table top. Kate grabbed the note and opened it but could find nothing to explain what she had seen. She smiled in bewilderment.

Peter smiled back: it was nice to have the upper hand on Kate and he found himself wondering what it might be like to have the lower hand as well. 'It's the same basic idea as the floating hypnotized ladies or light bulbs or metal balls.'

'That's it? That's every magic trick ever?'

'Every physical trick is based on one of those. There's a couple of mental effects as well.'

'What?' Kate grinned. 'Really crazy stuff?'

'No.' Peter fiddled with the fiver, unable to completely shake his last 'lower hand' thought which had fast become a fondle memory. 'Mind magic, thought reading, that sort of thing. And you know, those six tricks I did used just three different methods.'

Kate was suddenly a kid again, filled with wonder, watching her father. She felt that if she could go back to that time, maybe she could pick a different path through life. 'And you'll teach me how to do it?'

'If you really want to be disappointed. Yes.'

'I won't be disappointed, that's amazing.'

'Nobody thinks that they will be, until they are.'

There was a rattling noise outside. Kate killed the light. 'Shhh.' Quickly they rolled under the bed as they had practised.

♣

With an ear pressed to the door of the hut, Brown stood silently listening. He glanced back at the two officers who were perched in the shadows by the porch and gave them a slight nod. Brightly stood at the side. Technically she would have to make the entry; they wouldn't want Minola getting off on a technicality. Brown moved back as the two Black Ops cops inched forward. The leader held his leg up like a dog by a lamp-post, ready to put his boot in the door. Brightly held five fingers up and mouthed the word 'five'. Rhythmically she folded one finger down. 'Four.' And then the next, mouthing each number until she was down to one finger. She lifted it. 'One.' The finger fell and the black boot sprang, hard, smashing into the door.

♥

With a loud bang the door swung open and light streamed in. It blinded both Peter and Kate for a moment as they tried to peek out from under the bed. There was a maelstrom of activity outside, a tumult of shouting and crashing suddenly filled their tiny space, and then a clear voice booming.

'*Monsieur, mademoiselle, vous êtes arrivés. Allons-y.*'

The two slid out from under the bed and stared out of their furniture truck. The last time they had looked out of that door was when they had clambered in by the Brake Fast! Caff, a mobile chip shop in a sodden grey lay-by on the Portsmouth Road. Now, a busy market was setting up around them. Doomed poultry, not yet slaughtered, squawked urgently as traders set up stalls, clanking, clattering and cursing in the narrow *rue*.

Kate leaned out of the truck and, placing Clarissa's ring in the driver's hand, she gave him a kiss on both cheeks. '*Merci, merci.*' She grinned at Peter. 'So this would, technically, be called a "translocation". Right? Welcome to Paris, *mon ami.*'

44

'Tavasligh? No. I don't think so.' Paula's eyes returned to her computer screen.

'Look,' Verstehung waved the Lotus House brochure, 'here, can't you see Dr Tavasligh listed as a director?'

Paula looked up and swiped the brochure from his hand. 'It also lists HRH the Duke of Kent as patron,' Paula said, scanning it. 'I don't have his number either.'

'So you have no way of contacting Tavasligh?'

'No.'

'Is the manager here?'

'I'm the duty manager.'

Verstehung shrugged and looked at Wissenschaft. '*Oy vey*. What can you do?'

'Always with the bits of evidence, Dick?' Wissenschaft shook his head. 'How can you see the whole picture?' He turned to Paula. 'I don't think you understand my colleague, miss. He is not asking you *if* you have Tavasligh's details, he's asking you *for* Tavasligh's details.'

Paula stood up, surprising the two men with her towering blonde stature. Now there was a shiksa. 'I don't know any details so now please leave before I have to call the police.'

Wissenschaft was the first to recover. Big though he was, she towered over him. Unintimidated, he leaned towards her menacingly. 'Shall we see what the computer says?' He pulled her computer screen round and reached for the keyboard.

Paula grabbed Wissenschaft's wrist. 'Computer says no,' she said, less with irony than with steely metal. The iron was in her grip, like a vice, one of the more addictive ones. It held Wissenschaft so firmly he could not even twist his hand. With the other one he grabbed a pair of scissors from Paula's pen tidy and quickly swung it across towards the hand which held him. With the consummate timing of one who has survived years of domestic violence, Paula jerked Wissenschaft's trapped hand upward at the very last moment, neatly forcing him to drive the scissors into his own hand.

He cursed with the pain. Mostly in Yiddish but even Paula got the idea. She released his wrist, now dripping with blood. 'Go. Now,' she said, gripping the bottom of her desk as if pressing something. 'I've pushed the police panic button. They'll be here in less than five minutes.'

Verstehung pulled the scissors from Wissenschaft's hand.

'And I want those back,' Paula insisted.

Timidly, Verstehung placed the bloody scissors back on her desk and wrapped his friend's hand with his scarf. 'Always the direct approach, Dick?' he said as they headed to the door. 'Can't you tell not everyone likes it? Don't you have a feeling for the situation?'

Back in the Lexus, Verstehung phoned it in to Titus.

'Not here,' he said, 'we've looked thoroughly. Tavasligh's not in Christchurch.'

362

'So it's possible the lab is in Paris? As Paul11's claiming?' Titus's voice was filled with optimism.

'Is Paris in Christchurch?'

'Er. No.'

'Then why wouldn't it be possible?' Verstehung looked at his injured friend. 'There'll be extra charges for this one, OK?'

'Sure, sure.' Titus already sounded distant. He hung up.

Paul11's version of things seemed to be bearing out. Tavasligh's last known location before the Patient S. debacle was Christchurch but that was years ago. If Tavasligh had left the country to continue the research, Paris was right on the mark.

From: _Project Notebook 11.32_ p2

Verstehung did have a point though. Just because I wasn't, apparently, in Christchurch didn't make Paris any more likely. But the pattern-forming mind is full of leaps of imagination, synaptic gaps and conclusions. All the detectives had established was a negative, but that somehow, to Titus's mind, just went to confirm a positive. It is the same flawed thinking that occurs when you're considering buying a new car and suddenly you start seeing the model of car that you're interested in all over the place. Everybody seems to be driving the car you want. This, of course, is just perspective. There are no more nor fewer cars, it's just that your mind has established a flagging-up system based on that model that tells you to take a conscious note when you see one. Also, the area you live in and see most will, for most people, have many others in similar income brackets and even mindsets to you, so there may well be a slightly higher chance of seeing a car you're interested in because your neighbours have a social propensity for similar interests. Still, Titus took the lack of a Tavasligh in Christchurch as independent evidence that Paul11 was on the level.

The emails had carried on apace; slowly Titus was charming Paul11. Gradually hinting at an introduction to Tavasligh. For over two weeks the relationship had blossomed as Titus groomed Paul11. Eventually the email arrived.

Subject: Re: Tavasligh Memory Wiper Video
From: paul11@gmail.com
Date: 23 May: 12.42
To: iam@titusblack.com

Hi Titus   Got a bit drunk last night and told Tavasligh all about you. Said you were interested in the Alpha Wave Disrupter. Anyway, things have changed, think there might be a way now. We're moving on from the AWD and think financing next phase may be causing a change of heart re sale. Can you come to Paris? Asap?   Your mate, Paul

45

'Had it been . . . different circumstances, do you think . . . I mean, do you think we might have . . . ?'

Brightly looked at Brown as if he might be slightly mad. 'Listen, you're nice, I've enjoyed working with you and I'm sorry it's been such a massive waste of time, and overtime, and equipment, and police resources, and I think you know who's going to get blamed for all this. You've got a lot going for you, Danny, but, not to beat about the bush (I know you've got a plane to catch), on a policeman's pension? Really? When I get hitched I'm looking to hang up my badge, my sensible shoes and my quite frankly bloody itchy big underwear. I need someone better off. A lot better off. So unless you can tell me now that you've stashed away a fortune from one of your busts, you're not getting near mine.'

'You're pretty direct, Brightly.'

'It's one of the things you like about me.'

Brown heaved a big sigh as he fiddled with the strap of his bag. 'And that sure ain't the first time I've heard that.'

'Gate nineteen,' whined a voice taking the T out of 'tannoy', 'is closing. American Airways to New York. Gate nineteen.'

'You know,' Brown looked at Brightly, 'I've spent my life catching millionaire fraudsters and conmen. Most of them beautiful people, people that people like to like, with great smiles and feel-good repartee and they get tagged in their penthouses or they're sent to prisons with tennis courts and swimming pools for a few years because they're low risk and their crimes were "victimless" because the only people who got hurt were so far down the line they're invisible, people like you or me trying to pay the hike on our insurance premiums. And the assholes I catch? They bury their assets under a rock or in Switzerland or someone else's name and when they've done their time and they come out, their nest eggs are waiting and they've got a whole legally blameless jet-set life ahead of them. And the guy who caught them? The guy who brought them to book? Nickels and dimes. Nickels and dimes.'

Brightly tutted. 'You should have told me I was going to need a violin.'

'It's like I've facilitated their lives, they no longer need to be afraid of the law because they've got the loot and there's no more fear. Hell, I'm surprised they didn't line up to get caught. You know, there are times when I can't even think of an easier way to earn a million dollars than to stay in a prison that's like a five-star hotel for a couple of years. And if it weren't for my declining adolescent sense of morality, I think to myself, What's stopping any one of us doing it? What's stopping me from doing it? Why aren't I having a bite at that cherry pi—'

'Last call,' the tannoy interrupted, 'boarding gate nineteen, American Airways to New York, gate nineteen.'

'You've got to go.' Brightly tiptoed up and kissed him on the cheek with a force that burned. 'The Yard'll have my guts for garters if I let you miss your flight.'

'Hey, now you got me thinking of your garters.'

'Dream on, big guy. Safe journey.'

'Sure.' Brown nodded. 'Maybe if I came back one day, on holiday. Do you think we could . . .'

'Go,' Brightly ordered, pushing him through the security gate. She nodded to the metal-detecting officer who waved him through urgently.

Brown took one last pitiful look at Brightly and started running heavily in the direction of his gate. It wasn't until he was sure he was out of sight of Brightly, security or CCTV that he ducked into the arrivals corridor, filed along with a posse of red-eyed Texans and re-presented himself at passport control.

'Business or pleasure?' the scowling customs officer demanded, staring at his passport.

'Pleasure.' Brown smiled. He still had one lead and he wasn't letting go of it. He knew Titus Black was somehow involved and the bug he'd left in Titus's office would tell him exactly how. So he didn't have the co-operation of the Limey police. Who needed them? Catching Kate, the pleasure would be all his.

5,000 Milliseconds to Higham
(TEA *minus 11 months 19 days 8 hours*)

Kate

Just for a second. What if this is love? The gooey stuff in the books, the partnership that goes further, the mutual support, the soul partner. What if this is the only chance I have, what if Peter is it? How many other people could even get to first base in understanding who I am and how I think and operate? Look at him lying there. What if that bag of flesh is the only one I'll ever meet who can talk to me, to me inside?

So I grab the case, I get out. Will I be leaving the really important thing behind?

I've got to stay put. Give it a chance. This is it, the moment I change. The moment I put the heart above the moolah. Fuck you, Clarissa. This is it, a new life, a new adventure, with him. Together we scored this money, what else could we do? Great things. Straight or crooked. Always been an opportunist. Why have I been stopping myself seeing this, him, as an opportunity? A chance to become something new, to change, to escape the fake and . . .

But what if he makes a move for the case?

I'll kill him.

He won't. But, just in case. Shouldn't I get there before him? Maybe I just open my eyes but, if he does go for the grab, there's really no point in carrying on. The trust thing's out the window. If it didn't happen tonight it would still happen. Maybe not today, maybe not tomorrow but here's looking at you, kid.

I'll stay. I'll watch. Let's see.

46

It was too hot to get up. And too early. Unruly sunlight coursed through the shutter slats, coating the plain bedcovers in a racy zebra print. Somewhere distantly, across the city, a church bell tolled. The whole room seemed to drowse in milky brightness, all detail lost in the soundless white light. All was still except the fine dust slowly swimming and glittering through the shafts of light and the pounding torrent of neurochemicals that flooded Kate's brain. Not even conscious and the adrenalin was already surging through her body, as it always did on a sting day.

From: _Project Notebook 31.12_ p10

As the dream faded and the web of Kate's neural strands began to spark and leap from gamma to beta to alpha wave frequency, they ignited her sequence of nano-neuro-queries that generates consciousness: the round of checks and questions our brains are constantly asking as they continuously re-establish who we are through the waking day: Where am I?; Why am I here?; What am I doing?; How am I doing it?; Who knows I'm doing it? And within

the frame of our answers, each one of us hangs our identity. The amalgamation of our eternally shifting replies
answers the further, grander, eternally shifting question:
Who am I?

But these answers don't just determine our identity; as
the discreet building blocks of cognition, they are, put
simply, consciousness itself.

For Kate the answers came easily. 'In bed, Suite 63,
sixième à droite, Hotel du Nord'; 'to make a lot of
money'; 'scamming a minor TV magician'; 'by selling an
imaginary device'; 'Peter'. Only the last answer felt odd.
For almost two decades the answer had always been
'just me', but now there was another name and Kate
wasn't sure that she was comfortable with it being so
core to her self-identification. Having a witness.
However, Kate's less critical nervous system, having
found its initial answers and ascertained, as best it
could, who exactly she was, then allowed her to set her
more consciously directable neural patterning on to
future questions; all the 'what if's of the hours ahead.
Before her eyes had even opened she was choreograph-
ing the day to come, anticipating all the possible
variants and different ways each of her actions could
lead and how she would steer things back to her track
plan.

By the time the dream million had passed into her
hands, Kate was yawning. Her eyelids fluttered as they
conditioned her irises for the coming brightness of the
room. The drone of a motor scooter tore along the
cobbled street far below. Now and again a snoring
breath would mimic this vesparation. She rolled lazily

and looked over the edge at Peter curled up on the floor.

Lacking an invitation, or the ego to assume, to share Kate's bed, Peter had chosen to sleep on the chaise longue, a piece of furniture jammed into their tiny room not only to add an *ambiance très française* but to justify *le prix exagéré* for transforming the tiny room into a suite. Although Kate had no intention of paying any prix, especially not to the leery concierge in the lobby, she smiled at the thought that the chaise longue had finally found a purpose. It had always seemed to her that the invention of this totally unattractive and futile *objet* was, in itself, a justification for Waterloo and the deposition of Napoleon. It was a neoclassical misinterpretation of a Roman daybed, devised in desperation to forge links with the classical empire of the Romans. Any culture that could iconize a piece of furniture that tries to be a chair, a sofa and a bed, but utterly fails as a substitute for any of them while challenging all sense of symmetry and proportion, is a civilization that has already reached its nadir. When something so utterly useless can define an epoch, it really is time to move on. Not just for a night, Josephine.

For the entire fortnight that they had been staying there, each time Peter had fallen asleep he had almost immediately fallen off the chaise and spent the rest of the night splayed out on the rug on the floor. Now, dipped in tranquil morning, he lay on his back breathing heavily, peacefully, arms stretched out cruciform as Kate followed the sinewy contours of his frame. His bare chest rose and fell slowly, invitingly warm. She wondered what it would be like to lay her head on it. With an inexplicable fondness, like that of a mother inspecting her young, Kate traced the muscle masses that gently undulated beneath the skin of his arms and down to his long hands, and his quite beautiful, delicate prestidigitator's fingers.

It had taken a fortnight to prepare the scam and reel Titus in; it had been almost three weeks constantly in Peter's company. Kate had had marriages shorter than that. Most of them, in fact. Peter brought no money, no power, no intrigue, no challenge to the equation and yet not only had she not tired of him, it felt as if he had always been with her, like she had just never turned round to take a look.

Kate put her arms out to support her weight on the floor and then slowly tumbled off the bed, bringing the sheets with her entangled in her legs. Gently she eased herself beside Peter's sleeping form, placing her leg across his, an arm across his chest and allowing the heat of her body to slowly be absorbed into the cool of his.

Half dreaming, Peter's own nano-neuroqueries plagued him with tantalizing and preposterous answers. He willed himself to believe that the sensation of the warm bare body that seemed to be moving on to his was true, and yet dared not open his eyes for fear that it was a dream and he would lose it in the waking. He longed for it to be Kate and yet could not quite bring himself to believe that she would come to him like this. That really did feel like the light touch of a fingertip tantalizingly running along his arm, over his hand, tracing his hip bone and slowly running across and down towards his crotch. Unbearably real.

It was less than a touch, more than a touch, a wash of warm breeze, an impalpable wrap of scent, a force that left him struggling to remain unwoken and inert against the pulsing push and pull already straining between his legs.

Kate realized that she must have been wondering more about his body than she had dared admit to herself. Now so close, so naked, every rise and dip drew a nod of recognition, as if they were the landmarks of a country familiar only through the long study of its maps. From her low, close-up, perspective, his jutting collarbone seemed to expand to a mountain range, and even as the three dimensions that defined his body seemed to distort, so the fourth dimension of time seemed to bend; her imagination raced forward to the moments ahead as if the anticipation and what was anticipated were occurring simultaneously. So even as her finger idly ran up the centre of his torso, she was picturing him above her; now she was the one being rolled over on her back in the bright room with his sinewy outline bearing down on her, his shadow rhythmically, urgently, covering and uncovering her. The thought brought a burning twinge below the crest of her pubic bone and bore wetly downwards. Impulsively she sat up and set herself astride him, her knees cradling his hips. She leaned forward, holding herself over him, and examined his peacefully sleeping face. As much to tease as to experience, she slowly lowered her shoulders until her breasts hung over the slow swell and plunge of his sleeping chest, at the height of his intake the distance between the two of them no more than the thickness of Turkish toilet paper. Gently she began to swing her shoulders minutely, watching her hardening nipples brush like little more than the wind across his own tiny dark areolae. Within seconds his breath seemed to break and quicken. Kate knelt up again. Did she really want to wake him? Did she really want to go this way?

But now, rising, fluttering against her buttocks, she could feel that at least one part of him had been wide, and somewhat long, awake. And here, now, she realized was the parting of . . . ? Never had Kate felt so cursed by the eternal presence of her meta-mind, one that always has to analyse, objectify and examine as much as, if not more than, it partakes and indulges and participates. Even as she looked down at his naked body framed by her breasts that felt swollen with her longing, she also knew she was poised at the parting of the two paths their partnership could follow. Even as she felt the heat of his hips and the trembling against her backside she felt suspended between the practicalities of a working relationship with a job to be done and her own unutterable magnetic urges.

If he opened his eyes, she knew she was lost, she knew from the hot wetness that seemed to be streaming within her, aching, as she clenched her bum to try and stem the flow, suspended above him, she would have no choice any more. If he just opened his eyes there would be only one glorious way to go and yet was she ready to plunge herself into that, on to that, hold him within her and become just a part of a whole, a part of a beast where decisions were compromises? She swallowed as if she could stop the flood.

Now Peter was absolutely sure that he was just

pretending to be asleep. When had he felt more awake, more charged? He yearned for the next touch, imaginary or real. An irresistible energy seemed to be mounting, he could hear it in the rising pounding in his heart, the blood rushing and pounding in his ears. Somehow he knew, hardly touching him but pressing hard against him, it really was Kate. All he had to do was open his eyes.

Kate looked at him. She swallowed again, eager but anxious, frustrated but grateful to him for playing the sleeper. She knew he was trying to give her every out possible, to give her time to choose him, his body, the urgent weight of fulfilment or . . . alight while it was still feasible to do so without recrimination. Even if he was *sh*leeping; there, supine, his form still seemed to exert such a compelling pheromonal power she felt dizzy with indecision; a rare, exotic though not exactly comfortable feeling but, in that irresolution, she had already taken a little bit of him inside her.

Though it is little bigger than a thumbnail in itself, like most amygdalas, Kate's consisted of several nuclei which competed to inspire the best survival tactics. Her central nucleus told her to stop, her basal nucleus told her to fly, and her naughty limbic system right next to them tried to inhibit their responses, anaesthetizing them with glorious happy dopamine, anticipating the potential pleasures of the ready and willing body beneath her.

Somehow her basal nucleus won through, over-coming the neuron-inhibiting gamma-amniobutyric acid that tried to mute its cry. Thoughtlessly, silently, carefully, Kate dismounted and clambered back on to the bed. Rolling on to her back, she ran the heel of her palm hard over her pelvis and curled her fingers on to the warm wetness. When she had barely touched herself, a shudder shot through her, along her spine to her neck, her shoulders, and a tiny gasp escaped her lips.

But Peter's imagination had gone too far to hold back. His imaginary Kate drew a finger slowly down his chest, creeping along to the tensed lower stomach to induce a pleasure so intense it verged on pain. His buttocks contracted involuntarily and his pelvis shot upwards. He opened his eyes but as T. S. Eliot's poem about man's eternal search for a pussy eloquently put it, macavity was not there.

47

After the IRA, in the nineteen seventies, developed a penchant for placing bombs in London's dustbins, the city's refuse containers were redesigned to resemble stumpy black postboxes complete with little roofs and brick-sized holes in the sides near the top. These holes were supposed to limit the size of object that could be deposited, which, if you were making your bombs out of bulky fertilizer, would indeed render them more difficult to plant. Limiting the size of rubbish that could be left had the added virtue of enabling the councils to empty them less frequently, so everybody except the wicked bombmakers seemed to win with the new design.

Of course if you were to make your bombs from more compact materials like Semtex, or good old sticks of dynamite, there was nothing to stop you sliding as much as you liked into one of these bins and visual checks of the bins were less easy and less frequent. In fact, considering a blast follows the path of least resistance, the majority of your explosion would no longer be forced upwards, relatively harmlessly, into the air but would be funnelled horizontally outwards at waist height, massively increasing the radius of your killing potential by cutting everybody down at the hip.

If you happen not to be a bombmaker but a heavyset FBI agent, the hoods of these bins also make excellent places to hide things, affixed to the ceiling with a generous wodge of gaffer tape. The bin outside Titus's office in Soho proved an excellent home for a voice-activated memo recorder plugged into a small FM receiver.

Having retrieved his device and found a quiet corner of a stickily dark and beer-stained Soho pub in which to listen to it, Agent Brown felt somewhat upbeat. The recorder had faithfully picked up every word broadcast by the bug that he had placed under Titus's BAFTA award for Best Show Featuring an Arrogant Twat, an award for which every year the competition is stiff.

He rewound and wound through endless drivel but there was no mistaking the excitement in Titus's voice when contact was made.

'Ronnie. It's him again. He says Tavasligh's up for it.'

'Up for what?'

'You know. Showing me the wiper thing. Maybe selling it. And . . . look, that's why the boys couldn't find them in Dorset. They're in France, in Paris. He wants us to make an offer. Go out there and test the thing.'

'Titus, what the—? He might as well be selling you meds or trying to shift money out of the Bank of Nigeria. You've got no idea who this person is. It could be, no, it probably *is* a complete con.'

'Ronnie. You've got no faith. I've been talking to him for weeks. I know exactly who he is.'

'And that is?'

'He's Paul.'

'Paul who?'

Titus paused. 'Well, eleven.'

'Really, Mr and Mrs Eleven must be so proud of their son.'

'Look, it's worth going. The boys can check him out. This would put me so far ahead of the game . . .'

'Yeah. If it's true. But what if it's all bullshit?'

'But what if it isn't? What if I miss the opportunity? You've got to be open to opportunities. You've got to be looking for them. You can hide in a shell of cynicism but life and its riches will pass you by. You'll be safe in your cocoon and never get anywhere. I'm open, Ronnie. I grab opportunities when they come along. I get the chances because I know how to spot them, how to grab them. That's why I'm where I am, with my own telly series, and you're where you are, waving the applause sign.'

'Oh, it had nothing to do with the fact that your daddy was chairman of the TV company then?'

Brown stopped the recorder and looked at his watch. He fished his cellphone out of his coat and dialled New York.

'Hey, Larry. No. No, actually I decided to extend my stay. In fact I thought I'd take in Paris. Paris, France. Yeah. I've got a heads-up our little bird's flown there. What? Oh shit. I forgot. Yeah, the three things the French don't do: marital fidelity, oral medicine and extradition. Look. If it's OK with you I'm going to wait for my inform-ant to get back. If the lead's gone cold I'll be straight back. Sure. Yeah. Sorry. I know, they're always bitching about how much it all cost. It's what they do. Yeah, well, thanks for that. Yeah, I'll keep outta trouble. No, I mean it. See you later, Larry. Sure. Bye.'

48

It was another half-hour before either Kate or Peter would admit that they were awake. Then they rose stickily and silently fought for the bathroom. Neither spoke about what had happened or what they had imagined happening. It wasn't until they were sitting at a table crammed on to the narrow pavement outside the Café de la Paix on the corner of their street that they really spoke, and then it was all business. Two *cafés crèmes*, croissants from the *boulanger* across the road. Kate brushed the yellow flakes from the shiny aluminium table.

'It's all yours to play now, Magic. I'm just there to back you up.'

Peter nodded and sipped the muddy-looking coffee. 'It's your plan though, your script.'

'We've paced it out, you know all the moves, how to steer it. He's not going to hand over money like that for a couple of minutes in a sideshow, you're going to have to build it all up, the main event, the drama.'

Peter nodded. 'What I don't get though is how,' he put down his cup and looked at Kate with puppy-like awe, 'do you even start thinking about putting something like this together? It takes me a week to figure out how to make up a new trick and then I'll find someone's already got there three decades before me in the *Pallbearers' Review*. You're altering someone's very concept of reality and you've done it in a few days. How?'

'You ever wonder why murder isn't one of the seven deadly sins? Or paedophilia? Or rape? Or lying or bullying or what about just swearing, you ignorant fucker?' Kate dipped the end of her croissant into her coffee, where a diaspora of tiny flakes swam off across the surface. 'Seems a bit of an oversight.' A soggy sliver of croissant leapt out to lie over her lip. She brought the back of her hand up to push it in again. 'That is until you think how all those things don't happen in vacuums, they tend to be inspired by something. And you can bet, if you go to the heart of any of those crimes, it's still one or more of those hoary, archaic, centuries-old seven sins behind it all. They're like a list of motives rather than crimes in themselves and they're just about one of the greatest psychological insights religion has ever gifted the world, a definitive list of human weaknesses. It's certainly a gift for any of us who might make our living from deception.' Kate winked at Peter.

'Because they're humanity's soft spots,' Peter

concurred, 'the weak points on the dragon's underbelly which you exploit.'

'Me? I'm not the only one at this table who makes a living from deception,' Kate pointed out acidly.

Peter nodded thoughtfully. 'I suppose it's true. They're a part of the art of misdirection. The things that distract people, or get them to look in the direction you want them . . . The beautiful assistant is a bit of lust; coins and cards, the basics of gambling attract the attention of our greed and envy; the frustration of not knowing the secrets, what's that? Anger?'

'It's not just greed and envy inspired by card tricks and something for nothing, it's sloth, the good life for the minimum effort. And the challenge to your pride when you take the puzzle on, working out how the trick was done. What does that leave? Gluttony?'

'At kids' parties I used to make a cake appear,' Peter suggested.

'Gluttony isn't the sin it used to be. I mean in medieval times it might have had some point, but now? In this western world of cheap fast food, where the poorest are the fattest? It's kind of lost its place,' Kate slurped her coffee loudly, 'but in my book I replace it with a much more insidious sin.'

Peter looked at her with open-mouthed admiration. 'Only you could invent a sin.'

'Collusion, Peter. Think about it. The going along with others and their sins. The not thinking for yourself. Sinning because you are too scared or pathetic to challenge the orthodoxy or because you're desperate to be in with the cool crowd or the usual wankers. Collusion is the lack of independence, the lack of backbone, to stand up for yourself or what's right, it's what leads you to become a pawn in other people's crimes.'

' "All that is necessary for evil to triumph is for good men to do nothing," ' Peter quoted smugly. 'Burke.'

'Even if you are one,' Kate said sharply, 'you don't need to advertise it.'

'No, I meant . . .'

'Collusion, Peter, is the last and most important weakness every con and every magician who invites a spectator to pick a card exploits. You see it's this last great one that stops any mark going to the police. If they are collaborating in a crime themselves, to get their fabulous object, the grifter is home and dry long before any crime is reported.'

'So . . .'

'Peter, you asked how I put together a plan for a sting and I'm telling you it's like painting by numbers. Seven numbers. Nowadays, apart from the odd sensationalist horror flick, the seven sins get overlooked as serious psychological frameworks. And it's probably because they are a list of our weaknesses. Since one of our weaknesses is pride, we remain too proud to think about or admit them. It's when we give in to our weaknesses we end up enacting our crimes, or get involved with them. And it's through the indulging of our weaknesses that we are led to believe in the impossible. Which is, of course, what we're selling.

'Today, we keep to the script, everybody plays their part. Titus will be enticed to buy our perfect piece of junk because we will show him it fulfils his laziness, his greed, his lust, his anger and his pride. And last of all he will collude. The little slimy toad.' Kate drained her cup, fished into her pocket and dropped a few euros on the table. 'Come on, let's go to work.'

49

'Golem to Dybbuk. Have possible visual. Male, black hair, dark suit, rolled copy of *Le Monde*? Over.' Wissenschaft took his finger from his ear. The system was two-way, there was no need to touch the tiny invisible earpiece or say 'over', but then there's no need to wield handguns horizontally, start your car with a screech of the wheels or squint one eye when you light a cigarette with a Zippo, but the physical vocabulary of cool equipment usage has become so ingrained from the movies it takes a strong conscious decision to resist it. Wissenschaft's mind was elsewhere.

'*Vas?*' Verstehung whined in his ear. 'Why am I always the Dybbuk? Why am I the malevolent spirit and you're the Incredible Hulk defender of the faith?'

Wissenschaft kept his head glancing about to cover any tell-tale movement of his lips. 'You think I like being the zombie monster, Dick?' he hissed.

After passing the eight uniformed and absurdly smiling concierges behind the desk, the target stopped gazing around the lobby of the George V hotel and suddenly smiled. He embraced a woman *Chanel*ed from her shoes to her suit; even her tiny mouse-like dog, farting nervously as it peeked out of her handbag, wafted more the scent of No. 5 than No. 2. The couple kissed each other loudly, passing from cheek to cheek for several minutes in that Parisian style which surpasses even the Inuit for the least intimate form of kissing ever invented.

'*Oy vey*. That's a negative, Dybbuk,' Wissenchaft whispered, 'stand down.' He returned to surveying the large room, holding his phone out and pretending to read it through the dark veil of his sunglasses to avert the suspicions of the entire ingratiation of concierges. He knew that Paul11 would have, at the very least, a copy of the prearranged *Le Monde* but none of the men with copies in the lobby seemed alone or hungry with anticipation enough to be Paul11.

In a distant corner of the lobby Verstehung peered out to the side of the large floral armchair facing his own, and then leaned back again.

With his back to the action Titus was growing restless. He looked straight at Verstehung. 'Is all this cloak and dagger stuff strictly necessary?'

Verstehung met Titus's eye with some exasperation. 'Do you have half a motorbike in unmarked notes sitting in your room safe?'

'Half a motorbike?'

'A motorbike pillion. A million.'

'Oh right. Up the "apples and pears" sort of thing. So a motorbike is like a twenty-first-century "pony"? You know, like inflation.'

'That's crap.'

'Well, you might not agree but . . .'

'No, a "pony" is crap. Pony and trap, crap.'

'I thought it was like twenty-five pounds or something.'

384

Verstehung nodded. 'It is. But the actual rhyming slang for that is a "Godiva's sore". A fiver, a Godiva, plus a score, sore. But then it kind of developed because what made Godiva sore?'

'Of course,' Titus replied, 'her pony. It's as obvious as a drunk at a Tourette's conference.'

'So,' continued Verstehung, 'you've got all that money, in cash, upstairs and you don't know the first thing about the person you're handing it over to?'

'Might be handing it over. If it works.'

'OK, might be. You think a bit of cloak and dagger isn't necessary? How do you know he doesn't have a whole *khevre*, a gang, just waiting to jump you? This is our business. Trust me.'

At that moment the *portier* pushed the door open again. There was no mistaking Paul11. He gripped his tightly rolled newspaper stiffly in front of him like the pole of a ski-lift, as if it was pulling him through the lobby and if he took his eyes off it he might just fall off.

Wissenschaft chuckled quietly. 'Golem to Dybbuk. Target entered. It's him. Lab assistant's uniform: jeans, tie, Sta-Prest shirt, pens in top pocket.' The clothes followed every part of Kate's disguise dictum: meet every expectation. 'You got visual? Over.' Wissenschaft relaxed; if Paul11 was just what he had claimed then there would be no aggro, no need for the security detail at all.

Verstehung clocked Paul11 instantly. 'Dybbuk to Dick. I see him. You checking for baggage? Over?'

'Golem to Dick. You think I don't know my job? If he's come with bandits you think I won't signal? Over.'

Verstehung slipped off the armchair and stood up, an action which only served to decrease his overall height. 'Wait here,' he said firmly to Titus and strode towards Paul11 with a smile as broad as a thick four-by-two beard allows. 'Paul?'

Paul appeared taken aback. He looked around the lobby and then looked back down at the rabbinical character in front of him. 'Do I know you?'

'Paul. That is your real name, isn't it?'

Paul nodded.

'My associate and I . . .' He nodded towards Wissenschaft, who was staring at them by the door.

Paul followed his gaze and found himself smiling a greeting to the large Hasid.

'. . . we look after Mr Black's interests.'

Paul's face suddenly seemed to relax. 'Mr Black. He's not here then?'

'Oh no, he's here. It's just, before you meet him, I have to establish a few things. To make sure you're on the level. Some fans, you know, they're crazed, they can . . .'

'Right, yes,' Paul nodded, 'of course.'

Verstehung pulled out a black police-style notebook. 'So your real name? It's?'

For just a moment it seemed as if this was a difficult question. 'It's Paul.'

'Yes, yes. Paul?'

'Paul,' Paul hardly hesitated, 'Daniels.' And there was the master stroke. A classic double bluff. Something so unlikely it can only reinforce authenticity. With celebrities being so common nowadays the curse of sharing your name with one is as common as any Tom

Jones, Dick Cheney or Prince Harry. But what better than an attention-seeking name to throw off suspicions of deceit? After all, you wouldn't make up something that calls attention to you if you didn't want attention. Ipso facto, you're genuine.

Verstehung looked at Paul doubtfully.

'Yes. I know. Like the magician. And do I like it?' Paul said dolefully. 'Not a lot.'

'Look, Paul, before I introduce you to Mr Black I need to ask you: have you got the Alpha Wave Disrupter with you?'

'No, no. Of course not. It's not even mine. It belongs to Dr Tavasligh.'

'OK, so we're going to be meeting Dr Tavasligh, right? And we're going to be along with Mr Black every step of the way. You understand?' Verstehung extended his hand to Paul, who took it instinctively. 'Very nice to meet you, Mr Daniels.'

The pressure of Verstehung's hand increased until it began to crush Paul's fingers together, his knuckles painfully biting into each other with a force that seemed completely out of proportion to the size of the little man who exerted it.

'I do like it when we all understand each other.' Verstehung smiled.

Paul winced.

'No funny business. Not from you, not from us. We all understand. Understand?' One final crunch and he released Paul, who groaned softly and wiggled his fingers to check they still worked. 'This way.'

Verstehung waddled to the corner of the lobby and gestured to the chair he had vacated. Paul sat down quickly and only when he looked up did he realize that he was staring into that face he had dreamed of so many times. He felt as if his lungs had suddenly filled with sand; they would not move, not breathe in or out, heavy, uncooperative, still. This was the moment it could all fall through. If Titus recognized the clown who had made his eighth birthday the best he had ever had, the play would unravel quicker than the toilet paper in the Calcutta general hospital dysentery ward.

Titus had a fine memory, even if it wasn't quite as good as he pretended on a TV special that demonstrated he could memorize every word in the *Encyclopaedia Britannica*. An unwitting stooge in the guise of his librarian tester made it possible by being directed to certain pre-memorized 'force' pages.

From: *Project Notebook 15.2* p31

Even the healthiest memory has its limits: not because of the way that the brain is shaped – a baby's brain can make mnemonic connections as it sees fit – but because of the hierarchical systems we have evolved to organize what we put in it. It is possible that early humans recognized the benefits of hierarchies in the natural world: the food chain of ever more vicious creatures eating less aggressive ones, the superiority of height in battle or for getting the porno mags off the top shelf, the survival advantages of being first to get the hell out of somewhere dangerous or into the watering, shitting and pissing hole. We appear to have aped the hierarchies to make the potential of our memory manageable, to background it, so it won't over-whelm our present consciousness. Even as recently, in

388

evolutionary terms, as classical times, memory was so much more dominant to our brain function that the Greeks saw the past as stretching out in front of them and what they couldn't see, the unknown future, at their backs. The advance of civilization for thousands of years has been measured in the improvement of memory substitutes, from papyrus to the printing press, from sculpture to the hologram. We have struggled to prioritize our present and how it leads into the future at the expense of our past. So now, in our brains, it's the recent bits of information, emotional data, recurring material and the stuff we anticipate needing in the future that get priority in the hierarchy of our memories. The reason that we forget names, and quite often faces, is how they figure in our hierarchies. Egotists tend to put others beneath themselves and are inclined to have much worse name and face recall than more introverted people.

Titus shouldered a gargantuan ego and maybe, had he not just seen a clown, had he been in court and had to look at Peter across the room, rather than just see a judge on a video link, maybe he would have remembered the face, the way he sat, the mix of terror and loathing in his expression.

'Paul,' Titus smiled and leaned over to shake hands, 'you're older than I imagined.'

50

The Hôpital Lamartine on the Rue Morgue has few windows and they all face inwards. They overlook a small grey cobblestone courtyard that sits in perpetual shadow. The building lurks forbiddingly in a discreetly forgotten part of Paris's fourteenth arrondissement, an eighteenth-century monolith, its high walls mottled with cracked and peeling paint. Its dilapidated appearance belies its origins as one of Paris's premier *grandes institutions*. At the time of its construction it was the world's most advanced smallpox hospital, which, essentially, meant it was little more than an extravagant waiting room for those heading north to the Père Lachaise or south to the Montparnasse cemeteries.

By the turn of the twentieth century and the European eradication of the smallpox virus the hospital had had to extend its 'care' to a host of other diseases such as cholera, malaria and gonorrhoea. But as even these became rarer, a hospital whose chief facilities were a morgue and garaging space for hearses became increasingly superfluous.

During the Second World War, the hospital enjoyed a brief renaissance when, attracted by its thick walls and the efficient blood guttering in all its morgue rooms, it was taken over by the Schutzstaffel as a 'persuasion centre'. In the late forties, it was reinvented as a hospital for the mentally ill and thus it was able to reutilize some of the electrical equipment left by the previous occupiers.

In the sixties it briefly found itself a focus for the café intelligentsia, when Michel Foucault used it to deliver a lecture on the incarceration of the mad. But by the eighties it had become too expensive to house the insane any more. It was finally closed up in 1989; too big to be maintained and in too unfashionable a backwater to be sold to developers. Like so many of Paris's *grandes maisons* it stands as a best forgotten, abandoned conundrum, not even gruesome enough to be made into a house-of-horror tourist attraction, and there is a finite number of museums that even Paris can sustain.

However, with a new Space Age-looking flashing LED panel to cover the door's broken lock, and inside a few pinging bits of machinery, racks of testtubes, some microwave ovens, a few 'friends' with white coats, clipboards and glasses, the west wing of the Lamartine was transformed, overnight, into a very credible Tavasligh Amnesthetics Lab.

Paul swiped his identity card across the lock and a green LED lit up. He knew his card could just as easily have been a banana and still the LED would light up. He pushed the door open and waved at one of the assistants, who smiled back.

'This way.' He ushered Titus and the two Hasidim across the lab towards an office door and knocked. 'Dr Tavasligh?'

They waited but there was no reply. Paul knocked again. 'Dr Tavasligh, it's Paul. With those people we were talking about?'

Kate opened the door and peeked out sheepishly. She had thick glasses, a creased white coat and her hair done up in a tight bun. Without meeting any of their eyes she pushed the door open further and scuttled back to her desk, gesturing to the chairs opposite her. She stared at a cup of tea in front of her.

Titus and Paul sat as Wissenschaft and Verstehung stood by the door.

Titus began effusively. 'Dr Tavasligh, I just want to say I'm a real admirer of your—'

'It's a million pounds,' Kate interrupted, still not looking up. 'It's what we need to keep the lab going.'

Titus laughed gently. 'Well, that's a lot of money.'

'Paul says you can afford it.'

'It's not a matter of whether I can afford it, it's whether what you've got is worth it.'

'Do you know what the Alpha Wave Disrupter is?' Kate said, finally meeting his eyes. 'Do you know what it is we've developed?'

'Paul's shown me some of your experiments, it confuses people for a moment.'

'Oh, it does so much more than that. Mr Black, have you heard of interference?'

'In respect to what?'

'Waves,' Paul said. 'Like radio waves.'

'Yes, it's the altering of wave height without disrupting frequency. Look.' Kate dipped her finger into her tea at the side of the cup. 'The wave pattern that comes from my finger sends an even frequency of ripple rings all the way to the other side of the cup. Yes?'

Titus nodded. Verstehung and Wissenschaft edged a bit closer to peer at the tea, and even Peter found himself leaning over to watch the demonstration.

'Now although the height of the wave decreases as it gets further from the finger, the frequency, the distance between the up and down bits of the wave, remains constant, right?'

The entire room nodded again.

'So the opposite side of the cup is receiving a series of waves determined by the finger that created the waves. But if I put a finger in the other side, watch.'

Kate placed the index finger of her other hand just into the surface of the tea. This sent out a similar pattern of rings, which, on meeting the rings going the other way, seemed to cross but also made the centre ripples more pronounced.

'Now I'm creating two similar wave forms so that they increase the height of their ripples by adding to each other where they meet. But if my tea was just flat on the top and I could create an opposite wave form underneath, what do you think would happen?'

'You'd get quite wet?' Titus tried to break the intensity of the moment.

'No. When the opposite wave forms overlapped they would work as a form of subtraction and cancel each other out. Each would stop the ripple of the other, like noise cancelling headphones.'

Wissenschaft raised his chin. 'Ach, this is just a cup of tea.'

'You Dick.' Verstehung looked up at him. 'It's metaphor, it's a model, it's an example. Everything for you it needs to be the thing, but you can't see everything, sometimes you've got to understand by example.'

Kate continued above the bickering that had broken out. 'The brain in its conscious state works in a series of fluctuating pulses known as alpha waves. As it goes into its unconscious state it descends through wider, slower beta and then gamma wave patterns.' Kate stood again and disappeared into another room. They could still hear her voice. 'When I studied the brain's frequencies I found that, rather like the body's temperature, the alpha frequency has little variation in waking adults.'

Kate returned holding an object that resembled a mini FM radio wrapped in a coil of bare copper wire. It resembled it mainly because it was a mini FM radio wrapped in a coil of bare copper wire. 'The AWD,' she said, staring at it with some awe. 'Placed within an inch of the cerebellum,' she gestured towards the back of her head behind the ear, 'it can send an electrical pulse which interferes with and disrupts the brain's alpha wave pattern. For a split second it shuts down the system. Anything in the conscious mind at that moment is wiped. It's like rebooting your computer and clearing out the RAM.'

'Well,' Titus smiled, 'if it works it's a great little gimmick.'

'Gimmick, it's not a gimmick.'

'Forgive me. To a magician a gimmick is any device, however complicated or diabolical, that can create a moment of wonder.'

'Mr Black, you don't seem much of a scientist. I don't think you understand. This is the key, our key into the human mind. Right now it's a split second but the technology opens the door for better, more focused devices. Now we can do just this, but it's only a matter of development, of finessing, before we can, say, target particular bad memories and erase them, permanently. It will mean the end of suffering for millions struck down by psychiatric problems, haunted by their past. It will mean instant relief for those enduring the long onset of Alzheimer's. This Alpha Wave Disrupter is like the musket was to the arms industry. It's undirected, unreliable, limited in scope, but it is the start of an entire new way of dealing with the world. There are labs across the globe dying to get hold of this, to find out what I have done, but Paul assures me that you can actually pay the amount I need to keep this lab going and that you will sign a confidentiality clause promising not to sell on, exploit or divulge the technology used. You just want,' Kate looked at the wire-laden radio, 'this.'

'If it works I will . . .'

'You keep saying that. If it didn't work I wouldn't have asked you here. Of course it works. Paul told me that you've seen the tapes.'

'Yes but, well, before we give you a sum that big we're going to have to do some independent verification. A little bit of testing.'

Kate nodded.

'Could you use it on me, for example?'

'I'm afraid we have found that once the brain can anticipate the wave surge it can quickly shift in and out of a different frequency. Basically you can only use it on people who don't know that you are using it.'

Titus smiled. 'That's perfect. Well. Maybe a few field tests? Can we take it out of here?'

Kate considered this. 'Only if Paul goes with you. To ensure its safe keeping.'

'Certainly.'

'Mr Black, if you can't develop this, or sell it on, or reveal how it works, may I ask why you want it?'

'Because, Dr Tavasligh, Paul's told me all about you, I've read all your books and I believe in you. I believe you are right. I believe that you are holding the prototype of something that will change the world and I will be the man who has the pleasure of owning it, like the man who bought Stevenson's *Rocket*, Shakespeare's folio or Galileo's telescope.'

'Or the first Betamax video recorder,' Wissenschaft muttered under his breath.

Titus winked at Paul. 'I just want to own a bit of history in the making.' He was a charmer.

51

The Lexus was barely out of sight of the hospital when Titus patted Peter chummily on the knee. 'P-P-Paul my friend, I haven't had time to thank you, for the introduction, for t-t-telling me about this.' He took the AWD out of Peter's hands and looked at it more closely.

Peter could see Verstehung still eyeing him suspiciously in the rear-view mirror. 'I still can't quite believe I'm in the same car as you,' Peter enthused. He looked down at Titus's neck and remembered how often he had dreamed about wringing it.

Titus smiled indulgently. 'You know, you've been pretty good at keeping secrets so far. I w-w-wonder if you can keep just one more?'

Peter tried to look eager to please.

'We're not going to be doing any standard t-t-test on this.' Titus turned the little device in his hand. 'I didn't want to tell your b-b-boss but I'll let you into a little secret. I'm not really so interested in rebooting consciousness or whatever. But I do believe, if this really does what she says, it'll change my act, my career, every-thing.'

'How?' Peter said hesitantly.

'Maybe you saw my Emmy-nominated TV Special where I approach people in a car park asking for directions?'

Peter looked unsure. If this was going to be convin-cing he had to appear to know nothing.

'That's OK. You see, I have a map which is upside down and I ask them to hold my can of Coke so I can point and I get things muddled and then in the middle of it all I ask them to give me their car keys and, in the confusion, because everything has been benign and compliance has been established, they hand me their car keys and I leave them there. We then see how long it takes them to realize that instead of their car keys they're holding my can of Coke.'

Wissenschaft turned round in the passenger seat. 'You don't see anything wrong in exploiting nice people for cheap laughs on TV?'

'Nothing cheap about it. Give the market what they want, Vis. Bread and circuses.' Titus turned back to Peter. 'There's a moment, a condition I was using; it's used in rapid hypnotic induction. It's called the "confusional event". When you're trying to induce a trance, looking for a moment of heightened suggestibility, you ask something paradoxical and as your volunteer's conscious mind goes into overdrive to process the information their critical faculties go into neutral, and it's at that moment you can suggest that they act like a duck or stand on their head or whatever.'

'Wow,' Peter continued, apparently in awe, 'hypnosis, it's real.'

'Oh yes. But to do any of these things, you have to have the person's full focus. And then it's still not guaranteed. I can't tell you how many out-takes we end up with. Pick the wrong person, someone with a high-performing, multi-tasking, capable brain, and they can remain unsuggestible however confusing I try to be. But this.' Titus waved the device gently. 'This could change it all. If I can just induce that confusional event with this thing, without all the struggle and wordplay and direction, then I can concentrate on the suggestions and the act. This could be a godsend.'

'So what you're saying is, at the moment of the mind wipe, someone will basically be open to anything you suggest to them. Oh Lord, that's powerful.'

Titus seemed to realize that he was talking himself out of a job. 'Well, obviously you have to suggest in the right way, it wouldn't all be this thing.'

'But you could,' Peter grinned, 'I don't know, rob a bank if you wanted to.'

Titus laughed. 'I suppose I could.'

'So how are you going to test it? Can we go to a bank?'

'Slow down there, Paul. You can't just go and rob a bank. There is such a thing as right and wrong.'

Peter wondered if Titus had any concept of what he had just said. 'But money's the thing, isn't it?' Peter insisted. 'If you can convince someone to give you money for no reason, that's pretty much the deal.'

Titus was beginning to like the idea. 'Anyway, how would you get this thing to the back of a teller's ear? No, I'm not robbing a bank, there's CCTV, I'm a celebrity. Even as a stunt it's a risky business.'

'Oh, I know—' Peter stopped. 'No.'

'What?'

'Well, we could . . . No, it's silly.'

'Could what?'

'Well, what if you asked someone at a cashpoint for their cash? That's not robbing a bank.'

'I like the way you think, Paul. But that's still theft.' Titus fell silent for a moment as the car glided around the great obelisk in the centre of Place de la Concorde. 'But if I just asked for the card and pin number, I don't think that could be classed as—'

'Take a left here,' Peter suddenly barked at Verstehung. 'I know just the place.'

As the car veered and the two rear passengers were thrown together, Peter and Titus both grinned at their own brilliance.

Five minutes later, outside the Crédit Agricole on the Rue des Martyrs, Verstehung eased the Lexus into a minuscule parking space using the time-honoured Parisian technique of smashing into the cars front and back until it fitted. Opening the doors was like diving into a sea of noise, an ocean of commotion, wave upon wave of market traders shouting their prices, scooters grinding, crates crashing and the alarms of recently barged cars wailing. Radios blared from the open-fronted *charcuteries*, *fromageries* and *fruitiers*, a street vacuum cleaner monotonously moaned and some unseen roadworks filled any free audial space with the perfunctory rattling of pneumatic drills. People swarmed up and down the market at the height of its pre-lunch trading. Peter stood next to Titus near the cashpoint machines. Each breath seemed to be filled with the tang of fruits and camemberts and mingled with the rich, sweet aroma of dripping cooked chicken from the street-side rotisserie ovens. Here was the market that had been Peter's first glimpse of Paris.

'It's busy, people are on the move, if you want confusion this is it.' Peter spoke close to Titus's ear. 'There's so much going on, if this doesn't work nobody will notice. Two people arguing on a street corner is par for the course around here.'

It wasn't long before a young man wearing jeans and a torn T-shirt approached the machines. He clocked the two men standing by the Lexus as anybody planning to withdraw money might check who they were about to turn their back on. He leaned forward, placed a bank card in the machine and tapped in his PIN. As soon as the money was delivered into his hand, he turned and found himself looking straight into Titus's smugly smiling face.

'*Bonjour. Parlez-vous anglais?*'

'Er, yes,' the young man said in a thick accent.

'I was wondering if you could help me.' Titus brought the little radio up near to the man's ear and pressed the

400

one button on it. The device made a little squeak and the man momentarily seemed to relax every muscle before looking around. 'Perhaps you need to give me your bank card.'

The man looked at his right hand, still clutching the bank card. He put it into Titus's outstretched hand.

'And do you remember the PIN number, *le numéro de la carte*?'

The man was still casting about. '*Soixante dix-sept trente-cinq*,' he murmured absently.

'*Merci*,' Titus said, 'maybe you should head home.'

The man looked at Titus, looked down at the money in his hand and then shoved it into his trouser pocket before turning and walking away through the market.

Peter watched as Titus approached the machine. Titus's shoulders showed him inserting the card and tapping in the number. He hesitated and then triumphantly shouted, 'Yes!' and punched the air. Then, realizing just how illegal and visible what he had done was, he turned and ran back to the car.

'Quick,' Titus shouted with glee, 'quick, let's get out of here.'

They tumbled into the car and Verstehung crashed backwards and forwards again until they were out. With a screech of the wheels they turned into a side street and sped from the scene of the crime. Peter suppressed his urge to giggle. Jean-Baptiste had earned his money, the play was only going to get better.

Back at the bank, a couple of motorbike riders who had been parked across the road kicked their starters, flipped up their stands and set off behind the Lexus.

52

It wasn't until the Lexus was cruising along the banks of the Seine that Verstehung spotted the flashing light in the rear-view mirror. The front spoiler on the motorbike was marked 'Police'. Verstehung sighed. 'Trouble behind.'

A short siren burst and Verstehung slowed. He pulled over in the shadow of the Pont de l'Alma. The bikes behind stopped and in unison the two officers leaned them back on their stands. They dismounted and sauntered towards the Lexus.

The first policeman, whose moustache was so thick it seemed to knit into his nostril hairs, knocked at the window. Wissenschaft rolled it down.

'*Anglais?*' the policeman asked. '*Oui?*'

Wissenschaft nodded. '*Oui.*'

'I speak English then,' the policeman confirmed in a thick accent.

'Thank you.'

'We know English car, Lexus. *En dehors*,' he turned to his companion, '*comment est-ce qu'on dit "en dehors" en anglais?*'

The other policeman shrugged. '*Je pense que'on dit "outside".*'

'We know English car, Lexus, outside Crédit Agricole *dans la Rue des Martyrs*. Man he gets into car after how you say, robbery, he take bank card.'

Titus sat behind the blacked-out windows staring at the policeman. 'Shit, fuck, that's it, career closed. Down the pan. Shit, I feel sick.' He looked dizzy and his shoulders heaved as if he might just vomit there and then. Peter savoured the moment; he probably let it go on a little longer than he should have but finally he pulled himself back to the script.

'No, no,' he reassured Titus, squeezing his hand. 'We've still got a trick up our sleeve.'

'Are you mad?' Titus hissed, staring at him. 'We can't monkey about with the police. You're insane.'

'Do you remember *Star Wars*?'

'What?' Titus was shaking. 'You want to reminisce about movies when I'm about to be arrested?'

'Luke Skywalker and Obi Wan Guinness are in their like hovercar and they're stopped by some storm troopers and asked for ID.'

'Paul. You are nuts.'

'And Kenobi says to the storm troopers, "These aren't the droids you're looking for." And the storm trooper just repeats what he says. We've got the AWD. You see?'

'They're the police, you can't start doing the Jedi mind trick . . .'

Peter had grabbed the device and was already rolling down the window. '*Je parle français, monsieur*,' he said softly.

The policeman moved closer to him. '*Comment?*'

Peter quickly held the AWD up to the policeman's ear

403

and in a second the officer seemed to relax and then stiffen.

'*Ce ne sont pas les hommes que vous cherchez,*' Peter said authoritatively.

The policeman called over his shoulder to his colleague. '*Ce ne sont pas les hommes qu'on cherche.*'

'*Ils peuvent vaquer à leurs occupations,*' Peter said.

'*Ils peuvent vaquer à leurs occupations,*' the policeman repeated. He stood up again awkwardly and nodded to Wissenschaft. '*Au revoir, monsieur.*' Then with a flick of his wrist he waved the Lexus on.

Knowing that the police were still watching, Verstehung carefully checked his mirrors, indicated and pulled out back into the traffic.

Titus sat silently. An acrid smell arose, making Peter sniff, grimace and then stick his head out of the window for air. When he looked in again he noticed that a dark stain had appeared on the seat surrounding Titus, which went a long way to explaining the sharp smell of urine.

'I'm sorry,' Titus muttered quietly. 'That was just brilliant. I really am a fucking genius.'

53

To any passer-by, the group standing about clutching glasses of wine in Kate's lab would have appeared to be engaged in no more than a convivial after-work celebration among staff. However, since the windowless walls of the Hôpital Lamartine were over three feet thick and the only passers-by tended to be homesick lunatics, there was really no opportunity for such errors of interpretation.

With an empty bottle of champagne on the bench, the lab technicians had gathered around Titus. Fresh in a change of clothes, he was recounting the day's adventures, again, with some glee.

'So I said to Paul,' Titus grinned as smugly as ever, ' "Do you remember *Star Wars*, the old Jedi mind trick with the storm troopers?" And he said . . .'

Kate wandered out of her office as the technicians indulged Titus with some more laughter.

'But there she is,' Titus said, pointing at her. 'The most brilliant scientist I have ever met, that I will ever meet. She has made one of the world's most truly awesome inventions. Dr Tavasligh, I wish I had your brains, your knowledge and, the way you're looking right now, your number on my speed dial.'

Paul, the technicians and the two Hasidim clapped. Kate nodded sharply, keeping in character and with her eyes averted. 'The AWD met your requirements, I hear.'

'Well,' Titus said, 'ideally I would have liked to try it a few more times but apparently it had run out of charge.'

'Yes,' Kate said, more to her glass than to Titus, 'it uses a large amount of energy, we had to develop its own battery system. It's in my office and recharged now. Obviously, the charger will come with it.'

'Well, I'd like to spend a little more time . . .'

'The time, Mr Black, is to buy. Your browsing is done.'

'Well, I think this still needs a little negotiating.'

'In what way?' Kate brought her eyes to meet his. 'The price has been set.'

'But it sounds to me like my price is way beyond my competitors, and I'm not sure that I can agree to not getting some cut in this if other buyers are interested. We haven't even talked about exclusivity.'

She had expected this. Kate looked around the room at all the expectant faces of her shills, who had acted their little hearts out on the promise of payment. She needed to bring this in. She looked at Peter and thought about how brave he'd been: he had faced his demon, sat with him, been friendly to him, all day for this. She had to bring it in.

'OK,' she looked back down at her glass, 'let's take this into my office. The rest of you, pack up and head home. See you tomorrow.'

The technicians dispersed but Peter was rooted. 'Me too?' He didn't like this. Titus was a toad, a weasel, he wouldn't leave anybody alone with him, especially not someone he cared for. He was already trying to renege on the deal.

Kate nodded at him wearily. 'It's OK, Paul, we'll sort this out.' She pointed Titus towards her office. 'Come on, we'll talk about this.'

Titus drained the dregs from the bottle and shooed his security men away.

'It's OK, I'll take a cab when I need one.'

Verstehung was hesitant. 'We don't think leaving you is . . .'

'Go, it's an order.' Titus turned his back and strode purposefully into Kate's office.

Peter grabbed his coat and headed outside.

'You want a lift?' Verstehung asked him, his key already in the door of the Lexus.

'No,' Peter shook his head, 'it's OK, I'll make my own way. Thanks.'

'Goodnight,' said Wissenschaft over the roof. The two men got into the car and it slid quietly out and down the street.

Peter took a look at the forbidding walls of the Hôpital. Should he go back? She could handle herself if anybody could. How had she survived without him up to now? He trusted her. Suddenly the vision of Titus's sneering, cruelty-filled boyhood face loomed across his inward eye. Peter shivered, pulled his collar up and headed towards the Métro.

2,500 Milliseconds to Higham
(TEA minus 11 months 19 days 8 hours)

Peter

So make her honest, go for the bag myself, remove it from temptation. Kate wants to go straight, her cold turkey starts here. We're almost stopped now. Stand up and grab the case and get out, that's all I need to do. What happens? She wakes up, the money's gone. She realizes she's been burned and experiences how shitty it feels to be on the receiving end. That will be the nail in the coffin of her career. Find out what losing is like.

OK, get ready.

But then I will never see her again. Can I bear that? Really? I know love is about sacrifices for the other but it's also selfish and self-gratifying and fuck, do I really want to go on without her? Can I go on without her?

I've already stared into the waters and felt that icy temptation of oblivion. Without her, what would be the point? Just keep your eyes closed. Let her do what she must do. If she stays, she stays, if she goes . . .

If you love something, let it go.

54

Peter opened his eyes. The hotel clock said two in the morning. The light in the room was on and glaring. He twisted and sat up on the chaise longue. In his just-woken visual fug, against the light, he could make out the silhouette of a figure.

'Kate?' he said, though he sensed it wasn't.

'No, not your girlfriend, Peter.' Titus stood in front of him. He had been rumbled. 'Your worst nightmare. In fact your exclusive nightmare is what I've heard.'

Peter tried to swallow but found his throat constricted as if by a noose. 'Kate told you.' But why? Why would she do such a thing? The money? She didn't want to share it? So this is what she did? He felt sick and utterly betrayed, not by her, she had pretty much warned him that she was not to be trusted, but by his own foolish desire to believe in her. Had he been honest with himself, he'd always known her bottom line. The money. All the talk of transformation and change. The lure of the money was too much. Maybe it was true, you can take the girl out of the con but . . .

'Oh, you really think I wouldn't know?' Titus almost laughed. 'The moment I clapped eyes on you I knew. I didn't need to see you like that to remember.' Titus glanced up and down Peter's body.

Peter looked down and saw he was naked. Instinctually he tried to bring his hands in front of him, only he couldn't. His hands were tied or cuffed behind him. Again.

Titus put his sneering face right up to him. 'You,' he said. 'You.'

As he pulled at his bindings, Peter became aware that he and Titus were not alone. Wissenschaft and Verstehung were on the other side of the room. Their estjewry accents chimed in. 'You,' they chanted.

'Where's Kate?' Peter shouted. 'What have you done with her?'

Then a voice as familiar as his own breath spoke. 'You,' she said.

Kate was there too? She stepped out from behind Wissenschaft.

'You.' They all chanted together with taunting sneers, 'You, you, you're a dirty old man.' They sang and began to dance about, pointing and laughing. 'You, you, you're a dirty old man.'

Peter screamed defiantly, 'No.' He tried to stand but fell off the chaise longue.

He opened his eyes. The hotel clock said two in the morning. The room was dark. Peter listened to the silence. He listened intently, trying to pick up Kate's sleeping breath. Nothing. He steadied himself as he stood and wobbled towards the bed. It hadn't been slept in. Peter switched on the light and stared at the empty sheets.

Peter pulled his clothes on and grabbed his coat. He

ran down the stairs, past the dozing night receptionist and out into the street. A light but constant drizzle quickly encased him in a shroud of dampness. He cast around for a taxi but the street was quiet. He started to run up towards the Place Pigalle. A couple of taxi drivers stood outside a café arguing.

'*Excusez-moi*. I need to get to the Hôpital Lamartine.'

'*Où?*' The drivers looked quizzical.

'*Dans la Rue Morgue, la quatorzième arrondissement.*'

One of the drivers looked at him cautiously. 'Oh, it's the place for lunatics.' He rotated his finger in a circular motion near his ear. 'You missing the place, want to get back in?' The other drivers laughed at Peter and returned to their previous argument.

'*Je suis sérieux,*' Peter raged.

The driver who had spoken turned back to him. 'This time of night, that will be *cinquante euros*.'

Peter stopped and shoved his hands in his pockets. All they contained was a couple of Métro tickets, about seven euros in change, and his hands.

'Shit. Fuck,' Peter screamed, confirming the driver's initial analysis. Then Peter smiled sheepishly at them. '*Pardonnez-moi*. I'll walk.'

He was pretty sure that if he followed the force of gravity he'd end up at the river, then he was fairly confident he could find the right landmarks to take him to the Rue Morgue.

At the first side street that led downhill Peter turned and descended like Dante. He found himself moving through a chiaroscuro of street lighting, alternating between light and darkness as the antique lamps, attached to weathered walls, failed to spread their pallid beams more than a few feet through the precipitous haze before falling at the wall of wet darkness. At each corner Peter found himself leaping the deep gutters that gushed with rainwater. The narrow, uneven pavements and grit-textured stone walls seemed endless. Occasionally he would come across a street of shop fronts and would watch his reflection as he passed each dark shop window. It was nice to have some company but he wished his companion didn't look so bloody miserable.

Why? What? Where? Had she got the money and skipped off? Had she been attacked? Why couldn't she call him at the hotel?

By the time he reached the banks of the Seine, Peter was soaked through and his mood was pretty sodden too. He crossed over the wooden Pont des Arts and stared into the dark churning waters of the river and, despite a life which had held more than its fair share of misery and misfortune and terror and dismay, he realized he had never asked himself the big what-if, the 'If I died . . . ?' question. And yet, after almost three weeks which were, no doubt, the happiest of his life, he could see the black liquid death calling him from below as he leaned forward. He knew that all it would take was for there to be particular answers to his questions and he would return here to plunge into the seething dark beneath him. What a place to have come to in life. To be or not to be, that wasn't the question; to be and to live under certain conditions or not to be, that was the question, but it didn't really fit into the iambic pentameter so Shakespeare could be forgiven.

Peter tore his eyes away from the river. He remembered the Groucho Marx joke about being in Paris and jumping into the river, and everybody saying he went in Seine. And then Groucho Marx, as he always did, led him to thoughts of the Groucho-ho and the nightmare that had changed his life and he ran, ran off the bridge, towards the illuminated top of the Eiffel Tower visible over the rooftops.

An hour later, Peter's pace was barely a traipse as he finally turned into the Rue Morgue. He pushed open the door with the red LED still blinking steadily.

The lab was dark.

'Kate?' Peter called out as the fluorescent tubes flickered on. Then, realizing that the scam might still be on, 'Dr Tavasligh?'

He walked past the microwaves and the unpinging machines and the empty glasses by the sink and knocked on Kate's office door. 'Dr Tavasligh,' Peter said more softly.

He pushed the door open. Darkness. He moved to the desk and switched on the standard lamp, which threw a small pool of bright light on to it. There was a half-finished bottle of whisky and two empty glasses. Peter picked the glasses up and sniffed them. The whisky still smelled strong. Kate and Titus had been drinking but had left. To do what? Did he get her drunk, or drug her and get his henchmen to take the body out and dump it somewhere? He was pretty keen on the AWD. Could she be lying half dead in a gutter somewhere and he unable to help? The answers he had hoped to find here had not only not materialized but he was plagued by even worse questions and suppositions. Peter studied the glass with the lipstick stain. He took the bottle and poured himself a measure, careful to put his lips where hers had been. He drank. He poured some more and drank, and pretty soon the questions, unanswered, drifted away and in a few minutes so had he. Consciousness ebbed like the sea pulls back a wave that has rushed too far across the shingle of a beach; it ran back, washing across the pebbles of awareness until it was no more distinguishable from the great ocean of unconsciousness than the vague sensation of gentle breathing and then . . .

'Remember me?'

Kate shook Peter. 'It's fucking ten in the morning and we've got to get out of here. Now!'

55

Kate shook Peter again. 'No no no no. You don't close your eyes. You stand up, you sober up and we get out of here.' She pulled Peter's head up by his hair and a long string of dribble snaked down to the desktop. 'Come on. Walk it off.' She leaned in from behind and, inserting her arms into his armpits, she hoisted him on to his feet.

'Oh bloody hell,' Peter whined and wobbled. 'I think I'm going to be ss . . .' He burped. 'No. Maybe not. I think that was it. I'm fine. I'm oak.' Suddenly he turned his head and a spume of vomit splattered loudly against the linoleum floor. 'Oh God,' Peter said, wiping his mouth with the back of his hand. He seemed to gather himself. 'On the plus side, I feel a lot better.' He smiled.

'Come on.' Kate grabbed one of the abandoned lab technicians' coats and threw it at him. 'Clean yourself up, we have to go.'

'Where?' Peter wiped away the last bits of sick.

'La Marseillaise' suddenly rang out of Kate's coat. She pulled their mobile phone out and looked at the caller ID before cutting it off. 'I've got a cab waiting outside, come on.' Kate opened the lab door and beckoned to Peter.

He suddenly remembered all the questions and doubts that had been plaguing him the night before, and he slowed. 'Hang on. Where were you last night?'

Kate sighed. 'I'll tell you in the cab.'

Peter stopped. 'How did you know I'd be here?'

'Because,' Kate advanced to get him, 'it's the sort of stupid thing a complete amateur does; return to the scene of the crime. How long do you think it would have taken Black to work out the AWD was bogus? And where do you think is the first place he'd come looking for us, with his henchmen, or the police, or both? You pillock. And,' Kate's voice quietened, 'because I knew you would worry about me and come looking.'

Peter seemed to need time to process all this and he stood very still until finally he asked, 'What do you mean, "would have"?'

'What?'

'You said, "How long do you think it would have taken Black to work it out?" "Would have".'

Kate fell silent now.

'Why won't he?'

Kate hurried out of the door into the harsh Parisian sunlight. Peter followed. A rusty brown car reeking of diesel was idling outside, shaking with that trembling Carkinson's disease that old taxis seem to inevitably contract.

'What's stopping him, Kate? Why won't he have found it was bogus?'

Kate opened the cab door and got in. Peter was expectantly looking into the dark taxi.

'Just get in, you idiot.'

'Tell me why.'

'*Monsieur, Rue des Martyrs vite s'il vous plaît.*'

As the taxi started to move, Peter quickly clambered in and slammed the door behind him, only to be thrown across Kate by its abrupt acceleration. He pushed himself away and sat heavily down. 'What's happened?'

Kate stared out of the window. 'La Marseillaise' rang again, she looked at the phone and cut the caller off again.

'Kate?'

Kate mumbled something towards the glass.

'What?'

She spun to face Peter. 'The deal's off. He's not buying the AWD. Kiss the money goodbye, OK?' She returned to the window to stare at a rainbow crocodile of cagoules that traipsed along the pavement behind a Paris Perdu tour guide dressed in the uniform black beret, stripy jumper, string of onions and curly waxed moustache – which clashed with her lipstick something shocking.

Peter was reeling. 'What, why?'

Kate sighed into a silence. 'Don't,' she said quietly without looking at him, 'don't ask.'

'Why?'

'It will change everything. For us.'

'Kate, you're talking in riddles. It sounds like things have already changed. You have to tell me.'

Kate still said nothing.

'Look, all right, the money, it's not everything, it's—'

Kate turned back to Peter, with tears in her eyes. She fished something out of the pocket of her coat. It was their AWD gadget. 'He used this. On me.'

She passed the AWD to Peter, who stared at it for a moment then closed his fingers around it. 'What do you mean? He wiped your mind? Kate, this is just a bust mini radio with some copper wire. You can't even get the weather report on it, let alone wipe a brain or hypnotize someone.'

'You know that. I know that. But bloody Titus Black doesn't know that, does he.'

'So?'

'So I could tell he was wavering, he was going to try and renege, which was why I sent everyone home last night. We had had a drink and we were talking over the deal when he was playing with it and he leans over suddenly, uses it right by my ear. I couldn't stop him. He just zapped that stupid thing. And then made a suggestion.'

Now Peter had to look away. 'I get it,' he finally said. 'You either had to blow the whole scam wide open or conform to his suggestion.' He turned back to Kate but still tried not to look at her. 'What was it? That you just give it to him, gratis?'

Kate laughed a little bitterly. 'In a manner of speaking.'

Peter looked right at Kate, shock registering in his eyes. She nodded. 'You didn't forget lust was one of the seven come-ons?'

'And that's why the deal's off? You had to show that toerag it didn't work on you?' Peter sat back, suddenly feeling relieved. But Kate didn't agree. She didn't reassure him. She just sat there silently. 'Kate?'

She cast her eyes down and looked at her wringing hands. 'I . . . I went along with his suggestion. I wouldn't, couldn't let the scam down, us down, you down . . .'

'No, no, no, no,' Peter repeated, 'please tell me no.'

'Half a million quid.'

'Kate, no.' Peter could feel that lump of tears welling in his own throat.

'What wouldn't you do for half a million quid?' Kate spat bitterly at him. 'For half a million, tell me you wouldn't?'

They sat in silence, shaken by the engine, listening to the taxi driver's radio and Paris trundling past them. Neither could speak. Peter knew what he was calling her. Kate knew what Peter was thinking.

He cleared his throat. 'So why, if you, um, went along with his suggestion, why's the deal off?'

'Because you know what I did this morning, Peter?' Kate pushed her chin out defiantly but a glaze shimmered on her eyes. 'I woke up and I woke up to exactly what I am, to what I know you're thinking about me. To what you've probably been thinking about me right from the start.'

'Kate, of course I don't think that of . . .'

'Think what, Peter?'

'That you're, um.' Peter realized she had cornered him. 'Shit.'

'Don't bullshit the bullshitter. Of course you think I'm a fucking whore.'

Peter considered this and realized now that she wasn't completely wrong and he was so angry and disgusted at her and at himself he found it hard to listen to her any more.

'I woke up and I got dressed in yesterday's clothes of come-ons and come-hithers and you know what? I wept. I don't do crying, Peter. I haven't cried since the midwife hung me upside down and slapped my bottom.'

'I bet that's the last time,' Peter couldn't resist, 'you date someone in the health sector.'

'You know,' Kate sobbed and laughed all in one awkward gulp, 'I've worked so hard to change. I really have. And to then sink right back into doing anything for the sell. I'm starting to think what's the point? I'm doomed, like this, it's all too much. And you, you, Peter, you were the one, you were going to be the rock I'd anchor to and all I could do was drag you too into my silly games. Revenge and money.'

'I wanted it.' Peter smiled.

'Oh, I know you wanted it. It's my job to know what people want. It was my come-on to you. Don't you see? I knew I needed you, I wanted to use you so I tempted you in the only way I knew how. I made myself irresistible using all the old techniques. Nothing honest. And so this change, this project, this transformation was doomed from the start. It started in lies, it ends in

419

lies. I was never going to be what I wanted to be, not with you. If I ever can be, I have to start again, just me.'

Peter turned to her desperately. 'What are you saying?'

'You'll live, Peter. And I'll tell you this for nothing, you'll live a much better life without me.'

'But, Kate, no. Please.'

Kate's phone, resting in her hand, started ringing again and without even looking she cut it off. 'You know what? Just when I was leaving this morning that arrogant twat woke up. Do you know what he said to me?'

' "My God, I've just realized what an arrogant twat I am"? Er.'

' "So we still on for this deal?"' Kate imitated Titus's nasal voice. 'That's the first thing that was on his mind. What a charmer. As if I wouldn't know what had gone on. He had the fucking audacity to ask about the deal. And I told him exactly what sort of shit he was to use the machine on me. And I grabbed his precious gadget,' Kate pointed at the AWD in Peter's hand, 'and I left. And you know what? He'll never know it didn't work now and at least I know he will have to live the rest of his life with the fact that he fucked up the sweetest thing he'd ever seen. And you know what, I will too.'

'But it doesn't have to be that way. We can—'

'Peter, I'm a whore and a bitch and until I can start something honestly I always will be. And you deserve more.'

'Kate, give me a chance, I understand what you're—'

'I don't want your fucking understanding. I don't want your holier-than-thou. I don't want your fucking pity. *Arrêtez*,' she screamed at the taxi driver.

The taxi slowed from its dawdling crawl to stationary and Kate rattled the door handle. She opened the door and swung her legs out. Peter gripped her arm and she looked hard at him. 'What, Peter? What?'

Peter's mind raced and suddenly a terrible thought fell into place.

'Peter, let go before I have to make you sorry.'

'Is this on the level?' Peter squinted up at her. 'You sure you didn't do the deal already? You could have just decided to take all the money for yourself. Is this your kiss-off?'

Kate pulled herself sharply from his grip. 'You see,' she said almost smugly, more confident now that all her old armour seemed to be firmly back in place, 'you'd never know with me, would you? You don't deserve that. I don't deserve that. You don't believe me? That's all right. Who the fuck would? Certainly not my rock. You don't believe me? Fucking call the twat yourself.' Kate threw her phone at him. She turned and began to run, fast, right into the Left Bank crowds endlessly searching for the legendary Café de la Paix of Cocteau, Les Deux Magots of Sartre, and *le* Big Mac of *Pulp Fiction*.

Holding Kate's phone in one hand, the AWD in the other, Peter clambered out after her.

'*Où est-ce que vous allez?*' the taxi driver shouted, getting out of the cab. The fact that he was twice Peter's size became all too apparent as he grabbed him by the collar. '*Sept euros*,' he demanded menacingly.

Peter winced and, burying the gadgets in his pockets, began rooting around for money. He located his last coins and flung them at the driver.

The driver's grip loosened. '*Qui raffole, mais doute, celui qui soupçonne, mais aime éperdument!*' Peter's school French didn't quite stretch to this but he assumed that he was being given the all-clear. He set off in the direction Kate had gone. But she had done just that. Gone.

56

Tears began to blot Peter's vision. He had no idea where he was; in a busy street next to the river, stumbling through crowds of tourists. Every now and then he would see her and he'd shout. But she would turn or move and he would realize it wasn't her. She was the only one who moved like Kate, there was no mistaking her even from a hundred yards.

He turned, wandering on to a footbridge that spanned the river. Slowly he began to recognize the hollow echoing of his shoes on the wood. It was the Pont des Arts, the same bridge he had found himself on the night before, contemplating his mortality.

Peter lurched towards a bench and, resembling a drunken tramp on the verge of psychosis, he managed to terrify the young couple sitting there having a quiet word in each other's mouths. They gathered their loose words and scurried away as Peter sat.

Truth was, he would never know whether Kate had been playing him all along, or Titus, or both. And what was the point anyway? The illusion was broken. Yet again he had opened up the magic trick that promised the impossible, he had unravelled the illusion that pretended that the unfeasible escape from his shitty existence could be achieved, and found it was no more than a rubber band and a magnet. During his years of hibernation, he had made such steely armour, been so successful at protecting himself from contemplating the emptiness, from feeling the void. And then Kate . . . No. All Kate had done was show him what a dark abyss of meaninglessness his life was. He'd only been living because the alternative was too painful to think about . . . or do. But now it was all too clear. He would never be able to shut the door on it again. Never be able to pretend that he was content or happy. She had lifted him out of the morass and dangled him high above his own life and now he was to be dashed down again. Life with her might have always been a shifting sea of meaning, but without her . . . Oh fuck it. What was the point?

He pulled himself up again and staggered towards the railings. Leaning over, he looked into the fast-running, rain-swollen waters pelting at the foot of the bridge and spitting with white foam. It didn't seem so romantic in the plain light of day. That black invitation to sweet oblivion seemed more graphically painful. He imagined the intense pain of his lungs filling with water . . . perhaps fate would be kind and he would knock himself unconscious against the bridge's pillar footings.

Peter clambered on to the narrow iron railing, seating himself as precariously as possible; now only the tiniest movement separated him from the blissful nothingness of death. To slip or not to slip, to be or not to be . . . But if that was the question, the answer was easy: not to be. Obviously if you are so far gone as to be asking yourself the question seriously, you've pretty much answered it.

Not to be.

The question, Peter realized, for your unprincely, ordinary, everyday, ignoble suicide is never about the choice of slings or sleep, but rather how. How to not be? The journey into that unknown is so awful, so apparently painful. Peter stared at the gash of angry waves that opened and hissed about the pillar. The question the daft Dane should have been asking was: Is it harder to be than to do whatever it takes to stop being? Admittedly it wasn't quite as catchy as the original but as you're sitting there wondering whether, if you fall head first, you could achieve the right angle to dash your brains against the pillar before being pulled below by the undertow, the requirements of the iambic pentameter seem a little irrelevant.

The water was becoming hypnotic and as Peter found himself leaning towards it he wondered how invisible, hidden, even depersonified, how much of a non-person, a zombie living dead he had become even to himself if, sitting here at the very brink of death, he was not think-ing of himself, his struggle to see any light in the dark world, his family, those who might have to clean up or discover him or deal with the aftermath, or even Kate, but some inaccuracy in his GCSE set texts?

But now that question was even simpler, it was a basic problem of equilibrium, of balance. What was the point? This was the point, the tipping point, the point of no return. When leaning forward took him beyond the going back and he would no longer be able to stop the slipping. And that was the only point.

He should have had the courage to do this years ago rather than lead that pathetic non-existence for so long: walking the long way around town to stay away from schools; terrified if a child neared him; courting the adoration of old people who, by the next day, would not remember he ever existed.

If he slipped now who would remember, who would care? Cedric? There was a friendship that was a metaphor, if ever there was one, for the meaninglessness of his life. His best friend, a man who couldn't remember whether he put his underpants on, let alone if he possessed a friend or not. But was he his best friend? Or was it Cedric's daughter? O Kate!

He closed his eyes ready for that final push. Maybe the courage he needed now was the courage he should have had fifteen years before when facing the band of marauding eight-year-olds, or standing in the dock, or signing the sex offenders' register. He listened to the river gurgling beneath him, and the distant horns hooting and the shouting of tour guides, and the loudspeakers of an approaching bateau mouche belting out Edith Piaf warbling 'La Vie en Rose', the most morose life-affirming song ever sung, and the rumble of traffic and 'La Marseillaise' and the well-heeled souls of gay Paree clattering over the wooden bridge.

'La Marseillaise'? Peter fished in his pockets and pulled out the AWD. He flung it down in disgust as the French national anthem still rang out. He pulled the telephone out and looked at the caller ID: 'George V'. Could it be Kate?

'Hello?'

'Oh Paul. You've got Chris's phone, I mean Dr Tavasligh.' It was Titus. An anger suddenly raged in Peter. He wanted to fling the phone far into the raging foam even if the very action tipped him over the edge, and yet a peculiarly British instinct for inappropriate politeness held him back.

'I'm very sorry, she told me that she doesn't wish to talk to you.'

'No,' Titus agreed, 'no, I figured that. In fact you might be a better person to talk to.'

'Is that so?'

'Listen, do you think you could get your hands on the AWD?'

Peter looked down at the raging torrent. 'I don't think so. Hang on, what's . . .' Peter spotted the AWD dangling beneath him. Part of the copper wire that curled around the transistor radio, added to give it a steampunk look, had hooked around a bar of the bridge's ironwork.

'It would be difficult, but I probably could.'

'I was wondering if, perhaps, I could buy it from you?'

Peter allowed the slightest smile. Titus, true to type as ever. 'It's not mine to sell you.'

'No. No, I know that. I thought maybe you could just take it.'

'And you don't think she would miss it?'

'Well, maybe it's time for a change of career.'

'So I steal it, betray my boss, lose my job, and never work in the career I've trained all my life to be in . . . is that right? That's what you're asking of me?'

'Do you fancy a job in telly?'

'I would prefer not to be prosecuted by the police and sent to jail.'

'Well, maybe a financial incentive?'

'Go on.'

'Fifty thousand pounds.'

'You were offering Tavasligh half a million.'

'Oh, you know that, do you? OK, half a million pounds, for you.'

Peter hardly let a beat fall before answering. He glanced at the precariously balanced AWD. What would Kate do? 'A million,' he said. He felt liberated sitting there with quite literally nothing to lose.

'I'm sorry?' Titus said after a strained pause.

'A million pounds. Take it or leave it.'

'Paul, we're mates. A million pounds?'

'You know what you're asking me to do. You want me to conspire in a theft.'

'But a million, you must be joking.'

'I'll show you how I'm joking. I'm putting the phone down at the count of five, that's how long you've got to get over your laughter. One.'

'Paul, be reasonable.'

'Two.'

'Paul, look, maybe I could go to six hundred thousand.'

'Three.'

'That's enough money, tax-free. You'll never have to work again.'

'Four.'

'Paul!'

TOE

3. The Originating Event (TOE)

The Originating Event is the initial moment
that triggers the logical and apparently
inevitable set of conclusions and feelings
that overwhelms the subject's better judgement and even their natural fear of pain
and death. TOE occurs when, due to bad luck
or the subject's own shortcomings, something
goes wrong during TAC which then reinforces
all the long-term underlying negative feelings that were generated during TIC. If
suicide is to be prevented, intervention is
critical between The Originating Event and
The Expiry Action (TEA).

1

Light burst into the windows at the end of the carriage, illuminating the still wide-eyed passengers, and worked its way along, rhythmically, window by window until the entire Eurostar coach had emerged from the Channel Tunnel. The grimy jam of parked trains and the Gordian spaghetti of criss-crossing rails in Folkestone sidings fittingly greeted the continental travellers to England. A blonde woman sashayed down the aisle, following the path of the light to the back of the carriage. She passed a dishevelled-looking man sitting by the last window. He held a tatty business card in one hand and a mobile phone in the other. With the return of a mobile signal he started dialling with his thumb. He put the phone to his ear and waited.

'Hello. Message for Agent Brown. This is Peter Ruchio. We met a couple of weeks ago. You asked me to tell you if I had information about Kate Minola. I think we need to talk. Call this number when you get this message.'

Peter put the phone back on the table and looked out of the window. The faint trace of a smile was as visible as the faint trace of sunshine over Kent. Everything was different now. Now it was his game, his magic show.

1,000 Milliseconds to Higham

(TEA minus 11 months 19 days 8 hours)

Kate

Christ. The squealing brakes would wake anybody up. He hasn't moved. He's faking it. But then, he must be pretty tired. No. No. He is asleep. But.

Fuck. Why can't I be sure? I read people all the time, what is it with him? Is it the emotional thing getting in the way? Am I really just getting past it? Or, is he just that good at fooling . . . shit, he's a magician. I'd never know where I was with him. So I'm never going to exactly trust him. And that's the truth isn't it. Always was. Trust no one. Live the life. Die rich. Put money in thy purse. Grab the fucking case and get out of here.

Stopped. The train's stopped. It's now or never. What? Am I paralysed? I don't want to go, but I can't bear to stay.

What am I afraid of? No, what am I more afraid of? Life with him? Having to trust someone else when every fucker I've ever known in my life has let me down? Or would have if I'd given them the chance.

Or am I more afraid of never changing? Knowing I'm going to be faking it until I die. No. No. Got to stay. Stay still. Leave the case.

A million quid.

Courage. Courage to leave the money alone. I will. I will just pretend to be asleep. All will be good with the world. Goodbye Kate, hello Catherine. It's been a long time.

2

The location of London's most illustrious magic shop is, like its contents, a somewhat arcane secret. Simply trying to find it is the first challenge for any conjuring initiate. It may only be yards from the very centre of London, the cross at Charing Cross, it may have large windows filled with terrifying, staring, ball-eyed ventriloquists' dummies, skulls, silks, guillotines, iron maidens, straitjackets and numerous magic stage props resting on a background of dark red velvet, but few ever see it. It hides in plain sight. Thousands pass around it every day and yet never catch a glimpse. Ravenport's Magic Emporium for the Discerning Prestidigitator lurks beneath; at the end of a pedestrian subway that appears to go nowhere. At least nowhere anybody who is not in a tall hat with a chain of multi-coloured silk hankies trailing from his pocket would want to go. It is the only retailer still trading in a long-forgotten sub-terranean shopping arcade created to replace an entire street which the construction of the grand modern building above, spanning two blocks, destroyed. The street and the underpass have long been forgotten; people preferred to go round the building rather than down all the steps and up again the other side solely for the pleasure of being accosted by homeless people trying to keep dry and the particular acidic aroma of urine and Thunderbird that accompanies them. Nobody goes past Ravenport's unless they are looking for a warm place to doss the night or to acquire some object from, or knowledge of, the art of magic.

So central is Ravenport's to the magic community they even have, next door, their own 'studio' space where select shows are performed, professionals may rehearse and, every Thursday, the members of the London Young Magicians' Society meet to show off their faro shuffles and double lifts to each other.

It was here that the adolescent Peter had cut his magical teeth, travelling 'into town' once a week to pursue his hobby and meet other like-minded, cripplingly shy, awkward, socially inept introverts seeking the extra prop of astonishment to carry with them into the terrifying big world of socializing and relationships. Few of them aspired to be an Ali Bongo or Doug Henning; they just wanted the confidence to know that at any moment they could produce a pack of cards and ask someone to 'Pick a card, any card.' It somehow assuaged their almost paralysing fear of starting conversations, filling awkward silences or saying something stupid, and as long as no one asked why they were carrying a pack of cards around they'd be fine.

In the early stages of his enthusiasm for escapism, Peter had practised weekly on the lock on the Ravenport's Studio door. Now he returned to the old familiar lock with a nostalgic fondness and in less than thirty seconds he was inside the deadening, eerie silence of the soundproofed studio. 'In Ravenport's Studio,' Peter muttered to himself, 'no one can hear you scream.' It was the unofficial motto of the LYM Society, always whispered when a new member started presenting one of the hoary old tricks like 'Out of this World' or 'Oil and Water' as if no one had seen anything so spectacular in their lives.

The studio was one of the few places he knew in London and it felt like home as he switched on the small series of spotlights designed to highlight 'close-up' work. Some chairs were arranged around a green baize table as if it was a private room in a casino, but more astonishing things had been seen by these walls than any casino had ever witnessed.

He quickly set up the little laptop computer he had bought with the money Kate had left him at their hotel. He checked all his equipment, went through his patter, blocked his movements, pulling the chair here, putting a hand there. He was preparing for the highest-paying one-man show on earth.

The studio doorbell tinkled. He was early! Peter spun round to the shadowy figure who stood at the door.

'Remember me?' it said.

3

'Kate?'

Kate moved forward. Just watching the movement of her shadow as she slowly strutted towards him made his soul melt into a flood of emotions. His mind seemed to drown in questions and feelings as she swam into the light. She looked around the room appreciatively, nodding. 'Good location. When's he bringing the loot?'

Peter paused. How could she possibly know? 'The loot?'

Kate looked straight at him and the colour of her eyes seemed to repaint his grey world. 'Peter. Please don't tell me that you're just going for the revenge and not the money.'

'How? How did you know where I was?'

'I've been following you from France.' Kate sat on one of the stools at the table.

'Why?'

'A million reasons.' Kate stopped. 'No. No. A million and one.'

'How, how do you know about the money?'

'Because this is the way the game has to go.'

'This was all the game? Kate? Your game?' There was silence. 'You were playing me? You had no intention of going straight.' He could hear her breathing. 'And you just wound me up and set me going like a wind-up doll.'

Kate cleared her throat. 'It's not quite like that. We're a team.'

'No. We stopped being a team when you got out of that cab.'

'Are you sure?'

'Yes,' Peter snarled, 'and now all you want is the money.'

'Well, I suppose that's partly true. You're about to be a millionaire so, congratulations, you've qualified as much more my type. You're officially in my league, Peter. How does it feel?'

'What makes you think this is where I'm going to get the money?'

'Well, breaking into an old magic shop in the middle of the night is a bit of a giveaway. Nice and quiet, great place to meet for the handover.'

'I can't believe I never saw you.'

'Peter, I was in plain sight but we look for what we expect – you taught me that. Or maybe it was me who taught you that.'

'Kate, even if I do have the money, it's not like I could ever trust you.'

'You're the illusionist, you don't exactly score high on the trustometer. Always looking for the moment of mis-direction, looking to fool . . .'

'Yes, "fool", Kate, not con.' Peter sat down opposite Kate and pulled out his own trusty 'bikes'. He began a series of calming false shuffles.

'Peter, when you got the call from Titus and you saw that the game was back on, and you could profit from his shagging me, did you stop for a moment and think about what you were doing and what that might mean to me? I have to fuck that disgusting shithole and what do you do? Quadruple your personal profit from the game. Who exactly is conning who here?'

Now it was Peter's turn to fall silent. It was starting to dawn on him, the seven deadly sins. She had begun listing them at that café but they had only got to lazi-ness, greed and envy. But then Titus did sleep with Kate. Was that still part of her plan? Was that lust? And Titus was so smugly proud of the sneaky way he thought he'd bedded her. And she stopped the sale, which made Titus angry. And then he . . . Peter could barely bring himself to admit it. Peter had got Titus to collude in the theft of the AWD. All of Kate's seven sins in exactly the order she had predicted. All of it was just a plan and he had acted it out like an automaton at her bidding.

Kate's voice continued after a slightly overdramatic sigh. 'Peter, you're just going to have to work out whether to believe me or not but think about this. Half a million was never the goal, was it? The game was always a million and it was always going to be the last game, the one that set us up to live the lives we know we deserve.'

'So why,' Peter spat back, 'did you have to put me through that, why didn't we play this together?'

'Because, Peter, you had to be convincing, you had to use every ounce of your soul to act out the performance you gave Titus to double his money. You're too nice, Peter, you'd never have done it if you didn't feel that it was all or nothing.'

Peter absentmindedly began dealing out a poker hand, bottom-dealing the culled aces to Kate. 'What about America?'

'America, that's Kate the Con who wanted that. We're going straight, Peter. Fuck America.'

Oh, he wanted to believe her and, as even a novice con artist knows, the desire to believe is half the journey to self-deception.

'You know, I was desperate, Kate, I was going to . . .' Peter tailed off.

'You talking about your moment on the bridge? Really? You know it's bloody hard to drown when you

438

know how to swim. Unless you're miles from shore or something and the exhaustion gets you.'

'You saw me?'

'OK, depending on how you look at this, either I've been following because I was playing you and you're my link to the money and because I knew that Titus, with all our come-ons, would not only double his bid but, by apparently inducing you to steal the device, would also implicate himself in a crime that would prevent him from sending the police after us.' Kate stopped.

'Or?'

Kate looked down at the hand she had been dealt. 'Or I love you and didn't want you to come to harm.'

'And which one was it?'

'You think I'd give you an honest answer?'

'I hope so.'

'Both.' Kate picked up her hand, smiled and laid down the four aces.

'So what now?'

'Now you need to trust me and Titus needs to not see me. So I'm going. And you'll tell me where to meet you and maybe you will come carrying a million quid, or maybe you won't. If you don't we'll go our separate ways and that's it.' Kate shrugged. 'Or I suppose I could send a bunch of heavies to hunt you down, get my money and break your legs.'

Peter nodded, not trusting himself to know if that was a joke or a threat.

Kate stood up. 'So what's your exit strategy? Where are you going?'

Peter hesitated and swallowed. 'I planned to take the

milk train from Charing Cross, three twenty-three to Rochester.'

'Out on the estuary. That's nice.'

'Chartered a boat down there. Thought it best to get out of the country.'

'I'm proud of you, my little student. I'll get out of here. Head over the river. London Bridge, the station?'

Peter smiled and nodded at her.

'I presume you told him to come without the heavies.'

'Yes.'

'Well, don't do anything stupid,' Kate commanded. 'Just take the money and run.'

'What would you consider stupid?'

'The money is revenge enough. You don't have to do anything else.'

'OK,' he said non-committally.

Kate opened the door and the little bell tinkled again. She stopped and Peter peered at her shadow.

'This is it, Peter, this is the courageous choice I told you about in the meadow in Christchurch. This is it.'

The bell in the darkness tinkled again, and she was gone.

4

'Brightly.'

'Brown?'

'Yeah. How's it going?'

'Are you calling from New York?'

'No. No, I had a bit of a breakthrough.'

'You're still in the UK?'

'Yeah. And there's been a development and I've got to ask you a serious question and I want you to answer me completely honestly.'

'OK.'

'You know what you were saying, back at the airport, about a fed's retirement package?'

'Yes.'

'Well, Madeline. Can I call you Madeline?'

'This isn't official, is it?'

'No, no, it's very much not official.'

'OK, Danny, call me Madeline.'

There was a long pause. 'Would you, Madeline, would you reconsider my proposal if, if I, somehow, found the sort of financial package you were talking about?'

Now it was Brightly's turn to pause. 'Yes, Danny. Yes, I would.'

'Wow.' Brown breathed a long, low whistle. 'Well, I think we're going to be very happy together.'

'I'd have to see what you're talking about before I committed myself. Yes?'

'Sure, sure, I understand. When's your next shift?'

'Considering I'm no longer up for promotion I can take tomorrow off. As long as I'm back the next day.'

'I'm going down to the Kent coast tomorrow, will you meet me?'

'Where?'

'Where do you know?'

'Margate?'

'Sure. I'll find a hotel, book us a room and text you

the details. Should be there some time in the early morning. That all right?'

'Five-star?'

'Sure, honey.'

'It's money before honey, Danny boy.'

'Got ya. I'll see you there then?'

'I'll see you there.'

Click.

5

Titus arrived at Ravenport's Studio like a wraith, as silent as a shadow. 'You like magic, don't you,' he breathed at Peter, eyeing the cards on the table as he sat down. 'What a very fitting place. You have my little magic gadget?'

'Sit down.' Peter gestured to the stool that Kate had warmed just half an hour earlier.

Titus ingratiatingly obeyed.

'You've come without your bodyguards like I said?'

'Certainly. You can check outside if you like.'

'It's just that after what you did to Tavasligh, I don't exactly trust you. They could just jump me for the AWD.'

'Oh, don't worry, Paul,' Titus leaned forward with some menace, 'I'm perfectly capable of doing that for myself. And if I thought you'd be stupid enough not to hide the AWD until you'd seen the colour of my money I might well have.'

Peter sat down opposite. 'You know I've stolen from

my employer, I've ruined my career, I'm a wanted man in France. You've asked a lot.'

'On the contrary,' Titus sneered, 'it is you who have asked a lot.' He nodded to the case on the table.

Peter pulled it round and opened it. There, in neatly packed bundles of fifty-pound notes, was a whole lot of money. He pulled out a bundle as Titus watched him like a bird of prey, ready to swoop at the slightest odd move. Peter knew to look carefully through the wodge to check that they all were genuine notes and not just the top ones, a classic con according to Kate.

'The AWD is worth so much more than that, why would I bother to try to fool you?'

'It's your job.'

Titus laughed. 'So it is. So it is.' He scratched around in his jacket and felt the warmed metal of the stiletto knife he carried so close to his heart. 'What you have there is twenty piles made of five packets each and each packet containing two hundred fifty-pound notes.'

Peter counted as Titus enumerated. He checked some more packets and felt the paper, looked closer. It was genuine. This was a million pounds. It really was. Peter suppressed the glee he felt looking at his old enemy and playing the game better than him.

The next con he had to watch out for was the Switch. Punter sees and counts the money, he closes the case and somehow the magician switches the case for an identical one that's full of plain paper. He had already prepared a way to prevent this. He pulled a bright red silk hanky from his pocket and placed it in the clasp of the case as he closed it. Now a switch would be practically impossible.

Titus raised his eyes. 'Oh really! What happened to good old-fashioned trust?'

'You tell me,' Peter said.

'So the AWD?' Titus asked tetchily.

'All in good time. I've got a question first.'

'I didn't come for an interview.'

'Why magic?'

'What?'

'I've just always wondered. Why did you get into magic?'

Titus sighed but seemed to have to think hard about it. 'I was just good at it.'

'But it's quite obscure. I just thought maybe there was some magician who had inspired you.'

Titus shook his head. 'No. No. Anneman might have been an influence on what I do.'

'Did you have magicians for, I don't know,' Peter shrugged nonchalantly, 'birthday parties?'

Suddenly a storm seemed to cross Titus's face. 'No. Why do you ask?'

'Oh, your life fascinates me. But let me get the AWD.'

Titus grinned as Peter got up and walked around the table. Suddenly he stopped behind Titus. 'Oh, what's that on the leg of your chair?'

Titus felt with his hand even before his head turned to look. Instantly Peter took Titus's wrist and pushed it into the handcuffs that he had set up there earlier. It's all in the pre-show work.

'What the fuck are . . .' He pulled at the handcuffs and nearly wrenched his arm from its socket. Titus's free hand dived into his jacket and pulled out the stiletto knife. Peter was on his other side now and he lunged round at him. As the knife embedded itself in Peter's arm, he reeled with the shock of the cut and the presence of a weapon. As he fell backwards the knife was wrested from Titus's hand. To stop himself dropping to the floor, he grabbed Titus's arm with his good hand and pulled back. Titus screamed. 'You fucker, you fuck, what are you doing?'

Peter felt dizzy as he lost blood but he grabbed the other pair of handcuffs and jammed Titus's wrist into them, listening for the swish of the metal talon swinging round and the clicking ratcheting as the handcuffs locked.

Only then did Peter allow himself to collapse on to the floor. He breathed heavily as the pain of the knife started to connect with his brain.

As Titus continued to rant at the top of his voice, Peter pulled himself to an upright position and gripped the handle of the knife. He steeled himself to pull but could not. He tensed his muscles for the pull but felt too weak watching the blood pouring down his arm and he let go.

'You fucking madman, you fucking loony, I'll have you killed for this,' Titus continued.

'You know what they say,' Peter breathed heavily at Titus: 'in Ravenport's Studio no one can hear you scream.'

He knew he had to get the knife out and staunch the flow before he lost much more blood. Peter gripped the knife again and wrenched upward without stopping to think. Another wave of pain rocketed through his body and he experienced a moment of complete disorientation as he felt he might pass out.

Titus's full-volume stream of invectives kept Peter conscious. He got up and lurched towards his own bag, dripping a trail of blood as he went. He gripped a small silk hanky and, holding the end in his fist, pulled it out of his hand. It turned out to be knotted to another hanky and then that one was tied to another and so on until the entire string of twenty-two hankies had been pulled out. Titus had actually stopped shouting and struggling as he watched this improbable bit of first aid.

Peter slumped down on his chair again opposite Titus and started wrapping his wound with the string of hankies.

'Is this all part of the deal?' Titus sneered. 'We working through your trust issues? You finished yet?'

'Oh, not by a long shot, Titus. I can't believe you don't know who I am yet.'

'In my line of work you make many envious enemies. You're just one in the queue.'

'Oh, I don't envy you, Titus. And give me time, I will probably pity you. Meanwhile.' Peter picked up the bloody stiletto and advanced on the other man.

'Stop!' Titus screamed. 'I'll give you whatever you want.'

'I just want my cold dish served,' Peter panted.

He pulled the chair round to the side and placed the knifepoint on Titus's stomach.

'Please no. It wasn't me.'

Peter stopped and looked into Titus's eyes. 'What wasn't you?'

'Your, er, grandparent?' Titus guessed.

'My grandparent. What didn't you do to my grandparent?' Peter was almost smiling.

'They killed themselves. That's all.'

'Last I heard all my grandparents were in fine form.'

'You didn't have a relative, er, die recently?'

Peter shook his head.

'Fuck. Well, who are you?'

'I was about to remind you.' Peter placed the tip of the stiletto in the top of Titus's fly and ripped upwards, sending the button flying. Then, cutting at the trousers until they fell loose, he pulled them straight off.

'Oh my God, you're going to rape me. You're the fucking loony fan they all warn me about.'

Peter shook his head, smiling, as he cut Titus's Y-fronts off too, exposing a very scared and tiny penis. He turned to fetch something from his bag.

'Oh my God, stop,' Titus shouted desperately. 'It's not like I'm going to get a hard-on . . .' He stopped abruptly when he saw what was in Peter's hand.

'Recognize this then?' Peter held up the Groucho-ho.

'I. You,' Titus stuttered. 'Mr Noodles.'

'Oh yes.'

'That was just a joke.'

Peter nodded. 'And so's this and, frankly, so are you.' Peter jammed the Groucho-ho on Titus's penis.

'Oh well,' Titus tried to smile indulgently, 'good joke. Ha ha ha. You certainly got me back.'

'Oh no, Titus. I was exposed to the world. And so will you be.'

Peter brought round the laptop and placed it on a chair opposite. Titus's face froze as he saw the YouDude.com live video feed on the web page. The laptop's webcam showed his entire body. The big bold title read 'Titus Black Exposed'. That was bound

447

to send the search engines crazy. Titus stopped struggling lest the Groucho-ho should fall off. He smiled at the camera. 'Help,' he announced, 'I'm at Ravenport's . . .'

'Don't bother,' Peter said, 'the microphone's been muted. Unless someone's lipreading you'll have quite a wait.'

'You abominable fucker. They'll fucking hang you for this.'

Peter nodded. 'You know, I must find out more about these grandparents you talked about.' He was just jamming now, off script, impromptu, but it felt good. 'I wonder if they'll bring back hanging.'

Titus wavered between shouting more obscenities and smiling at the camera.

Peter was very careful not to go near Titus or into the camera's field of vision. 'Thanks,' he smiled, picking up the case, 'for everything.'

The bell above the door tinkled and Peter was gone.

Titus turned back to the vision of himself on the laptop screen. Beneath the ghastly video feed, messages were already being posted.

'Do you think he saw that coming?'
'You telling me his entire cock can fit in that plastic nose? LOL.'
'BTW he's not looking so f***ing smug now!'
'What a prick! Oh no, he doesn't seem to have one.'
'He's still gorgeous but wouldn't want to give him a blowjob with that staring at me. LOL.'
'I'm Titus Black and we've been sharing way too much!'

On the screens of thousands of internet surfers Titus bowed his head and wept.

6

At three in the morning the concourse of Charing Cross train station is eerily empty. In the disparity between its appearance and its usage, it resembles a movie set; fully lit with every essential detail of a modern urban transport hub in place: the ticket gates, the large clock, the arrivals board and the socks, ties and knickers franchise shops, but not a single passenger passing through. At the three main gateways into the station, heavy-duty contracting steel railings are firmly locked shut apart from a small gap left in the most western gate. Here stands Baldev Mountbatten Sarabha, 'Baldy' to those of his colleagues who feign chumminess in terror of overstepping the complex and unwritten rules of multiculturalism but still wonder if it might be derogatory considering he has more hair than the rest of the entire crew combined. He stands and mentally composes his forthcoming novel as he has done every night since he joined British Rail Security. He had joined in the days when trains not only had guards but guards had vans; full of ambition to travel his adopted nation, or at least the exotic parts with the evocative names he saw rolling up on the boards in the morning: Dover Priory, Tunbridge Wells, Battle, Westenhanger, Sandwich, Paddock Wood and the Ramsgate, whatever that was. But it was never to be. Before he could be promoted to rolling stock, the rail guards were phased out by the unsmiling black-shirted Transport Police who had no need of the man, the van or, indeed, the turban.

Unlike the contorted and labyrinthine plot of his yet-to-be-written Booker Prize-winning post-colonial magnum opus spanning several generations of a Punjabi family torn apart by the Partition and then ripped off by the ruddy builders who did the conservatory, the duties of his night job were blessedly simple: to check the passes of the track and stock maintenance staff, open the gates for the mail vans and usher in the cleaning staff. Meanwhile he was to keep away the tramps, the riff-raff, the terrorists and the late revellers wandering from the nightclubs under the arches dressed in silver foil and fluorescent bikinis.

'Buba, you know that I always respect you,' Nina clucked exasperatedly, 'but Ranjit is still your son.'

'Ding ding, just coming through.' The man who had disturbed his dénouement father-and-daughter dialogue flashed a post office badge at him. Baldev nodded him through and was about to return to *Peckham Popadom*, volume two of his *A Nightingale Singhs* trilogy, when the trail of blood that followed the interloper caught his eye.

'Excuse me, sir.'

The man stopped and turned. He looked down at the dark red line that traced a path from him back to Baldev. The wheels of his suitcase had criss-crossed the blood.

'Are you all right?' Baldev asked. Now that he looked hard at the man he could see that, beneath the coat on his shoulders, his upper arm was bandaged with multi-coloured hankies and haemorrhaging profusely. At the centre of the rainbow tourniquet was a blood-black scab wetly winking in the lights.

The man pointed to the suitcase he was wheeling. 'Just delivering this case to—'

'I mean your arm.'

The man looked at the arm. 'Oh this? I just cut myself.'

'I have a first aid kit. It has bandages.'

'No, no, please don't bother.'

It is when someone obviously grievously wounded tells you not to bother with a bandage that your suspicions may justifiably be raised. 'Can I see your pass again, sir?'

The man hesitated, seemed to think better of his first thought, and ambled back towards Baldev waving the card. Baldev tried to follow the path of the moving pass and suddenly his head filled with the blasts and screams, the blood and the bullets, of chapter 38, his depiction of the storming of the Golden Temple, concluding with the hero holding his dying guru in his arms as he whispered 'Khalistan' with his last breath. Baldev was so shocked, so caught between the expectations of his own dramas, the dramas offered by the 'War on Terror' and this tiny real event, he seemed to be in the moment and outside it at the same time. His conscious mind and his daydreaming unconscious reorientated themselves to try to take in what was happening. The pass was little more than a card with a tube logo and a photo on it; the man wheeled a heavy-looking case. This was it. This was what he'd been waiting for. This was the next 9/11, the next 7/7 . . . Baldev started trying to work out the date and whether it was something as neat as the others.

'I'm just dropping this off for John, John on the mail train.' The man seemed to be trying to bluff it.

Behind Baldev, in the station forecourt, a man with a long beard not unlike the guard's own got out of a black Lexus and ran towards them over the cobblestones.

Baldev didn't see him, but the bleeding man took one look over Baldev's shoulder and suddenly tried to turn. Baldev grabbed the stranger forcefully and pulled him, case and all, out of the station. At that point he spotted the bearded man from the Lexus, evidently an accomplice. The newcomer rushed up, barging into Baldev and making a grab for the bomb case. With heroic disregard for his own personal safety, Baldev swung round and put his elbow straight into the second man's face. He fell, shouting, '*Oy vey.*'

The first man scrambled up, took hold of his case and ran off. Baldev knew he couldn't leave his post and promptly sat on the conspirator, who had been rolling on the floor holding his nose, shouting, 'Dick, Dick, help me with this *shumphstusser.*'

'Oh sodding hell,' Baldev kept repeating to himself as the burly man beneath him struggled. He pressed his walkie-talkie.

'Yeah, Baldy?'

'Mr Sherings, sir.' He watched another identical but smaller man getting out of the Lexus. 'There is a ruddy bunch of terrorists here at north access.'

'Fuck off, Baldy.'

'No, it's true, I need back-up. Please call the police,' he shouted.

Hearing Baldev shout, the small man from the Lexus stopped and inched back inside again.

Baldev cast about, looking for the man who had started this all off, but he hadn't hung around. He was nowhere to be seen and neither, the guard thought thankfully, was his payload.

7

It wasn't long before there were sirens screaming down the Strand. Policemen tumbled out of the station on Agar Street, heading for the terminus.

Peter was already halfway down Villiers Street when he heard them. The street ran parallel to the station and the train lines. It dropped down towards the Thames, leaving the end of the station high above with the tracks and the platforms running out over the river on Hungerford Bridge. At the bottom of the road a group of men and women in orange boiler suits smoked outside the Embankment tube station, ready for their next cleaning shift. Peter tried to cover his sweaty, arse-clenching nervousness by nodding to them and hurriedly taking a right under the bridge. He looked up to a street sign to check where he was and suddenly felt inexplicably relaxed. He was on Northumberland Avenue.

There is a strange, warm familiarity whenever you

find yourself on a street from the Monopoly board. It's somewhere you may have built houses, hotels, even empires on and yet had always just thought of it as a green or pink rectangle. Deep in your hippocampus long-lost neural connections are rediscovered and electrified, feelings return, not a specific memory of an actual game but a pleasant amalgam of emotions brought back from a more innocent period; when you had both time and family or friends to play a game that served as a paradigm for good financial management in the same way Barbie serves as a model for a healthy body image – ritualizing capitalism as if it really had rules and regulations that competing developers and bankers always stuck to and enjoying the fantasy of how painless a life led in mortgaged servitude could be.

Peter found this sudden nostalgia calming him, letting him breathe, helping him think a bit straighter. The train he needed to catch, the one Kate had at least half a million reasons to be waiting for, was standing straight above him, ticking on the bridge. Its engine was against the buffers in the station, waiting for the mail sacks.

As he stared up at the bridge a flashing light, reflecting from the buildings, caught his eye. A silent police van turned out of Trafalgar Square, slowing as it entered the other end of the avenue.

Peter couldn't stop now. He turned towards the river and darted up the stairs to the Golden Jubilee footbridge, one of the two walkways that run along either side of the Hungerford railway bridge. Each footbridge is suspended from a series of leaning maypoles radiating thin spokes that distribute the weight and look like the skeletons of tepees. Now Peter was back on the same level as the train.

The cruising police van below him stopped. Peter ducked down to peer over the edge. An armed officer, dressed all in black, dropped stealthily out of the back of the van. And then another. As each policeman followed, the leader pointed to various positions, holding his fingers up to indicate how many men should go to each one. In a few minutes the entire area would be in lockdown. He looked out at the purple-lit bicycle wheel of the London Eye, the string of lights that bounced up and down along the Embankment to the Houses of Parliament, and floating above them the yellow moon-face of Big Ben's clock telling him he had just two minutes to get on the train.

Peter pulled back and turned. The last carriage of his train, the only train lit up and ready to run, was roughly four yards from him. Unfortunately the first two yards were the gap between the footbridge and the railway bridge across a vertiginous drop to the swirling river below, and if that was not enough – if he could make it there and clamber through the cast-iron railings – the following two yards would entail crossing a possibly electrified track. Peter looked down at the river. The view felt very familiar. Though much higher than his visit to the Seine, the stakes seemed pretty much the same.

Quickly he closed the case's drag handle and laced his good arm and then the more painful bleeding one through its carry handles. He hitched the case on to his back.

Now Peter could hear feet running up the stairs to the

bridge. He ran to the first maypole strut; he could see it was attached by a long white metal beam to one of the massive main piers of the railway bridge. With no time to think about balance or probabilities, he pointed his toes and stepped on to the beam, lunging towards the railings of the railway bridge.

Peter's hands made contact, his fingers laced with the cast-iron bars as his muscles braced to take the shock of the full weight of his body. Twelve stone and a million pounds. As gravity took over and his shoulder sockets wrenched, the muscles in his stabbed left arm seared with pain and he felt his fingers let go. He grabbed again with that hand, scrabbling to find a purchase lower down. He grabbed and gripped and stopped his descent. Peter caught his breath and then, angling his head to his left, he looked right into the eyes of the gun-toting policemen on the footbridge.

He froze. He waited for them to shout or raise their weapons but, while they were well lit, he was in the shadow of the bridge. Barely more than a few yards away yet they hadn't seen him. They looked about, peered over into the water, then the taller one word-lessly pointed two fingers to his eyes and then towards the other end of the bridge. The shorter one took off, stomping within feet of the hanging fugitive.

Just then the railings began to shake. Peter could hear an engine coming on to the bridge, shunting towards the station.

His muscles aching as they never had before, Peter dared not pull himself up in case his movement called attention to him. He waited, pain stripping his arms of their strength, his fingers stinging as they slowly seemed to be giving up on him. Trapped against the side of the bridge, he couldn't look down below his dangling feet. He swung them gently to see if there was any foothold but was met by empty air.

Now the vibrations of the heavy engine began to shake Peter violently, and worse, sparks where the wheels bridged gaps in the electrified track popped and lit up parts of the bridge in lightning flashes, black and white high relief, like the frames from a comic book. All too soon Peter and the railing he clung to were suddenly bathed in a blinding flash of light, his face caught in a contortion of fear and determination. For a few seconds he could see nothing. He listened for the shouts, 'Stop,' or a gunshot.

His eyesight came swimming back. He could make out the shape of the officer, closer now but with his back still to Peter.

'He's behind you,' Peter breathed as if playing in a pantomime of his own grim humour.

He could feel his fingers slip millimetre by millimetre towards the choppy, sucking water beneath. He considered the likelihood of surviving the fall, the direction of the tide, the noise of the splash . . .

A car alarm started and caught the attention of the officer, who turned back towards the Embankment.

Peter took his chance. He pulled himself up painfully, trying to suppress any grunting, and managed to clamber through the railings, tumbling over and on to the bridge. He lay for a moment watching the policeman return to his lookout position. Peter turned his head, trying to roll to an upright position, and stopped dead. The shiny metal track was an inch from his face.

Peter could hear a buzzing electric noise running through it. Carefully he pulled himself back and slowly stood, swinging his gaze between policeman and track.

At that moment the mail carriage at the back of the train gave out an ear-piercing squeak and started to move. Peter leapt the rail, then the next, and ran to the moving carriage. He reached up to the door and tried to turn the handle. It was locked. He jumped from sleeper to sleeper as the train gathered pace, still holding on to the handle. The window was open and he jumped, reaching out with his bad hand. The pain that hit the already aching arm was too much and immediately his grip slipped. He began to fall towards the track and the wheels, when suddenly he felt his still-raised arm caught by something. In a moment it took his whole weight and dangled him above the turning wheels. Peter swung his hand round to catch hold of what was holding his arm. A hand caught his hand and Peter was dragged up to the window. The door swung open and he was pulled inside. He fell to the floor, coughing with the effort and the exhaustion.

'Glad you could make it,' his saviour told him. 'I thought you were never coming.'

Peter looked up and met the dark eyes of Agent Brown.

8

'Nine hundred and fifty thousand, a cool million.' Agent Brown fished the last packet of notes from the bottom of Titus's case and kissed them. 'You know, I don't know what's sweeter: the money, or depriving Minola of her biggest haul.'

He flung the packet on to all the others in a grey Royal Mail sack.

Peter sat on a crate as the train slowly ground through sleeping south London. 'And your end of the bargain?'

'Sure, son, sure.' Brown pulled out his phone. He waited. 'Charlie, hey Charlie? Yeah. You heard I was on the way back? Got another lead so I stayed on a bit. Nah. They love me. Yeah? Charlie, listen, I've got good and bad news, my friend. Yeah. About Minola. The good news? I caught up with her, she ain't going to be a threat no more. Yeah. Yeah, after all this time. No, it feels good. The bad news? Yeah. The bad news is, she's dead. Yeah, Charlie, you heard right. Yeah. Bad fall. They're going to be dredging the river. Sure. Listen, Charlie, can you do me a favour? Can you get on to the Most Wanted guys? You know I'm retiring, man, I just want to see that page without her mug staring right back at me, finally. Yeah. Thanks, man. I'll be back to do the paperwork day after tomorrow. OK. Talk to you later.' Brown pressed 'End'. 'OK?'

Peter shrugged.

'We'll check the site in a bit.'

'I'll need a couple of thousand for the boat I chartered.'

Brown reached into the bag and stripped off a bunch of fifty-pound notes. He passed them to Peter.

'And you're staying on board until Rochester, right? Keep us safe from Titus's men, yeah?'

'I'll be right here but, son, if you think she'll be heading off on a boat into the sunset with you when she finds out that you ain't got the money she, you, worked so hard to get, you're pissing in the wind.'

'Perhaps,' Peter thought aloud, 'I'd better find the right time to tell her. Like when we're on the boat.'

Brown shook his head wearily. 'What a chump. You give up a million pounds to save her. Man, she'll be as loyal to you as she was to the thirty-eight other suckers she swizzed. Married most of them.'

'She's going straight, she's changing. She said.'

'Yeah? Did she tell you your cheque's in the post and no, your ass don't look big in that? I've known her a whole lot longer than you have and the girl don't change.'

Peter looked out of the tiny mail-van window as Brown checked his smartphone.

'There you go,' Brown said, still looking at the phone. He passed it to Peter. It was the America's Most Wanted page. He scrolled through it. The familiar picture of Kate was gone.

'And you promise, you're never coming after her again?'

'Listen, kid, a federal agent takes a bribe of close on one and a half million bucks, he ain't ever going back. I do, I go straight to the slammer. I got your money but you've got my balls.'

'She's free.' Peter exhaled.

Brown grinned. 'I really got to her, huh?'

'Not literally, obviously, but,' Peter nodded, 'I know what it feels like to be haunted, hunted, for fifteen years.'

'She's got herself a conscience? Hey. Maybe she can change, maybe I've done my job.'

Peter nodded at him enthusiastically. He was getting it.

'And maybe you're the biggest moron on this goddam earth. Don't you see? Minola's got no conscience so she's got you to act like one instead.' Brown leaned forward and tied up his mail sack full of money. 'But hey. It's your money, er, her money. Whatever. It's my money now. And if she wants to go back and screw the States again? None of my business. I got a feeling I'll be hanging out in Europe for a little while.'

Peter looked anxiously at Brown. 'I can trust you?'

'Woah. Way more than you can trust Minola. I'm like George fucking Washington to her. I'll stay on the train for you, you can try for your happy ever after. I've been looking at a more brightly future.' He winked at Peter.

The carriage wheels began to squeal as they slowed, easing into London Bridge station to take on more mail and one female.

'Anyway,' Brown mused, 'be good to get one more look at her. Closure, you know.'

Peter took a last wistful look at Brown's mail sack, then grabbed a few more envelopes from the pile they had made and stuffed them into his own case before locking it shut. He nodded to Brown and headed off through the train to one of the empty carriages. He hauled the case on to one of the overhead racks and leaned out of the window.

In the distance, down the platform, Peter could make out a familiar form. She had her long raincoat on and her hair tied back. As soon as she saw him she began to run. Peter had barely opened the door when she pressed into him, hugging him and kissing his cheeks, his mouth, his neck. Holding his head between her hands she looked at him with that dazzling smile.

'You know I doubted and I'm sorry, something deep inside always told me you could do this. For me. For us.' She kissed him again and pushed him back into the carriage.

Peter winced and she saw his arm.

'Fuck,' she said. 'Titus do that?'

'He came armed. I should have—'

Kate put a finger on his lips, shut the door and led him to a seat. She untied the hankies, ripping off the blood clots that had congealed around them, and looked at the bright red knife wound. She laid him down and, tearing off some of the unbloodied hankies, cleaned the flesh about the lesion. Then she leaned back and started to pull up her skirt.

Peter watched spellbound as Kate slipped off her stockings one by one, straightened them and then slowly spun them around his arm, binding tight the laceration.

As Peter tried to sit up, Kate pushed him down again and lay beside and on him. She kissed him and he strained his neck up to kiss her. There in the empty carriage each relished the ecstatic, exhausted relief of finding each other again. The tension of the last forty-eight hours flooded out through every touch and look, the release of emotion through motion and sighs of sweet home. Yes, that was it, home. Home for two fellow travellers who could barely remember the idea of home; never felt at home in their own skins but for this

462

minute they were at home in each other's, wrapped in each other's. And only when their tired frames could kiss and hug and hold no longer did they fall apart on to opposite seats and stare at each other. And it was minutes, hours and eternity before either one noticed that the train was already rattling through the window's mirror-black countryside with just tiny distant lights floating past.

Kate looked up at the case on the rack and smiled naughtily at Peter. 'That it?'

Peter nodded.

'A million?'

He nodded again.

'And no trouble from the Torah Twins?'

Peter shook his head. 'Nothing I couldn't handle.'

Kate stood up unsteadily and put her hands on the case. Peter tensed. Everything would change now, when she saw what was inside. It had all seemed so clear just an hour ago but now, now he wasn't so sure he'd made the right deal. She saved him from his ghost, he'd save her from hers, that was the idea, but at the cost of losing her? Could he face that? Not now, not now.

'Don't you trust me?' he asked.

Kate stopped and looked down at Peter.

'I don't trust Titus Black.'

'I saw it, I checked it, I haven't let go of it.'

Kate sat down again, grinning. 'You know, you're right. I know I don't need to look. And that feels' – she screwed her lower lip into her upper one as she tried to find a word for this astonishing new feeling, the one most of us recognize as 'trust' – 'good,' she continued, and smiled. 'I like it. It doesn't matter, it's not what's important. It's there. You're here.'

To a more objective observer in possession of Kate's history, such a statement might smell terribly of fish but Peter ate it as if it were sushi, relieved to stave off the moment and enjoy the intimacy a little longer.

Kate slipped down against the back of her seat, putting her feet up on the seat next to Peter. 'I'm just so tired,' she smiled lazily and closed her eyes, 'and so happy,' she whispered.

Peter watched her for a while as her breasts gently rose, gently fell, and the carriage swayed from side to side as he began to realize how horribly tired he was and he too began to close his eyes, listening to the heartbeat of the tracks beneath the wheels rhythmically pacing their way towards Rochester.

Higham

The station was quiet, the train was quiet. Kate opened her eyes. Peter still had his shut. His chest undulated as if he was sleeping. The money sat above him, on the rack.

Maybe I should just count it, Kate thought. Just have a look.

She peered out at the dark station. It would be so easy. Just to get out. Peter would carry on to Rochester. And it would be time for a new life, a new sting.

No. No, Peter was the new life. He had shown her it wasn't all about the money, there was something more.

She looked back at the bag, stood up and reached for it. Peter remained asleep. It felt so good, the weight, the idea of all those notes.

Kate lifted down the bag and now everything was back on automatic. Quietly she turned the handle of the door. Silently she stepped out on to the platform and noiselessly she turned the handle and closed the door again.

Rehabilitation could wait. A million pounds couldn't. She stepped into the shadows and watched Peter's sleeping form through the window. Slumbering and bathed in the light of the carriage. For a moment she thought that was it. That was the test of his innocence. He was the one. For a moment she wanted to open the carriage door and wake him and kiss him and tell him how sorry she was. But the weight of a million pounds in notes on her shoulder dug deep. The train sighed and started to move again. She watched the window move slowly at first and gather speed and the little red lights at the end of the train disappear down the track. She was alone. She was a fucking millionaire!

9

'Don't make me say it, man.' Agent Brown strode into the carriage.

Peter wiped the streaming tears from his cheeks and tried to regulate his breathing against the irregular spasms in his chest. As he had seen her close the carriage door quietly behind her, he had felt paralysed. It all seemed fated and he just couldn't find the will or the spirit to move or even show his wakefulness.

Now he just felt woozy, as if he'd just been punched, as if he might throw up. He found he couldn't even sit up, he felt winded, nothing making sense. It was like he'd been drugged, which, in a way, he had been. Watching Kate suddenly open her eyes and silently rise up to reach for the case, his brain flooded with adrenalin and seventeen other detectable chemicals which combined in a neurococktail of dizzying, mind-altering complexity. He had anticipated, half expected it, certainly knew it was possible and yet hope had kept him there, hope had teased him with fruitless possibilities. But now she was gone it all seemed too unreal.

From: *Letters* Tavasligh mss. 14.9

DR C. TAVASLIGH MSC PHD
CHANGE IN MIND ORGANIZATION
CHRISTCHURCH
DORSET

This was it, Peter. This plunge into hopelessness, the vortex of despair, the moment that connected beginning and end; the two hypoemotional points in your life: from the handcuffs at the party to the parting on the train. Kate's abandonment was the edge-tipper, the life changer, the death bringer. Just at the moment of your greatest victory, you found yourself tumbling into the abyss. Your mind making connections it had rarely done before, uncritically drawing your fatalistic conclusions: there is no escape from tragedy, the journey to excise it is futile, to stave off one demon is to invite another.

Aristotle said that tragedy was like a wheel; each time the tragic hero reaches the top he is merely turning the wheel that drags his predecessor to his nadir. And as the next hopeful rises, the hero topples down to his own lowest point and the wheel turns through another cycle.

How could you see life as anything but inherently tragic, an endless onslaught of anguish and dejection? Conquering Titus? What did that mean? Losing Kate. And what would you need to stand again, to conquer this loss? She would be long gone and if you ever found her again, what then? And even if you got together again, what then? You could never trust her; whatever lives of dissembling you had led, you had believed, and it was the belief in and of itself that was the splendour, the joy, the happiness.

468

Even if it is an illusion, the process of belief, the total conviction that if you fall the other will be there to catch you, the confidence it gives you is the bedrock of happiness in life. And the miracle that failed, and buggered belief and proved it was unfounded? That. That was stomach-churningly and, more importantly, mind-alteringly terrible for you but in turn it raised me up on that wheel.

Because it was this mindset, the persistence of despair, that would lead you back to me. Put you in the frame of mind I needed to change it for you for ever. When I next saw you, it was clear you were ready, you were ideal to undergo my treatment. The key to your memories stemmed from these two emotional peaks, or troughs, in your life. It was the two moments of Peter's life which cemented an unshakeable expectation that, for you, misfortune was unavoidable.

And for your mind to totally accept a new identity, the infection of hopelessness was ideal. It's when we are hopeless that we are most subject to suggestion and belief.

From the poor who were promised better lives in the hereafter if they just believed in a supreme being, to the death-bed conversions of rakes, belief is the last resort of the hopeless. And you, Peter, were without hope.

Brown helped Peter sit up. For a long time all Peter could do was breathe heavily as Brown sat, his hands resting on his lap, observing him and waiting patiently. The train had almost come to the next station before Peter found his voice again. 'It,' he panted, 'it was her own choice. She had to choose. If she hadn't had a choice it wouldn't have been . . .' Peter stopped, the last

469

thing he felt qualified to talk about right now was what was 'real'. This all felt too dreamlike. His unconscious mind was buffering him from the full impact of the emotional hit. It's kind like that.

'Oh man,' Brown sighed, 'I kinda feel sorry for you. What was it? The love-conquers-all delusion? Can you really have got to your age and not found out what really conquers all?' He rubbed his thumb against his first finger in the international sign for money – or Parkinson's. 'Kate went for it. I went for it. I know DI Brightly's going for it. You see, Peter, I'm not here just for your little drama with Minola, I've got Brightly meeting me at the other end. And with that money we'll never have to work again, the sweet life, no tricks, straight up. And you know what? I can trust her. Police stock through and through, I'll always know where she's at. Confidence, trust, it's a beautiful thing. But you with your magician's tricks and your sleight of hand and illusions . . . what the fuck? You know I was telling you: look, she's just smoke and mirrors, but you couldn't, wouldn't see it. It's fucked up.'

Peter thought about this and put his hand out to Brown. 'Lend me a coin.'

Brown fished in his pants pockets and flipped a two-pound coin to Peter. Peter caught it and it flashed as he placed it squarely on the palm of his other hand, closing his fingers around it.

'Look. We're so used to the usual story,' Peter said, 'the narrative of one thing simply passing from one place to another, that our minds resist accounting for the unlikely, even if we know there's going to be a trick. We totally unconsciously block the unlikely. Having to keep an eye out for it clutters the mind; the unlikely has no evolutionary benefit so we've developed filters for it. And because we're so good at ignoring the unlikely, the unlikely process creates the impossible effect.'

Peter moved the fist holding the coin closer to Brown. He unfurled his fingers but the coin was gone. Brown laughed and pointed at Peter's other hand.

'The illusion's called the persistence of vision, a retention vanish.' Peter flipped the coin back to Brown. 'The glint of the coin, the plausible angle, the casual finger positions, the naturalness of the action, all work together to make you believe the coin has been left in this hand by the other one. It's an optical illusion, but you know what, it still fools you even when you're expecting to be tricked.'

'Ah huh?' Brown nodded, not really seeing where all this was going or caring much, somewhat distracted by the little voice singing in his head, 'I'm in the money, I'm in the money. I've got a lotta what it takes to get along.'

'The coin vanishing is impossible, right?' Peter said. 'And the coin being dragged back out of the hand by the casual-looking fingers is, at best, just unlikely. But still we ignore the unlikely as a possibility and then are surprised by the impossible. The unlikely becomes invisible. That's what magic is, an unlikely process creating an impossible effect. You see?'

Brown shook his head.

'I knew Kate's trick, I encouraged it, I even set it up, but my persistence of vision, my basic human need for life to be made up of likely events, still had me thinking that the unlikely was impossible.'

'Now here's the thing,' Brown leaned forward, 'Kate

ripping you off? That was by no means the unlikely action, it was the probable course.'

'Every day,' Peter sighed, 'the unlikely happens, planes fall out of the sky or long-lost twins bump into each other or money is found in the street or Christ appears on a cracker but . . . but what if you led your life expecting every lottery ticket would win you the lottery? You can't live a life expecting the unexpected, knowing that the wool might be pulled from your eyes at any moment, that at any time the persistence of your vision might be shown to be completely wrong. All illusion. You can't lead a life like that. I don't want to lead a life like that. She said she didn't want to lead a life like that any more.'

'So the case full of money. It was a test? Huh? You didn't have the balls to just tell her what you'd done. You couldn't tell her you were buying her freedom. You stuck the case there and you closed your eyes because you wanted to believe in Kate's better nature?'

'I still believe in it, it's just . . .' Peter stopped and looked out at the trees pacing by as the earliest dawn light began to make them softly visible. 'It's just I don't think Kate believes in her own better nature.'

Brown shook his head with disbelief. 'But you were testing her and even a test is a doubt, is a trick. Be careful what you wish for.'

Peter bowed his head, his shoulders heaved, the first wave of reality was hitting him. Hard.

'You crying?' Brown said in amazement. 'I'm sorry, I forgot to pack my Kleenex, but then I didn't know I'd find such a giant asshole needing wiping. For crying out loud. You're like the rabbit roadkill that claimed it didn't see the juggernaut coming. Man up to it. You were ridden by Minola, you were suckered. It's happened to both of us. End of story.'

Peter couldn't meet Brown's eyes any more so he turned back to the window. He was right, it was the end of his story. End of everything.

They were five minutes from Rochester when Peter's phone beeped. Brown looked up as Peter looked down to read it.

'Rmber me? Sry had 2 go. Tx a million. N0t. FYI gt out B4 Rochstr. TRAP.'

Any brain over the age of fourteen takes, on average, two seconds longer to interpret 'txt' than anything written in plain English. Brown picked up the hesitation; it was like Peter had to read the message twice and it seemed to electrify him.

Peter looked up at Brown, unable to hide the sudden panic in his eyes. Trap? What sort of trap? Brown only stayed with him to retrieve the money? The police were waiting at Rochester? Brown said that he was meeting DI Brightly. Fuck fuck fuck. There were no more stops before Rochester. Not only does Kate piss off, leaving his life in total shit, but he's going to be arrested at the end of the line? Peter's future flashed before him. His heart seemed to crash as he began to hyperventilate. He'd be stuck in prison and then . . . oh, what was the fucking point? Then he wouldn't even have the choice about his own life. He had to get out of there, make a jump for it. Death or freedom and what was freedom but to choose your own death? In all his years of living in that tiny dump in that damp little town he would never have believed that his life would come down to such a stark polarity, but now he looked at it that was all there was. Two paces to the door. If he lived he'd find another way, if he broke his neck then that would be that. A blessing, free from all the crap this shitty little life he had led had continually thrown at him.

Without a word Peter stood. Something wild in his eyes alerted Brown and he reached out to Peter, who instantly tore away, lunging for the carriage door. Peter turned the handle. It was all too much to bear, he'd played completely the wrong card, given up the money for nothing. The lock had already clicked open before Brown had a hold of him. What had he got? Who would mourn? Who would fucking care? He'd lost his family and friends and future to Titus, and now he'd lost the only hope he'd ever had, all there was was darkness to look forward to. Just fucking darkness. He felt Brown's iron grip on his shoulders as he stood close behind him and Peter stopped, offering no resistance.

'What are you doing, man?' Brown shouted in his ear.

It is well known among the fighting classes that every man will involuntarily pause before he kicks another man in the bollocks, it's an act of unconscious empathy and it is a hiatus that every fighting man fears. Peter allowed his shoulders to be pulled back from the open door, just long enough for him to pay his respects to Brown's tackle. He swung his left foot backwards and up, sharply, the heel of his shoe catching Brown's testes and striking the area hard. Coming from below and a little behind, without even his penis to disperse some of the force, this moment was crushingly painful for Brown, who staggered back trying to find breath.

As soon as Brown's hands released him Peter pushed

the door open; he saw the tracks flashing and twisting as they rushed by, the sleepers beating to the rhythm of his own racing pulse. Was this another trick? Did Kate, finding no money, text him about a trap to get him to do something like this? What was the truth? With her was there ever a truth? The train rattled on to the bridge high above the mouth of the Medway and suddenly the ground fell away to the choppy waters petulantly clashing with the grown-up sea waves of the wide Thames estuary. With Kate life would be constantly searching for the real within the illusion, within the deception, within the sleight, within the delusion. He stared at the glittering water catching the coruscating light of dawn on the harbour and for a moment everything seemed clear. There were only two facts, solid as concrete: live or die, stand or jump. Only decide. No mind games, just one or the other. Truth or lie, live or die. Just one courageous choice. The iron beams of the bridge flashed past his face, counting down the moments before they were over dry land again and the chance gone. This was the third time he had looked at his watery end but this time . . . This time there was no holding back, no last-minute save, no trains to catch, only air and freedom and final peace. Peter bent his knees, pushed away from the doorway and leapt.

TEA

4. The Expiry Action (TEA)

When all is done, the subject is ready for TEA. It is no longer a matter of whether they will take their life, only how. The chosen method will have become clear through TIC, TAC and TOE.

Postscript

It was a dark and stormy night – no, really, it was –
when I saw Peter again. He stumbled into Lotus House,
dishevelled and not just a touch inebriated. Paula didn't
recognize him but who could blame her? His clothes were
torn and fetid, his hair unkempt, the beginnings of a beard
veiled his chin and I never saw him look less like the
immaculate Magicov; more tragical than magical. She
called me down to reception and I stopped on the stairs as
I caught sight of him, unsure if it really was him. But he
stared at me with those pale grey eyes, milky and crazed
with red. 'Can't even kill myself,' he said.

Back in my study we eventually found our old voices
and we talked and he told me this story, and I took
notes.

He couldn't kill himself. That was to be my job. On
that night he still had almost a year to go.

The one phrase in my notes I underlined again and
again at that session was 'suicidal ideation'. The opportunity was too providential.

'You know, Peter,' I said, 'it's not all just about living
or dying.'

He sat in my sunken 'patient' armchair, bowing his

head with exhaustion, as if talking to his own stomach. 'No, I know it's not,' he said, 'it's about regretting, and failure, and a world not even just enough to let me take my life.' He looked up at me. 'I found what it's all about, then I lost it. It was her.'

'But,' I said, 'Kate's not here, she's not in front of you, so if you couldn't remember her, you would never know she was not here. Right?'

He shrugged to show both his agreement and his ambivalence but he sat and listened and I believe I even saw the traces of a smile forming on his lips.

'For the past five years, while you've been playing the mad Russian for the residents, I've been working on false memory syndrome and methods for its induction. I have found protocols in the use of hypnosis, electrolysis and certain chemicals that allow not only for the removal of the ability for long-term memory. I believe I've also discovered a way to create new memories.'

'New memories?' A moment of wonder, his mind re-engaging with curiosity, brought the slightest flush of colour to his face. 'Really?'

'The healthy brain is a great big pattern-finding connections machine. Now imagine I induce amnesia. If I then introduce the right balance of false new memories your brain will do most of the work itself, make all the assumed connections on its own, as it does when you regain consciousness every morning. The fact that the memories are false will not occur to the brain as long as they all agree with each other, and the environment you wake in, and the people around you who believe that they know you. Peter, ask yourself, what makes us who we are? How do you know who you are?'

'I don't know,' he laughed a little nervously, 'I just am.'

'Your identity is far more fragile than you think. Imagine it like a bottle. It's filled with memories and corked with your five senses, giving you a continuity of conscious awareness. Surrounding the cork is the foil of your community, the people around you who remind you of who you are in relation to the world. Now strip off the foil of surrounding people and you become like a prisoner in solitary confinement going crazy, banging his head against the wall to reaffirm that his senses are still there to keep his identity intact. But then pull out the cork of the senses as you do, partially, when you sleep, and there is nothing to keep the memories in. They can all flood out and away with nothing to keep them inside, the bottle is empty, meaningless, all it has is a label, and then when we peel that off? What I believe I can do is empty your bottle and blow you a whole new bottle, refill it with new memories and cork it right back up again.'

'You can make me become, what, someone new?'

'You'd just wake up with no idea that you'd had any other life. You'd believe you were Tom or Dick or Harry, whoever I'd have decided, and you'd have both long- and short-term memories, you'd remember all the rags of time, a day, a week, a year, a lifetime before, whatever you needed to affirm that you were you. Tom or Dick or Harry. It's not just a new identity, it's a new start, a rebirth, a new beginning and with absolutely no idea that you've ever been anybody other than who you are right then.'

'So,' he said a little slowly, piecing it together, 'this

shitty fucked-up life of mine, I wouldn't remember?'

'Gone for ever.'

'And the nightmares? I'd never have to wake up screaming again?'

'No more amphetamines, no more ProPlus, no more desperately trying to stay awake to avoid the returning demons. Nightmares gone. Demons gone. Peter gone.'

And when we were done that night, when he had understood what we could do, he took my hand and shook it with strength and warmth.

'Yes,' he said, 'yes, yes. Let's do this.'

♠

As easy as that. We agreed. I would take Peter's life. But I would give him another. As simple as a handshake.

To put everything in place was considerably harder. I had talked the talk, now I had to perform a neurological experiment of mind-blowing complexity. Mind-blowing. I like that.

Preparation for this would take me nearly a year. Creating new bank accounts, a passport, old photos, the material reminders of identity, was relatively easy. In fact I created several identities. Even, in a moment's fit of envy, some for myself. The audio, video and olfactory new memory programme that I created to automatically bombard Peter once his mind was in the blank-state fugue took over two months and considerable fine tuning. But most time-consuming of all was the altering and preparation of what is our most stable reminder of identity, our foil, our community of people whose memories and recognition correspond with our own.

I will, of course, be providing fuller details in the publication I am planning, *Subject P. – Amnesthetics and New Identity through False Memory Syndrome*. However, put simply, over many months I inveigled myself into a group of people, I must not say where or who. But after taking careful histories, through the judicious administration of Rohypnol, neuro-inhibitors and the surreptitious use of Ericksonian hypnosis, I was able to suggest to each one of them that, after his introduction date, they had always known the person who appeared, Peter, that someone who was a stranger had always occupied a certain corner of their own memories. At first glance they might have a moment of puzzlement, just for a second, but their brains' own will to find the patterns, to make the connections, would quickly place him in the depths of their memories.

◆

In the days and weeks that followed our agreement Peter would come for sessions where I could explore his mind, mechanically, verbally or quite often both. It was there we found Titus's party and Higham as his memory touchstones, the emotional moments that every other memory he had was anchored to. Suppressing the synaptic patterns that occurred when he remembered these would set his entire mind adrift.

For a long time he never wavered in his resolve. He never went back to performing to the day room but he sat doing card tricks with Cedric every day. Until, one hot summer's afternoon, in the middle of a torn and restored card routine, Cedric's stroke-induced arrhythmic heart missed a beat and never found another one. Never afraid of performing with irony, Cedric died, one hand clasped tightly to his pack of 'bikes', in the other the remnants of the unrestored ace of hearts.

I left a message for Kate on her answering service and, at the funeral, I never saw a more nervous mourner than Peter. He stood at the side of the grave, glancing around as if she might materialize at any moment. But she didn't. El Sid performed his last vanish, into the earth, with his only friend standing there beside him.

And nearly every day, before dusk, Peter would take the bus out to Hengistbury Head and walk the two miles to Mudeford beach. He'd sit in the sand near their old hut and look out at the empty sea as the sun set over distant Purbeck, or he'd be swaddled in sea mist with only the hissing wash of the waves to mark the passing time, never able to rid himself of the memories. Kate was never far away, but always over the horizon. That's what memories are.

Peter had picked the date for our 'mind-blowing' day with a curiously unenlightened attitude towards superstition: the anniversary of his meeting with Kate. I was just happy to have a deadline, pun unintended (for once).

Then, with just a month to go, Peter came to my office looking red-faced and agitated. At first he said nothing but paced about, occasionally jerking and turning his head. Every now and then he would look at me, open his mouth and it seemed as if his tongue was forming a sound but nothing came out.

'What if I don't like it?' he said at last. 'Death is at least final. But with this, what if I want to come back?'

He was standing with his back to me, looking out of the window, playing hard to gauge. 'It's just, I mean it's hard to imagine . . .' His voice tailed off.

I got up to see what held his gaze but the town outside lay quietly in order, neat burnt-orange rooftops on either side, occasionally punctuated with the erratic black and white arrows of aspiring dormers. I put my hand on his shoulder.

'Can't you think of anything,' Peter turned to me, 'anything that might set my mind at rest? Something that could give me hope to, I don't know, find a way back. What about your notes? You've got my life down there. You've got all my memories.' He pointed at the reams of paper scattered across my desk.

I laughed before I could stop myself, then, rather inexpertly, tried to turn it into a cough as I returned to my desk. 'It would be useless,' I said. 'With pleasure, you could read my notes but they'd mean nothing to you. What we're going to do, it's so, so thorough. Do you understand, Peter? You wouldn't take them personally; you wouldn't see them as you. You would read them like they were about someone else. Meaningless. The problem with the notes is that it is impossible to emotionally connect with them. They'd never remind you of anything. You see, our deepest, our most lasting memories are the ones embedded in emotion. You might forget where you put the remote control because you attach no emotional depth to it. But a single moment as you watch a girl in a train carriage can last a lifetime.'

'Yeah,' he snorted, sitting down heavily opposite me, 'tell me about it.'

'You're haunted, Peter, by memories that were made

at a heightened emotional time. Our emotions are governed by the amygdala, buried deep beneath our cerebellum. It's your emotional attachment that keeps you from forgetting them. Notes as notes would be useless. You do this, you're not coming back, there will be no idea of a back to go to. It would be, well, the end of you.'

'But it's not the end, it's . . .' His eyes cast upwards for the right word. It's difficult to find the correct vocabulary for something that has never happened before. I took his hesitation as an opportunity to finish the entire argument once and for all.

'The end,' I said, banging my pen down on the desk with a loud and definitive clap.

From: _Letters_ Tavasligh mss. 56.9

Dr C. Tavasligh MSc PhD
CHANGE IN MIND ORGANIZATION
CHRISTCHURCH
DORSET

17.15 (TEA minus 2 hours 45 minutes)

That, Peter, was your life. My notes, your notes, pushed
into the TIC, TAC, TOE and TEA time of a narrative
structure. A novel, no less. You are a third person, as you
will be by the time you read this. Now I've written it all
down here and though some veracity may have been lost
for the sake of a continuous narrative – scenes guessed at
because neither of us was actually present, conversations
reassembled from snatches and some of the characters
rather badly drawn – this was your story.

Almost.

In just under three hours you will lie down on my
examination bed. I will run the false memory programme
on the screen above you and give you just one injection in
the nape of the neck. You will still be perfectly conscious.
And I will take you to your new home, your new people,
and you will go to sleep. Then, then when your brain logs
on in the morning, then you will wake and be someone
incredible, someone new. Entirely.

You will turn up here this evening, an hour after the
sunset you insist on seeing, and tonight Peter will die.
Tomorrow —— (I must not say in case you really wish to
stay as who you are) will be born again. Maybe as part of

a family, maybe on your own, maybe with a lover, and your conscious mind will start fitting the jigsaw of your memory together and everything will fit, only it won't be Peter, it will be, you will be, someone else and I will have finally finished my work.

I wish you luck in your better life.

Chris

19:45 (TEA minus 15 minutes)

Peter!

You haven't turned up, you bastard.
The window of opportunity, the
electrodes, the chemicals, the
journey to your new life, it's all
closing. Where are you?

I can't let it end like this. If
you're not here in the next ten
minutes I will put myself through the
programme, I will wire myself up if I
have to, I must see if this will work.
I can still drive myself to the new
community. A little tweaking for me
instead of you. I have all the
papers and bank accounts set up.
Numbers ready. Just in case.

I don't know what's happened to
you. Could you really have got cold

feet at this last moment? Could you really let me down like this?

Peter. If you do come. If you do find this. Please realize that I had to take your place. It had to happen tonight, now, or all the work would go to waste. Tonight I go to sleep as Chris Tavasligh, tomorrow I wake up as —

No I will not tell you. I will know if this fails, but if it succeeds, in order for it to succeed, it must work totally.

Please send these documents to my publishers.

Despite this, it was a privilege knowing you, Peter.

I hope you find a better life another way.

Best

Chris

Marius Brill
c/o Transworld Publishers
Ealing

Dear Marius

How's it going? It's been a long time. Don't suppose you thought you'd ever hear from me again.

But seriously – a 500 per cent return on shares in a West African gold mine? Did that really not wave any red flags for you? I guess you've worked out by now that there's no such country as the Independent Republic of Bulimia.

Anyway. I'm really sorry. I'm honestly trying to turn over a new leaf. I can't reimburse you but in these boxes is something that might help repay a bit.

I saw you've written a book. Looks good. It's not my kind of thing but I've ordered it on Amazon. I'll give it a go.

That's kind of why I'm contacting you again. I know you're not exactly going to be predisposed to help me but you're the only person I know who might have some contacts in publishing.

Do you remember the fuss in the press a few years ago about Dr Tavasligh? The brain scientist who disappeared? Well, for reasons that will become clear if you read this stuff, Tavasligh's last papers, research notes, etc. have all fallen into my possession.

I realize you're hardly going to trust me but I promise these are genuine and they do explain, at least in part, what happened to Tavasligh, and how I, and a guy called Peter, ended up with all this.

We were the first to enter the lab, literally the day after Tavasligh disappeared. There was a note on top of all this, asking us to get this stuff to a publisher. We've held on to it for a while but I think it's time this came out. Can you help? Can you show it to your editors or whatever they are?

I'm also attaching some stuff Peter and I have written to clear up some of the holes in Tavasligh's story. It ends with Peter not turning up to see Tavasligh but that's not quite how it ended. I mean, I'm sure Peter was going to turn up and everything. But it was me who buggered it up for him. Again!!

Just thought, in the interest of truth, which is what I'm all about nowadays, honestly, I better put down how it all ended. I'm not a writer, but then neither was Tavasligh. Please see the attached chapter I've written, and Peter's letter, because Tavasligh, and Peter, missed quite a lot they didn't see behind the old smoke and mirrors.

Yours apologetically

Kate Minola

Kate Minola

Additional Material by
Kate Minola

Peter looked sweet with his eyes quivering and pretending to be sleeping. The train was sitting panting in the station and I really thought he'd stop me the moment I laid my hands on the case. I think a part of me just wanted to see how we were doing on the trust side of things. But then, when he just lay there and I knew he was still watching me and I had my hands on a million pounds, I just couldn't let it go. It was like I had to carry out the action I'd started.

In the back of my head I was still wondering what had happened to Wissenschaft and Verstehung. I know he had told me about the fight at Charing Cross but you don't escape security boys like them quite so easily.

I don't know, maybe I thought that if I took the money I would lead the sniffers away from Peter and maybe that was my way of showing him I loved him because, well, I did. Which was still something I was having difficulty admitting to myself. And then again, maybe that's just hindsight justification for the fact that I stole the money and couldn't break my habit of going for it. Anyway, whatever it was, however it was about to play, I got off and I took the case with me and as far as I knew there was a million quid in it because, well, Peter hadn't given anything away to make me doubt it. Superb misdirection, great acting, whatever it was, he'd have made a fabulous grifter.

It was just starting to get light when I tiptoed on to the empty platform of the tiny station. A couple of cars were still in the car park, dirty stop-outs still in London. I had no idea where I was, just knew what I was. Very, very rich. I walked out past the little ticket office with the 'Closed' sign behind the glass and breathed in the crisp night air.

Left or right didn't seem to matter, I'd walk until I found a sign. But I'd gone less than twenty paces when the lights of a car came gliding down the narrow country road. Even then, I was sure it was more than just coincidence. I jumped to the side, but there was nowhere to hide. The car stopped, the full beam of its headlights on me.

I heard the door opening and a short man with a long beard appeared in front of the lights.

'May I?' Verstehung pointed at my case.

I looked at it casually. 'No, I'm fine.'

He came closer and I could see he was holding a nasty-looking knife. 'Dr Tavasligh? What a lovely surprise. I believe that belongs to us.' He put his hot sweaty hand on the case handle and ripped it forcibly from my grip. Then, putting the knife in his belt, he gripped my arm with his free hand and marched me to the Lexus, shoved me into the passenger seat, pulled a pair of handcuffs from the glove compartment and before I could think he had cuffed me to the door handle.

Taking the case round to the driver's seat, he got back in and smiled at me. 'You see, doctor, or whoever you are, we put a satellite tracker in the case.' He tapped it. 'We've known exactly where it was all the time. My colleague drove down to Rochester while I followed the case, just in case you made an early exit.'

I nodded as I tried to get my fingers around to the cuffs' lock as Peter had taught me.

As we sat in the silent car on the dark lane, Verstehung unzipped the bag. As the case fell open, so did his mouth and, well, so did mine. It was stuffed with letters and envelopes and every one of my beautiful million was gone. In an instant Verstehung pulled the knife out again and had it to my throat. I could feel the stinging prick as it pushed into my skin.

'Where is it? Where's the money?'

'I don't know,' I breathed, trying not to move my throat as I spoke. 'I thought I had it. It's Peter, he's done a switch.'

'What?' Verstehung snarled.

'He's switched the money out, classic con. The little bastard screwed me.'

I couldn't tell if he believed me but he pulled the knife from my throat, started the engine again and we roared down the lane. He dialled on the dashboard phone and Wissenschaft's deep voice echoed in the car.

'Yes, Dick?'

'You in Rochester?' Verstehung shouted.

'At the station.'

495

'I picked up the woman, Tavasligh, she was sneaking off with the case.'

'You got the money, Dick?'

'No. The money wasn't there. They've taken it out somehow. It's Paul, he still—'

'Peter,' I whispered, 'his real name is Peter.'

'Peter. He's still heading towards you. Look out for a bag or something. I'm on my way there now.'

'What you done with the girl?'

'Oh I'm right here,' I shouted over the crunching gears as we took a corner at speed.

'Well, dear,' Wissenschaft said with a patronizing lilt, 'if we don't get your boyfriend, the next time he wants to see you he'll have to go scuba diving.'

Verstehung and I looked quizzically at each other for a moment. 'Is that an allusion to a mafioso "sleeping with the fishes"-style threat?' I asked a bit fatuously but, since he wasn't there and his mate was preoccupied, I wasn't exactly worried that he'd slap me for it.

Verstehung floored the pedal on a straight section and agreed. 'She's right, Dick, you really should leave the allusions to me. You're good with your hands. Always have been.'

'Right,' Wissenschaft said angrily, 'if you're so smart, Dick, how come the money's coming to me and you were suckered?' The line went dead and I smiled at Verstehung before being flung into the door again as the Lexus took another corner on two fewer wheels than it was designed to.

It was at this point that I realized I could get my fingers into my pocket and dig out my mobile phone. If

Peter had the money I still had a better chance of getting to it if these Hasidim from hell didn't get to him first. Jolting and swinging through the Kent countryside in the purple light of a new day, I managed to send a text.

'Rmber me?' That had kind of become our catch-phrase. 'Sry had 2 go. Tx a million. N0t. FYI gt out B4 Rochstr. TRAP.'

It was the best I could do under the circumstances. I just sat tight, or at least wishing I was so I wouldn't feel the full terror of this man's insane driving.

When we screeched into the car park at Rochester station, we were ahead of the train. From the car's clock I could see it was due in a few minutes.

Verstehung jumped out, slamming the door behind him and leaving me in peace to work on the cuffs' lock.

From where I sat I could watch the train pull in. As it stopped at the buffers I saw Wissenschaft and Verstehung run along the platform. And then I saw someone who sent a chilling shiver through my heart. Getting off the train with the casualness of an InterCity day-tripper was Special Agent Danny Brown.

I tried to drop down in my seat in case he saw me. That really would be the end of the road. Did he get to Peter? Did Peter sell me out and take the money as well? Could I have misjudged Peter so badly? Had I really slipped so much as to have been played so well, right from the start, by a two-bit prestidigitator from a one-whore town in fucking Dorset? Was everything Clarissa said in New Zealand spot on? At that moment I hated Peter with every inch of my heart but, my God, if I didn't admire him as well.

Brown stood on the platform without an apparent

care in the world as Verstehung and Wissenschaft desperately searched every carriage. He seemed to be more interested in the post office porters throwing the sacks of mail off the train. When they had finished he ambled outside to strike up a conversation with the post office van driver waiting to take the mail. Even through the glass I could hear his loud American tones.

'Hey,' he said, 'I'm a stranger to these parts, do you know where Margate is?'

The van driver spoke at an English volume, one designed to match the proximity of the listener and not the whole of East Kent.

'Yeah?' Brown answered. 'I'm down here to surprise my girlfriend, you know, get to her hotel real early? Do you think you could give me a lift?'

The van driver shook his head as he replied.

'Oh well, gee, look, I can make it worth your while.' Brown peeled off a couple of fifty-pound notes from a large wad, and that made me sit up. A wad of fifties? A federal agent bribing someone? My mind flooded with possibilities but it was clear from that very moment. He had turned. The bastard who had made my life a living hell had taken the money. And now I knew exactly where the money was. It was being loaded into the back of the van as I watched.

I strained at the cuffs angrily and suddenly noticed my door handle was beginning to wriggle. It was a lot less secure than the cuffs themselves. It was coming loose. I bashed the chain at the handle repeatedly. Brown. Taking the money. I was livid but I wasn't sure if I was angry with Brown or Peter or just myself for being such an idiot and not offering a substantial bribe

498

like that years ago. No one's untouchable. The money speaks. I had told Peter that and didn't even listen to myself.

I gave another hard yank to the door handle and it flew off. My hands were still cuffed but at least I could move. Now I could get out or . . . I watched the post office van start up and drive slowly out of the car park with Brown in the passenger seat.

I wasn't letting the money out of my sight. If I could just hot-wire the Lexus I could get after them.

Unfortunately, even as I shifted into the driver's seat Wissenschaft and Verstehung came running through the car park. With no Peter around and having found a case of mislaid mail, they had obviously drawn the same conclusion. Wissenschaft climbed into the back as Verstehung pushed me on to the passenger seat again.

Verstehung looked at my door, the lining hanging half off.

'What have you done to my car?'

'Oh, what? I was supposed to just sit here?'

'Yes, this is the velvet-range interior, it cost a bloody fortune.'

'You talking about a fortune, Dick?' Wissenschaft chimed in from the back. 'That's what's driving off up that road. Start the sodding car.'

Verstehung turned the key and spun the wheels as he set off in pursuit of the post office van. I was thrown back into my seat but this was the journey I had been planning so I had no problem with being chauffeur-driven.

It was somewhere just before Canterbury that we finally caught up with them. We saw the van in the distance, pulled up on the verge. Verstehung stopped at the crest of the hill and we watched. Brown stood at the back of the van. He appeared to be holding a gun or something, the doors of the van were open and the postie seemed to be searching through the bags on board.

Now. What happened next I am not proud of. I had no idea what Brown had done to Peter. I had no idea of the deal Peter had struck with Brown. I only saw that hateful man stealing my money after ruining my life and suddenly all that rage that I laughed at in Peter, all that wishing for revenge, all that repressed anger, boiled up in me.

We drove slowly down to the van. No doubt Little and Large intended to get out and pull a gun and take the money. Even if they succeeded, I had my doubts that Titus would ever see it again.

Verstehung cruised down the hill towards the stationary van while I steamed until it was impossible for me to just sit there any longer and not act.

I grabbed the steering wheel with both cuffed hands and locked it straight, then I jammed my heel hard on to Verstehung's shoe. The Lexus squealed and accelerated towards the back of the van.

'Stop, you crazy bitch,' Verstehung screamed.

Brown barely had time to turn towards us, and I can still see the most gratifying look of terror in his eyes as we ploughed into him and the back of the van.

The noise, the most incredible crunch, hit me first, then the airbag.

I pushed my door open and toppled out, stumbling and running round to the front. Brown was there, unconscious or dead, stuck between our crumpled bonnet and the van.

The postman was lying among the bags, shaking, and money, fifty-pound notes, fluttered here and there into the wind. Packs of fifties were scattered over the road and in the field next to us.

Wissenschaft was first to recover but his door was jammed shut. He pounded at the glass and shook Verstehung. Verstehung seemed to regain consciousness and began to shout something in Yiddish as he staggered out of the car.

I knew I couldn't hang around. Hoovering up the money would take them a while. Explaining to the police why their car had killed or maybe injured an American federal agent would also take some doing.

I grabbed what notes I could and set off across the fields.

'You fucking crazy shiksa,' Verstehung shouted after me.

I turned and laughed. 'Cheer up, Dick. You're in the money!' I shouted and set off towards the woods.

Fortunately most garages tend to have bolt-cutters. Fifty quid at Stan's Breakdowns near Faversham and the cuffs were gone.

Peter was not so easy to lose. At first I hated him. Either he'd been so stupid as to be bag-switched by Brown, or he had given him the money on purpose. Scared little twat. It was a couple of months – I was in the Algarve – before I checked my status on America's Most Wanted. I scrolled right down to the bottom but I had vanished, as if by magic, which, in a way, it was.

I crawled through old news, googling my name, only

to find that I had disappeared, presumed dead, somewhere in the Thames on that night of the slow train. For the last two months and for the rest of my life I was free.

It's hard to describe how elated I felt. Not only could I go back to the States but I knew that that freedom was what Peter had bought me. And I realized what a terrible, hate-fuelled mistake I had made crashing into Brown.

Still, I'll live with it.

I think I guessed where Peter would go, almost immediately, but I wanted to move on, move away from my grifting history, and now he was firmly a part of it. I travelled, I went back to the States, I pulled a few scams but it never gave me the pleasure that one night on the train to Higham did.

I did OK. But, as autumn approached again, and the anniversary of our meeting began to haunt me, I could no longer fight myself, my past, my memories. They were a part of me, they were what made me me. Whether you can remember more or less, the important memories stay. They're not pictures or smells or events. They're feelings.

I was all ready to head back to Christchurch when I got the message about Da. I don't know what it was but I was such a beginner at all this emotional stuff. I didn't think I could face a funeral and a reunion all at the same time.

Da would have understood.

But when it was twelve months since I'd met Peter I knew where I would find him. Beyond the long grass and the swaying reeds and the wild gorse that shakes and whispers around Hengistbury Head. As the sun set and the stars burst into the darkening sky I saw his figure sitting up in the pale sand by the beach huts, looking out at the sea, our sea that washed with a purple ease, breathing in and out across the sandy shingle on the beach. And my shoulders ached and my stomach filled and I stood so close behind him I could hear him breathe and I knew I was where I should be, where I always should have been, where I would always want to be. I looked at his neck and the arms that wrapped me and knew they were the only home I'd ever want.

'Remember me?' I said.

Additional Material by Peter Ruchio

So now you breathe and take in this stillness, this lulling moment, now with the world ebbing softly back again from this distant quiet. The noise and busyness that has been far away, deadened like the hush of fallen snow as you followed the dark prints across these white fields, silently tumbling into inky meaning. It returns. And maybe now you'll notice how your head is nodding, faintly, as if invisible chains are gently releasing you from these pages. Perhaps you can feel how your neck is almost imperceptibly tensed to prevent your dropping head from being drawn towards the paper, the black scratches on the bright page. And now, perhaps, as you hang between the last and first, you can sense that tiny rhythmic movement of your body, slightly rocking with your breathing, pitching ahead with the weight of your head and shoulders, and pulling back, then pitching forward again with the rhythm of your breathing ... perhaps you don't just finish a book, you soar away, pull back from these uncertain arms of sense and feeling, back into the sphere of time and notion.

And now I only wonder when you will try to let go

504

completely. I wonder how long it will be before you loosen your grip on this world of Kate and me and take wing back into that immediate world of your conscious senses. To tumble away. To fly headlong into that other life and find yourself there again. Because it is only when you are there, with part of your brain already altered to accommodate this story, that there's just a chance you might start to remember. Remember what happened, remember who you were, and remember, my friend, why it was you who were so desperate to forget.

And now. Somewhere. You, who are reading this, you are waking up each day just as you woke up one morning a little while ago and remembered who you were. But you weren't the great memory expert, the doctor, but someone else. You were someone else. You were you.

And maybe a lover kissed the morning away. Maybe a child came to hug you. Maybe you were on your own, or woke up on the sofa with the TV still on. And you pieced together who you are from the memories and the stuff around you and remembering where you're supposed to go today and who you're seeing or what you're supposed to get done, and you have no idea that a little while ago you were someone else entirely.

And I don't know enough about your old life to write your 'story'. But sometimes I think maybe if you read this you'll get a flashback and you'll remember writing this.

And then I find myself hoping that you won't. Because if you do, then your great experiment will be over. If I saw you again I hope I'd have the strength to just pass you by, that I could just watch you go with your new family or friends or just on your own, un-disturbed, just being someone else. Because unlike anybody else on this planet, it's what you chose.

So wherever you are and whoever you are now, I . . . Kate and I, hope you're happy. That you're leading a happier life than the lonely one you so much wanted to escape.

Live well, doc, whoever you are now.

With love

Peter x

Bibliography

Banachek, Steve, *Psychological Subtleties* (vols 1–3), Magic Inspirations, Houston, 1998.

Brown, Derren, *Pure Effect*, H & R Magic Books, Humble, 2000.

Burger, Eugene and Neale, Robert E., *Magic and Meaning*, Hermetic Press, Seattle, 1995.

Busch, Richard, *The Destiny Response*, Richard and Cynthia Busch, Pittsburgh, 2004.

Carter, Rita, *Mapping the Mind*, Weidenfeld & Nicolson, London, 1998.

Chelman, Christian, *Capricorn Tales*, L & L Publishing, Tahoma, 1993.

Corinda, *13 Steps to Mentalism*, D. Robbins & Co., New York, 1968.

Erdnase, S. W., *The Expert at the Card Table*, Frederick J. Drake & Co., Chicago, 1904.

Fitzkee, Dariel, *Magic by Misdirection*, Lee Jacobs Productions, Pomeroy, 1975.

Fulves, Karl (ed.), *The Pallbearer's Review*, Karl Fulves, Teaneck, 1965–77.

Gardner, Martin, *The Encyclopedia of Impromptu Magic*, Magic Inc., Chicago, 1978.

Goldstein, Phil, *Focus*, Hermetic Press, Seattle, 1990.

Goldstein, Phil (writing as Max Maven), *Prism*, Hermetic Press, Seattle, 2005.

Gregory, Richard L. (ed.), *The Oxford Companion to the Mind*, Oxford University Press, Oxford, 1987.

Harris, Paul, *The Art of Astonishment* (vols 1–3), A-1 Multimedia, Rancho Cordova, 1996.

Hilford, Docc, *The Book of Numbers* (vols 1–3., Docc Co., Bal Harbour, 2006.

Hollingworth, Guy, *Drawing Room Deceptions*, Mike Caveney's Magic Words, Pasadena, 1999.

Hugard, Jean and Braue, Fred, *Expert Card Technique*, Carl W. Jones, Minneapolis, 1940.

Jermay, Luke, *Seven Deceptions*, Kenton Knepper Presents, Phoenix, 2002.

Jillette, Penn and Teller, Raymond, *Cruel Tricks for Dear Friends*, Villard Books, New York, 1989.

Jones, Lewis, *Seventh Heaven*, Lewis Jones, London, 1993.

Kennedy, *Tell Tale Factor*, Kennedy, Newcastle, 2005.

Knepper, Kenton, *Kentonism*, Kenton Knepper Presents, Phoenix, 2002.

Kyriakides, Robert, *The Master Conman*, Headpress, Manchester, 2003.

Lamont, Peter and Wiseman, Richard, *Magic in Theory*, University of Hertfordshire Press, Hatfield, 1999.

Macknik, Stephen, Martinez-Conde, Susana, and Blakeslee, Sandra, *Sleights of Mind: What the neuroscience of magic reveals about our brains*, Henry Holt & Co., New York, 2010.

Mahood, John, *K.E.N.T.*, Kenton Knepper Presents, Phoenix, 2003.

Marlo, Ed, *Revolutionary Card Technique*, Magic Inc., Chicago, 2003.

Neale, Robert E., *Magic Matters*, Theory and Art of Magic Press, Sherman, 2009.

Neale, Robert E., *Life, Death and Other Card Tricks*, Hermetic Press, Seattle, 2000.

Poncher, Jheff, *Ultimental*, Profits Publishing, Sarasota, 2004.

Sadowitz, Jerry, *The Crimp Magazine*, Choob & Eejit Publications, Glasgow/London, 1992.

Sankey, Jay and Sanders, Richard, *When Creators Collide*, Ben Harris Magic, Queensland, 1987.

Voodini, Paul, *Reader of Minds!*, Paul Voodini, Sheffield, 2008.

Waters, T. A., *Mind, Myth & Magic*, Hermetic Press, Seattle, 1999.

Acknowledgements

John Donne said, 'No man is an island,' but then he never saw this author taking a dip after years sitting on his arse writing a book. So let me, at least, be a tropical island, as warm and lovely as the people who have tirelessly supported me all this time, because nobody deserves a holiday on the white sandy beaches of my belly more than my dazzling family: Claire Scudder, George McCrae, Roxana Brill and Jezebel Brill.

Those never to be forgotten include my brilliant editor, Jane Lawson, and the magnificent Robert Caskie, my agent at PFD. Others whose contributions have been immeasurable, mainly because the Society of Authors still haven't sorted out a standardized unit of acknowledgement, include Adam Markwell, Adrian Gill, Anna Pasternak, Avy Joseph, Bobby Allen, Caroline Calder-Smith, Caroline Kohn, Caroline Michel, Christine Kelly, Claire Beezem, Claire Farrow, Dean Ricketts, Emma McFee, Emma Rea, Francesca Brill, Harry Burke, Jean Markwell, John Henderson, John Kelly, Kevin Adams, Laura Bondi, Leo deMyers, Lucy Dundas, Matthew Harris, Meera Shah, Rachel Mills, Rebecca Bowen, Robert Moore, Stafford

Gregoire, and the seminal magicians Jerry Sadowitz and Lewis Jones. Lastly, I must thank the mentalists Kennedy, Max Maven, Andy Nyman and Derren Brown for their inspiration as performers, magicians and thinkers.